The Silent Sisterhood

a novel by

Trudie-Pearl Sturgess

authorHOUSE®

AuthorHouse™
1663 Liberty Drive
Bloomington, IN 47403
www.authorhouse.com
Phone: 1-800-839-8640

© 2010 Trudie-Pearl Sturgess. All rights reserved.
No part of this book may be reproduced or transmitted in any form
or by any means, electronic or mechanical, including photocopying,
recording, or by any information storage and retrieval system, without
the written permission of the author, except where permitted by law.

First published by AuthorHouse   1/13/2010
ISBN: 978-1-4490-5949-1 (e)
ISBN: 978-1-4490-5950-7 (sc)
ISBN: 978-1-4490-5951-4 (hc)

Library of Congress Control Number: 2009913232

Printed in the United States of America
Bloomington, Indiana

This book is printed on acid-free paper.

To Chrissel and Torian Sturgess,

who are where my hope lives,
and who show me that forever never dies.

That is how much I love you both:

with all my heart and soul,

my sweethearts.

Thank you, Dr. Sally Brun-Jackson
for editing the book.

Chapter 1

After an exhausting day at The Buzz, Tia Sharp and her best friend Kate Lee are walking to South Croydon station to take the train home. They have so many dreams and one of them will come true in a few weeks with the opening of their very own clothing store. It's a small business venture for the girls and their girl pal Brooke who is the brain behind "Urban Style". The anticipation is killing them. It has been a long dream since they were ten years old to open a fashion outlet one day, and when they meet Brooke, the dream has become a reality. Brooke is the go-getter of the group. The other two girls are dreamers. Brooke likes to put ideas into reality, and at twenty years old, she has been working for her mother's real estate company since she graduated from college.

As soon as Kate mentions the idea of the girls having their own shop, Brooke wastes no time to do some market research. Before they know it, they are out looking for a commercial space to rent before they even have start-up money. With no money whatsoever between the three of them, Brooke encourages her friends to give her fifty percent of their weekly wages so they can open a business account. By her calculation, in six months they should have enough money to launch their business. True to her word, it's all about to come true.

Kate is the older of the three girls: she is twenty-one years old and about to graduate from University in two months, a fulfillment of her mother's dream to see her daughter educated. Kate is the creative one of the group, having designed her own line of clothes. As a little girl, she watched her mother make clothes for her and Tia, so she is not a stranger to the sewing machine, nor to cutting fabric without using patterns.

Tia, the youngest of the group, is nineteen years old. Tia has just returned from New York with her mother. While she was in New York, she saw how the American urban community dressed differently from the urban style in the UK. Urban, she advised her friends: they needed to tap into that kind of style to set them apart from the very popular Karl Kain wear that everyone at their college was wearing.

In the summer of 1994, everyone is into the American fashion style they see in the videos of R. Kerry and the Jodece. "They are 'it' in the music and fashion industries," Tia tells her friends, "Hot, hot hot!"

"I don't like it," said Brooke. "Our target should not just be for the urban. We should also do old-fashioned, classy, British fashion, not like Vivian Westwood, but let people know that it's okay to see a teenager in a well-made, affordable, three-piece suit or a dress, not just street clothes all the time."

"Who the hell is Vivian Westwood?" Kate asks.

"Kate, how can you have passion for fashion if you don't who is who in fashion world?" Tia asks, teasing and laughing at the same time.

Brooke does not see what is so funny: "Vivian Westwood is one of our very own British fashion designers. She has made dresses for Lady Di, Jerry Hall, and others," Brooke explains.

"We don't have the kind of budget that Vivian Westwood has," Tia points out, still laughing about Kate not knowing who Vivian Westwood is.

They all agree with Brooke. They should try to set themselves apart because they are British; and although hip hop has taken over the teenage culture and half of the fashion industry, they want to be trendsetters. After all, they live in a country where every young person still wears a blazer and a tie to school. Why not embrace it?

Kate makes all the clothes they need for the show with help from her mother and her two girl pals. They spend two weeks going back and forth from the East Street market, Liverpool Street looking for earrings, bags, purses and sunglasses to buy for the show. They have a very small budget and they don't want to exceed it. Finally, they have all the accessories they need. The girls discuss and share ideas about which designs Kate should make as well as what kind of fabric, and the embellishments for each garment. Accessories – shoes, purses, jewelery – become a hot debate between Brooke and Tia.

Tia is in charge of the fashion show; she has posters all over the campus about the fashion show; and she has arranged the auditions for models and DJ's music. The tickets are sold out with half of the sale going to the Drama Club at the college, the only way they could use the collage auditorium for free. Brooke is not happy that Tia agreed to give up half of the ticket sale to the Drama Club without telling them first.

"I'm not a student here and I don't want our hard earned money going to them!" she snaps at Tia.

"We are saving money having this done at the college." Tia snaps back at Brooke and walks away so upset.

"I am so sick of Brooke's know-it-all attitude, Lola," Tia says to Mrs Lee, who is in her kitchen cooking as usual. The two girls join them in the kitchen.

"Ladies, I don't want to put my two cents in your business... but you girls have done well and your show is in two days. Please don't fight over money now. It will tear you apart," Mrs Lee advises.

Tia is still upset, but thinks about what Mrs Lee has said. "I should have talked it over with you guys before I agreed to give half of the ticket sale away. I am sorry," Tia apologizes.

Brooke and Kate respond simultaneously, "It's okay."

"There's one thing I need you all to see," says Brooke. "Here is the floor plan of the shop. I have completed a 3-D layout of the fixtures design for you guys to see so we can approve which to go for. If you – we – all like it, in less than a week I can have it created and the product will be delivered. Assembly and set up in one afternoon when we all have time."

She turned on the laptop and faced it toward her friends. They were seeing the impact of the new fixtures, showing the four seasons: autumn, winter, spring and summer.

"This will make our merchandising solutions simple for us to do stock takes and at the same time know what we have sold and how much we should produce," explains Brooke.

"Wow! I love it !" exclaims Tia.

"Well, Kate. What do you think ?" Brooke asks.

"Great quality work, Brooke. I appreciate your ability to customize to meet our needs at a reasonable price. I am so proud of you, Brooke. I didn't think we could do this."

"Good job, Brooke! You came through for us," Tia adds.

The next day they rehearse everything and set up a station for food and drinks. The three girls spend the night at Brooke's flat, unable to sleep and not quite able to believe their vision is about to be realized.

"Are your mum and dad coming tomorrow night?" Brooke asks Tia.

"Yep, and my sisters, too," Tia tells her friend.

They are sitting in a bubble bath together drinking white Maria Christina wine, while Kate chats on the phone with her boyfriend. She tells the two girls in the bath to be quiet so she can hear her man.

"Is your mum going to come Brooke?" Kate asks.

"I sent her some tickets. I don't care if she does or not. Tomorrow is about me and my girls and the beginning of our own empire. No one is going to spoil it for us." She raises up the bottle of wine and toasts with Tia. In the back of her mind, she wishes that her mother would show up – even for five minutes – and say that she is proud of her.

The next night the show is right on time. The auditorium is packed, so Tia tells the DJ to keep the music pumping. Back stage, all the models are dressed and lined up ready to hit the auditorium stage. As the lights dim, "I Wanna Be Down" by Brandy plays as Tia walks onto the stage with a microphone in her hands. Tia, dressed in a pale, ice pink, silk jersey, bandage dress that Kate made for her that morning, looks so sexy; her hair is done up like a bow tie up-do with the bangs out. She wears black high-heeled shoes and long, white gold earrings: it is very Jessica Rabbit and quite beautiful.

The music stops. Tia's voice softly welcomes everyone. As she moves to the left corner of the stage, Keith Sweat's "How Do You Like It" comes on the loud speakers. When she starts introducing the models and what they are wearing, the whole crowed goes wild and stands up clapping, whistling, and dancing to the music. Some of the students have seen British Fashion Week on TV, but the Urban Style fashion show at the college is better than TV. They are on their feet as the models work the runway with one outfit after another. For Tia, the auditorium is like a night club with a famous band playing live music. The audience can't get enough of Kate's designs.

Back stage, Kate makes sure that the models are wearing the right outfits. Brooke is in charge of make-up and hair. The two girls take a peek every now and then to see the audience reaction. Every time she takes a peek, Brooke secretly hopes that for once her mother will be in the audience. It breaks her heart that Sarah does not make it to the show.

The last two models are a boy and a girl, both wearing suits. As they walk backstage, Brooke and Kate walk hand-in-hand to the podium to join Tia. Kate is wearing a silk printed chiffon, lilac and winter white dress with her long hair down. Brooke wanted something unified with her friend. The asymmetry of Brooke's dress and the one-shouldered dress speak to each other. They thank everyone for coming and invite some of the people to the backstage for snacks.

The night has been nothing they ever imagined. They are blown away by the response. The show has given them the buzz they need: after the show, half of the students are ready to purchase some of the clothes.

"This is our target audience, girls! And as you can see, we were a hit tonight!" Tia screams as she runs to hug her two friends. They have worked hard for this and in four more weeks their diligence will pay off by the look of things when Urban Style opens. Expecting Brooke's mother not to show up, Tia asked her father to videotape the show. She also had one of her friends take photographs so that she could put them on the Urban Style website she is designing for them. Tia knows the power of Internet, and she wants to use it as their marketing tool to increase their sales potential.

Chapter 2

The next morning, Tia slides the videotape of the fashion show into an envelope and drives to Gemini Real Estate where Brooke's mom works. As she pulled into the parking lot, she notices Sarah Williams getting out of her BMW. "Good morning, Mrs Williams!" Sarah is on her cell phone but flashes Tia a smile even though she has no idea who Tia is. Tia thinks Sarah looks tired.

"My dad made this last night at our fashion show. I thought you would like to see what your daughter, Kate, and myself did." She hands the tape to Sarah, who has forgotten about Brooke's little fashion show. "The show was last night?" she asks.

"Yes ma'am, the show was last night," Tia says as she gets into her car and drives off before Sarah can say anything. It's almost midnight and Tia is still not asleep, drinking iced tea in her father's study. She can't stop thinking about Kevin and their meeting in the morning. They have been talking on the phone for almost a month now. Tomorrow will be the first time they meet face to face. In the morning, she wakes first and heads straight to the bathroom. She doesn't want to dress too sexy, so she dons white paddle pushers and a black t-shirt, typical Tia fashion, lowers the neckline to make it sexier and adds large earrings. She's ready for her lunch date. In the rush to catch the bus to the Brixton tube station, Tia has forgotten to charge her cellphone battery. As she jumps on the northern line tube to Seven Sisters, she thinks, "Oh, well! I can find a phone booth to call Kevin when I get there." Rummaging through her bag, Tia finds Kevin's number and dials. "I am here," she says to the person on the line and hangs up. Five minutes later, feeling a tap on her shoulder, Tia turns around and meets his smile: five feet eleven inches tall and about a hundred and sixty pounds – not bad at all. He looks a little bit like Will Smith without Will Smith's big ears. He sports a blue Oxford shirt and black pants with one hand in his pocket. Kevin looks nervous.

"I am Kevin," he extends his hands to shake Tia's. "Allow me," he says as he reaches for the laptop case Tia has placed on the floor. They walk out of the tube station toward his flat. The flat has some kind of a smell there, but Tia doesn't let it bother her. The dark living room has a love seat and a three-seater sofa. Tia chooses the sofa. Kevin comes in with what looks like books. He hands them to Tia. They are family photo albums.

"What do you want on your pizza?" Kevin asks.

"Anything will be great, Kevin. I am not fussy about what I eat," Tia replies.

"We will have lunch in forty minutes. How about a movie while we wait for the pizza? Or you can tell me about yourself," he suggests with a half-way smile.

"Miss Tia Sharp. There is really nothing to tell. What you see is what you get, no mystery or surprises here!" Tia says evasively. "What about you? What can you tell me about you that I don't already know?"

"A lot, if you have the time. I live here with my brother, Aaron, who is at work now. My sister, Ola, lives in Tottenham. She is going to get married in two weeks. Can you come with me to the wedding? I mean, will you be my date?" he asks anxiously.

Tia looks up and says, " I'd love to, but I am leaving for Amsterdam tonight for three weeks." While waiting for the pizza, Kevin takes the opportunity to provide some background information about himself. He points out special memories captured in the pictures of the albums. He tells Tia about his favorite family events as they look at the pictures together. Tia enjoys lunch with him, and by the time they are done with lunch, Tia has already fallen in lust with him and he doesn't even know it.

"I had a good time, Kevin. Thank you for lunch."

"You are welcome, Tia," he says. "Em....... I'd like to take you out on a proper date when you come back, if you are up for it," he offers.

"I will give you a call when I get back, Kevin, and you can let me know your schedule."

He smiles. "The tube is here." He reaches in and kisses her goodbye on the forehead. He is still standing there when she sits down on her seat. Their eyes never leave each other as the tube moves out of the station. Tia exhales slowly and closes her eyes for the train ride, but Kevin never leaves her thoughts. It turns out to be the longest three weeks Tia has ever spent in Holland with her mother because of the endless shopping. By the time she returns to England, Tia couldn't wait to see Kevin again.

The phone is ringing as Tia and her mother open the front door. "I think it is your phone darling," Naana says.

Tia drops her backpack on the floor and runs. By the time she gets up to her room, the phone has stopped. She sits on her bed almost out of breath. She is about to put her head down and scream when the phone starts ringing again. She picks the phone up with an attitude, but when she hears Kevin's voice, she immediately loses the attitude.

"You are back, I see. How was your trip?" he asks.

"You don't want to know. Trust me: my mum and her friends are so annoying and all they wanted to do was shop, shop and shop, so how have you been doing?" Tia asks.

"Good. My sister's wedding was good. My dad and step-mother came from Nigeria. At the wedding, there was a fat lady sitting by herself, so I danced with her. My brother said I was brave."

"Your brother don't like fat women, I trust?"

"I wish you were there, Tia. I mean, I told my parents about you, and my sister really wants to meet you soon. Can I see you again?"

"How about you come and visit me? Pick any day you want and I can pick you up at Brixton station. There's a Tower Records there. I can pick you up right from there. So what do you say?" Tia asks. She was full of anticipation waiting for his response. He wasted no time suggesting a date. Kevin has thought of her every day since they last met and there's so much he wants to tell her.

"Sounds good! I am free tomorrow. I can be there around noon, if that's okay with you?" he says.

"It's settled. Tomorrow at noon, it is," Tia confirms.

They stay on the phone for two hours and it is hard for either one of them to hang up. Finally, Naana Konadu-Sharp comes into Tia's room and tells her to hang up and go to bed.

Kevin doesn't know what to make of Tia: she is different from all the women he has dated in the past. He can't put his finger on it. That night after he finished talking to Tia, his brother discovers Kevin smiling to himself.

"What's up?" Aaron asks. "Did you win the National Lotta?"

His brother seems to be in a better mood since he met Tia.

"No man, I am going to Tia's house tomorrow. She is back from Amsterdam. We just got off the phone a minute ago," he says.

"So that explains why the phone was busy all this time! I was trying to find out if Marie called." Marie is Aaron's girl friend from Iceland. She is only a little over five feet tall, but easily weighs one hundred and forty-five pounds with blue eyes like the sky and beautiful blonde hair.

"Oh, sorry mate. She didn't call." Kevin informs his brother.

His mind returns to the girl he has only met six weeks ago. If only he knew how she felt about him. He walked to the living room where two of his brother's friends were watching MTV and playing video games at the same time. Kevin hi-fives them, and says, "Good-night, guys. I have an early start in the morning."

Sam looks annoyed at Kevin. He's winning the game and now he has to leave. "How rude!" he thinks. "Okay, guys. Let's bounce. Later dude," he rolls his eyes as he walks through the narrow hallway to the front door.

When Kevin woke up the next morning, before it got too hot, he took a run around the park. Jogging with his head phones on, all he can think about is seeing Tia that afternoon. He does not pay much attention to where he is running, so he almost gets hit by a car. Playing it safe, he decides to stop running and walk back home to take shower and made himself some breakfast.

Later, at Tower Records, Kevin is about to go inside the shop when he sees Tia sitting in a Ford Escort, looking more beautiful than he remembered.

"Hey, you!" she exclaims.

"Hey, yourself!" Kevin replies.

They drive to her house in silence. Finally, "We are here," Tia says. "Come on in."

Tia lives with her family in a big detached house in Croydon. "Straight up" she says to him "and make yourself comfortable. I am coming."

"Lisa, are you home? Come on down!" she calls out to her sister.

Lisa, just turned sixteen, is at home for mid-term break. "What's up?" she asks.

"I need you to take this to my friend. He is in our living room." Tia hands her a glass of juice to take to Kevin. Tia is working in the kitchen when Kevin enters to ask whether he can help.

"I am baking a cake for your brother. Lunch is already made. You can set the table if you want." Tia points to the cutlery drawer and the china hutch.

"Show me around your house," he says.

"Okay, follow me. I must warn you my room is very messy!" Tia replies.

They go back to the family room and then to the living room. "The bedrooms are upstairs. Come."

They go to Tia's room first down the hall.

"Wow! You must love music!" Kevin exclaims. "Are all these CDs yours?"

Tia smiles. He sits on the bed and grabs a pile of CDs from the bed. "May I?" he looks up at her.

"Of course!" Tia responds, and then asks "Are you a jazz fan?"

"Yes, ma'am! I love jazz." he enthuses.

They listen to CD after CD. They didn't really have much in common: just jazz music.

"So where is your mother?" Kevin asks.

"She will be here soon. She drove Claire, my baby sister, somewhere. They should be home soon anytime soon."

Naana Konadu-Sharp is a banker. Her husband, Bobby Sharp, works at Bankers Trust in risk management. Both have lived in England since their teens. Originally from Bristol, and now in his early forties, Bobby met his wife at college and until now he cannot remember how he got the courage to ask out the African beauty. He didn't waste time getting down on his knees and asking her to marry him. To his surprise, she said "yes". Their three girls – Tia, Lisa and Claire – are as close as sisters can be. When Bobby Sharp arrives home, he calls out "Hello is any one home?" as he normally does.

"Up in my room, Daddy," Tia replies.

Kevin's heart starts to beat faster as Bobby Sharp's footsteps got louder and closer to Tia's bedroom. He knocks on the door as he asks "you home alone, sweetie?"

"No, Daddy. Lisa is here. Come and meet Kevin, my friend," Tia invites.

"Glad to met you," Bobby says as he stands on his daughter's doorway.

Kevin get up and shakes his hands, "You, too, sir," he responds.

"Claire and Mummy still out?"

"Yep! You want to join us for lunch, Daddy?" Tia asks her father.

"No, thank you. I've had lunch already. I'm going to be in the study after I check on your sister. See you two later!"

Kevin was relieved, but Tia started laughing out loud: "You should have seen your face!"

"Oh... you think that was funny. Ha, ha, ha." He gets up and grabs hold of her, as they both laugh. Suddenly, Kevin stops laughing.

"God, you are so beautiful," he whispers. Their eyes lock with one another. Slowly he kisses her softly on her lips. Her whole body is floating as she puts her hands on his shoulders and kisses him back with tender, sexier kisses. He has never been kissed like this before. Her lips are so soft, they taste like strawberries. Kevin has never felt this way and he doesn't want the kiss to stop. When she finally pulls away, he discovers he is aroused to the point of no return. She somehow knows it and loves every minute of his discomfort. They are still holding hands when he pulls her close to him and she stands on her toes and softly kisses him behind the ears. Whispering in his ear, Tia asks "are you hungry?"

Speechless, Kevin smiles. He is not thinking about food right now... no man would be thinking about food after that kiss!

"Let's go have lunch!" says Tia playfully.

Chapter 3

At nearly five months pregnant, Kate Lee has big things on the way. She still lives at home at the age of twenty-one. Her mother wishes that she was married by now, preferably to a Chinese man or to have a Chinese boy-friend. Kate is preparing for her new arrival and overseeing the launch of her newly designed dress collection being retailed by Urban Style. She and Jaden Blake have been dating for two years now. They have a lot of similar qualities and the relationship works, including their shared laid-back vibe.

"Jaden has asked me to move in with him," she tells Tia and Brooke.

"Move in where?" Brooke asks sarcastically.

"Don't tell me you going to move into that pit he calls a flat? Girl, are you out of your mind?" Brooke adds.

Tia shouts, "Brooke, please! Stop it."

Brooke stands up. She puts one hand on her waist and the other one brushes back her blonde hair. Then, she pulls down her super-short shorts and throwing down the fabric she exclaims, "Just because you are going to have a child by him doesn't mean you have to move in with him in that pig-sty of a flat! You should think twice before you go and do this, Kate. Having a baby and moving in together is not a joke." Brooke heads straight to the kitchen after venting her feelings.

"Wow! I think you're really brave. Brooke can be pretty mean when she wants to," Tia remarks. "Listen, sweetie. You do what you feel is right for you. I am here for you if you ever want to talk," Tia murmurs.

Tia always knows how to balance their friendship: Kate and Tia have been friends since primary school. They are in different colleges now, though still friends, and in a few weeks about to open a shop together.

"Your mum did not make any rice today, Kate?" Brooke shouts from the kitchen.

"Yes! There's a large, square Tupperware container in the fridge, the one with the red lid!" shouts Kate in reply.

Brooke loves Mrs Lee's fried rice. Although she hates Chinese food, Mrs Lee's Chinese food is the best. She often wonders why Mrs Lee doesn't open a Chinese restaurant. Brooke is the business brain in the group. She is always coming up with business ideas, some not so good. She is very out-spoken and doesn't know when to stop sometimes.

"Darling, perhaps I was a bit harsh about what I said before – oh, my God, this is delicious! Kate, your mum should really think about opening a restaurant. This rice is better than sex," raves Brooke.

They all laugh out loud and Tia teases, "when was the last time you had sex to know how good it is?"

"You are such a child, Tia!" Brooke screeches.

Meanwhile, laughing hysterically, "I am scornful about everything!" Tia says.

Brooke sits down and puts a plate of food on the table in front her. Crossing her legs and with a forkful of food in her mouth, she raises the glass of wine and says, "as I was saying, if you are so determined to move in with Security Officer Jaden, the best thing I can do as your best of best girl pal is make sure that I help you two find a flat in a decent area, so my god child can be safe and I won't have to worry about the poor darling all the time."

"Whoa!" Tia exclaims. "Since when are you her best of the best of her girl pals?"

"Ladies, please. I have to break the news to my mum first," Kate says.

It's been a great strain not to be able to tell her mother that she is pregnant. Kate has been anxious about telling her mother. She puts on a happy face for her friends, but Kate is seriously concerned about the impact her pregnancy will have on her relationship with her mother. She can't let them see how nervous she is. As thrilled as she is about having a baby, Kate knows her mother will not be happy at all. She is stressing out so badly that she's having panic attacks, which she desperately tries to hide from her friends. Kate is totally freaking out and it's weighing heavily on Kate, keeping her up at night. Although, her mother is amazing and understanding, Kate hasn't told her everything about her Jaden and their plans for the future. She doesn't want to worry her friends, so she's holding a lot of her fears inside. She suddenly feels a pain in her lower abdomen and screams in pain.

"Oh, sweetie! You don't have to be afraid of telling your mum. She loves you and she will understand," Tia re-assures Kate. She stops mid-sentence and stares at Kate, "what's wrong with you?"

"No, something wrong with me.... am in so much pain," Kate starts to cry as the pain strengthens.

"Brooke get the car! We've got to go now!" Tia commands.

"We still have lots to do, girls, if we are going to open in two weeks. We cannot be messing about any more. We are not going anywhere until the labels are put on the dresses, and Tia, you need to call your Dad and see if we can get some kind of business loan. I called your mum's Bank and she told me she don't loan money to family. Besides... her rate was too high." As Brooke walks into the studio, she sees Kate on the floor crying in pain. "Mary, Jesus, and Joseph! I will get the bloody car! Hold on darling!" Brooke runs out and pulls her car in front of the house. Impatiently, she gets out of the car to help Tia assist Kate. They pile into the car and in just a few minutes they arrive at Croydon Hospital. Anne Lee was there, too.

Ann Lee, a personal support worker, is visiting a client at Croydon Hospital when Brooke calls to say the girls are on the way and can she meet them at the emergency door. Mrs Lee's mind was dull of worries, when she gets Brooke's call. Brooke, Tia, and Mrs Lee have been at the waiting room for almost five hours and the doctor finally comes out to talk to them. The doctor joins Mrs Lee, as the girls walk out to the examination room where Kate is resting for a brief visit. Mrs Lee and the doctor stroll away from the waiting room and chat in the hallway, while the doctor describes Kate's condition.

"Girls, I need to talk to the doctor alone," says Mrs Lee.

As she's walking out, the doctor says to Annie Lee, "I just want you to know that your daughter and the baby are fine. An ultrasound test was done to check for the baby's heartbeat, but Kate is still bleeding."

"Oh, no, I think you are mistaken. My daughter is not pregnant."

Kate mumbles, "Mum, I am," and the doctor says, "Obviously, you guys need to talk."

Annie has a lot to consider: the fact that her little girl is pregnant; that she has been through a lot by herself, and hasn't been honest with her is a lot of information to process. Annie Lee has always thought she and her daughter are as close as any single parent can be with her child. They have been through a lot together, the two of them. She couldn't think, so she kisses her daughter on the cheek and says "it's okay".

How can Kate be almost five months pregnant and not tell her? She leaves the room not wanting Kate to see her disappointment. Annie's mind drifts back to when she first arrived in London as a refugee in the eighties, with a six-year-old Kate, an adorable kid, even though they both didn't speak much English. But two months after they arrived in London, Annie decided that she didn't want to be on welfare, so she started school to learn English. One day at the job center there was an advertisement for a housekeeper at the Ghana High Commission House. Annie applied for the job and got it. Over time, Annie became friends with the ambassador's wife, Gertrude, and one day Gertrude told her that her granddaughter, Tia, who is the same age as Kate, would be coming to stay with them for the summer, so if Annie likes, she can come and stay at the guest house with Kate. The two girls have been like sisters ever since. Annie feels confused.

"Lola, Lola," Tia calls out to her, the Chinese name meaning "auntie" that Tia has been calling Annie since she was a child. "What did the doctor say?" Tia asks with a worried look in her eyes. "Are Kate and the baby okay?"

Jealously, Annie thinks, "Of course, she knows. They are like sisters."

"Yes, Tia. They both fine," Annie mutters.

Both Tia and Brooke throw up their hands in relief and hug Annie at the same time.

"Why didn't you girls tell me she was pregnant? And how long? Don't you girls know you cannot hide a pregnancy?" Annie demands almost in tears.

Tia asks Brooke to leave them alone. "Oh, Lola. I'm sorry. She was going to tell you today. It's just that everything has been happening with exams and the launch of the clothes... we all have been very busy. I'm so sorry we didn't tell you sooner, Lola. Really, she was." Tia explains as she holds Annie.

"I don't know what to say to her, Tia. I had so much hope for her and so many dreams for her, too."

"All the dreams that you have for her are all going to come true, Lola. You will see. Right now, she needs you." Tears roll down Lola's face as Tia lets go of her embrace.

"You have always been a good girls." Annie stands up and returns to Kate's room. She gets into the bed and holds her little girl just like she used to when she was five. With her mother holding her, Kate easily falls asleep.

"Someone should let Jaden know that Kate's is in hospital," says Brooke.

"In the morning. He is working a twelve hour shift and his cell phone is probably switched off. I will call him in the morning. Let's go," Tia says.

She and Tia return to the room to see their friend. She is sleeping and has her mum with her, so the two girls leave. On the way home their friend never leaves their thoughts. As Brook pulls the car into the Sharp's driveway, the two girls sit in the car with their own thoughts about their friend.

"What are we going to say to Jaden?" Tia wonders.

"Right now, we hope for the best. That's all we can do. The baby and Kate are both doing well, which means we can all have a good night's sleep and worry about what's ahead tomorrow. There is nothing we can do now, Tia," advises Brooke.

Jaden Luke Blake is a security guard. He attends London School of Law and Economics, and has just finished his second year studying Law and working hard to save money for the summer so that he and the love of his life, Kate, can move in together. Kate is the best thing that ever happened to him. In four months he is going to be a father. He is determined to do his very best for Kate and their child. He wants to give them a home and a family life he never had. Jaden has recently reconciled with his alcoholic father, a graduate of the school of Hard Knocks, who has moved in with him and has happily settled into Jaden's second bedroom. Jaden was raised in London by his mom, Joyce. The Blake's marriage started promisingly enough: adultery, addiction to marijuana and alcohol, abusive behavior, physical abuse, sexual addictions and frequent abandonment. Joyce always put up with Luke's moods, but she reached her limit of what she could take when Luke became addicted to heroin. She and Luke, a former school teacher, divorced and Joyce got custody of Jaden; she filed a restraining order against Luke and moved to London, away from the bad influence of Luke's habits.

Most of their family members could not understand why Joyce would go that far. The breakdown of their marriage came as a surprise to most of their friends as Joyce always appeared content. Luke would often drink during the day and would stagger back to their flat if he wasn't driving. The boozing had a serious impact on their marriage and on Jaden. Joyce would get upset about Luke's drinking, the lack of money, his behavior, and they would frequently argue in front of Jaden until one fateful afternoon during one ferocious fight Luke hit his young son and knocked him out. Luke was lucky that he didn't kill the boy. Jaden was only three years old at the time. Luke later relocated to a small town in Surrey. He and Jaden reunited four months ago after Jaden learned he was going to be a father. Luke claims he has kicked his drug habit.

"We both have similar tastes," thinks Jaden. "Living in close proximity, we get into little battles... over the fridge, over supplies... just everyday average stuff – toothpaste, clean towels – it becomes a little overbearing. Kate is a godsend," he often says to himself. Classy, intelligent, beautiful, his exotic beauty Kate. It's a serious relationship for the both of them. It's amazing to be in an adult relationship. It helps that they have been friends for two years before becoming intimate. Jaden is ecstatic that Kate has agreed to move in with him. They have been spending more time in his flat the past two months anyway, so they decided Kate should just move in her stuff. It's a big move for both of them, but they're very much in love and with a baby on the way, Jaden absolutely adores Kate and fits right in with her friends and lifestyle.

Jaden has just finished a twelve hour shift with a partner he doesn't like and has come to his flat for some peace and quiet. Instead, he finds the place looking like a tip. How is it all going to work when Kate moves in? He notices how the Lee's live: their house is so clean and tidy, he often wonders how Mrs Lee manages to keep the house so spotless with Kate and her girl friends always in and out. Maybe he should start and look for a three bedroom flat somewhere near Kate's mum's house. Jaden knows just who to call for help. He takes out his cell phone and as he switches it on, he decides to call Brooke first to see if she can help him find a place for them before he calls Kate.

The cell phone begins to ring as soon as he switches it on and it's Brooke calling.

"Hey, you! I was about to call you. I need your help to find a three bedroom flat in the Croydon area. Please say you will help me?" Jaden says.

The person on the other line tells him to slow down and she is not Brooke, but before Tia can tell him that she is using Brooke's cell phone he hangs up.

"What the hell's wrong with this boy? He just hang up on me!" Tia tells Brooke, who is still sleeping at ten in the morning. "Brooke, Brooke did you hear me?" Tia says.

Brook wakes up and sits on the bed. "You and your family are so loud in the morning! Don't you think it's time you move out and get your own place? This is not an ideal romantic atmosphere for you and Kevin – if you know what I mean!"

Tia gives her one of her nasty looks. "Jaden just hang up on me," Tia complains.

"Well, the way you look, any man will hang up on you, darling," Brooke says. "What are you doing calling him this time of the morning anyway? Shouldn't you be calling what's-his-name sweet-lips-Kevin?"

"I was calling to let him know about Kate being in hospital," says Tia.

Brooke had forgotten that Kate was in hospital. "Oh, good heavens! I forgot he doesn't know! Give me the phone, darling. I'd like to see him hang up on me!"

"No, I think he thought he had a wrong number. He wanted you to help him find a three bedroom flat."

"Well, that's a good start!" She dials Jaden's number which he answers on the second ring. "Hey! I tried to call you a little while ago, but it was a wrong number," says Jaden.

"It was Tia calling you, but you hang up on her. Kate is in Croydon Hospital since last night. She and the baby are okay, but we are going there to see her soon. Do want us to pick you up?" Brooke asks.

Jaden is shocked and cannot talk. He has no idea what Brooke has just said. The only thing he can remember is that Kate is in hospital.

"Kate is in hospital!" he repeats.

"Yes, Jaden. Do you need me to come and pick you up?" Brooke asks again.

"Why is Kate in hospital? Do you know why?"

"She was feeling pains, and we thought it was the baby. Do you want me to pick you up?"

"Yes. Please. Thank you, Brooke."

Hanging up the phone, Jaden sits down on the floor, the tears rolling non-stop down his cheeks. What had happened? She was fine yesterday when they had lunch and she looked so beautiful. She was glowing and the dress she wore looked so sexy. He rushed outside to the nearby florist and got some flowers before the girls got there.

As they were pulling into the parking lot of the hospital, Brooke's cell phone was ringing. As she answered the call, Mrs Lee blurted out, "I don't know how to tell you this, but Kate lost the baby last night." Brooke's face went white and she was speechless. She drops the phone and lets out a loud scream "that's not fair." Both Tia and Jaden hearts start to beat faster as they both ask, "What's wrong?" Brooke could not talk and when she turned to face Tia, her expression told her the inevitable. They got out of the car without saying a word to Jaden.

Mrs Lee met Jaden and the girls outside Kate's room and she said to Jaden, "I am so sorry she lost the baby." Even though Jaden went from the high of impending fatherhood to the depths of grief when he learned Kate had lost their baby, Jaden never lost sight of his need to be strong for her. When Kate's mother delivered the devastating news, Jaden was stunned. "How did this happen?" he asked.

"The cervix, I mean the bottom part of the Kate's uterus was opened. She was having painful cramps after Tia and Brooke left. After her miscarriage, there were some tissues left in her uterus, which the surgeon removed using a D & C procedure because the residual tissues can cause infection. There was nothing the doctors could have done to prevent her miscarriage. However, she can still get pregnant again and have a healthy baby. She was bleeding very heavily last night after Tia and Brooke had left. I am so sorry Jaden," said Mrs Lee. Mrs Lee hugs Jaden because she doesn't know how to soften the blow for him. His grief is evident to the girls, who also don't know how to react to the bad news.

Jaden is devastated. Joyce Blake is there, too, because Mrs Lee called her earlier. Slowly releasing pent-up tension with a deep exhale, Jaden's eyes and the husky tenor of his voice conveyed the depth of his suffering; yet, Jaden held in all the pain and focused on comforting Kate. Jaden kissed her forehead and whispered," I am so sorry, darling."

Kate could not stop crying, so Jaden holds her as she cries, while her friends and her mother watch with their own grief.

Later, at the Lee's house, Jaden continues ignoring his own grief to dote on Kate. When she goes for a nap, Jaden's face is a mask of confusion. Jaden looks lost, and there is a note of frustration in his voice as he sighs and admits he doesn't know how to help her.

Tia tells him it will be okay, that he is not alone, but it is alone with his mother that Jaden finally admits his pain. "We lost the baby," he croaks as his eyes well with tears. After showing that brief vulnerability, Jaden quickly reverts to stifling his feelings, but Joyce reminds her son that he, too, has suffered a loss, so Jaden allows himself to open up a little more.

"I feel like I lost someone I loved with all my heart, and I never got a chance to meet him," he whispers, his facade of strength cracking right along with his voice. Joyce has never seen her son in such pain and she wishes she could take it away. She is so proud of him: only twenty-two, he is in university studying law without a government grant and has found it in himself to forgive a father who abandoned him for drugs and now this. Why? Her son doesn't deserve this. He is a good boy. "Why can't God give my son a break?" she asks herself. "How is he going to get thought this? He was so looking forward to becoming a father."

"Jaden, I would like for you to come and stay for the summer. Please, think about it. I don't want you alone in that flat of yours," Joyce says to her son. She makes an effort to console him. Jaden has not told his mother about his father living with him. "I guess now is not the right time to tell her," he thinks privately. "I will come home on the bank holiday weekend, Mama. I have that weekend off, " and with a kiss and a hug, he leaves.

Jaden's flat has been a pig-sty since his father moved in. The flat is becoming increasingly untidy. Going to the fridge, Jaden takes out a beer and sits on the floor drinking. He is thinking what he could have done to prevent the loss of the baby. Kate did not fall, or do drugs, so how can she miscarry the baby? He feels enraged! He feels helpless, too, just as he did as a boy when his father beat his mother and there was nothing he could do to help her. He throws the beer bottle against the wall in anger. He sits down on the dirty living room floor and cries.

Chapter 4

Sarah Morgan-Williams was the only child of Ethan Morgan, a real estate mogul in the sixties, and Sarah's mother, a fashion magazine editor who believed that one should not run to the altar and get married for the sake of a child. Ethan adored her and gave in to her wishes, so they were not married when Sarah was born and she died soon after giving birth to Sarah, so Ethan raised his daughter all by himself in a huge mansion in London's Kew Gardens. He was often seen at work with the infant at a time when women looked after babies. Although he had plenty of money to hire a nanny for his daughter, he refused to do so. He had many romantic interests from actresses to duchesses. He told one of his charms from Oxford that "no woman was fit enough to raise his daughter." He would take her with him when he played polo with his aristocratic friends, who often thought little Sarah Morgan was a well-behaved child. They all watched her grow to be a beautiful girl and an extraordinary young woman. And still, Sarah was the only teenager in their circle of friends who did not talk back to her father. Sarah did whatever her father asked without questioning him. They also shared a passion for art. After graduating from Oxford University, it was not surprising when she followed his footsteps and turned the Gemini Real Estate Company into a multi-million-pounds empire. Rumor has it that her first marriage to Ted White was arranged by her father. Again, Sarah obeyed her father even though she had hardly been on a date with a man her own age.

Ted White was in his fifties. An over-weight Irishman, with a big ego to go with it, he worked for the London Weekend Television as a producer on the Cila Black Show, "surprise, surprise." He has more money than he can ever spend before he dies. The duo first met at a charity event, but they actually didn't start dating until two weeks before they were married. The Cila Black Show was pre-taped during the week and shown on Saturday evening on ITV. Ted White is a workaholic, who works from seven in the morning until ten at night. The union with Sarah turned out to be a farce for all involved, as Sarah filed for an annulment two months after the wedding, citing "fraud" as the reason, a claim that has never been explained by either party. Her beloved father died soon after the annulment of complications from bacterial pneumonia. Sarah has always missed him dearly. She was prepared for her father's death, so was better able to cope with her loss.

Jackson Williams was an old friend of the family. When Jackson was looking to buy a home in London in 1976, he asked his old friend Sarah to help him and sparks reignited. They began dating. Every Monday, Jackson would send her a present with a note attached which would always lead to a romantic rendezvous between the two love birds. Although they were both in their mid-twenties and had had previous sexual relationships, they decided to wait until they got married to become intimate, and were together for a year when one day Jackson asked Sarah to go to the mail box and get his mail for him while he get changed his clothes. She found a single yellow rose and a tiny white box with a card written in a red ink: "Please say you will marry me." She turned around with a surprised look on her face when she saw Jackson on one knee, "what do you say?"

Jackson and Sarah are perfect for each other, and he would do anything in the world for her. A year later they welcomed a new addition to their family, Brooke. Jackson says Sarah has given him many gifts, but the best one of all was the birth of their daughter. Jack died in the Lockerbie plane crash and Sarah turned to work to assuage her grief. She put Brooke in a boarding school at an early age, and they have been growing apart since Jackson died, as if part of them died with him.

Brooke Williams thought of the time when she was living at home and started acting out. She was just like any other teenage girl, and her mum, Sarah, had had enough! Sarah is putting the brakes on her out-of-control daughter's bad attitude, snotty comments and flirting with boys and older men. Sarah Williams grounded the seventeen year old Brooke, forbidding her to use her computer or the phone, and no sleepovers! Brooke is getting too big for her britches and has to be taken down a notch or two. That summer Sarah told Brooke, who has been in boarding school since she was six years old, that she will be going to the local secondary school to finish her A-Levels. Brooke now attends a nearby college and works part-time with her mother.

Sarah was concerned over her daughter's nonstop rudeness. Brooke continues to rebel. Once, she found a box of condoms in Brooke's room, and when she confronted her, Brooke snapped, "Get off my back, Mother!" She also has been using inappropriate language, swearing and yelling. Sarah has had enough of that. She called Brooke into her study one day and said, "I want to show you something. Come with me."

Brooke thought they were going do something together for a change, as mother and daughter, so she didn't make a fuss when her mother asked her to get in her car. They drove to a neighborhood called Charlton in the south east of London. Brooke did not see any of Gemini's for sale signs and asked, "What are we doing here?" Sarah did not reply. They took the lift to the ninth floor and Sarah opened the door and invited Brooke inside. It was beautiful open-concept apartment with a spectacular view of the Thames River and also of the planes taking off from London City Airport. Brooke was in love with the place already. Sarah went to the kitchen and came back with a bottle of Coke for Brooke, who was standing by the window looking at the view. Sarah has put Brooke on a strict allowance and even taken away her driving privileges. And Sarah has even more radical plans to keep Brooke on track.

"You are seventeen years old, Brooke, and as much as I love you, I cannot live with you. The way things are going, it's only a matter of time before you run away from home. This is one of my flats and now it is yours. You want to be a grown up? This is your chance to become one. Go to college, don't go to college. Show up for work and respect the job that provides for you, or don't. It is all up to you." Sarah threw the keys on the table and left.

Brooke was not shocked or saddened. This was like a dream come true. For once, she felt like her mother had read her thoughts. There were two bedrooms: the main bedroom had a double bed and two bedside tables and two double-sided wardrobes with all her clothes in it; the second bedroom was a bit smaller with a computer and a printer on a corner desk. The living room had a peach sectional leather sofa and a dining table with six chairs. There was a washing machine and dryer in the small kitchen, with a small fridge. The hall closet had a chest freezer. The bathroom was smaller than her bathroom in her mother's home.

Brooke didn't have any friends in London, so she couldn't call anyone to have a party. She put the music on and took a bath with the bathroom door open. Afterward, she wandered around the neighborhood. She discovered a fish and chips store, so she went in and bought herself fish and chips for supper. Brooke did not discover anything else of interest in her new neighborhood.

The first two days she stayed home and listened to music. From time to time, the phone rang, and whenever it was her mother on the other end, she immediately hung up on her. The phone rang again and again. She got sick of hearing the phone ringing nonstop, so she left the flat. As she came out, Brooke saw bus 54 going to South Croydon. She got on and went upstairs on the bus. She had never before been in a double-decker bus. She had no idea where South Croydon was, but felt game for anything as long as she wouldn't have to hear her mother's voice telling her to grow up.

The last stop of the bus was a big shopping mall. Brooke strolled around the mall and discovered a shop called The Buzz. There was a Chinese girl behind the counter who was talking and laughing with a black girl, whose back was turned to Brooke, so she couldn't see her face. It looks like they are good friends the way they are talking and laughing. Brooke forgot what she was doing, so the black girl came and said, "are you alright?" She had a tiny little voice like a little girl. Brooke wondered if she could sing at all with voice like that.

"Yes, thank you," says Brooke.

"Is there anything I can help you with?" Tia asks.

"I'm not sure. I got bored at home, so I took a bus ride and here I am. You have nice things here." says Brooke.

"Are you looking for a job, or are you doing window shopping?" Tia prompts.

"A little bit of both," says Brooke. Brooke figures if her mother can't stand being in the same house with her, she might as well not work with Sarah, even though she loves the real estate business.

"I am Tia. Come meet Kate. She does the hiring. Who knows? You may go home with a job! Kate, are we still looking for sale associates?" Tia asks.

"I'm not sure. I have to call Nicky and see. Who wants to know?" Kate asks.

"Hi! I'm Brooke. I am in desperate need of employment. I'm a fast learner and I can work any day you give me. I can get references, if you want... I do have work experience as well good interpersonal skills."

"Nicky is the owner, but she is away until next week. I'll talk to her first, and see. If you leave me your number or a CV, we can call you." The phone was ringing. "Please excuse me." Kate says as she answered the phone. It was Jaden. Just then a bunch of teens came into the shop and one of them asked Brooke for help. She showed them what goes with what and what doesn't, and the teens were taken with her. Tia and Kate watched Brooke make three sales. Clearly, she was a natural salesperson. After the teens left, Kate said, "You are hired!"

Tia ran to hug her and they started to laugh. Brooke stayed until they closed. When Kate asked for her phone number, Brooke replied, "I just moved into my flat two days ago. I don't know the phone number yet."

When Jaden arrived at the store, he wanted to take them all to movies, but he didn't have enough money. Brooke offered, "Since you guys have given me a job, how about you all come to my place for a house warming party?"

"I have to call my mum first and tell her. I have my driving test in three days, so I may not be allowed to go with you guys, if she says no," Tia says.

"Cool. You can call her from my place. That way you can give her the address, and maybe she can't say no," suggests Brooke.

It is not long before they arrive at Brooke's flat. When they go into the living room, Sarah is there and Jaden immediately recognizes her. "You're Sarah Williams, the real estate queen!" he exclaims.

"You cannot just come in here whenever you feel like it, mother!" Brooke snaps at Sarah.

"But… I was worried about you when you didn't answer your phone, Brooke." Sarah notices Tia, but Tia didn't recognize her. Sarah Williams and the Sharps have been very good friends for years. Sarah refers most of her clients to the African Mortgage Fund, Tia's mother's company. She thought Brooke was in good company for a change, so she tried not to make too much fuss.

"Where have you been?" Sarah asks.

"I don't live at home anymore. I don't have to answer to you, but if you must know, I went job hunting and these are my co-workers. Please leave, Mum," says Brooke.

"You want a second job? That's fine, I expect you at work on Monday – if you want to keep your flat!" Sarah warns her.

Brooke lashes out at her mother, and pours out her feelings in front of her new friends. Sarah is embarrassed by her daughter's outburst in front of the strangers. Sarah glares at Brooke and then storms out of the flat.

"You live alone?" Kate asks.

"Yes," she pauses for a minute. "I got kicked out of my house two days ago and here I am, living in one of my mum's flats."

Brooke turns and goes to the kitchen, telling to them to make themselves at home.

"Oh, Tia, the phone is right there on the center table if you want to call your mum." Brooke points to the phone.

They could not believe that Brooke lives in this fabulous flat all by herself, nor could they comprehend the way she talks to her mother. Jaden, Kate and Tia could never talk that way to their mothers – ever. They would be killed. They somehow feel sorry for her, how lonely it must feel to have a mother like Sarah Williams who doesn't care because the three of them all have a close relationship with their own mothers. They all follow Brooke to the kitchen and help her fix a meal, and before they know it, they have a meal fit for a king.

They end up staying the night and from that point forward, they have all become like a family.

Chapter 5

When Brooke returns to her flat in Charlton later that evening after work, her flat is so quiet she wishes Tia would move out of her home and come share with her. She never understood why any nineteen year old would want to live at home with parents and siblings. Personally, she could not wait to leave home when she turned sixteen and she has not looked back since. Although with everything that has been going this weekend, she sort of envies her two friends and their close relationships with their mothers, something she has never had with her own mother. Brooke saunters into the living room, feeling sad as she thinks about the baby Jaden and Kate have just lost and she starts to cry. She knows how much they have been looking forward to the baby. She wonders what Tia is doing.

Kevin is watching the World Cup in America. Argentina is playing Nigeria and when the doorbell rings, he doesn't want to go and get the door. At the second ring, he gets up and runs to the door. It's Tia in a yellow dress.

"Thank you, God," he says in his head.

She kisses him right on the lips as she enters the flat. She smells so good. She has grocery bags and Kevin takes them for her. "How are you?" he says.

"I been good... and you?" she asks. "Can I use the kitchen?"

"Yes, of course! Do you need help?"

"No. Go, watch your football. I am fine," Tia says.

"It's okay, I'm taping it for Aaron because he is working tonight. So... what do you have in the bags?" inquires Kevin.

"I want to make dinner for us, is it okay?"

He kisses her on the cheek, "yes, yes."

After dinner, while they are sitting on the sofa, Tia falls asleep. She did not sleep the night before with Kate being in hospital. Kevin carries her to the bedroom and puts her to bed. Later, Tia wakes and as she sits up in the bed, she sees Kevin sitting opposite her. She is unusually quiet. Kevin doesn't know what is wrong with her. Finally, he asks if she feels alright. Suddenly, they are kissing passionately, Tia undresses him and asks him to lay face down on the bed. Tension melts away as Tia massages warm oil into his back and runs her tongue all over with soft kisses. She makes love to his back as she rocks her hips in slow, small circles, pressing her mons directly against his tail bone. She slips away from him on the bed, and as Kevin rolls over, he watches while she peels down to bra and panties.

Fully aroused, he walks towards her and pulls off her lingerie. Her bare breasts feel like velvet as he touches them. Tia slides her hand down his arms, braids her fingers into his own, and he lifts her up onto the bed as he kisses her neck all the way to her thighs. Tia becomes more aroused as Kevin teases and fondles her, strokes her.... he slips inside with a ride slow and easy while the steam starts to build. The head of his penis is riding across her G-spot with every stroke. He feels her hot breath and warm mouth on his neck. With desire, burning with anticipation, they drove each other to an intense and very powerful climax.

"Will you marry me ?" Kevin asks.

"It was not that good !" Tia kisses him with a smile.

"I am serious! I want you to be my wife. Tia, I have not stopped thinking about you since day one. Making love to you is nothing I have ever experienced. You have my heart. I don't know any other way to tell you." He is almost in tears. Tia kisses him and now they are making love again. They stay up all night talking and Tia tells him about Jaden and Kate's loss and how helpless they all feel. They fall asleep in each other's arms. Later, Kevin is the first to wake and when he realizes that Tia has spent the night, he feels aroused all over again. As he reaches over and kisses her, she opens her eyes and says good morning with a kiss.

"I can't keep my hands off you," Tia says.

"I don't want you to keep your hands off me. What would you like for breakfast?" Kevin asks.

"Make love to me," she says.

"I thought we were doing that already," he jokes. They stay in bed until after lunch when Tia finally says, "I have to be at my friend Brooke's at four so we can find a way to help Kate cope with her loss."

"What is Brooke's number?" Kevin asks. As he picks up the phone, Tia tells him and he dials the number. "It's ringing," he says to Tia.

"Hello, may I please speak with Miss Williams, please?" Kevin says.

Brooke is not feeling well that afternoon when she answers the phone, and no one calls her Miss Williams, so she snaps, "What can I do for you?"

"I have your friend here wants to cancel your date tonight. I will pass the phone to her." As Kevin passes the phone, Tia is laughing out loud.

"Who the hell is this?" Brooke snaps again.

"Hey, Brooke! It's me, Tia. How are you?"

There is a beep on Brooke's line, so she takes the phone off her ear to see who is calling. She sighs deeply when she sees the number and takes a deep breath before she pushes the hold button, and with an even tone she says, "Hello, Mother. One second, please, Mother," as she puts her mother on hold. "Tia, darling, I will call you right back." Hanging up on Tia, Brooke walks to the kitchen, opens the cupboard, takes out a wine glass and pours herself some before going back to her study. She sits in the love seat for about a minute before resuming the call with her mother.

"Sorry to keep you waiting, Mother. What can I do for you?"

Sarah Williams senses some sadness in her daughter's voice. It reminds her of when she was a little girl and often felt sad. Ethan would sit her on his lap and hold her and kiss her on the head. How she missed him so and wished he were here.

"How have you been, darling?" Sarah inquires.

"I am alright, mother," Brooke says as she takes a sip of the ice-chilled wine and closes her eyes.

"I just finished watching the video of your fashion show. You look so beautiful, darling. I am so sorry I missed it."

Brooke almost spilled the wine on herself as her mother's words travel through her whole body like an electric shock.

"What are you talking about Mother? What video?"

Sarah is a little confused. "Are you alright, darling?" she asks again.

"Yes, Mother. I am fine. What video are you talking about?"

"Tia Sharp brought a video tape of the show for me last week. I just finished watching it. I thought I'd call and touch base and see how you are. I have not seen you in the office lately," said Sarah coolly.

"I have two closings on the tenth and both clients' lenders are about to pull out because of the down payment issues. I should be in the office all day Monday. I was hoping Tia's mum could help, but she is still in Ghana," she tells her mother.

The relationship between them is still so strained. There is not so much anger between them since Brooke left home three years ago, but both women secretively wish things could change, even though they are both scared and have never dealt with the death of Jackson until now. They talk on the phone a long time. It was good for the both of them. Sarah has always felt she abandoned Brooke when Jackson died by putting her in a boarding school, but there was not much else she could do. Jackson was her rock, and after his death getting out of bed was like climbing a mountain. Also, Brooke looks so much like him, she couldn't bear to be around the six year old. She didn't want to be the kind of a parent her father was. How she wished she could turn back the clock! She would do things very differently. She has missed her little girl's childhood. "Fifteen years has gone by so quickly," Sarah thought. She agreed to a shaky truce with her once-estranged daughter when Brooke asked to work full-time with her. Sarah likes Brooke's work ethic, and Brooke seems to understand the business a lot more now. Before they say good-bye, Sarah advises her daughter: "Do give Jason Grey at Mercury Asset Management a call. He might be able to help your clients to secure a mortgage."

Chapter 6

As soon as she ended the call, Brooke went to the bathroom and ran a bubble bath, got into the bath tub and dialed Jason Grey's cell. On the second ring, he answered. Brooke wasn't sure if it was the effects of the wine, but Jason Grey had the sexiest phone voice.

"Jason Grey here… what can I do for you?"

"My name is Brooke Williams. Mr. Grey, I was hoping I could meet with you on Monday with my clients who are trying to secure a mortgage."

"Are you a broker?" Jason asked.

"No, Sir. I'm the real estate agent."

"Oh. Please call me Jason. Um… who referred you, Miss Williams? I mean, how did you get my private number?" he asks.

"My boss just gave it to me a few moments ago. She thought you might be able to help my clients."

"How about Tuesday at one?" he invites.

"Sounds good," Brooke affirms.

"I'm at 33 London Bridge Road. It's the first building on your left if you are coming from the Borough."

"Thank you, Mr. Grey, I mean, Jason."

"I'll see you then."

Jaden has not been himself since the loss of the baby. He has been drinking and going to the pubs a lot more. He has grown a beard and looks unkempt. He calls Kate, but on the second ring he hangs up and throws his beer bottle across the room. It almost hits his father. Luke has not seen his son for weeks. Now, he is trying to avoid him for some reason he can't quite identify. "What could be going on with Jaden," he wonders.

"Are you alright, son?" asks Luke.

Jaden stands there expressionless. He doesn't respond to his father. Instead, he goes to the balcony and lights up a cigarette, inhaling slowly. Tears drop as he sits down on the chair and looks up the sky. "It is so blue," he thinks. He remembers his father using marijuana and getting high on amphetamines. The drugs seemed to made him happy. The thought outrages Jaden. "How could his father do that to him and his mum? Pathetic," he says to himself as he opens the door and goes into the living room. He is greeted by a smell he knows well but can't place. He walks into the small kitchen where Luke is smoking something that looks like a cigarette. "No smoking in the flat, Dad. Go outside like everyone else," he snaps at his father.

His father has a goatee, thinning gray hair, his blue eyes hidden behind dark sunglasses. He is obviously in a good mood.

"A lovely afternoon," he says to his son. "Want a drink with the old man?"

Jaden stands alongside his father as Luke hands his son his smoke. As Jaden takes a puff, he feels the smoke go straight to his whole body. "What kind of cigarette is it?" Taking another puff, he inhales more slowly this time and feels relaxed as he drinks his beer.

"You know, Dad, Kate lost the baby two weeks ago."

"Oh, dear God. No, son, I didn't know. I am so sorry. Why didn't you tell me?" Luke was shocked to hear about the miscarriage. He can see the whole thing has taken on a heavy toll on his son. Perhaps giving his son pot is not such a good idea, given the circumstances.

"I don't know how I am going to get through this. Dad, I don't know how to help Kate. I am going to lose her," he says as he nearly collapses from the emotional strain. He falls into his father's arms as Luke carries Jaden to the bedroom and puts him to bed. Afterward, Luke lounges in the living room contemplating what he can do to help his son. After all, this is his second chance to be a father to him.

The door bell rings. Luke looks through the peep hole to discover Kate at the door. "Just a minute! I will be right there!" he shouts and starts to pick up some of the mess and open some windows.

"Hello, Kate! Please come in, sweetheart," invites Luke.

"How are you, Mr. Blake?" Kate replies.

"The flat smells bad," she thinks, "and it looks like they've not cleaned up for a long time." She goes into the kitchen to put away the food she brought for Jaden, and starts doing the dishes in the sink.

"Jaden is sleeping. I'll go and let him know you are here, love," offers Luke.

"No, it's okay. Please, don't wake him up yet, Mr. Blake."

"I was on my way out, love." says Luke awkwardly.

"See you later!" says Kate.

She tidies up the living room, and as she mops the kitchen floor, she hears someone using the bathroom. Kate walks toward the bathroom door, and initially does not recognize Jaden with his beard. They both stand there a long time not saying a word to each other. Jaden turns and closes the toilet seat, and as he sits on it, he buries his face in his hands, fighting back the tears. Kate stands still for a while, watching him cry. Turning to the cabinet, she takes out two towels and she raises the bath tap and starts to fill the tub with water. She, then, opens the cupboard under the sink, and takes out shaving cream and starts applying it to Jaden's face. He has missed her so much but the words won't come out. He feels so emotional he cannot stop crying. Lightly, softly, Kate brushes her lips across his eyelids as she shaves him.

With a quiet ecstasy, she undresses him and takes his hands and guides him into the bath. While Kate undresses, Jaden watches her, studying all the places that he wants to touch. She sits on the opposite side of the bath tub and rests her head on his chest.

"I am so very sorry, Kate," he says softly.

She turns to face him, kissing him lightly on the upper lips, saying "it was not your fault. It wasn't meant to be."

Tears are coming down from both their eyes as they hug, and they soak in the bath tub for a very long time. After they bathe each other, he carries her into the bedroom and lays her down on the bed. Laying next to Kate, Jaden holds her close under the covers while he kisses her neck, nipples and belly. He tries to find new erogenous zones; he observes the way Kate's skin reacts as he trails his fingers tips across her warm flesh.

"Are you okay?" he asks.

She brushes back his hair and kisses him on the forehead. "Yes. Please, don't stop." She presses her fingers deeper into his skin as she massages a rich oil into his rising manhood. She observes his penis in its various stages of arousal. She wants to stroke him until he comes, but Jaden has other ideas. It was not like their usual love-making, but it was an absolute lust with each other and they both knew it. His mouth nibbling on her breast was a sensation that intrigued and delighted. It wasn't predictable sex, which was warm and very rewarding, but wild, fantasy-filled sex that's like fireworks and champagne. It was not grief sex. Emotions are swirling, though it's the worst pain ever for them losing the baby, making love numbs their pain. Jaden wakes up and Kate's gone. He has a headache, so he calls in sick again at work. He showers after a cigarette. He is so disgusted with himself after promising to quit last summer. Jaden has stared to smoke again since Kate lost the baby. He has no idea what his father gave him to smoke last night, but it lifted some of his mood. He is under intense pressure these days. It might look like he is effortlessly holding it together, but he has been hiding the loss of the baby and hopes no one knows about the drugs.

At least, he thinks no one knows. If Kate finds out Jaden has been experimenting with drugs, it will be the end of their relationship. He feels more guilty now that he thinks it may be the reason why Kate lost the baby. He tries not to let himself think of that anymore. He is done with it. "I'm nothing like my father," he says to himself. "I have lost too much already."

Chapter 7

At the opening of Urban Style, there is a long line up before the girls open and it is almost three in the afternoon before they have a coffee break.

"Wow! At this rate we may need to hire a sales associate!" says Kate enthusiastically.

"No, no. We can't! We need to make sure we break even first and let's not forget our loan payment is due in two weeks," Brooke advises.

"I hate to agree, but she is right. We need to be very careful with the money, and the three of us can't be here all the time. I have to help my mum around the house and there's my part-time job at British Telecom, too. And Brooke's job at the real estate office."

"We need to start dividing the jobs today, ladies."

"I call for a day off tomorrow," says Tia.

"Oh, no you don't, I'm older than you," Brooke says, "and I have a meeting tomorrow with a mortgage broker I can't blow off. You have to be here to help Kate in the afternoon. I can open and be out out of here by eleven, but I will come back after my meeting."

"I'm working until one tomorrow and am meeting Kevin after that" says Tia.

"What about you, Kate? Who do have a meeting with tomorrow?" Brooke quizzes.

Kate is in her own little world. She has no idea what her friends have just said. Everything is falling apart in her life. Her mother is still upset that she did not tell her about the pregnancy, Jaden has started smoking again, and even though she did not want to fight with him last night, she needs to talk to him about that, too. They realize that Kate is preoccupied. They have not talked about the loss of the baby and none of them wants to raise the subject. They can all see it's tearing her inside and they don't know how to help her.

Brooke glances at Tia and says, "I'm moving back home with my mum."

"You can not be serious!" Kate shouts.

They all started to laugh, "Good to have you back!" Brooke chuckles.

"What is happening with you? Is everything alright?" Tia asks with concern.

"Oh, nothing. I'm fine," Kate replies.

"It sure doesn't look that way," Brooke remarks. "If something is bothering you, we want to know now. We cannot afford any mistakes. We can put our heads together and deal with it, but we can't have you spacing off now you are the backbone of this business, Kate."

"Wow! You really starting to sound like Mother. Lay off her!" Tia snaps.

"Look, Kate. We're trying to do something special here. If your heart is not in it, let us know."

"If my heart is not in it?" Kate asks teary-eyed. "Since when?"

Tia has been the only one operating and meeting their customers' demands. Through her girlfriend, Lock Washington, Tia knows the professional footballer, Ashton Wentworth. The cool couple are in the tabloids all the time, so Tia invites them to visit Urban Style. They agree to come and have a look. A photo and caption noting where they got their duds will definitely boost Urban Style's sales. Kate is still sewing for the shop, each outfit custom-made for each customer, but it isn't working well. Losing the baby and regaining her health has prevented Kate from performing well for the store. They now have a supplier from Thailand for their clothing line, thanks to Tia's efforts to make their store successful.

"Well, I think you are really brave," Tia pipes up. "Brooke can be pretty mean when she wants to be." Tia turns to Brooke, "She's been through a lot. The least we can do is support her and be there for her."

Brooke frowns slightly. No one knew that better than she did. "You think I don't?"

Before anyone can respond she comes and pulls the two girls apart and stands between them, trying to control her anger. Brooke says, "We can't forget our loss, we cannot let things over which we have no control manipulate our lives and decide our fate. We just can't." Turning towards Kate she murmurs, "It hurts that you lost the baby, but it will get better. I promise you, darling."

There are tears in all of their eyes as Brooke screams, and in her voice and in her eyes Kate and Tia see something they've not seen in their friend before: Brooke being emotional. Brooke never shows emotions. It's hard to say whether she ever felt any pain in her life, but this is not her usual rant and rave business. Her voice breaks down as she begins to cry. Brooke continues, "I have not stopped thinking about what you and Jaden have lost. Just like I have never stopped thinking about my father's death. I just don't know how to help you Kate. I feel if we don't learn to deal with this …" she purses her lips, "Tia, I'm sorry if you think I don't care. You are my family and when one of you hurts, I'm hurt, too. Working and bringing all this to life is what I can do." She begins to walk off.

Kate grabs her by the arm and so does Tia.

"I am really okay, you guys, and doing a lot better. It's just some days are a lot harder than others. That's all. And I love you guys very much. You are right, Brooke. We have to take control of our fate. I won't keep things to myself, I promise."

They hug and wipe each other's tears away. "It was good to have that little talk and cry. It helps. I will be all right by myself in the afternoon. I can ask my mum to come and help out, but we have to pay her for her time," says Kate. "We can start to put the posters up on the walls and let people see what we are all about."

Tia was sorry now that she had scowled at Brooke. She felt a slight twinge of guilt for her comments to Brooke. Brooke is not the crying type. She is more of a get over it type. Of course, it all makes sense now! Tia realizes that her mother's observations about Brooke and her mother have a lot of weight: they have never dealt with the death of Brooke's father. How could they? Tia thought she understood Brooke a lot better now.

"Hey, Tia! Stop day-dreaming about that Kevin. I hope you've been practicing safe sex with him!" Brooke chastises.

"I hate you Brooke! Damn, don't you get sick of telling me what to do?" Tia snaps.

"No, it's called being an older sister. He better not give you any STD!" Brooke says bluntly.

Kate couldn't stop laughing. "Are you alright?" Both girls turned their attention to Kate.

"Keep telling her about safe sex, big sister!"

"I hate you both."

They all agreed that Tia should slow things down with Kevin and that Tia is too young to be having a sexual relationship with him. Tia and Kate went to the back stock room to bring out more merchandise to fill the space. By the time they return, Mrs Lee is laughing and eating with Brooke.

"Lola! Good to see you!" exclaims Tia as she runs to hug and kiss her auntie. Kate follows with too many things in her hands. She does not see her mother, but as she puts the products down on the display counter, Kate sees that Lola has a big smile on her face – the kind she has not seen since that day in the hospital.

"I brought some food and came to see if my baby needs my help," says Ann Lee.

Kate stands still as she cries.

"What is wrong sweetie? Did I do something wrong?" Mrs Lee asks.

Kate hesitates in confusion. " No, Mama. I'm happy to see you, that's all. You always know when I need you," Kate says as she hugs and kisses her mother.

They walk hand-in-hand around the store and Kate shows her mother where everything is.

"I am so proud of you." Mrs Lee says, hugging her daughter and crying at the same time.

"Any more crying out of you Lee women and I'm leaving!" threatens Brooke good-naturedly.

Later that the day, Brooke adds up all the sales and Tia does the stock take when they're not busy; Kate creates more designs and makes a schedule they can all bear.

"We need to put the posters on the wall tomorrow."

"I look like a dork in that picture," Tia groans. In the photo Tia is wearing a pink and green polo shirt and jeans, her hair in a ponytail. She doesn't look like a dork: she just doesn't look sexy – at least not in the way Brooke does.

"No you don't," Kate re-assures her. By six, the shop is closed and Brooke brings in three bottles of water for each of the girls and they toast to a job well done. They made more than they hoped in the first day's sales.

"I'm going to Holland in three weeks for the long weekend and I asked my grandfather already and he said it's okay for all of us to come. And my grandmother said yes. She can't wait to meet you and Jaden," says Tia. "Before you all say "no"... we need this, guys. It's just the weekend and you cannot say "no" because I have already booked us on the Euro shuttle and I was thinking Brooke could drive if we all chip in with gas."

"Well, Sin City of Europe, I'm in!" crows Brooke.

They all turn to Kate laughing.

"Okay, okay. I'm in, too. I have to talk to Jaden when he comes to dinner tomorrow night. You all are coming right?" she confirms.

"Of course! I can't say no to Lola when it comes to her cooking. You all know that!" enthuses Brooke.

Next day, Brooke opens the store. There are not as many customers as the first day, but the sales are steady. Kate arrives near eleven o'clock and says, "we may have a big wedding order to do if we all agree. It's not going to be easy and I will need everyone to help."

They know most businesses fail in the first six months and they are determined not to fail. They agreed to take the order.

"Of course, darling! I've got to run to my meeting, but tell me all about it when I come back, okay? You can reach me on my cell if you need me." Brooke kisses her friend on the cheek and leaves. She comes back a minute later: "How do I look"?

"To die for, darling!" Kate giggles.

Traffic was not bad as she picks up her clients at the Elephant and Castle and they drive to Mercury Asset Management. They approach the security guard and Brooke informs him that they are here to see Jason Grey. They are told to sign in the visitors' log and go up to the seventh floor. They take the lift and up they go.

They are shown to Jason Grey's office, where he sits behind a huge desk talking on the phone with headset on. He has more products in his hair than Brooke. Brown eyes, clean shaven, with a pink shirt – no tie – the first two buttons of the shirt collar are open, a double-breasted jacket: very smart, indeed. He extends his hands to greet Brooke's clients and introduces himself. They all shake hands and he directs them to a conference room in the corner. Before he sits down, Jason announces, "I have a lender for you for a second mortgagee based on the the information you faxed to me." He hands a copy to Brooke and two more copies to the clients. While everyone is busy reading the mortgage forms, Jason cannot take his eyes off Brooke. "She has more products in her hair than I do," he finds himself thinking. She is sporting sexy, carefree locks that make her blonde hair much more beautiful. "The starlet's sizzle pants suit she wears makes her look super smoking hot," he thinks. He quickly takes his eyes off her and clears his throat.

"What do you all think?"

The client husband says to his wife. "I love it, sweetheart. How about you?"

"The same here," says the wife.

"Okay, if you excuse me, for a minute, I will get you a commitment form to sign, and I can fax everything to your lawyer this evening."

As Jason leaves the room, Brooke draws the couple's attention to the proposed interest rate: "His rate is three percent lower than our last one."

The client husband thanks Brooke for a job well done.

"It's all in a day's work," says Brooke, " but you are welcome."

Jason returns with the papers. As he gives the couple their copy, he says, "I will get this to your lawyer ASAP!" He hands them his business card and walks them to the lift. Brooke shakes hands with Jason and says "thank you, Mr. Grey." "It's Jason," he says with a smile.

As soon as Brooke gets into her car, her cell phone starts to ring. Thinking it was Kate, she flips it open: "Darling, I am coming. I will be in the store soon with lunch," and she hangs up. The phone rings again. This time she says "hello?"

"I am hurt! No 'darling'?" – it is a man's voice.

"Okay, freak! You have a wrong number," she snaps.

"Miss Williams, it's Jay... em... I was wondering whether I could buy you dinner tonight?"

Brooke quickly changes her expression and doesn't know what to say. Recalling her promise to close the shop and then the dinner date at Lola's with her friends, she thinks, "Darn! I'm busy." There is complete silence for a while.

"Brooke, are you there?" Jason asks.

"Oh, sorry. I am driving. Thank you for the invitation, but I have to work late tonight. I'm closing my shop. Some other time maybe?"

"Where is your shop?" Jason asks.

"It's in South Croydon, Urban Style," she replies.

"Okay, um...er ....maybe, I will call you, some other time to see what your schedule is like. You have a great day now."

"Sure. That sounds good, Jason."

Chapter 8

Brooke hangs up before Jason can finish what he's saying. He throws down his head set on his desk with a disappointed look. Most women usually throw themselves at his feet. They don't usually say, "I have to close my store" and hang up on him. Still… there's something about Brooke Williams besides the obvious physical attraction. "She is… *well!*" he thinks. Jason clicks the mouse and his day-book appears on the screen. He doesn't have any appointments left and not much to do at the office. His assistant comes in and asks for a file. He double-clicks the mouse and waits. Suddenly, the computer shuts down.

"Oh, man! It crashed!" Jason exclaims with a curse. He pushes a few buttons and turns on the computer again.

"It's all right. Just pull up the file and try again," the assistant calmly urges him.

Jason nods and begins searching, but after a few moments he frowns, "It's not here. I mean, I can't find the file. It's missing."

"The file just can't be missing," the assistant insists.

"I know," Jason agrees. "It's probably just in a different folder or something. It's going to take some time, but I'll find it," he assures her as he shuts down the computer.

"I gotta go. You take the rest of the day off," Jason tells her.

"We will miss the deadline," the assistant objects.

"Don't worry. I'll find it," Jason promises again as he grabs his laptop and runs out of his office.

Meanwhile, Kate is in the shop with her mother when Brooke returns. They are talking in Cantonese but switch to English as soon they see her.

"How was your date?" Kate inquires.

"You sound like me," Brooke laughs. She pauses for a minute. "I went to see a mortgage broker with my clients, and when he asked me out to dinner, I declined." She takes one of the cookies from Kate. "Mmm," Brooke sighs as she licks the cookie crumbs from her fingers. "That was yummy. Can I have some more?" Before Mrs Lee could hand her a second bag of cookies, Kate comes out from behind the display unit and grabs her by the arm, dragging her friend toward the exit. "About the dinner date… I know you try to act like it doesn't bother you being by yourself all the time, but sometimes – "

"But sometimes it gets to me," Brooke says, finishing her sentence. "I know exactly how you feel."

Oblivious to Kate's comments, Brooke opens and closes the shop door in complete shock. Kate follows her glance. She can't see what is distracting Brooke, so she leaves her and walks back to the display unit. As she sits down, Kate says to her mum in Chinese, "she is crazy." Mrs Lee laughs heartily as they watch Brooke, but cannot figure out what is upsetting her. It looks like something has got her attention or she is in her own little world. They catch a glimpse of Brooke biting her lips and kicking at the floor. Then Kate figures out what is bothering Brooke: "Whoa!" There is a good-looking man standing by the door talking to Brooke. She watches in amazement as he writes something on a slip paper and hands it to her. She nods and then tucks it in her purse.

Nudging Kate's arm, Mrs Lee asks, "Is that Brooke's boyfriend?"

"Since when did Brooke have a man?" Kate replies. She walks toward the door in a blatant attempt to overhear their conversation. "Are you not going to introduce me to your boyfriend?" Kate whispers in Brooke's ear.

Brooke giggles and introduces Jason to Kate. She glances over at Mrs Lee to see if she has noticed how weird Kate is behaving. It is kind of obvious that she, too, has been watching them. Before she knows it, Kate and Jason are walking hand-in-hand towards Mrs Lee.

"This Jason Grey, Lola," says Kate.

Mrs Lee extends her hand to greet Jason. Just then Brooke comes rushing over to them and announces, "Mr. Grey has to leave now, guys." She carries a pile of posters and some masking tape. "Come on, you guys, start putting these up," plopping the posters into Kate's arms. She's nervous, so she shouts. Brooke places one of the posters on the wall across from Jason. He frowns. The photograph on Brooke's poster features her in a long black dress with her blonde hair pulled back in a tight bun. She looks like a model.

"Can I offer assistance?" Jason asks.

Before Brooke can respond, Kate hands him a pile of posters and says, "Please, do you mind?"

"No, not at all. I am not in a rush. Actually, I was hoping to take Brooke out to dinner tonight," he says with a smile.

Brooke insists they don't need his help. Just then Mrs Lee announces she is leaving and that they should all join her for dinner at her house tonight, and Jason should come, too. Mrs Lee continues, "Tia and her boy friend are coming, so you must be there, too. Please?"

With that, Jason looks at Brooke, who nods her head 'okay' that he should come to Lola's for dinner. Brooke feels very uncomfortable. She has always chosen whom to bring to dinner – not that she has always told herself not to mix business with romance. Admittedly, she felt a connection with Jason Grey the first time she spoke to him, but she put it down to having too much wine, and that any idiot on the phone would've sounded sexy. Twenty-two years old and she has not been on a proper date, or had a good shag with a lad. She thinks, "what a loser I am!" Brooke supposes that love is not what she needs. She only has to look at her mother's life to know that love could potentially cost her everything. Nope, don't need it! Her life is perfect the the way it is, she surmises.

Kate's excitement over meeting Jason has more to do with being happy for Brooke than anything. She has always been alone when it comes to romance. It's like she hates men, Kate muses. Even better,

Jason is totally Brooke's type. Kate hopes Brooke don't blow this chance. Kate thinks she owes it to her friend to help her make it happen and with her mother's delicious cooking, the relationship should have a good kick-start. Although, Brooke has not indicated whether she likes him, Kate can tell by her body language that she does. No one can make Brooke this edgy. After all, Jason did follow her here, so he must like her despite turning down his dinner invitation. Kate chokes back a laugh. She looks up the ladder to hand some more posters to Jason and clears her throat, then says in a whispering voice, "so how long have you been seeing my girl? You have got to tell me everything."

Jason, laughing, turns and looks at Brooke who is busy doing something on her laptop. "I met her for the first time today... um... I asked her to dinner and she turned me down cold. And here I am."

"Whoa!" exclaims Kate. "That sounds like my girl!"

"So... tell me. Is she seeing anyone?" Jason quizzes.

"No. She is all about work."

"So what are my chance with her?" he asks.

Kate laughs. "I bet Brooke's really surprised someone had the guts not to expect no from her! She is a great girl when she lets people in."

"I don't know what it is about her, but I am drawn to her," he confesses to Kate.

They both exchange a glance and a smile.

"We've been friends for four years now. The three of us are like sisters," she tells Jason.

Jason looks at the poster on his left and sees Tia's face – like she is looking right at him. He turns back to Kate and smiles.

"And you tell me about yourself. Are you seeing anyone?" she asks.

Jason smiles nervously and says in a low voice, "nope, not seeing anyone."

"Please, excuse me," says Kate. As she enters the stock room at the back of the store, less than half a second later Brooke is standing in front of her. "What are you playing at?" she demands nervously. "The man is a freak, and whatever freaky conversation you two were having about me, I want to know right now!"

Kate throws her hands around her and says, "I can feel it, he is the one! And he is so into you, I can tell. Oh no! I've got to call Tia and tell her."

"This is ridiculous!" Brooke exclaims. "How could you say that about him? You just met the guy. We don't know anything about him." She pauses for a minute. " uh –huh. I don't like people making decisions for me or pushing me to do things."

Kate could see tears forming in Brooke's eyes. "I'm going home!" She glares at Kate and then storms out. Kate comes out of the stock room and grabs her by the arm before she closes the back door. "I'm not really good when it comes to stuff like this."

"Well, I am supposed to know. What you are talking about?" Brooke asks.

Kate sighed, "remember when I lost the baby? You said life goes on and things happen for a reason. And people come and go in our lives for a good reason. It is time for all of us to stop running and give romance a chance, Brooke. Please, come to dinner. I need you there. Jaden is coming and I need to have a talk with him about something. I really do need you there."

Brooke looks up to her friend. She can hear in her voice that she really needs her attention.

"What the hell! An empty flat, or a home-cooked meal with my family, and a man I hardly know!"

The two were quiet for a while, then they both say simultaneously, "I love you." They go back inside the store and Jason quips, "my ears have been burning!"

Brooke is a little more relaxed and says, "Well, Mr Grey, that's what happens when you follow a strange woman into her store!" Both Jason and Kate laugh.

"I'm going to call Tia. She is late and it's almost six-forty five. Where could she be?" Kate wonders aloud. She grabs the phone and dials Tia's cell phone number. Tia has spent the whole day with Kevin.

They don't waste time taking each other's clothes off as soon as they reach his flat. It's been like a like a sexual marathon between them all afternoon. Kate was about to hang up the phone when Tia rolls over and answers groggily.

"Where are the hell are you?" the voice on other end demands.

Kevin is kissing behind her ears. She tries to talk to the person on the phone, but she is so turned on that she does not realize that the phone is still on. She drops it by the bed and starts responding to Kevin's kisses. Meanwhile, Kate puts her on the speaker phone. She waves her hands to Brooke, who is now relaxing and talking to Jason, to come over. She and Jason approach the counter.

"Did you reach her? What is up?" Brooke asks.

"I'm not sure if she is alright. She sounds weird," Kate says, "so I put her on speaker."

"Um, ...em darling, she is fine!" Brooke is a little embarrassed. They listen to Tia and some guy on the phone having sex. She hangs up the phone.

"What did you do that for?" Kate shouts.

Jason could not stop laughing. "I like these ladies," he says to himself.

Brooke gets serious and pouts, "It's not funny!" Jason, who is still laughing at poor Kate, is still clueless. "Darling, Tia is with Kevin. And ..." she purses her lips for a second, "and I think we've been listening to them shagging!" She clears her throat again. The look on Kate's face is priceless as both Brooke and Jason start laughing together. Before they both know it, they are holding each other's hands. As soon as Brooke realizes she is holding his hand, she quickly pulls back her hands, and says, "Let's go! I'm starving."

"I think it's safe to say Tia will not be joining us for dinner tonight." She writes Mrs Lee's address on a piece of paper and gives it to Jason. He reaches for the paper, briefly touching her hand, and this time she does not pull back as she says in an even tone, "We will see you at Lola's in ten minutes."

"Sure! See you guys soon," he says as he heads towards the door. Brooke is about to close the door when he turns and says, "This the right address. I mean, I'm not going to end up in the boonies somewhere?" he asks jokingly.

She turns her head and looks at him, but it is impossible to read his expression in the warm darkness. She holds her breath.

"Funny! Very funny. It's the right address, Jason."

"She calls me Jason! Later.... Brooke."

Chapter 9

Jason glances at his watch. It is almost seven-twenty when he arrives at the Lee's house. He stands by the door with one hand in his pocket and the other holding a bottle of wine and a bouquet of flowers. He exhales and pushes the door bell.

"Come on in!" welcomes a warm voice from the door way.

Tia turns her head to see an attractive man. She instantly thinks, "the man has more products in his hair than Brooke!"

"I'm Tia," Tia smiles, "and this Kevin. You must be Jason."

"Yes. How do you do?"

They dash through the hallway into the kitchen where Ann Lee chats with Jaden.

"Welcome, Jason. Where are the girls?

"They will be here shortly," replies Jason.

"You've met Tia and Kevin, I trust?" affirms Mrs Lee.

"Yes ma'am."

"This is Jaden, Kate's young man." Mrs Lee points to Jaden.

"Hello." says Jaden.

"Nice to meet you." Jason extends his hand to greet Jaden.

"This is to thank you for inviting me to dinner." Mrs Lee accepts the flowers and the bottle of wine: "Thank you! You shouldn't have, but they're lovely."

Both Jaden and Kevin have brought her flowers, too, so she puts them all on the table.

She calls out to Tia to set the table while she hands Jason a glass of wine.

"Thank you," says Jason. "Is there anything I can help you with?" he offers.

"Yes. How good are you at making salads?" Mrs Lee inquires with a smile.

"Very good."

Jason is impressed with the Lee's house. It isn't what he expected. From the outside, the ranch-style house seems small. Inside, the house has split levels: you can see the living room on the second floor from the eat-in kitchen, nicely upgraded with a huge brick fireplace adorned with a photo of Kate, Tia and Brooke on the mantel. Their pose shows how close they are. Jason also loves the mix of old English medieval and Oriental design. "Very charming," he observes.

Back in their store, Brooke turns to Kate with a concerned voice and asks, "what's going on with you and Jaden?"

"I'm not sure, but I think he is drinking too much. And it looks like he's taken up smoking again." Her voice breaks down and she looks about to cry. "I don't want to be complaining, but I am worried since his father moved in. He's changed a lot!"

"I thought his father died when he was young?" Brooke asks.

"No, his parents divorced when he was just a kid," Kate says. "His father came to London a few months ago and he's been living with Jaden until he sorts himself out."

Brooke senses that there is something about the father that Kate is not sharing. She sits down, crosses her legs, and clears her throat with a sip of water: "Is there something about dear old Dad that you're not telling me?" she demands. Kate does not respond. She hates it when Brooke demands to know everything like a mother would – and they're both the same age!

"Look, darling, you might as well tell me before I hire a private investigator to find out what there is to know about Jaden Blake and his whole family tree!"

"Uh-huh," grunts Kate.

Brooke sits back in her chair, feeling more in control. "Kate, let's get one thing straight here. I am not joking. I mean it: you tell me or ..." she purses her lips when she sees the look on her friend's face.

"Oh my god, what is wrong with you, Brooke? Must you always think everyone has a dodger past? The Blakes are good people. You have no right to jump to this conclusion!" Upset, Kate grabs her purse and heads towards the back door.

"I'm concerned, Kate!" Brooke shouts. "Stop it," Brooke scolds herself silently. She felt certain that Kate could not handle what ever was developing with Jaden. "On second thought, perhaps it would have been wiser to sit and listen to what's troubling Kate," she said to herself. She reached for her keys and turned the store lights off, switched the alarm on and locked the door as she left the building. Kate is sitting on the hood of Brooke's car. As she looked up in the dark night Brooke can tell Kate is still upset with her.

They have been driving for more than ten minutes when Kate exclaims, "Oh no, I forgot to pick up the wine at the off license!"

"It's okay. I keep a case of Californian white wine in the trunk of my car. We will take that, unless you want to pick up some beer for Jaden?" Brooke asks.

Kate brightens. "Oh, good! That will do for the night."

Brooke feels an overwhelming need to find a logical connection to bring Kate back to the subject of Jaden before they reach the house. She could not think of what to say until just before they pulled into the Lee's drive way. She says, "I am sorry about before, Kate. Sometimes I do tend to be a little over-protective of people I love and let's face it, there's not many people in my life that I care about. I don't want you to get hurt, Kate. I didn't mean to come off like that before about Jaden and his father. I have been worried about you, and things always come up every time I try to have a talk with you. I am here for you if you still want to talk, Kate."

Kate could not fight the tears coming down and Brooke could see it. She turns off the radio and holds Kate's hands in her own.

"I am so sorry. Brooke, something is wrong. I just don't what to do. I don't want to lose Jaden," Kate confessed.

"Oh, darling! You won't. He loves you just as much as you love him. You will never lose him."

There was a shadow in the dark and it caught Brooke's attention, so she started the car and put the lights on to discover Jaden standing at the back of the house smoking. Kate saw him, too.

"Come on, we are late. Let's not keep our guest waiting. We will talk later. Please, promise me?" Brooke insisted. She turned off the car and before Kate could open her door, Jaden appeared at her side, so happy to see her he didn't even let her out of the car before he bent down to kiss her.

"For the love of god, not in my bloody car! Can't you two ever keep your hands off each other for a second?" Brooke shrieks.

"Oh, and how are you this evening, Brooke?" says Jaden mockingly as he pauses mid-kiss.

"Why don't you drop dead, handsome! … Ha!" says Brooke as she gets out of the car and walks to the rear of the vehicle to get the wine. "I can do with a little help here, people !" Brooke shouts from the trunk of the car. Jaden walks around to the back of the car and gives Brooke a kiss on the cheek, "I miss you, too, Miss Playful!"

Brooke and Kate glance at each other. Jaden was too hyper, not his usual quiet self.

"Are you bloody high?" Brooke demands as she grabs his arm.

"Don't be ridiculous, love! When was the last time you brought a boy-friend home to have dinner with us?" Jaden asks.

Brooke has momentarily forgotten about Jason Grey joining them for dinner. She is more confused about Jaden's behavior now, and she quickly remembers that Jason is already in the house.

"Listen to me, happy boy. That man is not my boy-friend. Pick up the wine and let's go before I make you cry!" she snaps. Both Kate and Jaden start laughing at the same time.

Meanwhile, inside the house, mixed scents of peanut sauce, garlic, peppery hot and sour soup, and black bean sauce poured out on the steam with the hot, sizzling spice smell all over the kitchen.

"Something smells good, Lola!" Brooke exclaims as she walks through the hallway towards the kitchen. Jason is in the kitchen wearing an apron and making salad. Brooke feels a little uneasy again because Jason looks so very comfortable, like he is at home. Then again, Mrs. Lee knows how to make people feel comfortable.

"em… I see you make yourself at home, Mr. Grey," she says.

"It's Jason. Please call me Jason. My father is not here," he says with a smile. "You made it! You know, I was beginning to think you stood me up," Jason jokes.

"You, I will stand up any day, but not Lola," affirms Brooke.

Before Jason could respond, Jaden, Kate and Lola entered the kitchen. Brooke went over and gave Lola a kiss on the cheek, demanding to know why Jason got to help when she never lets Brooke help. Mrs Lee laughs and says, "I couldn't say no to him." They all laugh in response.

"Is dinner ready yet, Lola?" Tia shouts.

"She's here?" Brooke asks incredulously.

"Yes, Tia and her young man were the first to arrive," says Mrs Lee.

Tia and Kevin are in the family room, cuddling and watching TV. Earlier, Jason caught the pair smooching. "Cute," he thought as he watched them. Tia looks up at Jason and their eyes meet. They both couldn't stop laughing. Of course, Mrs Lee did not understand, but she simply thought "young love."

"I am surprised they could tear themselves away to join us," observes Brooke sarcastically.

"I'm right here!" came Tia's warm voice from the hallway.

Brooke turns her head and sees an attractive black man walking behind Tia.

"I'm Brooke," Brooke smiles.

"You must be Kevin," says Kate.

"Yes, he's alright," Brooke thinks. "How do you do?"

"Dinner is ready everyone," calls Mrs. Lee.

Everyone assembles at the round table except Kate and Jaden. The food looks and smells good. Brooke puts her glass down, taps Tia's shoulders and says to Kevin, "will you please excuse her for a minute?" Mrs Lee is too busy talking to Jason to notice the girls have left the table.

"What's up?" Tia asks.

"You seen Kate around?" Brooke queries.

"She was on the deck with Jaden earlier – why?" Tia looks worried when she sees Brooke's expression.

"What is going on, Brooke?" Tia demands.

"I am not sure, but let's go find them. Come on," she says. "Kevin is handsome. By the way, the next time you go to Kevin's flat and you two are shagging, don't answer your cell phone!" Brooke says.

"I hate you!" says Tia.

The door to the deck is wide open. Kate is sitting on the hammock alone. They stop and look at each other for a moment. For reasons Tia doesn't understand, Brooke is getting angry. She turns to Tia and says, "why don't you go back to the dinner room. I will be there in a minute with her. And make sure Lola doesn't come out here!" she tells Tia.

"Stop telling me what to do, Brooke," Tia snaps at her.

"Please, Tia, for all our sakes, just do it." Brooke is almost in tears as she grabs hold of Tia's hands and begs her to go back inside.

"Alright! I will go back," Tia says petulantly.

Tia pauses as Brooke sits down next to Kate. She couldn't hear what they were saying, so she turned to head back to the house. She was about to close the doors when she saw Brooke and Kate hugging each other, and it looks like they are both crying. She opens the door and without thinking who could hear her, she says, "What's going on that you can't tell me?"

Brooke smiles coldly. Kate looks nervous, and Brooke seems slightly mad.

"You can't do this to me. Please, tell me what's going on?" Tia pleads.

"Nothing is going on!" Brooke says softly.

"You two want to keep things to yourselves – fine!" Tia says loudly. "I am leaving! I am going to get Kevin and we will leave!"

Brooke jumps to her feet, scowling furiously at Tia. "Keep your voice down you stupid little brat! Does everything have to be about you, Tia?" Tia tries to respond, but Brooke silences her with a look. "Be quiet, Tia, for once. Just be... I am sorry, Tia. Why am I being angry with you? I am going to kick his butt!"

"Jaden has been drinking too much, and it's not the first time. He has been vomiting for the last ten minutes," Kate murmurs.

Tia is clearly taken back by Kate's disclosure. "What are you talking about?" Tia asks.

Brooke steers Tia into one of the two chairs and takes the other one herself.

"Are you? This is an on-going thing? I mean, maybe he has had one too many tonight..." suggests Tia, staring at Kate who is now visibly shaken. "Where is the son of a bitch now?" Tia demands.

"He is upstairs, sleeping it off," Kate replies frantically.

"There is nothing we can do now! Lola can't find out. We need to get him out of here quickly! Since everyone knows that I'm a party-pooper, I will come up with something. I need you guys to help me get him in my car," suggests Brooke.

They went back to the house and dragged Jaden to Brooke's car.

"Try and stay focused, darling," Brooke whispers into Kate's ear.

"I see you guys are enjoying Lola's cooking!" says Brooke. Turning to Mrs Lee, she says, "Sorry, Lola. I had a little problem. I needed the girls to help me. I do apologize."

Mrs Lee can tell that her daughter looks flushed. "Are you alright, baby?" She asks Kate.

"Yes, mama."

"Where is Jaden?" Mrs Lee asks.

"He is going to take care of something for me. I will take some food for him when we leave," says Brooke.

"I thought you were going to spend the night?" Mrs Lee asks.

"Not tonight, Lola. We will come home on the weekend. We have a meeting in the morning. It will be better if we spend the night at my flat, so we can beat the morning traffic."

Brooke hates telling lies to Ann. It would break her heart if she knew what's going on with Jaden. The whole situation has made Kate frustrated and edgy.

"Hey! How about you guys go. Kevin and I will stay to help clean up and join you later," Tia suggests.

"Can you stay for coffee?" Mrs Lee pleads.

"We don't have to leave right away, Lola. Relax." Brooke says as she puts a spoon full of pudding in her mouth. Everyone looks at her and laughs.

"So Kevin... nice to finally meet you," says Brooke.

"Thank you all for inviting me to dinner," Kevin says.

"You are very welcome," says Mrs Lee. "You're not eating, baby! Are you sure you are feeling alright, Kate?"

"I'm not that hungry, Mama. I will take some food with me to Brooke's for later," Kate reassures her mother. Ann Lee has been worried about her daughter since she lost the baby. She thanks God everyday that she didn't lose Kate, too. Ann wishes Kate would let her help her through the pain, but she has Brooke and Tia. How fast they are growing up before her eyes.

Chapter 10

Jason enjoyed the dinner just as much as he enjoyed watching Brooke eat. Although most of the women whom he meets seem to be afraid of food, Brooke is not. He likes this girl and her friends; they have a lot of love for one another which is easy to see by watching them.

Tia and Kevin are holding each other's hands under the table. Brooke will tap Kate's knee every now and then to remind her to stay focused.

"It was nice to have dinner with all of you tonight. My mum loves dinner parties, and giving doggie bags afterward," Kate tells Kevin and Jason.

"It's true! You should see what I have for everyone to take home," Mrs Lee says.

Kevin and Tia clear the table while Jason and Brooke make the coffee.

"You know, I have never had an evening like this before. Thank you, Brooke."

"Well, I didn't invite you. Remember?" Brooke says softly. She passes him the milk and their eyes meet again. This time they can't take their eyes off each other – so much so that Kate walks in and sees them. She forgets about her troubles with Jaden and whispers to her mum: "They are so perfect for each other." Mrs Lee agrees. Jason is great for Brooke.

Brooke has always been impressed with how Mrs Lee warms up to strangers. She is so different from her own mother. Kate is very lucky. Although Brooke sort of sees why Kate is worried about Jaden, there is no way he is going to drag them into his habit. She glances at her watch. It's been almost two hours since they put Jaden in the back of her car. They have forgotten about him. Back in the family room, Jason thanks everyone and says "good night." Brooke grabs her purse and walks out with him. Kate shouts, "I will meet you in the car!"

"Which one is your car?" Jason asks.

Brooke pushes the button on her keys, unlocking the car and turning on the lights.

"Nice! I like it!" says Jason. He walks her to her car and suggests tentatively, "I don't suppose I can follow you home for coffee, or you and Kate want to come by my place for coffee?"

Just before Brooke could respond, Tia chirps, "Why don't you join us at Brooke's? We all are spending the night. Kevin and I will ride with you. If you don't mind?"

"I'd love to. I have missing documents on my computer I need to retrieve, but I can drop you guys off though," says Jason.

Brooke is relieved. Although she didn't really get to spend any time alone with Jason, he wasn't so bad after all she thought.

"Good night Jason. Thank you for joining us," says Brooke.

He smiles. "Stop.. ha... em... okay, how about you let me take you to lunch tomorrow?"

"We'll see! Good night, Jason," Brooke shakes hands with him.

He takes her hand and kisses it. "I will call you."

It was nearly midnight by the time they finally made their way out of Mrs Lee's home.

"You okay?" Brooke asks Kate.

Kate nods, but her body starts to shake, and she finally begins to sob against Brooke's arm. "It's all right, darling. It's all right," murmurs Brooke as she consoles her friend. Brooke puts one hand on the steering wheel to drive and the other on her friend's hands. A few minutes later, she parks and turns to Kate. "I called ahead to see if they have room for the night for Jaden." Kate looks confused.

"Who has a room for Jaden?" she asks.

"I don't ever want to see you or Jaden go through anything like tonight again. He needs help at least for tonight. This is "Better Day." They will help him come to terms with what he needs to do and we will be back in the morning if he wishes to go home. I will drive him home, then, and if he wishes to stay he can do so. Kate, he needs this before his drinking gets out of control. He may be on drugs for all we know and mixing up those two can be dangerous," Brooke says firmly.

There was dead silence in the car for a while. Jaden awoke to the dead sky light and had no idea where he was. He felt pain all over his body.

"I can do with a bloody drink!" he said out loud.

Brooke got out of the car in a rage. She opened the back door and dragged him out of the the car by his shirt. "You want a fucking drink? Go the fuck ahead, you son-of-a-bitch. Do have any idea what you have put everyone through tonight?"

Jaden started to laugh. He has never heard Brooke swear before. She always talks properly. Brooke pushed him to the ground, and got into her car and drove off. Kate was in her own world still thinking about what Brooke had said, so she did not pay any attention to Brooke and Jaden.

"I cannot let him spend the night with us at the apartment. I don't want to leave him here, but it has to be his choice to seek help. Let's drop him off at his flat." she said.

Brooke is still angry. "It's time his bad ass learned a lesson! After everything, the son-of-a-bitch wants to drink! You don't need this, darling. It's madness. Let him take himself home or to the nearest off license and buy all the buzz he wants. I don't have time for this."

"What are you talking about?" asks Kate.

"Did you not hear him say he could do with a drink?"

"He's sleeping, Brooke. You are losing it. Don't be too concerned. I am okay," says Kate.

Brooke glances over at her friend and realizes that she had no idea what happened a few minutes ago. She turned the car around and went back to the parking lot at "Better Day." Luckily, Jaden was still there on the ground where she had left him.

"What has gotten into you?" he shouts, still laughing at Brooke's cursing.

Kate finally looks out the window and turns to Brooke. "How did he get there?" she asks.

Brooke did not respond.

"Come here and give big daddy a kiss!" Jaden is yelling to her. Kate gets out of the car, heading towards him.

"I want to do you, right here! In the parking lot, love. Come, come to daddy."

Kate, in tears, stops for a second sizing things up. Brooke sits in the car. Feeling full of rage, she wants to get out of the car and kick the shit out of that bastard! She closes her eyes and tries to stay calm.

"Stop it! Please," Kate cries out.

"We've never done it in the parking lot, or under the stairs before, love," he says.

Kate turns and runs back to the car. "Please drive! Let's go!"

They drove home in silence that night. Tia and Kevin were already at Brooke's apartment. "I am off to bed," Brooke said. "Oh, no sex in the flat. I am the only one allowed to have sex in the flat, and if I am not then you two are not either! You two need air. Good night!" She closed her bedroom door behind her.

Kate looks like a car has run over her. She waved good night at the two love birds and closed her door, throwing herself on the bed still fully dressed. Tia was concerned, but she felt it was best to leave things alone until morning. Kate's cell phone rang all night. She did not answer it, and finally, Tia and Brooke knocked on her door. "Come in," she said.

When Tia and Brooke entered the room, Brooke turned off the cellphone and got into the bed with Kate. "It will be all right." Tia said, joining the girls in the big bed.

Later, the ringing of the phone awoke Brooke. She was not in her bedroom. "Hello?" she answered the phone with her eyes closed. It was the door bell. The voice said, "Breakfast for the lovely lady." She had no idea who that was but she buzzed in the person anyway.

"Kate, what time is it?" she shouted.

There was no reply. Someone knocked on the door.

"For the love of God, one of you get the bloody door! I am still sleeping!" She shouted.

The person at the door kept knocking, so Brooke got out of bed, strolled into the hall and opened the door shouting, "I heard you fifty times already! Put a sock into it!"

"Wow!... this is what I call a good morning, indeed!" says Jason.

Brooke takes the coffee from him, saying, "Do you always turn up on people's doorstep uninvited?"

She is wearing nothing but a pair of white lace underwear and a bra which Jason couldn't stop ogling. "You may come in," she says. Brooke takes another sip of the coffee he has given her. "Mr Grey, you seem to have a lot of time on your hands," she observes.

"Uh... em...," Jason cleared his throat. He could not get his words out as his mind was focused on not looking at Brooke's lacy underwear. "Is she doing this to get a reaction?" he wondered. Jason ran his hands through his hair. "Em, you are one sexy woman, Brooke Williams. Do you mind putting on some clothes before I am charged with rape?" he quips.

Brooke stops in mid-sentence as she realizes that she isn't wearing a bath robe. "Please excuse me."

"Of course," Jason nods. The view got his attention, but he still couldn't get Brooke's facial expression out of his head. Brooke was embarrassed, but she also wondered where the girls and Kevin were. She glanced at the clock on her bedside table: it was almost eleven.

"Is everything okay in there?" Jason cried out. "I mean, do you need help getting dressed?"

"Very cute!" Brooke shouts in reply. "What brings you to my door, Mr. Grey?"

"I called your office and the shop. Tia told me you were at home, and that you could do with a decent coffee. She told me how you take it, so I thought I would bring you one."

"I'm gonna kill her," she thought to herself. She opened her bedroom door, stuck her head out and said, "I am going to take a quick shower, do you mind?"

"Can I use the kitchen?" he asks.

"Knock yourself out," she says as she closes the door, puts the music on and heads to the shower.

Jason took off his jacket, smiling to himself. He called his office on his cellphone and informed his assistant that he would not be back at the office for the rest of the day. She should cancel all of his appointments, and she should take a day off herself. Before she could ask if everything is all right with him he hung up and turned the phone off.

By the time Brooke emerged from her bedroom, she looked stunning as usual. There was a pleasant aroma in the apartment. Jason was standing in the dinning room with both hands on the chair.

"I made lunch," he gestures toward the food-laden table.

Brooke sighs and says, "I thank you, but I am already too late for work."

"Today, Miss Williams, is a national day of rest." He takes Brooke's hands and says, "There will be no work, no phone calls, no friends or family: just the two of us and anything you want to do – within reason."

Before Brooke could say anything, he sat her down and handed her a fresh cup of coffee, "So, Miss Williams... how is the coffee?"

"Just right, the way I like it," she replies.

"Good, drink up, so we can go."

"Go where?"

"It's okay, you will love it," he says re-reassuringly.

She reaches for her ringing cellphone, but Jason takes it from her, shutting it off before she can say a word. He asks, "where are your keys?" She points to the wall, and he grabs the keys and Brooke's hands and steers them out the door. As he locks the door, he says, "let's go!"

Brooke is speechless. "Tia, you are dead," she says to herself.

They drive in his car in silence to the supermarket. First, at the produce section, he selects different kinds of vegetables. "He seems to know what he is doing," Brooke nervously watches Jason shopping. Jason saw her unease and asked, "fish or meat?"

"Neither."

"What about chicken? I love chicken," he says.

Smiling, she couldn't believe she was in the supermarket with a man she hardly knew. It was easy to give in to him. "Hmmm, chicken sounds good," Brooke replies.

The shopping was done before she knew it, and Brooke began to relax. Jason liked that. They put everything in the trunk of the car and went to HMV where they brought all kinds of DVDs and CDs, like a long-connected couple. On the way back to the car, Jason took out his cellphone, but Brooke took it away saying, "no cellphones on national day off!"

They both laughed.

Back at Urban Style, Tia has spent most of the morning alone, and finding she couldn't get Kate out of her mind. When the phone rang, it was Kate calling to say she had missed her train.

"We're not that busy," Tia says to her.

"Then, I will pick up lunch. Ask Brooke what she wants for lunch, would you?"

Tia tells her Brooke is spending the day with Jason.

"How did that happen?"

"Oh, with a little help from me. I'll tell you all about it when you come. Got to see to a customer!"

Kate was a bit happier. She had started her morning with intentions of going to see Jaden, but changed her mind and ended up at St Mark's Church where she helped at the Women's Center to feed the needy and to sort out the donations. It took her mind off her problems with Jaden. Her phone rang as she was about to get off the train. It was Jaden calling.

"I am so very sorry, my love. I have no idea what happened last night, or how I ended up in my flat. Please, I will make it up to you, love." He was crying as he spoke. "Kate, you are my world. I would rather cut off my fingers than hurt you. I feel so embarrassed. I can not remember anything about last night. My love, please say you will forgive me?" He begged.

Kate was in tears, but she fought them back and said with her eyes closed, "You were a perfect gentleman, my love."

Jaden breathed easily, "Oh thank God! I felt I did something I wasn't suppose to. I have been worried."

"Get some rest. I'll see you tonight. Love you!"

"I do love you so, Kate!"

She hung up, and sat down on a park bench across from the store, lost in her own thoughts. She could see Tia, looking so happy because a UPS guy has just given her something. Meanwhile, her own life is spinning out of control since the loss of her baby. "Why has God abandoned me?" she wondered.

"Tell me why you are so happy?" Kate was standing across the counter from Tia. Tia handed her an envelope in which there were five return air jet tickets to Holland.

"I thought Brooke was going to drive? When did we decide to fly?" Kate asked.

"No, we did not. Jason Grey sent them. His friend owns an air jet. I was telling him about our proposed trip last night on our way to Brooke's. Remember, he dropped me and Kevin off?"

"You asked him to get us the tickets?" Kate asked incredulously.

"No! Read the note, Kate."

"Wow! Brooke is not going to like it. You should return them and thank him for the kind gesture." advised Kate.

"Why? Forty-five minutes, we will be there, instead of the long drive," Tia objected.

"It's very sweet of him, but you know we can't expect it. We hardly know the guy. I don't think it is a good idea. I'm sure Brooke will agree, too."

"Okay, I will return the tickets only if you help me invite him to come with us. Come on! You know Brooke likes him and he likes her. Please!"

"Okay, let's eat first. I can't think on an empty stomach! Afterward, we can start Operation Love," giggled Kate.

Tia ran to hug her and said, "Good to see you happy again! I have been so worried about you!"

"I am fine now. Everything is going to be okay," Kate assured her friend.

Chapter 11

Brooke has never been on a date, alone with a man she hardly knows, in her apartment. She started thinking about all the things she has done growing up. Then again, she has lived a different life compared to many people her age. She endured the pain of losing a loving father at a young age, and her mother has not been much of a mother to her since her father's death. It often brings tears to her eyes when she thinks about it.

"Well… not in front of a stranger," she said to herself as she wiped away the tears.

Jason watched her, wishing he knew her pain. He would like to take it away but he knows Brooke finds his company good, it makes everything so much better. There is a maturity about her that he likes which he has not found in any other woman.

"A penny for your thoughts?" he says.

"I'm good. Thank you, Jason."

"For what?" he asks.

She put her fork down and sat back in the chair. "I live in my own little world except for the time I spend with the girls. I hardly ever take time for anything. I needed a break and you did that for me today. I appreciate it."

"Well, the day is not over yet! I should thank you for doing this with me. I am just as much a workaholic as yourself, as you can see," he says.

"You hide it very well," observes Brooke. "He is so handsome and full of self-confidence," she thinks.

After lunch, he makes popcorn and they watch *Jungle Book* because they both enjoy cartoons. "I used to spend all day as a child with my father on Saturdays watching cartoons," she said.

"You can still do that with him, you know," he said.

She smiled and said, "he passed away when I was six."

"Oh! I am sorry."

"It's all right. I am not a TV person anyway!" she tells him.

"What about your mother?" he asks.

"We are not very close, although things are a lot better between us these days. Are your parents both alive?"

"Yes. They live very close by you. I believe they are in Spain for two weeks. They are both lawyers – been together since their teens."

"Wow! Sounds good." She slips off her shoes and leans back in the sofa. Jason wanted to reach out and hold her, maybe kiss her, but he didn't want to scare her off. Instead, he goes into the kitchen and comes back with a bottle of water for her. Their hands touch and he doesn't want to let go. He sits down close to her and swings one of his legs over so that she is locked in between his legs. He lays down on the sofa and pulls her close to him, wrapping his arms around her. She does not resist. Brooke closes her eyes and can not stop crying, remembering that the last time any man held her like this was her father.

Jason sighed and kissed her on the head, "it's okay to cry, Brooke. And if you want to talk, I'm a good listener."

She felt safe with him, and she liked being held by him. She noticed that he was not in a hurry to let go. He shared some of his childhood with her as well as college memories and past relationships. She thought he had lived an interesting life and she was amazed how comfortable he was sharing all those private things with her. Jason told her about his first break-up with his college sweetheart whom he loved passionately. "After that, my only relationships have been one night stands," he confessed. "I had an on-off relationship with one of my co-workers for three years, but it just didn't have the commitment we both wanted, so we called it quits."

"She must have been a very special lady," Brooke said, hoping for more details.

"Yes, she is. She has been through the loss of a great love and I don't think one can ever get over that kind of love. As the next guy, it is certainly difficult to measure up to a grand passion," he tells Brooke.

"My heart goes out to her. It's like some one I know, but I never understood until now. You must really care about her?" Brooke asked, wondering whether Jason and his co-worker were really over.

"I do. Not many of us go through something like that and remain human. When the long-term relationship with my college girl-friend was over, all I wanted to do was hurt any woman I met and I did. She made me a better man."

"Were you in love with her?" Brooke asked.

"No, I was not. I would not be here with you if I was. Please believe that." He let go of her and stood up. Kneeling in front of Brooke, Jason said, "I can not put to words how I have felt since I met you. It's like something is pulling me towards you." He kissed her on the forehead and said "may I use your bathroom?"

"Of course! First door on the right."

Brooke started to think about her mother and her great loss. She reached for the phone and dialed her number. The answering machine picked up: "Hello, Mother! I was thinking of you. I just called to say I love you and em… I have missed you so very very much."

Sarah Williams was about to close her door when she head her daughter's voice and ran for the phone. Her voice was full of tears of joy, "B.B.! Are you there?"

"Yes, Mother. I was just, em…, leaving you a message," said Brooke.

"I tried to call you this afternoon, but your cell was turned off. Are you all right?"

"Yes, Mother. I took a personal day off from work," she says.

"That's good! We all need that sometimes. B.B., I love you and I miss you so, my sweetheart. If I could turn back the clock, I would do things very differently."

Brooke looked up and saw Jason standing there, "Mother, I will talk to you soon," and she hung up.

"You broke the rule about national day off," Jason joked.

"Thank you so much, Jason."

Kate hates to be a burden to the people she loves dearly. It seems to her that lately that is all she has become. She has never told a lie, but in the last twenty-four hours she has told lies to her mother and to Jaden. She needs to fix things; otherwise, everything she is suffering now could transcend bitterness. "How do I do that?" she asked herself. Kate thought of Brooke, fiercely independent and yet with everything going on in her life, she always holds things together.

"I need to think more like Brooke, now," Kate thinks.

She stood with her head on Jaden's door, all kinds of thoughts going through her mind. A neighbor passes by and says hello, but she does not respond. She puts the keys in the lock and opens the door. Not the welcome she expected – the flat was clean and covered with all kinds of flowers and lighted candles everywhere she looked. Kate closed her eyes for a brief moment to see if she was dreaming or in the wrong flat, but instead, a familiar scent she has forgotten and a soft tender kiss on her cheek confirmed she was in the right place.

"Hello love!" Jaden said.

She could not stop the tears rolling down her face when she opened her eyes. He wiped them off ever so gently with his hands. "Please don't cry, my love. I will make it all go away. I do so promise you," he said.

"What is happening to us, Jaden?"

"It will all be all right, my love, come sit. I will get you a cup of tea," he offered.

Did last night really happen? Was it all in her head? Kate wondered.

"I met one of my old school chums this afternoon. He told me sometimes in life things happen to test our faith and our strength. You know, he's a Christian! and I believe that is what has been happening to us, Kate. Please, don't lose faith in us, in me. I can see it in your eyes, that you feel tested." Jaden was now holding her hands and crying at the same time.

"I feel like something awful happened last night, although I cannot remember what it was. Please, love, say you will forgive me and not lose faith in me. I cannot lose you, Kate."

Last night was astonishing: he was like a different Jaden, not the one she knows and loves. The Jaden she is talking to right now is so full of love, one can't help but feel such graceful combination of empathy even. It is true their faith and love has been tested. Between them both, there are so many emotions, it is hard for either one of them to recognized the other's pain.

"Please, love, say something," he pleaded.

She throws both arms around him, "You are right! Our faith and everything that we are to each other is being tested. I am afraid of what's to come next."

"It will be alright," he promised her.

Back in north London, Kevin has just told Tia that he cannot go to Amsterdam with her. Tia is not very pleased.

"I want you to stay with me for the summer, Tia," he says.

He did not give her any reason why he could not come with her.

"I need to get going," she says.

"Please, stay the night," he begs.

"I'd love to, but I can't. There is so much to do before we leave tomorrow. I don't want to miss the last train because my dad is picking me up from Thornton Heath Station. I must not keep him waiting."

Chapter 12

Brooke is not happy at all that Jaden is coming with them on the trip. At least she is not going to be completely alone as Kevin did not come, so Tia will also be single. They drove to Dover Port where it took no more than forty minutes to cross immigration and board the ship. They purchased a lot of things from the duty free store, mostly gifts for Tia's grandparents, but Jaden did not waste any time buying alcohol.

"There will be no alcohol in my vehicle," Brooke told him.

"This is a fifty year-old whiskey! It's for the old Gasser. Keep your knickers on!" he snapped at her. The cashier couldn't help but laugh.

Less than three hours later, they had crossed the English Channel and disembarked in Ostend, Belgium.

"There is a place in Ghent. I have to stop there and buy some chocolate for my mother," Brooke said. Tia turned her head and looked back at Kate and Jaden.

"Of course, love," said Jaden. "You don't even talk to your old lady, and you want to buy chocolate for the old fart!"

Brooke stopped the car, went to the back and opened the door and said, "I want to have a private chat with you outside the car."

"I am sorry," said Jaden.

"Outside. Now!" Brooke demanded.

"I am very sorry, can we please go?" he said.

Brooke got back in the car and turned to him, "If you ever call my mother an old fart, or any other names again, your pretty-boy face will not see daylight again! Understand?"

"Understand," said Jaden contritely.

Just before they reached the border between Belgium and Holland, Tia felt sick and asked if they could stop the car.

"There is gas station half a mile away. I will stop there and we can get gas and something to eat." said Brooke.

"I got to go now," Tia insisted.

"I know you are African. You can't go anywhere you fancy, you are not in Africa. There's a loo there you can use," says Brooke, gesturing up the road to the gas station.

Jaden thought it was funny.

"I am going to vomit in the car if you don't stop!" Tia protested.

At the gas station everyone ate while Tia stayed in the loo throwing up. Kate sensed that Tia may be pregnant, so she went to the bathroom to check on her. Tia was washing her face and said, "I think I got food poisoning, but I'm okay now."

"Oh, thank God!" said Kate.

"We will be in Amsterdam in forty minutes," Brooke informed them.

"I'm going to call my grandpa and let him know that," Tia said.

"You all right, then?" Brooke asked.

"Yup! Bloody food poisoning," she replied.

"There it is – Varermasters Straat 198!" Tia said. "We are here! Wake up, love birds!"

Osei Kofi, an older gentleman in his late sixties, stands in the big hallway about six feet tall, not more than one hundred and seventy pounds. He speaks perfect English with a strong English accent. Looking at him, one would say he might be in his early thirties. "It is true what they say about the Africans: they don't age at all," observes Jaden. "My dad just turned forty-one, and he looks like a bloody hundred year-old gasser! Not to sound gay or anything, but your Granddad looks very young for his age," he adds. Both Tia and Kate thought Jaden's comments were funny, but Brooke told them all to stop that foolish talk. And they laughed. Osei Kofi took both Tia and Kate in his arms and kissed them.

"My darlings, I have missed you so much! You two have grown since Christmas!" Turning to Jaden and Brooke, he says, "Come, my dears! You are beautiful just like Sarah," hugging and kissing Brooke on both cheeks. Brooke had no idea he knew her mother. Of course, her mother knew Tia's parents before she did.

"And you, my boy, you must be... don't tell me... Jaden!" He hugs Jaden. "Welcome, my dears. Let's go inside. Guntar will take care of your luggage. Getty is waiting in the family room for you."

The house was different from the English houses that Jaden had seen. Beautifully decorated with French and Italian furniture, the flooring was made from different kinds of tiles like the ones in big office buildings in England, "but these are different," Jaden thought. The walls are covered with all kinds of art – African masks, Japanese water colors, but about the rest Jaden had no clue. He could not help but stare like a child at Christmas in Oxford Street when the Christmas lights are lit up. It was amazing.

Tia ran straight to the bathroom again.

Gertrude Osei looked so much like Tia's mum they could have been twins not mother and daughter. She was talking to Tia parents, but paused to greet the girls with the same warmth as Kofi. Tia's parents were wondering where Tia was.

"She gone to the bathroom, Naana," says Brooke to Tia's mum.

"I wish Sarah would have come with us. You must be hungry! Come, let's go eat," she says.

It was like a potluck party: every food was there. "It's better than Mrs Lee's," Jaden thought privately. They all grabbed plates and started to dig in.

"I hope the drive down was not too much for you," Gertrude asked.

"No, ma'am," said Brooke.

"Oh, my dear, call me Gertrude," she says. "Oh, before I forget, a young man by the name of Grey... Jason Grey has been calling after you. He is in Amsterdam. I have sent Guntar to go pick him up from his hotel. Daddy says it will be okay if you all are under one roof so we can enjoy your visit. I hope you don't mind, Brooke?"

"Oh, you didn't have to do that. I'm sure Mr. Grey doesn't want to impose."

"No, my dear. You are family. This is a family vacation, so we must all be together. Mr Grey is your friend, and you are family. Besides I'm introducing African Arts at the university on Monday, so I'll be out of the house and you'll need something to entertain yourselves, right? Sarah and Naana tell me that you are knowledgeable on art matters. They are so proud of the work you have done with Urban Style. You know, my dear, I think you have the creative edge that I need in this project." She smiled and patted Brooke on the shoulder.

Brooke put her plate down and grabbed Kate by the hand. They met Tia in the hallway.

"Are you guys okay?" Tia inquires.

"No! Bloody hell! You will not believe it! Bloody hell! What am I gonna do?" Brooke asks frantically.

Kate and Tia both look at each other. They have no idea what Brooke is going on about. She sits on the toilet.

"What are you going to do about what?" Tia asks guilelessly.

"Jason Grey is on his way here!" she cries.

"Oh, good! I did invite him to come. I didn't think he would," Tia remarks innocently.

Brooke's face is red with anger as she stands up, ready to confront Tia. "Let's all calm down here," says Kate, playing peacemaker between the two friends.

"When did you invite him to come?" Kate asks.

"Oh, my God. I have to throw up again!" exclaims Tia.

They stood there while Tia emptied her stomach.

"Are you pregnant?" Kate asks bluntly. "You know, nausea and vomiting is very common, especially in early pregnancy," she informs Tia.

"What? What are you talking about? I think I have food poisoning," Tia says.

"No one cares! Why did you invite Grey?" Brooke screams.

"Oh no! I can't be pregnant. I don't like kids. I think Kevin has gone off me. I can't be, I just can't be! My mum and dad will kill me and then kill him!" Tia cries out.

"Before we get our knickers in a twist, we need to get a test done to know and then you can get your knickers in a twist. And I will kill you before your mum and dad do," Brooke snaps.

Jaden is enjoying the food when Jason arrives. "The girls have disappeared to Gods know where," he says to Jason.

Naana Konadu -Sharp gives Jason a glass of red wine. "Please make yourself at home. There is plenty food to eat. Whatever you fancy, Rose will get it for you."

"Thank you," says Jason.

"I will not kick that one and her mother out of bed, I tell you that much," says Jaden.

Jason ignores him. "Where are the girls, Mrs Sharp?" he asks.

"They are around somewhere in the house. Rose, my dear, would you be kind enough to call Tia and the girls for me?" she asks the maid.

"Of course, Madam!"

"They often do this when we have guests," she says to Jason.

Tia walks into the room just as the maid is about to leave. "Hey! Mummy, how was your flight?" she bends to kiss her, "Jason, you've come, too! I'm so happy to see you!" Tia exclaims.

"Jaden, put the plate down, we've got to go. Good night, Mummy." She grabs Jason's hands and before her mother can ask where they are going, they are out of the room.

"I need to go to Pharma-Plus before it closes!" Tia tells Guntar the driver.

"Yes, Madam," he replies as he opens the car door for her.

Jaden and Jason get in the back of the car with Kate and Brooke.

They drive to Armsterveen and the girls run into the Pharma-Plus. Tia speaks in Netherlanders with the cashier. She gets the pregnancy test kit. "We are going to a club. I will do the test there and if I am pregnant I can kill myself there before my parents have to do it!" Brooke tries to say something, but Tia would not hear it.

"Guntar, cent rum! Amsterdam spot," she yells.

The girls run to the bathroom as soon as they enter the club, leaving Jason and Jaden to their own devices. Jaden wastes no time ordering drinks and smoking and flirting with any girl his eyes meet. Jason sits down quietly at the bar with a bottle of Coke, wondering what is going on with the girls. Poor guy, he has not said a proper hello to the woman he has come to surprise. After the last break-up, he promised himself he would never fall in love again and yet, here he is.

Back in the bathroom the stick has turned blue. Tia has said to the girls, "Tonight, we enjoy ourselves. I will cry about my pregnancy tomorrow. I hope to God that it is not too late for an abortion."

"Oh ,Tia, no!" Kate cries out. "You must not, you can't!"

"I don't want any one to know about this!" demanding their sworn promise of secrecy. Brooke leaves them in the bathroom and catches up to Jason. "I'm so sorry to have abandoned you, Jason. I am surprised to see you!" Jason is relieved to hear her say that. Taking her hand, Jason leads Brooke to the dance floor. He holds her close as they dance.

Meanwhile, at the bar, Jaden is mixing all kinds of drugs and alcohol together offered to him by some of the people he has met. He does not see Tia watching him making out with some girl. He is drunk out of his mind and having the time of his life. Tia is so disgusted with him. She tries to find Kate before Kate finds Jaden. The night club is fully packed, the light are dimmed and the music is pumping loud. Tia can't see Kate or Brooke anywhere.

"I've been looking everywhere for you!" Kate suddenly screams in Tia's ears.

"Well, you find me right here! I'm eating for two, so let's go get something to eat! We can come back later for the others." She steers

Kate out of the club. They walk to Sea Palace and go on the boat. Tia orders a Vietnamese noodle soup for them.

"Uh-oh. Got a bad feeling about this," says Kate.

"You what?" Tia asks.

A jolt of unease passes through Kate. She glances at the clock, "It's that time already?"

"Yes, Amsterdam is one hour ahead of us. It's two in the morning in London," says Tia.

"We must go and get the others, and think of a possible explanation for our departure to your mum."

Tia was not thinking about that because she had unsettling thoughts about what she saw Jaden do moments ago. Maybe Kevin is doing the same thing and that's why he didn't want to come away with her and meet her family. "My mum knows where we are and we will all have breakfast together – not to worry Kate."

"Yeah, look on the bright side: Jason and Brooke get to enjoy a quiet time together. That's more than any other man has accomplished in her twenty-two years," Kate says sardonically, and then she changes the subject. "You're not really going to kill the baby, are you?"

"Uh-oh, Kate. I am so sorry. I didn't think – you wanted your child – Jaden did, too. It's not the same as me and Kevin. I'm not in love with him. He's seeing someone else. The man I'm supposed to spend the rest of my life with is somewhere out there. He could be right here in Holland, searching for me!" says Tia, gesturing at the horizon.

"The man of your dreams is searching for you?" Kate laughs.

"Yes! My perfect man. A handsome, romantic man, who will give into my every wish." Tia exclaims.

"You have gone nuts! You should see your face talking about your fancy man that don't exist!"

"Oh, but, I can assure you, Kate, he does!" Tia winks at her friend.

"Maybe if Kevin knew that you are expecting his baby, he might stop seeing the other girl. You never know. And you have us, too, so you're not going to be alone."

"Kevin is not the one. I don't want kids now – maybe one day, Kate, not now. I'm not going to keep it no matter what! Stop worrying and eat."

At the club, the music has stopped. "Come, let's get out of here," Jason suggests.

Brooke is fuming as she has just seen Jaden all over some girl. As she walks out of the club, Brooke slaps her purse against his head, but Jaden is so out of it, he turns and says to Jason, "you need to give her some!" Jason is disgusted by Jaden's remark as he runs after Brooke.

"Kate deserves a lot better than this," she says as she wipes away the tears. Jason doesn't know what to say. He gently takes her in his arms and says, "You're right! She does and she will be fine."

"God, she smells so good," he thinks as he lets go of her and tries to change the subject. "Are you mad at me for coming to Holland?"

She takes a long breath and says, "yes and no."

They had walked about half a mile when they saw Sea Palace. "Will you let me buy you a late dinner right there?" he pointed to the boat.

"How can I say no?" She laughs.

They are escorted up the stairs to the boat. Jason does not eat much because he enjoys watching how Brooke nicely cleans off her plate.

"I like how you eat," he says.

"Well, I'm not like most women." They order coffee to go, and on the way out of the boat they notice Kate and Tia.

"Oh, sorry! I hope you're not looking for us?" asks Kate.

"Are you guys ready to head home?" Tia asks.

As they jump into a taxi, Kate asks, "where is Jaden?"

"He will meet us at home," Brooke says quickly to change the subject.

Meanwhile, Jaden was in the bathroom having sex with some tart. When they finished, he felt sick and vomited into a bucket. Looking around the room, he had no idea where he was. He later remembered coming to the club with the girls and Brooke's old man. Though he doesn't remember Brooke's boyfriend's name, Jaden thinks "he's just a tight-ass like Brooke." Right outside the club, Jaden sees a cab and he jumps into it. He tells the taxi driver the name of the street, but he cannot recall the number. The driver informs Jaden that the street is in a gated area and that he can only take him there if he knows the family name. Fortunately, his cab arrived at the same time as Jason and the girls. "Nice of you to wait for me!" he snaps.

Brooke glances at Jason and Tia saw the look. "You saw him, didn't you?" she demands.

"Tia, not now! Kate will sort him out. Let's go."

Chapter 13

First awake in the morning, Jason sits by the pool drinking coffee. Thinking about where he is right now, he could not get Brooke out of his head, even though he knows very little about her. How is he going to tell her that he is falling in love with her? He stands up and dips his feet in the pool, and suddenly he feels the shock of the icy cold water as he plunges into the pool. When he surfaces, Brooke is standing at the pool's edge looking surprised.

"Oh, no! I thought it was Jaden. I'm so sorry," she apologizes, but as she extends her hands to help him out of the pool, he pulls her in and they kiss. It felt nothing like she has ever imagined and she didn't want to stop. Half of the thrill has to do with the unknown, while the other half of the thrill has to do with the myriad possibilities of seduction. She pulls away because she feels a little vulnerable. Jason couldn't resist that vulnerability. He got out of the pool, grabbed a towel and pulled her out of the pool, too. He sat down and gently sat her on his lap as he wrapped the towel around them. They were both lost in their own world about the kiss they had just shared. They sat there soaking wet, enjoying the early-morning sunshine. Jason's temperature was rising as he carried her straight into his room and gently put her down and turned on the shower. He kissed the back of her neck – short, soft kisses on her eyelids and nose, long wet kisses on her lips and neck. He kissed her nipples, kissed her thighs, all while she's still dressed! He massaged every inch of her skin as he pulled her clothes away from her wet skin. Slipping his fingertips under the elastic of her panties, he stopped to catch his breath. Brooke slipped her hands under his wet t-shirt and slowly peeled it off; she rubbed her index fingertips on his lips as she kissed and rubbed his back at the same time. Jason was aroused, and she was burning with curiosity! She slipped her hands into his pants; he was swollen and hard, so she continued with her sensuous stroking of him. Kneeling, she slid her tongue over his exposed penis. She caressed and stoked his thighs as she pulled off his pants. It was incredibly different, incredibly arousing, incredibly sensuous as they both took their time pleasing one another. Suddenly there was a loud knock on the door.

"Mr Grey! Mr Grey, sir!" It was Rose, the maid.

Jason could not respond. "Uh - em what - what can I do for you?" Jason murmurs, as he catches his breath.

"Is there anything you particularly like for breakfast, sir?"

"A beautiful woman under the showers with me, would do nicely," he whispers into Brooke's ear, but to Rose, he says, "No, thank you, Rose."

"Breakfast is in ten minutes, sir."

"Thanks Rose."

"A man can die in this stage. I want you. I want you for breakfast," he kisses her again and again.

"I must go and get ready."

"You do know you have aroused me to the point of no return?" Brooke turned the shower knob to cold and stepped out. "We can't have you at the breakfast table with a hard-on, now, can we?" She wrapped a towel around herself and left.

Tia had called Kevin, but his cell phone was turned off. She was still feeling sick when Rose knocked on her door to remind her of breakfast. She felt like throwing up just at the mention of breakfast. Brooke walked in the room with only towel around her.

"How was your swim?" Tia asked.

"I wasn't swimming," she said.

"You just walk around with towel on and wet? Yep! And I am not pregnant. We have to be downstairs for breakfast in ten minutes. Don't spend all day in the bathroom."

"Good morning, ladies," said Kate cheerily. With a big smile on her face, there was something different about her. She was like her old self again. Tia wondered what had happened to change Kate's mood as she got up to hug her.

"Are you all right ?" Tia asked.

"Never better," Kate replied, "Where is our queen? And did the handsome Mr. Grey gave her a good night kiss or what? If he did, I'd like to know all about it."

"Who are are you?" Tia asked with a concerned look on her face.

"Yeah, who are you?" Brooke shouted from the bathroom. "And what you done with our Kate?"

Tia was thinking maybe she told Jaden to sling his hock, she hoped. Tia ran to the bathroom to vomit again.

"Jaden was so romantic last night. We stayed up all night talking and making love. Making more love he was like an animal that couldn't get enough of me. I have worn him out! He will not be joining us for breakfast because he's sleeping like a rock," she told her friends.

Brooke was mad as hell. "What do you mean you made love to him all night? Are you out of your mind?" She screamed as she threw the wet towel at Kate.

"Things have been bad between us since I lost the baby and it's like our faith was being tested." She explained defensively. "Look, Brooke. I know you don't believe in God. Things happen for a reason. It either makes us stronger or we fall apart. Both Jaden and I strongly believe that. That's why we have decided when we get back to England, we would like you to find us a flat. I mean, Urban Style is doing well. All our loans are paid for. I will tell Lola when we get back. So, what do you say? Help us find a decent, affordable flat?" She begged.

"Not in this life time! You better pray to God that that idiot has not – " Tia covered her mouth and assured Kate that Brooke would help. She hugged Kate and gave Brooke her not-now-leave-it-alone look.

"So are you going to tell us or what?" Kate demanded.

"Tell you what?" Brooke snapped.

"Did he kiss you last night?"

"I think between the three of us we've been kissed enough! And we don't need to talk about it before breakfast. She is expecting, in case you've forgotten, and you are just green in-love with that idiot. You have lost all sense," Brooke shouted. "Go to breakfast and let everyone know that I am running late," She told them.

Both Tia and Kate laughed and agreed that Jason did give her a good night kiss last night.

Everyone was downstairs eating, even Jaden. He had a huge headache, and had no idea what Tia said to Kate about his behavior in the club. Tia whispered in his ear, "You were out of control last night, that was not acceptable and a very disrespectful thing to do to Kate."

"What is he going to do?" he asked himself as his heart started beating faster and the plate he was holding was shaking so badly he immediately put it down on the table. He has lost his appetite all of a sudden.

Brooke was the last guest to arrive downstairs for breakfast. Everyone turned their heads as she looked as stunning as ever. "She looks like she's a cover model from Vogue Magazine," Gertrude thought as she is very fond of fashion herself. Gertrude immediately stood up and met Brooke by the door. She sensed that out of the girls Brooke perhaps needed to feel more at home.

"My dear, you look absolute fabulous morning. Did you have a good sleep?" she asked.

Before Brooke could answer, there were good morning hugs and kisses from Naana and Bobby. Brooke sat down and wasted no time filling her plate up with food. Jason got up and made her coffee and planted a kiss on her cheek and everyone took notice of the chemistry between them. The two of them didn't even notice they were not alone. Jaden pulled Tia aside on the patio, demanding to know what she meant by the comment she made earlier. He was mad as hell and he couldn't control his anger. He began to shout. Tia got scared as he grabbed her and started shaking her violently. Jason came with Brooke and told him, "let go of the lady right now, Mr. Blake" in a commanding tone, which he did. Brooke wanted to kick the living daylights out of him, but Jason asked the girls to excuse them for a minute.

Jaden was so angry and not a bit remorseful about his behavior toward Tia. "I am sick of their constant interfering in my business," he turned and blustered. Jason did not respond, as he pulled up a chair and sat down. Jaden lit a cigarette. "They need to mind their own business. Where does she get off telling lies that I was kissing some girl last night? When all I did was feeling sick as a dog and throwing up in the loo the whole time while you all left me there."

Jason started to laugh, and he raised his eye brows and looked at Jaden.

"Oh, so you think this is funny?" Jaden asked.

"This is Amsterdam. Do you have any idea how much drugs there is in this town? And – and anyone can get their hands on it in the clubs. It is not illegal. It's like going to the pubs back in England and asking for a pint or fish and chips."

"I was sick as a dog and you all left me!" Jaden accused.

Jason looked up at him and asked, "how long have you had a drug dependency?"

Jaden face went red. He was almost about to pass out. "How can you accuse me of doing drugs?" he thought. "What – what are you talking about?" he mumbled. "I've never done drugs in my life, mate."

"Well, that's good to know," said Jason affably. "But you did plenty last night and hit on most of the women in the club, too."

"No, no. I didn't, I couldn't have. Mate! I was sick as a dog. Kate, believe me," he said tearfully. "You have no idea what you are saying, mate. I would never touch drugs in my life. You must believe me. You saw someone who looks like me. I wouldn't do drugs," Jaden kept saying.

There is one thing Jason dislikes about people who lie and who do not take responsibility for their actions. "You did not fuck a bride you met in the club? In the fucking bathroom, too, but you did. Her number is in your pocket." Jason got up to leave him with his lies as he had had enough. Jaden grabbed his hands.

"Let go of my hands, Mr. Blake!" Jason said calmly.

Jaden was still holding onto Jason's hands, crying and pleading incoherently. Tia and Brooke came back outside. Jaden looked pathetic.

"Mr. Blake, please calm yourself," said Jason. "You, sir, have a problem. And you did do everything that I said you did last night. I'm sorry you don't recall. Please seek help before is too late."

Jaden's heart started to beat faster. He was so nervous he began to believe that everyone was out to get him. "Why is Jason Grey trying to poison the girls against me? I don't do drugs. I have been drinking a lot, but not drugs. Fuck a bride I hardly know in a night club toilet? That is so disgusting. I could never do that to Kate. She is my life! Jason Grey is a liar!" he told himself. He saw the girls. And they, too, had the same disgusted expression that Jason had. It was like he was having an out of body experience as his whole body stared to shake and tremble. "Why can't I remember what I did last night in the club?" he wondered aloud. The girls did not respond because they were also wondering why Jaden could not remember last night.

"I am sorry, Tia, Brooke, so sorry. I have no idea what I did. Please, I can not lose you all. It's not just Kate. I love all of you. I can not lose you. You are my family, the only family I have."

Tia and Brooke were crying, too, as they both put their arms around him and tried to console him. Jason watched with disappointment. "This is not what I flew to Holland for," he told himself. He couldn't take any more, so he left them. He was enraged to see Jaden lying his way out of a bad situation. He thought Jaden would become a good lawyer since he lied so easily. Jaden's nose started to bleed, so Brooke gave him a tissue. He told the girls that he has been drinking more than normal. Since the loss of the baby he has not been coping well.

"I can't get it out of my head, if it was a boy or a girl. That's all I think about," he mumbled.

Tia suddenly put her hands on her stomach when he said that, and her eyes met Brooke's who had tears running down her face. Brooke has never really cared for Jaden, or his feelings. She has often thought that Kate could do much better than him. Listening to him telling them how much he missed his and Kate's child brought back the pain she normally tries to hide.

"It's not easy to lose someone you hardly know, but love with your whole heart, Jaden. I know that feeling more than all of us. If you let it, it will take away everything you love before you realize it. You can not allow that to happen!" Brooke asserted.

"I don't know how to let it go. I wish I could!" Jaden said frankly.

"You have Kate and us, Jaden. Like you said, we are family – the four of us – and we all have been upset about the baby, but we can't let it take over our lives," she paused. "I love my mother very much and for years I hated her because my father died. I didn't get a chance to know him. I didn't even know their true love and how it felt until I found you guys. Drinking is not the answer, Jaden." She was crying, too.

"We all forgot about your feelings, we have been so worried about Kate, Jaden," Tia added.

"I am going to get help before I lose it all." He thought Brooke was right. It explains how she and her mum are not so close.

Chapter 14

"Listen, Brooke. I am sorry for calling Mrs Williams an old fart. I was bang out of order what I said about her. She is a babe, you know!" he laughed. Tia hit him on the head. "Everyone can see how much she loves you. I'm glad you are making an effort with her. I don't regret forgiving my father for leaving me when I was little. And thank you guys for everything and I promise I will not do anything to hurt Kate or disrespect what we all have."

The two girls both throw their arms around him.

"Is this a private party or can anyone join in?" asks Kate.

"Please, don't say anything! I am going come clean to her now. I love you all very much," Jaden whispers to the girls.

"Why are you all crying?" Kate asks.

Jaden quickly went to hug her and said, "I'm so very sorry, but I must go home immediately as my mum needs me. Please, Kate, forgive me."

"It's okay if your mum needs you; I must come with you, too. I don't want you to be by yourself, Jaden," Kate said.

Tia and Brooke looked at each other more confused than ever.

"No, it's okay. I want you to enjoy yourself, Kate. Please say you will?"

"Of course, but I'd rather go back with you," Kate said.

"Hey Tia!" He called out to her, "Do you think you can drop me off at Armstel station this afternoon? I want to see if I can get the Euro-line bus home tonight."

Tia came and pulled him aside from Brooke and Kate.

"Running away is not going to solve your problems!" she pointed out to him.

"I am not running away. I need help, but if I don't go now, I may never get the help," he said. "Please, Tia?"

"Oh, okay, okay. I suppose I have to be proud of you. You have been through a lot and we all forgot about your pain. I am so sorry Jaden. I wish you would have talked to us."

"I know, Tia. I'm so sorry."

"It's all right. You are doing the right thing, you know."

"My dears," said Gertrude, "Do you all mind if I borrow Brooke for ten minutes?"

"No, Grandma. It's okay," said Tia. She turned to Brooke and said, "I will fill you in later. You go. I will go and see to Jason."

"Jason is okay. Daddy is so busy telling him about all his adventures all over the world. Go see them in the study."

Gertrude and Brooke went to her studio where she has an even bigger collection of African art. All the paintings were hand painted oils on canvas. She showed Brooke some of the pieces and told the history behind most of them. Brooke could not believe some of the stories behind the paintings. She was very impressed. Gertrude told her about her plans to open an art gallery in the center of Amsterdam. She has the building and everything ready but she has been having health problems, so the project has taken a back seat. Brooke's face lit up as she sat down and crossed her long legs, and said "Well, Grandma, we just gonna have to put back life into it starting right now!"

Gertrude had no idea what she meant. Brooke shouted loudly for Guntar. The poor driver almost had a heart attack as he ran into the studio almost out of breath.

"I want all these pieces in the car, Guntar, please. You must be very careful, very careful, indeed, as they are very important pieces. I want them all in the car within the next twenty minutes."

"Yes – yes madam," said the driver.

Gertrude was speechless, "My dear, I didn't mean we should do it right away. It is almost lunch and your young man – "

She did not give Gertrude a chance to finish. "Please excuse me for a minute, Grandma." Brooke came to the family room where she found Naana, Tia and the two men.

"Where are Jaden and Kate, Tia?" she asked.

Before Tia could answer, she told her to go and call them.

"Yes, master!" said Tia jokingly.

How she hates it when Brooke bosses her about like that, like a child even though Brooke is not much older. Jason came to her and she immediately hugged and kissed him, without paying attention to where she was and said, "I am so happy." Jason, being a man with a big ego, thought he had something to do with her being happy.

"May I please have everyone's attention?" she said. "I need everyone in this room to help me for two hours, to help me help Grandma do something this afternoon. I am not going take no for an answer. We will have lunch in town – my treat – after we are done. Come on, everyone, please." Bobby and Naana both know Brooke too well and they both laughed when Naana's father said to his son-in-law, "Isn't she adorable when she is giving orders and bossing people around?"

"I don't think Tia is going to like this," Bobby observed. Bobby Sharp often tells Tia to listen to Brooke and that they must not fight about the silly things they often do. He and his wife both have come to love Brooke just like they have loved Kate as their own. They have been very worried about Sarah. They, too, wanted Sarah Williams to join them in Holland this weekend, but she could not find the time. They have formed a close friendship with Sarah. "She would be so proud of Brooke if she were here," Bobby thought.

Brooke pulled away from Jason and went to the studio where Gertrude was still sitting down and sat on the chair next to her. "Would you like to show me the gallery right now, Grandma?"

"Oh my dear, it's almost lunch time," Gertrude dithered.

Jason helped Gertrude up and Brooke informed her that her husband, son-in-law and her daughter are all in the car waiting for her. Brooke and Jason will follow them in her car.

"Oh, my dear, how can I say no?" said Gertrude.

Jason still had no idea what had just happened.

"I need your help too, Jason," Brooke said as she extended her hands to him. He pulled her towards him and said, "I have been falling in love with you, Brooke, but I don't want to scare you," he said softly. Brooke was scared of what he had just said. She stared at him for minute, smiled and tried to stay in control of her feelings. She kissed him softly and said, "You hardly know me, one blow job under the shower and you are in love? Come on! I need your help, please!" He kissed her. "It's okay to be afraid. I am, too. Let's go make your Grandma's dream come true."

Tia demanded to know what was going on. Brooke was in her own world, but she, too, has been falling in love with Jason Grey without knowing it. She cannot name the emotions she feels when she thinks about him, so she has tried to hide it ever since they met. "I don't want to be in love. People lose themselves when they are in love," she thought about her mother. Brooke has been thinking about her mother a lot lately.

"Are you going to tell us where we are going?" Tia shouted.

"Keep your knickers on Tia! We are there. Come on, everyone, come!" Brooke said excitedly. She looked like a child on Christmas morning. The building was about a hundred years old, a two story with very high ceilings. It was already painted dark gray inside, featured a huge sky light in the middle, and it needed to be cleaned.

"I love it!" Brooke said. "Grandma, I want the sky light removed. Do you have a contractor I can call?"

"Yes, my dear," said Gertrude. "I will call next week."

"No, Grandma. Call the contractor and have him meet me here now! Tell him there's one hundred guilders for him if he shows up in the next half hour. The building has an alarm system, I trust?"

"Yes, my dear."

"Grandpa, I need you and Bobby to go the hardware store," and she handed them a list of items to purchase. "Please take Jason with you." She kissed Jason on the cheek. The two other men went and kissed their wives without asking questions.

"I don't want to be here, Brooke. Give me the car keys. I am going home," said Tia.

"Too bad! We are all here to do our part. I don't want to hear any of you bitch, or I am going to have a bloody cow," Brooke declared.

"Jaden, help Guntar with the paintings. He is too bloody slow."

"Ladies, help me sort out Grandma's paintings. They all tell a story, so we must group them accordingly. When people come, they can learn and feel the emotions and the story that each painting tells. I want them to take home a piece of Ghana's history and the part the Ashanti tribe played in Ghana's independence," she said with care on her face.

Tia and her mother were amazed how much Brooke cared. It was like she knew Gertrude's dream. "She suddenly understood," Naana thought. Naana glanced through some of the paintings. They were so elegant, the details quickly overwhelmed her. "You know, my mother studied art at NYU in the sixties," said Naana.

"These are extraordinary works," said Brooke.

"Thanks Brooke," said Tia.

"She is not just your grandmother, you know?" She bitches at Tia.

Naana quickly steps in between the two girls and puts her arms around them, "You two can fight about which one is the boss of your relationship as you always do – later."

"We don't fight!" said both girls simultaneously and then they laughed.

"Come on, lazy buggers! We have work to do!" Brooke said, "I'm going to see how Grandma is doing with the contractor."

"You know, Sarah is very proud of you, Brooke." Naana told her. "She meant to come with us this weekend to visit mother. She and mother share the same tastes in art and they both are crazy about you." It made Brooke's heart warm to hear that her mother was proud of her. She tries not think of her mother much, but she has been in her thoughts lately and Tia has been encouraging her to try and make an effort with the "old fart" as they all called their parents.

In the corner office by the second floor door, Gertrude was crying. Brooke quickly ran to her. "What's wrong, Grandma? The contractor can't make it?" she asked.

"No, my dear. He will be here with his four sons. I took the opportunity to tell him that we want the sky light removed and covered, and he wants to go to the hardware store and get some four by fours, nails and roof tail so he can finish it tonight," Gertrude said.

Brooke hugs and kisses her. "We must not waste time, then. Grandma, I want you to tell me your vision and also tell me about the Ashanti kingdom and their strength. You have a name for this place, I hope?"

"Yes, my dear. The sign is already made. Come! I will show it to you."

Jaden and Guntar brought all the paintings indoors. She pulled Jaden aside and handed him money instructing him to go with Guntar and get all kinds of food and drinks for everyone. "The contractor is coming with his four sons and I want them well fed so that the job will be finish by supper time."

"Jaden, I am proud of you. You are doing the right thing for yourselves," Tia told him.

By the time the three men returned from the hardware store, all the paintings were placed in their designated area. There were sheets on the center of the floor.

"May I ask why you chose these colors?" Brooke inquired.

"These are the colors of the Ghana flag," said Gertrude. "The red represents the blood that was shed for independence; the gold represents the gold Ghana produces as one of our main resources; and the green represents agriculture. There is a black star in the middle of the gold, which we often say represents the black star," Gertrude told Brooke.

"It is ironic. I have been to all the museums and most of the art galleries in England and you hardly ever see African art there even though the British occupied most of the West African countries," observed Brooke.

By the time Brooke and Gertrude emerged from the office, the downstairs paintings were on the walls already and Jason and Naana were finishing hanging the last one on wall. Osei Kofi came and swept both his wife and Brooke into his arms and said, "a job well done, my dears" as he planted a kiss on the cheeks of both ladies.

Bobby Sharp was talking to Jason by the time Brooke reached upstairs. She overheard Bobby telling Jason Grey that if he does anything to hurt Brooke, he will answer to him. "Brooke is just like one of my daughters and I will not let anyone hurt one of my girls. So you behave like a gentleman with her at all times or I will have your guts for garters, Grey. Do you hear me?"

"I will never do anything to hurt Brooke or the girls, Bobby," Jason assured him.

Brooke stopped and stood still a second for and said, "Thank you, guys. Jason, do mind if I borrow Bobby for a bit?"

"No, go ahead, sweetheart," Jason smiles.

She took Bobby's hand and they headed down the stairs to Gertrude's office. Bobby sat as Brooke stood. She was a little speechless. All the time the Sharp's have known Brooke, she has never been short of words.

"What is it, sweetheart?" Bobby asked with a concerned tone.

"I just want to thank you and Naana for making me a part of your family. You two have always been the parents I never had and I really appreciate it, you know," Brooke murmured. Bobby was very moved himself.

"You never have to say thank you as Naana would say if she was here. We are family and as I said to Grey a while ago... if he hurts you, he will answer to me," Bobby said proudly.

Jaden entered the room before Bobby could finish. "Sorry, the food is here and the contractors are here, too."

"Thank you, thank you, gentlemen for coming on such short notice. We really appreciate it. Now how much will all this cost?" Brooke asked as she joined the workers in the main room.

Grandma translates the Netherlands for her. "He says they want twenty-five hundred guilders," Gertrude told Brooke.

"Grandma, tell them I say thank you for coming, but my budget is fourteen hundred and, of course, the extra one hundred that was promised over the phone," Brooke said to the old lady.

"Oh, my dear, I think it's a reasonable price," said Gertrude.

"It's okay, Grandma. Tell the gentleman what I said," Brooke insisted.

Poor Gertrude! She told them, and the younger man was upset, so he came and talked with Brooke in English. He went back to his father and brothers and they all came and shook Brooke's hands. The family sat down to eat and drink while the contractor and his sons worked. By the time they were done with lunch, it was almost two o'clock and the sky light was off and the roof was almost done. The contractor and his sons cleaned up all the mess they made and they told Gertrude they would be the first ones there when the place opened.

The afternoon helped take Kate's mind off Jaden going home that night, although he never did say what the emergency was with his mum, though Kate knows he and his mother are very close.

"Tia, did Jaden say what was the emergency with his mother was?" Kate asked.

"No, sorry, are you okay about him going home tonight?" asked Tia.

"I wish Jaden could stay. I'll talk to him later," said Kate. "Have you spoken to Kevin yet?"

"I have called four times. I have left two messages with his brother, Aaron. The last call was to his cell phone and some girl answered, so I hung up. He knows my number, Kate. I am not worrying about him. I don't know why they call it morning sickness when it's been all day! Kate, how did you cope?" said Tia.

"Oh, sweetheart! You are going to be okay," said Kate sympathetically.

"I am in so much pain, it's hard to keep anything down," said Tia.

"It will soon pass. Hang in there, you'll see. I'd love to come back and see this place when Grandma opens this joint. I love all the pieces. I can't believe we were able to put all this together in half a day. Look at her! She looks so happy," said Kate.

Chapter 15

"Grandma, we are going to leave now. We will see you at breakfast. Kate and I want to show these guys around the city," said Tia.

"Oh, my dear, but you will join us for dinner? Cook is making all your favorites and more," said Gertrude.

Tia turned and looked at Jaden and Kate, "Okay, we will."

"Tia, your mother and I need to know soon which university you are planning to attend. We need to sit and talk about it. If you're going out, make sure you eat something, Tia," said Bobby.

"Yes Daddy, I will. Love you!" said Tia.

"Daddy can be like bloody John Major sometimes. Who the hell does he think he is? I'm not going to no university, Mr. Prime Minister. Shouting my business out to everyone like this is question time at Westminster. I hate it when he does that. Sometimes I wish I could tell him where to go: I'm nineteen years old and he still treats me like a five year old. Wait until I tell him that I am going to have Kevin's bastard child!" Tia ruminated. "After a year and he goes and does this, I hate him! I wish I knew who the girl was who answered his cell phone. I thought he loved me!" she thought.

"Where were you just now?" Brooke asked.

"Just thinking about Kevin," Tia admitted.

Brooke hates to see Tia unhappy because of Kevin. She sits next to her with one arm affectionately around her. "I am always going to be the big sister you never wanted, Tia... And you, darling, are going to be the little sister I always wanted, Tia, that is how it is," Brooke told her.

"Whatever it is you are going to say – don't! I am not in love with Kevin. You have bossed me about enough for one day. Piss off and leave me alone!" Tia cried.

Brooke smiles and kisses her on the forehead. She gives her the cellphone. "Call him!"

"Here, call him now and I will go and round up the others," said Brooke.

She took the cell phone from Brooke and dialed the number. On the second ring he answered.

"This is Kevin," he says.

"Hey – it's Tia."

"I was just thinking about you," said Kevin. "I lost the number you gave me. Every time I come home I'm told you called. I miss you like crazy."

"Me, too, Kevin," she said. "I have to go now, but I will call you tomorrow."

"No, please don't go – unless you are going to call me again later, Tia," he pleaded.

"I will try," she said.

"I love you, princess, 'bye. I'll talk to you later. Love you!" he said.

"So all is well I trust?" asked Brooke.

Tia looked more confused than when Brooke left her. "Why is everything falling apart now?" Brooke wondered. "This is supposed to be the best time of our lives." Their business has taken off and they are about to open a second shop next week. She has finally met her Mr. Right. "I should think about the whole Jason Grey thing," she says to herself. She is right about love. It changes people or it dies on you and you forget what's important and before you know it, life has passed you by. She thought about her mother and how much she must have loved Jackson. Then Brooke thought about Jaden and Kate. Jaden has always been a perfect gentleman, even though she likes to give him a hard time sometimes. He has recently let alcohol take over him, and she hopes he pulls himself together soon because poor Kate can't handle it. And now Tia seems to heading God knows where with Kevin and the baby. "I can't fall into the same path," she said out loud. Jason heard her.

"Can't fall into the same path, what path?" asks Jason.

She turns to face him. He looks so handsome and it seems that he has more product in his hair than she does. She tries her best to fake a smile, but he doesn't buy the smile. Instead, he is concerned about the girls and what he had witnessed earlier that morning. Clearly, Jaden has a drug problem and a violent temper. He wonders what would have happened to Tia if he and Brooke had not walked in on the incident between them this morning. Jaden not remembering his actions means he has been doing this for a long time and the substance abuse is beginning to affect his thought processes. Someone needs to educate these girls. Love can't fix his problem. Jaden is long gone, he thought.

"Listen, Brooke, about this morning with Jaden. Promise me you will stay away from him," said Jason.

"He will not cross that line again. It was a one-off thing. He's been through an awful lot in the last six months. We all abandoned him and he, like most people, has turned to alcohol. He's a good lad. I would not take him home to meet my mother, but he is a good lad. He was really embarrassed. I dare say he will not do that again."

"Will you take me home to meet your mother?" Jason asks.

Brooke flushes crimson.

"You have already met everyone I love," replies Brooke.

"What about your mother?" Jason insists.

"I'm afraid we are not that close and we don't have the kind of a relationship most girls my age have with their mothers," she says, ducking the underlying question.

Jason can't discern that Brooke wishes she was as close with her mother as Tia is with her own. He doesn't want to intrude anymore. Instead, he puts his arms around her. She moves next to him and rests her head against his shoulder.

They went to WH Smith. It was a little different from the stores in England. Tia browsed the candy section for mints. Kate saw a finger-ring she wanted to buy for her mum. Jaden asked the sales girl to give him two of them. The girl wrapped them up neatly and placed the package on the counter. He kissed Kate and handed her one of the gifts. His eyes were clear with affection, exposing the hidden shadow of Jaden's personality. And no matter how uncomfortable he gets when he shows a public display of affection, Kate finds that side of him irresistible, even though he doesn't like to expose it much. On this occasion, Kate adores him.

"This one is for you, love, and this one we will take home for your mum," he says.

"Uh - I love you, but you didn't have to," says Kate.

Next, they went on "the Dutchman," which took them cruising all over Amsterdam. While cruising, Jaden stood gazing at a man drinking beer. He put his hands in his pockets and discovered a piece of paper with a number and address written on it in red lipstick. He quickly put it back in his pocket as his heart started to beat faster. Suddenly, he started to throw up in the channel. "What is happening to me?" he thought.

Jason ordered cocktails for everyone.

"Tia is under age, so she can't drink," said Brooke.

"I hate your big sister ways, Brooke," she snapped.

Speaking in Netherlands, she told the waitress to bring her iced tea.

"Tell her to make it two," said Jaden, "whatever you ordered." He did not want to go near any alcohol.

"Take her away," said Tia.

"No, I think it's time we get off this boat and head home for supper," said Brooke.

Tia glances at her watch and it is almost half-past five. She recalls her promise to call Kevin back tonight. With a shrug of her shoulders, Tia decided not to call Kevin.

Naana Konadu-Sharp is in the garden talking to Gertrude about the whole afternoon, expressing her amazement over what Brooke and everyone was able to accomplish. When they returned, Rose brought them cocktails and announced that supper would be ready in ten minutes. Tia was not looking forward to food at all. Bobby came and kissed her on the forehead. "I want to see you eat, Tia. You look rather thin, sweetie."

It was nine o'clock when Kate asked Jaden to stay, promising to leave with him the next night. He told her he wanted her to stay and enjoy the long weekend. He had asked Guntar to drive him to the Euro-line station later. The two of them went up to their room after supper to say their good-byes.

Tia couldn't avoid her parents as both Bobby and Naana asked to have a quiet word with her right after supper. She informed them that she was not going to university in October. She wanted to take a year off to travel to Canada. Naana was not very pleased. She asked, "why Canada?"

"There is a big software giant called Nortel Network. I am thinking of getting a job with them," she told them.

"Since when, Tia?" her father asked.

Tia didn't respond.

"Tia, you've said you want to work in television or write. Computers are a subject you took for fun. You're not even passionate about them!" her mother reminded her.

"I will pursue that when I go to university. Right now, Nortel Networks is big and I want to be a part of it. Mum, you always say I should apply myself to things that I am passionate about. I am passionate about Nortel and I believe there will be a job offer for me." Her mother asked, "without a degree?"

Bobby didn't force the issue too much. He said they would support her if that's what she wanted to do. He reminded his wife about the Canadian weather as they both knew it very well. "Tia has lived a very sheltered life. She will not last in Canada more than a week without Kate and Brooke. Most nineteen year-olds her age leave home, Naana. Tia still lives at home even though Brooke has this beautiful apartment for them. Even so, she still lives at home with us. We are not just the old fart they called us!" they both laughed. He kissed her and said, "I promise you, dear, she will be home and in university before we know it."

Brooke was left by the pool with Jason.

"Spend the night with me," he says as he kisses her.

"No, it's not very appropriate since we both are guests here," she says.

"Do you regret this morning?" he asks.

"No, do you?"

Jason put an arm around Brooke in an unmistakably possessive move, whisked her through the lounge and reclined with her on two of the padded loungers. Brooke braced herself as she did every time things got quiet between them.

"I have been on cloud nine since I met you. I told you I am falling in love with you, Brooke. We don't have to spend that kind of night together here. I agree we will have plenty of time for that. I just don't want the night to end, that's all. How is any man supposed to sleep knowing you're just upstairs? God only knows what you wear to bed," he smiles.

"I sleep naked," she teases.

Jason folds his arms behind his head and raises an eye brow and smiles. The silence deepens.

"I'm weird, Jason. I am not like most girls my age," Brooke blusters.

He turns his head on the padded lounger to look at her, but it is impossible to read her expression in the warm darkness.

"It has occurred to me," he stops in mid-sentence to gather his nerve. "This is probably the first time you've been this close to any man," Jason pauses. "I am not in any rush. We can take things as slow as you want, Brooke."

"You're sure about that?"

"Positive."

He framed her face with his hands. "It will be wise to take it slowly, get to know each other." He traces her cheekbones with the tips of his fingers. She feels his body responding to hers, and she catches her breath. "Well, I have to go to bed now." He glances at his watch and says good night. "It's time you go to bed," he said. He watches her go up the stairs.

Tia was sitting in the bath tub drinking water when Brooke returned to their room. She was in deep thought as Brooke picked up a towel and said, "Okay, Miss Sunshine, come out before you prune up."

Tia did not respond.

"Tia, come out of the bath before I drag you out," Brooke demanded.

"I'd like to see you try. I can't believe the old farts telling me I am lazy, and I don't apply myself to anything. Oh-oh- hear this! In my mum's opinion, taking a year off school is just being plain lazy. This is coming from the African Princess born into a life of privilege, married to the man of her dreams. What does she know about my life, an old fart?" she says as she takes the towel from Brooke.

"Tia can be a child sometimes," Brooke thinks. She grabs another towel and follows Tia to the bedroom where she wraps the towel on her wet hair.

"Tia, darling. What is it you want for yourself?" Brooke asks.

Tia does not respond. She hates when Brooke is all over her like a bossy big sister, which she always is. She reclines on the bed and puts her head down on the pillow as the tears start to drop. Brooke whispers to herself, "it is going to be a long night," as she gets into the bed and puts her arms around Tia. There is a knock on the door.

"Please come in," Brooke says.

It is Naana. She feels unhappy about how the discussion ended earlier in the study with her daughter. She has come to smooth things out with Tia. Kate is right behind her as she enters the room.

"I came to say good night, girls, and – " She stops in mid-sentence as she can see that Tia is upset and it looks like Brooke is consoling her. "Tia, I am sorry for what I said earlier, sweetie. You have grown up now and your father and I will support whatever it is you want out of your life, sweetie," her mother says.

Tia still does not respond. Both Kate and Brooke say good night to her as she closes the door and leaves them. Naana senses there is something going on with her daughter, and she wishes that Tia would trust her enough to talk about it. She hardly sees Tia at home anymore. "We are growing apart," she has told Bobby a while ago.

As soon as Guntar drove off, Jaden wasted no time taking out the number in his pocket that some bird had given him the night before and called it. When a woman answered, he almost put the phone down, but some how picked up the courage to say, "Hi! You asked me to call you last night after the club."

She told him to come on over to her place, "there is a party going on."

Jaden hung up and took a taxi to the address, and before he knew it, the girl opened the taxi door, paid the driver, and in an instant was all over Jaden. He was a little confused as she handed him a bottle of beer and took him to the back of the apartment into her bedroom. She lit a joint and put it in Jaden's mouth and kissed him at the same time. He inhaled with no hesitation and handed it back to her. She left the room. Jaden sat on the bed and closed his eyes for a second. He's never had a joint before. His drug of choice is ecstasy. The pot went straight to his head and he immediately felt the buzz. The woman came back with what seemed to be alcohol. He grabbed her and put her against the wall and ripped off her panties. He took out a condom and popped it on, and when he parted her legs, they were at it for hours.

He popped some more ecstasy and left just in time to board the mid-night bus to London. The bus driver announced that he would be stopping at Rotterdam to pick up some more passengers, and that he would stop at Ghent for twenty minutes. "We will arrive at London Victoria Station at ten fifteen in the morning." Jaden was asleep as soon as he sat down. He slept the whole trip. They reached the Port of Dover and the driver asked everyone to take their bags and go through immigration. "I will be parked at gate number ten," he announced to the passengers. Everyone on the bus got out when the customs officer came in the bus with the dogs. They immediately ran to where Jaden was sleeping, but he was so out of it that when the police put the hand cuffs on him, he didn't feel a thing.

When Jaden finally opened his eyes, he was told to stand up. They escorted him to a room and searched him. They asked for his shoes and belt. He was so dazed that he lay on the bed and slept some more. The police didn't find any drugs on him, but the backpack on his lap, however, had enough drugs to send him to prison for ten years. The customs officer and the police constable who arrested him were puzzled. Why did Jaden have so many drugs in plain sight in his bag? It was uncommon in their line of work to find drugs in plain sight like that – like Jaden wanted to get caught.

"Look at him," said one of the young constables. "No, a junkie and he's not too smart, thinks he can just walk in with a bag full of drugs and not get caught, not today mate! He is going to be banged up for a long time for these." The older police man ignored the younger one because they always get over excited on their first big bust. He looked through Jaden's wallet as he wrote down all the things they found in his possession. There was a bottle of prescription medication, a packet of chewing gum, half-opened condoms with only two left. Inside his wallet, there was a photograph of him and three girls. "They can't be his sisters," he thought. One was a mixed race, the other a white girl and the third a Chinese girl. There was another photograph of him and the Chinese girl. "This must be his bird," he thought. There was a student ID from the London School of Law and Economics. There was another ID for a security company. His driving license says his birthday will be in four days and that he is going to be twenty-three. The policeman's heart broke as he thought of his own son the same age as Jaden. "Why would someone with a bright future ahead do something like this?" he wondered. When he looked in on him after his shift was over, Jaden was still sleeping. "Poor lad," he thought.

Chapter 16

Back in Amsterdam, the girls spend the better part of the morning at the art gallery, organizing the rest of the art and the paintings they didn't get the chance to finish the day before. In the morning, Tia lashes out at Brooke that she doesn't want to spend her long weekend off working in some stupid gallery. Brooke promises it will not take them more than two hours at the most. It's been almost four hours and Tia is fed up already. She continues to be so sick and still cannot keep down any food.

"I'm going to go to Canada at the end of next month," she announces.

"Running away is not the answer, Tia! You have no idea how lucky you are," Brooke told her. "Naana and Bobby adore you and are always there for you. Do you want to give up all of that and run off so you can get rid of a baby you don't want?" Brooke asks.

"Shut your mouth, Brooke," Tia mutters.

"That Kevin may be a good fuck, but the son of a bitch is not worth all this confusion. You were looking forward to this trip for months and you let him mess you up like this? Go back to the house and talk to Bobby and Naana about what you are going through before I do. I can still remember what Lola said the last time we tried to keep Kate's baby to ourselves. I don't want to see the same look on Naana and Bobby's faces when they learn this later!" Brooke reminded them.

"I hate to agree, but she is right, Tia. You must go home and try to talk to them," said Kate. Tia did not respond.

"Tia, please, let's go home now. Brooke and Jason can finish this. I will ask Guntar to pick you guys up later," suggests Kate.

Brooke stands up and holds her hands out to Tia. She helps her up and hugs her, whispering in her ears, "it will be alright, darling. Tia, we all love you even though you are a royal pain all the time."

"I hate it when you are right, but you are right. I love you and I'm sorry I invited Jason without asking you," Tia mumbled.

"You did good asking him to come. We look out for one another no matter what because we are sisters," Brooke told her.

Jason stood in the middle of the gallery watching them. They are all so very close one would think they really are sisters. He's never met a group of people who truly care about one another like these girls and their families. He wondered whether Brooke's mother had the same relationship with the two girls as Mrs Lee and the Sharps do? "I wonder what kind of a woman Brooke's mother is?" he says to himself.

"Are you okay?" Brooke shouts.

"I am fine. Thank you," he replies.

"I'm almost done. Do you want to grab a late lunch?" she asks.

"Later... I want to you to show me around the building first," he says.

Brooke drops the painting she is holding on the floor and walks toward him. He looks so handsome, she thinks. She flashes him a smile as he takes her hand and kisses the back of her hands.

"This is Gertrude's private office," she says as they walk in.

Jason goes over to the desk, looks around and sits on the chair, "I like it."

He puts his hands out to Brooke to come him. She does so without hesitation. He guides her over to his lap and she slides her hands sensuously over his neck. She whispers, "You're irresistible." He holds her by the waist and kisses her neck so softly behind her ears. He loves her fragrance.

"You are making me totally hot," he says.

Brooke began with long, slow licks, as if she was eating an ice cream cone. She unzipped his pants and couldn't wait to take him in her mouth. It was like she knew this has always been Jason's all-time fantasy. The phone on Gertrude's desk started to ring, and he whispered, "don't stop." The phone was still ringing when she stopped and answered with one hand. Her other hand kept rubbing Jason, teasing and flirting with him. She hung up the phone and kissed him gently on the lips, whispering "that was Kate. Guntar will be here in an hour to pick us up," she said. She kissed him on the full lips and put her fingers in his mouth. It felt warm and she loved it. He pulled her into his arms and slid his hands under her skirt. These feelings were unknown to her, as she felt sexually helpless at his touch. Brooke Williams is not one to feel helpless in anything, but it was like Jason had taken her as a prisoner, and she wanted desperately to tell him to stop. Nevertheless, his face felt warm against her breast as he brushed his lips against it and squeezed it gently circling it with his tongue. He was aroused. He felt her nervousness, so he dropped his hands and stopped kissing her. "I want to make love to you in my bed with glowing candles everywhere in my loft. A bucket of chilled champagne at hand, too," said Jason.

"Will it be quite as shattering as this?" she asked. It sounded so romantic when he said it. She loved his idea about making love with candlelight. She teased and flirted with him. She told him to come and he did as he was told. They kissed for a long time and this time Brooke pulled away from him.

"I have fallen in love with you, Brooke. I know you are scared. Please don't be, Brooke," he pleaded.

She kissed him and he responded to her kisses.

"You must show me around before Guntar gets here," said Jason.

"My flight leaves at six in the morning. Since I can't take you to dinner tonight, how about – How about I take you shopping?" he offered.

"What is it with you and shopping?" asks Brooke.

As she put on lipstick, he watched her, biting his lips.

"Not like our last shopping," he said. "I have something different in mind."

"You can take me shopping some other time. We are going to the casino as soon as Guntar pick us up, darling," she said.

"The casino?"

"Yes, Gertrude has already rented a tuxedo for you. I'd love to see your sexy self in it, Mr. Grey," she said.

"When do you get back to London?" he asked.

"We leave tomorrow afternoon. Should be in London by five. Why?"

"Have dinner with me. I will pick you up at seven, no excuses!" he insisted.

She kissed him and said, "how could I say no?"

AT THE PORT OF DOVER – Jaden was still banged up in jail. He opened his eyes and was so confused about where he was. It was not long before he realized that he had landed in jail. His heart rate went up. "Oh no – oh no," he said. "How did I get here?" he asked himself. He had a huge headache. The last thing he could remember was Guntar taking him to Armstel station to get the bus to England.

"You awake then?" the constable asked.

Jaden did not respond.

"You want a cup of tea, mate?"

Jaden still did not respond. The constable left what looked like a cheese sandwich on white bread with a cup of tea in between the bars and left.

"I am in jail for what?" he asked himself. "How long have I been here?" His watch, shoes, and belt were gone. He tried to remember but couldn't, and his nose started to bleed. As he looked around, there was no sink for him to wash his face. There was a stainless steel toilet. He took some of the toilet paper and wiped his nose. He laid back down on the bed and faced the wall. "What have I done?" he asked himself again.

"Mr Blake!" the voice called.

Jaden turned and sat up on the bed. There was a man in a suit standing there with what looks like a file in his hands. He opened the door.

"Mr Blake, I am Detective Inspector Greenford. Would you come with me, sir, please?"

Jaden got up and walked out of the cell. He asked Jaden to wait as he closed the door on the cell. Then he asked Jaden to stand against the wall with his hands up against the wall. Jaden was almost in tears as he did what he was told. The detective searched him and put hand cuffs on both his ankles and asked that he put his hands behind his back. Jaden sighed. He closed his eyes and did what he was told.

"This way, Mr. Blake," said the detective.

They walked down the hall and the detective opened a door asking Jaden to enter the room. Jaden entered. There was a long brown desk, which has seen better days, with a tape recorder on it. There were three chairs in the room, two on the same side and the other one on the opposite side of the desk. Jaden was told sit in one of the two side by side chairs. He sat down and a few minutes later another man in a suit walked in and sat next to him. The detective sat on the other chair across and he pressed a button on the tape recorder, saying, "It's 10.30 pm on 27th of August, 1996. We are at the Port of Dover Detention Center. I am Detective Inspector David Greenford."

The other gentleman next to Jaden said, "I am Duty Solicitor Edward Mercer."

He turned to Jaden and said, "Please state your full name."

Jaden did not respond.

Edward Mercer asked the detective to stop the recording, which he did.

"Young man, I am here to help you," Edward Mercer snapped at Jaden.

"Detective Greenford, sir. Would you would be kind enough to give me a minute with Mr. Mercer?" Jaden asked politely.

The detective felt sorry for Jaden. As he paused for a second and looked at the lawyer, he said, "Of course, Mr. Blake." He left and closed the door.

Jaden did not say a word for a minute.

"Young man, I don't have all day here, what is it you want?" Edward Mercer asked.

"Why am I here?" Jaden asked.

"Mr Blake, you were found with illegal drugs in your backpack this morning on the bus from Amsterdam," he said.

"Thank you, Mr Mercer. Can you please ask the detective to come in?" said Jaden.

"Young man, did you understand what I just said, and the seriousness of it?" Edward Mercer asked.

Jaden did not respond: he frowned.

Edward got up and called the detective into the room. The detective started from the beginning with the date and time and his name and the duty solicitor's name.

"Jaden Luke Blake," said Jaden.

"Mr. Blake, you were found with a backpack full of drugs at seven o'clock this morning by two customs officers, and two of the Metropolitan Police in Euro Lines bus 198."

The detective picked up a backpack from the floor and showed it to Jaden and the duty solicitor.

Jaden clears his throat and said, "Detective Greenford, that is not my pack, sir. I had no backpack with me when I boarded the bus last night."

The solicitor tried to talk, but Jaden raised his hands for him to be quiet.

"Mr Mercer is not my lawyer. There are cameras at the Euro Lines station in Amsterdam where I boarded the bus. They will show that I had no backpack with me," said Jaden.

"Mr Blake, I must advise you to stop," said the duty solicitor.

Jaden ignored him. "I went to Amsterdam with my girlfriend and two of her friends. One of them is a granddaughter of the former Ghanaian ambassador. My mother has become sick and taken to Greenwich Hospital when I called two days after my trip. I took the bus a day early to come home as she doesn't have anyone else. I took two tablets of ZOLOFT antidepressant medication. I do have an anxiety disorder. I usually sleep through the whole night when I take the medication. I only had a Nike gym bag with me, which I put in the bottom of the bus. I had no other bag with me, sir!"

There was a knock on the door, so the detective stopped the recording and left the room.

"Mr. Blake, you must listen to me!" said the duty solicitor.

"No! Mr. Mercer, you must listen to me. I am not a junkie or a drug dealer. If you really are concerned and wanted to do the job you have sworn to do by law, you would have known that my rights have been violated. I have been in police custody for more than twelve hours with no food, no drink, and no phone call. And on top of it all, I am given you as a lawyer!" Jaden shouted. "Tell me, Mr. Mercer, did you even bother to ask what evidence they have other than that the alleged backpack was mine?" Jaden asked rudely.

"Mr. Blake, it's bank holiday weekend. I drove all the way from London to come while my son is in a coma as we speak, and I am sitting here listening to your lies that the drugs are not yours! You don't do drugs? Mr. Blake, I have been here the last six hours looking through the evidence they claim they have against you. I laughed at first until I saw you sleeping there. I knew it, Mr. Blake. You have been doing drugs, maybe not trafficking drugs, but you do have a drug problem, son. You let this be a lesson to you when you leave here, and know that next time you may not be so lucky. Drugs destroy people's lives and not everyone gets a second chance in life," Mr. Mercer said with an expression of loathing on his face.

"You can say whatever you want, Mr. Mercer. I am not a junkie and that is not my backpack," Jaden pointed to the bag. He leaned his head back against the wall and closed his eyes. He felt his nose bleeding again. The hand cuffs were still on him, and the lawyer saw his bleeding nose and handed Jaden some tissues. "God... I need help!" he said aloud, seeing the lawyer was almost in tears.

The lawyer stood up, slapped his hands on the table and left the room. Jaden was left in the room for what seemed like forever. The lawyer and the detective returned to the room. Jaden could not read the expression on the detective's face.

"Oh – no. God, no please don't let the drugs be mine. It can't be mine!" Jaden could not hold in his emotions any longer and he started to cry. "You must believe me, the backpack is not mine, Detective Greenford!" said Jaden.

The detective sat down and he put both his hands on the table.

"Detective Greenford, you either charge Mr. Blake, or I insist you release him now, or I will be forced to file a complaint," declared Mr. Mercer.

"I am so very sorry, Mr. Blake. We have got all the camera footage requested by our office this morning from Amsterdam Euro Lines station. I was just told that, in fact, you did not have any backpack like you said when you boarded the bus this morning. You are free to go, Mr. Blake," said Detective Inspector Greenford. "I am so sorry, Mr. Blake. We needed to make sure that the bag wasn't yours."

⸖ *Chapter 17* ⸖

Jason arrived at London Gatwick airport on schedule. He wasted no time cleaning up his east London bachelor loft. He was still on cloud nine about his weekend in Amsterdam, especially last night at the casino. Brooke looked like someone from a movie premier, when all the stars dress up, he thought. He has never brought a woman to his loft. He drove to Sheaped Bush market. He had no idea what he was looking for, so he bought a whole bunch flowers, vegetables and fruits. Then he went to The Body Shop in Bond Street and asked one of the sales assistants to help him find some scented candles, bubble bath and massage oil. On his way out, he saw Marks & Spencer, so he quickly crossed the road and went straight to the ladies' department. There, he bought all kinds of women's underwear, night gowns and bath robes. Afterward, he drove to London Harrods and picked up a whole line of women's clothing including shoes and purses.

Meanwhile, the girls had lunch and were already driving through France.

Jaden awoke trying to put together the events of what had happened over the weekend. He had no shirt on, and he was sitting up in his bed with a blank look on his face when his father came into the room.

"How was your trip, son?" asked Luke.

Jaden did not respond. Luke has been concerned about son's behavior lately. Although, Jaden didn't appear to be drunk, like he has been the last few months, Luke sensed that he was troubled. They are not very close as father and son. However, Luke sat down by Jaden and he raised his hands to put around Jaden but suddenly dropped his hands and took a deep breath.

"Jaden – I have not been much of a father or a role model to you all this time, and maybe it is too late now. Whatever it is that is troubling you, son, I'd like to know. Maybe I can offer some assistance – if you let me, son?" said Luke tentatively.

"I was banged up last night, Dad," Jaden said softly.

Luke's whole body was shaking as the word "banged up" went through him like he had been shot by a gun. He couldn't get son's his words out of his head.

"I was banged up in jail, Dad." This time he said it with an even tone as he stood up and faced his father. He saw the shocked look on his father's face as he continued. "I left Amsterdam two days ago. I have been doing drugs and drinking very heavily since I got there. I may have even cheated on Kate while I was there with some bird I hardly know." He sat down on the floor and leaned his head back against the wall. "I waked up in a jail at Port Dover last night about to be charged with drug trafficking, Dad," he said.

Luke got up and was almost walking out of the door as his worse nightmare was about to come true. Jaden grabbed hold of his hands.

"You need to hear this, Dad!" Jaden insisted.

Luke sat down as the tears rolled down his face. He has seen his son "high," but Jaden has always maintained he was not doing drugs even though he had all the symptoms of a drug user. He has seen Jaden full of energy then very nervous and believing that everyone is out to get him. "Why didn't I get help for him?" Luke asked himself.

"A bag full of illegal drugs was found on my lap in the Euro Lines bus I was in from Amsterdam. I was detained for the whole day. A solicitor by the name of Edward Mercer helped me. I have no idea how I got home, Dad."

He was holding on to Edward Mercer's business card. Luke sat down by him and he put his arm around him. They sat down for a long time without saying a word.

"What kind of drugs you been taking, son?" Luke asked.

"I don't know, Dad, all kinds," he said.

"Jaden, son, please don't lie to me now!" Luke begged.

"Honest, Dad, I don't know," he said.

"Do you have any drugs on you in the house?" Luke asked.

"I don't know, Dad," he replied.

Luke got up and ran both hands through his hair and over his face. "You need help, son. You need help to quit and we can't go to the doctors," said Luke.

Jaden got up and went to the kitchen and took out a beer out of the fridge and opened it. Luke walked in and saw him. He screamed "put the bottle down, son!"

"You can't tell me what to do in my own flat, Dad." Jaden shouted back.

As he put the bottle on his mouth there was a knock on the door. He looked at Luke and he went to the door and opened it. A man in a suit stood in the doorway.

"Good afternoon, Mr. Blake," he said.

Jaden had no idea who he was. He stood there looking at him trying to remember how he knew him. The man asked, "May I come in?"

"Of course!" Jaden says.

Luke quickly goes to greet the man and introduces himself.

"I am Edward. Sir, I brought your son home last night. I stopped by to see how he was doing," said Edward.

Jaden did not pay any attention as he opened the fridge and took another bottle of beer and opened it. Luke excused himself from talking to Mr. Mercer. He took the bottle of beer out of his son's hands. "For the love of God! Jaden, show some respect!" He snapped in a whispering voice at Jaden.

"Respect to whom?" Jaden snapped back.

"Perhaps I came at a bad time?" said Mercer.

"No, sir. Please sit down," says Luke. "I must thank you for looking out for my boy. He told me what you did for him last night. I had no idea you brought him home, too. Thank you, sir, very much."

Luke was in tears as Mr. Mercer could see. He wished he could help, but he doesn't normally get involved. There is something about Jaden, and now his father, that inspires him to reach out and help them somehow, but he doesn't know how.

"No, it's quite okay, sir," said Edward.

He gave Luke's his card and said, "if you and Jaden ever need any help – sir." He stopped, "Please give me a call any time, sir." He stopped by the kitchen and said to Jaden "I'm glad you are well, son. Take care, Mr. Blake," said Edward.

Luke thanked him again as he closed the door. Jaden was standing in the kitchen with no expression on his face. Luke emptied all the beer and the alcohol out of the flat. When Jaden finally asked what Luke was doing, he was pissed off and told his father to get out of his flat.

"I am not going anywhere, son," Luke said.

Jaden pushed past him and went to his room. He locked his door and put the music on loud. Luke saw Mr. Mercer standing by the lift when he opened the door to take all the alcohol bottles to the bin.

"Need help?" Mr. Mercer asked.

"Yes, sir. I do, but – I cannot impose. You have done enough already, sir," said Luke.

"Please tell me what I can do to help?" Mr. Mercer asked.

Luke invited him into the flat and he quickly wrote a list of things he needed and he handed it to Edward with the money. Edward took it and read through the list. He was quiet for a second. "I will be right back with this," he promised.

Luke went to Jaden's door and knocked, but there was no answer. He sat down in the chair with both hands in his lap crying.

The girls had arrived in London in no time.

"So did you sleep with him?" Kate asked.

No one responded.

"Well! Brooke, have you?" Kate asked.

"I hardly know the man, behave yourself!" she snaps at Kate as Tia laughs.

"I wouldn't be laughing if I were you, you little brat! You'd better tell your mum and dad about the baby before I do!" Brooke threatens Tia again.

"Why don't you mind your own fucking business, Brooke? I am sick of you always sticking your big gorp in my fucking business all the time," Tia shouted.

Brooke was about to respond when she saw Jason standing by his car in her parking lot.

"What in God's name is he doing here?" Brooke wondered.

The girls started to laugh. She parked her car next to his. Tia was first out of the car to kiss him. Kate followed and kissed him, too. Brooke sat in the car, mulling over this development. She put one leg out of the car as she took off her sunglasses. Jason came to the car and lifted her up into his arms and turned to the girls saying, "Do you mind very much if I take your sister out to dinner?"

"Please do!" giggled Tia as Kate laughed.

"She doesn't speak for me. Please put me down!" demanded Brooke.

Tia quickly runs to open Jason's car door for him as he gently puts Brooke in the front seat. As he closes the door, he kisses Tia, "Thank you!"

Tia said "No... Thank *you!*"

Kate and Tia laughed as Jason drove off with Brooke sulking in the car. They went into the flat and Kate called Jaden's cell phone, but it was turned off and there was no answer on his home phone, so she couldn't leave a message. She called her mother and they spent over an hour talking on the phone. Meanwhile, Tia took a bath and jumped into Brooke's bed. By the time Kate got off the phone, Tia was sound asleep. Kate made herself some popcorn and watched a movie on TV.

Jason and Brooke drove to the East London loft without a word. He parked in the underground lot and opened the car door for Brooke. She refused to come out of the car. Jason pleaded with her and finally she took his hands allowed herself to be guided to his condo. When he opened the door, Brooke saw a foyer opening into an expansive loft with rich, dark, hardwood floors. She can see the big kitchen from the threshold. Jason put his hands on her waist to guide her through the loft.

The living area was big, but there was no TV or sound system that Brooke could see, though she could hear chamber music, Beethoven's "Serenade in D major." The walls were all painted in white with oil paintings adding splashes of color on the walls, accompanied by tasteful accent lights. The center of the room had natural light coming through the huge skylight, which got Brooke's attention.

"I'm impressed," she said.

Jason smiled at her. She looked stunning as usual, and he couldn't take his eyes off her. She turned to face him. "Are you going to feed me after kidnapping me, or will I have to call the Old Bell?"

He smiled and walked towards her. Taking her by the hand, Jason lead her to another section of the loft and commented, "You must be so tired after the long drive." He opened a door which lead to the bathroom and let go of her hands. She watched him pour bubble bath into the tub and fill it with water. He also lit some candles. Brooke began to feel uneasy and he sensed it.

"Why don't you get in," he invited. "By the time you're done, dinner will be ready."

"Thank you, but I will take a bath in my own flat when you take me back," she asserted.

As he kissed her gently on the neck, Brooke felt her knees weaken. When he kissed her on the full lips, she responded. He stopped long enough to take a good look at her and said, "I have missed you like mad. I have not—." She didn't let him finish. Instead, she kissed him and whispered, "So do I."

He stopped kissing Brooke long enough to undress her, lifting her gently into the bath tub. As he let go of her, she kissed him and murmured playfully, "I hate you." He smiled at her and left. Back in the kitchen, Jason checked on the meal in the oven. He turned off the oven since it seemed to be ready. He set the table for two and lit some more candles, placing them all over the loft. He went to the fridge and took out a bottle of wine and opened it.

"Are you okay in there?" He shouted.

Brooke did not respond. She was enjoying the candlelight, and the scented bath oil was just what she needed. She spread her legs under the faucet, putting her feet up on the wall. She carefully adjusted the flow of water – not too hot, not too cold... She was relaxed. Jason came and handed her a glass of red wine, which she sipped. Jason piled up some of the big towels as a cushion for her head and rubbed oil on her shoulders.

"You are completely turning me on," he said.

Brooke was really enjoying his reactions. Watching him undress was just incredibly sexy. She teased him with her hands; slid his finger into those delicious, sensitive folds of flesh, and finally opened her lips and drank some of the wine he had given her earlier. She lifted her left feet and placed them on his shoulder as he washed and caressed her. She stroked herself as he watched her. He was excited and then a little surprised when she said "make love to me Jason." He straddled her in the tub and knelt right above her face, but did not let her take him in her mouth. He kissed her as he picked up a towel and jumped out of the tub. The stimulation under the water has swollen her clitoris and she felt out of control as she got out the tub and took the towel from him.

"What's the matter Jason?"

"You are so beautiful," he sighed.

"That's not what I –," he kissed her before she could finish her sentence.

Before Brooke knew it she was in his bed, his mouth was exploring her breasts and he was sucking on the nipples like a candy. She felt herself entering an unreal world of erotic dreams... wild, mysterious. She drew close to his ear and whispered.... "Don't stop," she moaned... Jason is so aroused he is not thinking about stopping. Suddenly, it was hard for him to think about resisting her. He knew this was the very first time for her. He wanted to build her sense of anticipation as he parted her legs gently, kissing and sucking on her most private place as she ran her hands in his hair. He let her feel his arousal against her as she opened her legs and kissed him. He gently thrust into her as he watched her close her eyes with the very first ride. He kissed her eye lids and whispered "Are you okay?" She opened her eyes, smiled and said softly "yes", moaning until she came. He rolled her over on top of him and framed her face with both of his hands, "I didn't plan for this to happen tonight, are you sure you're okay?"

She kissed him on the nose, "Tell me if you are okay first!"

"I am. I need to know if you are okay," he paused. "Uh – can I get you anything? What I mean is … did I hurt you?" Jason asked, concerned.

"I don't need anything," she said. "What about you?" she teased.

He smiled as he kissed and rubbed her back. Brooke couldn't stop. The more they kissed the more she wanted him.

"You must be hungry by now?" he said.

She kept on kissing him.

"I went shopping by myself today, since you wouldn't let me take you shopping in Amsterdam," he sat up on the bed. "I don't want you to be afraid. Brooke, please," he was pleading now as she, too, sits up in the bed. She kissed him and said "I am not afraid; otherwise, I would not be here." She kissed him again, slowly, deeply, passionately.

He pointed to the wall of closet and said, "on the left is yours – I mean everything you may need is there." Brooke was quiet and did not say anything. Jason's heart beat faster, "That's it. I've gone and done it, scared her off," he started thinking.

"Show me," she said.

He almost did not hear what she had said; he was in his own little world. Brooke saw it on his face.

"Where were you just now?" she asked.

"I know we agreed to take things slowly. Please, please, Brooke. I am falling in love with you. I do not know when or why and I know you don't feel the same about me, I just can't lose you," he confessed.

Brooke was almost in tears and Jason could see it. She put her hands over his face and kissed him. She walked over to the closet, opened it, and immediately saw a pink satin robe she just adored. She took it off the hanger and putting it on, walked back to the bed. Jason was still sitting on the bed holding his heart in his hands as he watched her she looked so beautiful in the robe. She sat down and leaned back against the headboard.

"I am ... I, too, have been falling in love with you, Jason," she said softly.

Jason almost had a heart attack as he heard the words come out of Brooke's mouth. His jaw dropped. His heart rate raced as he listened to her telling him that she was in love with him from the moment she heard his voice on the phone the very first time she called him and that she has not been able to get him out of her mind and all she has thought of was him.

"Why didn't you tell me?" he asked.

Before she could answer, he answered: "You were afraid of your feelings for me? Please don't be. I have waited my whole life for you, Brooke. When I told my mother about you, she advised me to do everything I can to show you how much you mean to me, and not let you go. I am sorry I took upon myself to go shopping for you. Please don't be mad," he said.

"You know for such a sexy man, you are very insecure," Brooke teased. "I am very hungry," she said.

Jason put on his robe and they went to the kitchen to warm up some food in the microwave. They ate and talked, both very happy like nothing else mattered. The food was delicious. Jason asked if he could get Brooke anything. She got up and threw one of her legs over Jason's lap. He liked that about her. She fed him ice cream as she rubbed him between his legs, and he tried to kiss her. Every time he tried to kiss her, Brooke put a spoonful of ice cream in his mouth. She put the dish of ice cream on the table. She held both his hands behind the chair. A big strong man, slightly helpless and restrained... "Wow," he thought. He buried his face between her breasts, kissing, nuzzling, and licking her neck. She raised her hips as he entered her and she rode him gently on the chair, she was exceptionally wet. She seemed to know his every sexual desire and there were no limitations. He enjoyed her taking the lead; he enjoyed the seduction in the chair, and as she let go of his hands, he stimulates her clitoris as she rides him. Later, he laid her on her tummy on the floor, legs apart and hips slightly raised. He took his time, exploring her vagina so slowly that when he slipped into her, her juicy flesh felt warmed through. He was not sure who did who, but he was breathless by the time they both came.

Briefly collapsing on the floor, Jason and Brooke ran straight to the shower and into the bed. Brooke fell asleep in a few minutes as Jason held her in his arms. He could not believe it was real, the whole evening, the girl of his dreams in love with him right here in his arms. It's been so long since college that he thought that he would never have this again. He tried to think of the last time he spent an evening like this with a woman and couldn't remember. He has had so many one-night stands since college that was all he was used to, brief sex. In marked contrast, Brooke was perfect in every way. He watched her sleeping. She is by far the most beautiful woman he has ever been with. She is sexually irresistible, and looking at her aroused him. "I cannot mess this up," he told himself.

Chapter 18

Tia was awakened after midnight by the ringing of the phone. She answered to discover Kevin anxiously waiting for her call. She wanted to hang up when she heard his voice.

"I am sorry. I went straight to bed as soon as we got here," said Tia.

Kevin is not completely sure, but he has a feeling Tia is mad at him, and has no clue why that might be. He wishes she would tell him what he has done wrong so he can apologize. "I miss you, Tia," he says. Tia did not say anything, though she cries quietly, breaking his heart with her silence.

"Tia, babe, please tell me why you are crying? Is something the matter?" Kevin asks. "Tia, please. I have been out of my mind with worry about you. Please tell me what is wrong with you or I am going to come over now."

"I'm fine," she lies. "I am just so very tired. I miss you too, Kevin. How was your weekend?"

"I really did miss you. I wish I could have gone with you," said Kevin, deftly avoiding the question.

Tia didn't say anything. In fact, the conversation seemed dead. The more Kevin tried to get Tia to open up, the more Tia was not interested.

"How about a movie tomorrow?" Kevin asked.

"Sorry, Kevin. Good night. I will call you in the morning," she said as she hung up the phone. She got out of bed and went to the living room where she found Kate sitting on the sofa watching a movie. Tia sat down next to her. "Is Brooke home, yet?" she asked.

"No. I think she may be spending the night at Jason's," Kate said.

"I hope he has enough hair products for the both of them!" Tia joked and both girls burst into gales of laughter.

"Have you spoken to Kevin, yet?" wondered Kate aloud.

"Yes, just now on the phone. He wants to take me to the movies tomorrow, but I'm just not interested," Tia confessed. "All I want to do right now is sleep and sleep and sleep." Privately, Tia knew she needed to think about her future. She has a job offer from Nortel Networks and it is official. She is definitely going to Canada in six weeks. "Wow!" she thought. She didn't really think she would get the position at Nortel. She has been on their web site over the last four months reading about the company and hoping and wishing for a successful application. Ottawa sounds like a good place to live. She likes the fact that Carlton University has a broadcasting department. Apartment rentals are a lot cheaper than England, too, she thinks. She feels sick again and runs to the bathroom to vomit. She tries to eat something, but can't. "How could mother have three kids with this pain?" Tia asks herself as she closes her eyes and tries to sleep.

Jaden woke up a little after two in the morning. Craving a smoke, he discovered he was out of cigarettes. He grabbed a t-shirt from the pile of laundry in his room. He saw Luke in his bed fast asleep as he unlocked the front door, but couldn't get it opened. Agitated, Jaden kicked the door.

"Going somewhere, son?" Luke inquired.

Jaden had a headache and his nose was bleeding again. He turned angrily to answer his father. Luke saw his bleeding nose, and knowing full well what Jaden was going through, he stood firm and pretended he not to see Jaden's bloody nose or his agitation to take the edge off. Jaden was becoming jittery, so Luke sat down.

"I fancy a pint. I am off to the pub to get one, you wanna come?" He asked his father.

"No thanks, son," said Luke.

Jaden turned the door handle, but the door would not open.

"Dad... I am having trouble opening the door. Can you help me?" Jaden asked.

Luke got up and he put on the lights. He stood still for a second, then firmly replied, "You aren't going anywhere, son."

"Did you say something, Dad?" Jaden asked.

"Yes, I said you are not going anywhere, son," Luke repeated.

Jaden was laughing aloud as he came towards his father.

"What did you say to me?" Jaden asked threateningly.

Luke did not respond. Jaden went back to the door and he saw that there was a padlock on the top and the bottom of the door frame. He began to laugh aloud again. He went into the kitchen and opened the drawer. There were no knives, spoons, or forks. He closed it and went into the hall closet where he kept his tools: they were gone. He went back to his room to get his cell phone, but it was not in the charger. He looked for the house phone to make a phone call, but it was like someone had cleaned up the house.

"Where is my phone, Dad?" Jaden hollered.

Luke did not reply.

"You are sad, you know that!" he screamed. "I'm a grown man. Dad, you cannot lock me up in me own flat! Fucking hell, Dad! You think after sixteen years you can be a father to me? You are sad, mate! Get up and open my fucking door before I have you banged up in jail!"

Luke still didn't respond.

"You don't wanna open my door? Fine! Fuck you, Luke! You old fart! If you think I'm afraid to jump from the eleventh floor, you are fucking crazy, old man." Jaden yelled at his father. Luke sincerely hoped that Jaden wouldn't try to jump. He knows from experience how unpredictable the boy can be.

Jaden went to his bedroom and tried to open the windows, but couldn't. He put the light on and noticed that the windows were all boarded up with four by fours. He looked more closely at the whole flat and discovered that all the windows were covered with four by fours. Likewise, there was nothing in the flat to use to smash the windows. He kicked the door again and went back to his room, slamming the door as hard as he could behind him.

A few minutes later, Luke went to the kitchen, made a sandwich, and poured a glass of milk. He knocked on Jaden's door before entering the room with the food. Jaden was sitting on the floor.

"You need to eat something, son," Luke said gently.

"I'm sorry, Dad," said Jaden.

He ate the food his father had made for him, but as soon as he drank the milk, he started to vomit. Jaden was sprawled on the bathroom floor by the time Luke got there. Luke quickly took off Jaden's pants and got him under the shower. In a few minutes, Jaden was feeling a bit better. He stood in the middle of the living room with the towel in his hands and took a deep breath, "I am really sorry for earlier, Dad."

"I know, son. Get some rest, son," said Luke.

"Dad ... Can you spare a smoke?"

"No, son. I quit," said Luke.

Jaden went to his room and threw himself on the bed, but couldn't sleep. He could not understand why his father would behave this way. "It's not like I have a drug problem or I've hurt any one. I am not a junkie," he said to himself. Jaden tried to sleep, but still couldn't, so he went to the bathroom to look for some pain killer, but there was nothing left. He passed by his father's door and saw that he was asleep and his jacket was on the floor. Quietly, Jaden searched the pockets of his father's coat, but there was nothing – no smokes and the keys nowhere to be found. He looked everywhere in his father's room but found nothing. As he closed the door behind himself, Luke got up and sat on his bed crying, knowing just how desperate the things were for his son.

Jaden managed to sleep a bit. A few hours later, Jaden found his father sitting in the small kitchen reading the newspapers. The front page headline says, *"PRINCESS DI HAS DIED!"*

"Is that true, Dad?" Jaden asked.

Luke was far away. He had not realized that his son was awake. He was still thinking about Mr. Mercer and his family. Edward had come by that morning and brought the newspapers and some milk for their breakfast. His son had died that morning, poor man. After six weeks in a coma for ecstasy use, the boy, only nineteen years old, died of his excess. Luke was afraid of what might come for Jaden in the next few days. The poor man had offered to help Luke mainly because he didn't want to see Jaden end up like his son.

"Good morning, son. Sit down, and let's get some breakfast," Luke suggested.

"Oh my God! Dad, did you see this?" Jaden showed his father the headlines. "Why were they running? Everyone in England knows she was shagging that dude. Why run?" Jaden asked. He read through the newspaper. "Dad, I got to get ready and go see if Kate's back yet."

"Son. Please sit," said Luke. He was quiet for a while. Jaden was wondering whether his father was alright. "Dad, are you alright?" he asked. Luke was still in deep thought, and he did not immediately reply. "Dad, whatever it is, it has to wait. I have to go and see Kate. Alright? We will talk later. How about we meet down at the pub later and you can tell me all about it, eh?" he suggested.

"Jaden, you are not going out of this flat for the next three weeks, son... not for Kate, not for anything, and not for anyone!" said Luke firmly.

"Look, Dad, are you back on drugs? In case you haven't noticed, this is my flat. I am not a six year old who needs supervision." said Jaden petulantly.

He pushed past his father as he went to his room and got dressed. He couldn't find his phone anywhere. He came to the living room to call Kate, but the phone was not there either. "Dad, have you seen the phone?" he asked. Luke did not respond. "He better not be back on drugs. I cannot deal with this now, and I don't need it," Jaden muttered to himself. "Dad, where is the house phone?"

"Son, you have a problem, and you need to deal with it before it is too late," said Luke gently.

Jaden was angry now: "How dare you compare me to you?" he shouted. "I went to Amsterdam. I banged a few 'E' here and there, and then all of a sudden I have a drug problem? I want you out of my flat now, Dad," Jaden demanded. He walked to the front door and tried to open it. He saw the padlock on the door, "What the hell is this?" He pointed to the door, frowning.

Luke stood there watching his son. It was like looking in the mirror sixteen years ago when Luke would go on a drug binge and would not remember a thing the next day. Poor Joyce: "She was a good woman," he thought. "Son, where you are standing now, I was there sixteen years ago... and... I... my Joyce was standing where I am now. I will not lose you to drugs. Mr Mercer's boy died this morning after six weeks in a coma. He is dead! Ecstasy has claimed yet another young life. Joyce has suffered enough! She put up with my bad behavior. I don't want her to have to go through all that again with her son. Now, sit down and eat your breakfast, son. Save your energy: you will wish you had it, later."

"I am nothing like you! Open my fucking door, Luke. And don't be here when I come back," warned Jaden.

Luke sat down and drank his coffee. Jaden continued to scream at his father. He got so frustrated that he came in to the kitchen and began kicking and beating Luke black and blue until Jaden could not hit his father any more. Jaden was like an animal. He left his father on the kitchen floor in a pool of blood and went to his room and slammed his door shut. Luke dragged himself up but he fell back down. He could not get up. Luke finally managed to get up and he cleaned himself in the kitchen sink.

He drank some water, went to the bath room where he did not recognize himself in the mirror he was in so much pain. The last time he took a good beating like this, he was in secondary school after getting caught having sex in a flat with a sixteen year old girl. The girl's father gave him a good beating, and said he would not call the Old Bell for him. It was worth every bit as Joyce fall madly in love with him; afterward, he fucked it up. He thought. "Well! ....This will all be worthwhile too when I have my son back." He went to Jaden's room and found the boy sitting on his bed shaking.

"You look like shit, Dad. What happened to you?" he asked. Luke sat next to his son, gave him a hug and pulled his hands behind him by force and put the handcuffs on him. "I love you son," he whispered.

Jaden was mad as hell. He began to scream and called his father all kinds of names. Luke simply closed his bedroom door and went to bed. He did not sleep a wink because he kept going back and forth to check on his son all night long like one checks a new born baby.

☙ Chapter 19 ❧

There was a knock on Brooke's door. When Tia answered the door, she found Kevin waiting, so she let him in. Kate had gone to her mother's in the morning and Tia has been sleeping all day.

"Hi ... you don't look too good," observed Kevin. He kissed her on the cheek, determined that she did not have temperature, and immediately felt relieved.

"I am sorry to come without calling. I've been worried about you, Tia," he said.

"It's okay. I'm fine."

"I was not sure what to bring you, so I picked up some Chinese food."

"Thank you. I can't really eat anything, Kevin, but thanks anyway."

She went to the living room and lay down on the sofa. Kevin went and sat next to her.

"I'm so sorry. I've been thinking the worst. I thought you were cheating on me," he said.

Tia began to laugh out loud. Kevin did not know what to think, so he took off his shoes and lay next to her, holding her as she fell asleep.

Brooke and Jason were sleeping through the better part of the morning without interruption as all the phones were turned off. They were cuddled up close all night. When Brooke slipped back into dreamland, Jason crawled out of bed and called Tia to let her know he would not be bringing Brooke back to the apartment. Tia reminded him that she gets cranky in the morning when there's no coffee. After chatting with Tia, Jason headed to the kitchen to make some coffee. Returning to the bed, Jason held Brooke as she drifted in and out of that drowsy half-awake state. He tried hard not to wake her, but he couldn't resist running his tongue right across her belly. She moaned as the passion built, and pulled him up greedily kissing his mouth. Disengaging from the kiss, Brook slipped out of bed, put on her robe, and softly kissed Jason again. "Please come to bed," he pleaded, but giggling merrily Brooke walked down the hall toward the luxurious smell of the coffee. A few minutes later she returned with a cup of coffee for him.

"Coffee in bed is good, but I... I'd rather eat you all up," he said.

"We have all the time in the world to eat each other up. I have to call home," Brooke said.

"Tia knows where you are. I told her we will have dinner with her and Kevin later. She is not feeling well," said Jason.

He dialed Brooke's home number and was about to hang up when Tia answered.

"Darling, how are you?" asked Brooke.

"I am fine. I'm doing some research. I will tell you all about it when I see you. How is Jason? I hope you've not worn him out yet?" Tia asked.

"No, darling, I have not worn him out yet! One second, I will give the phone to him. I love you! Call me if you need me to come home, darling," said Brooke.

She passed the phone to Jason and took the coffee cups back to the kitchen. When she returned, Jason was done talking to Tia and had logged onto his laptop.

"Oh God, no!" Jason screams aloud.

Brooke stood still as she saw the expression on Jason's face was so sad. He was reading something on his laptop. Brooke didn't want to interrupt in case it was something to do with work, but he kept saying "why?" Jason lean over and grabbed a remote control, and the closet door opposite the bed opened revealing a huge television. He turned it on and there it was on every single channel: Princess Di was dead. Brooke held on tight to Jason's hands as they watched the news together. People were standing in front of Buckingham Palace and placing flowers on the gates. They showed a shot of Kensington Palace where the Princess had lived. There were flowers everywhere. CCTV footage from the Ritz Hotel in Paris showed the Princess, her companion, her driver and two body guards leaving the hotel from a side door to avoid the paparazzi. Finally, a photo of the crash site in Paris was shown, too. Brooke's mind immediately went back to 1988 and the Lockerbie plane crash which killed her father. She thought of Princes William and Harry. She remembered the day her father passed, as she cried for the two princes and her father. Jason did not know why she felt so much emotion, but in deference to her feelings, he turned off the TV. Jason could not console her because he was in tears himself. Just then, the phone rang and when he picked it up Sarah Williams was on the phone. She asked to speak to Brooke.

"Miss Williams, do you mind if I have her call you back? This really is not a good time," Jason said.

"Please, tell her it's her mother," Sarah replied.

Brooke is Sarah Williams's daughter? Jason privately exclaimed. "I will, ma'am," he said. Now he understood why Brooke had been crying non-stop. He didn't know Sarah Williams had a child. Sarah and Jason's mother have been friends for as long as he can remember. He often has dinner with them. Why didn't he know about Brooke? Today is going to be one difficult day for them: what a reminder! Jason finally lifted Brooke into his arms, crooning softly, "Sweetheart… Please, please… Look at me… It's going to be okay. I am here for you… Please don't shut me out…" He rubbed her back as the tears rolled down his face. Brooke felt him crying and put her forehead against his.

"I can never get over my father's death," she mumbled.

Jason did not know what to say.

"I've been doing a lot better since – I" she stopped. "I have to go home."

"Please don't, I need you…I need to be with you, Brooke. Please, I can't be on the outside looking in. We are a team now, things have changed, sweetheart. You can't… you just can't … Brooke… Please!"

he pleaded with her. Brooke did not say a word, so she cuddled up to him and Jason felt somewhat relieved.

"You must call your mom. She called earlier. I'll hang out in the living room, so you can talk privately." He kissed her and handed her the phone.

Brooke dialed her mother's number and she answered on the first ring.

"B.B.! I was just thinking about you, my sweetheart," Sarah whispered. "How are you today?" she inquired.

"I'm good, Mother, and you?" Brooke replied.

Sarah can tell her daughter has been crying. Her heart breaks over and over again as she fights the tears in an attempt to pull herself together. She wishes she could hold her daughter. She wants to tell her to come home. Tia had said Brooke was with her boyfriend and given her the number to call. She didn't know Brooke had a boyfriend. Sarah has missed so much of her growing up.

"B.B. – can you come home?" Sarah asks.

"I will stop by the house tomorrow. Grandma Gertrude gave me a painting to bring to you."

"I know. She called me today to see if I was okay and to ask how you are doing," Sarah told her.

"I am well. We will call her later," said Brooke.

Sarah was confused, "Who is 'we'?"

"I was in Holland with Jason over the weekend. We have not had any time to thank her for her hospitality," Brooke explained.

Sarah was quiet as she thought of the Sharp's, and how they have made her daughter part of their family over the years and have extended the same courtesy to her, too. They have been very good friends to her little family.

"So Jason is your boyfriend, then? You must bring him home for dinner soon, my sweetheart," she said.

"Will do, Mother! ... are... are you going to be okay, Mother?" Brooke asked, concerned.

"Yes, my sweetheart, I love you," said Sarah, and she ended the call.

Brooke entered the living room and found Jason standing by the window. She watched him for a second before walking over to him and giving him a hug. She thanked God for him. They lay down on the sofa, and she told him how her mother would like to me meet him soon. Jason tells her he already knows her mother very well.

"You didn't have a one-night stand with her, did you?" Brooke asked jokingly.

Jason almost had a heart attack, "Ah, no…. Sarah Williams is one of my mother's dearest friends. I had no idea she was your mother. I mean, I didn't know she had a child."

Brooke told him that she and Sarah have been drifting apart since her father passed. "When I was seventeen, the relationship was too strained… so I moved out – actually, she put me out. We hardly see or talk to each other, even though we work for the same company and our offices are just a few feet away from each other. She gave me your number to see if you could help my clients when they were stuck for financing," she said.

"When you said your boss gave you my number, I forgot to ask for your boss's name," commented Jason. "She always advises me to stop working for other people and start working for myself. She is one classy lady! I wonder why I didn't make the connection?" He wondered aloud.

They spent the afternoon talking about Brooke and Sarah. Jason was even more surprised that Brooke could cook as she made them lunch and pre-prepped dinner for later.

Kate has been calling Jaden's cell and home phone, but there is no reply. She decides she will visit his flat to tomorrow. She has a lot to do with the new store opening soon and she wonders how she and Brooke will cope once Tia leaves for Canada. She hopes Tia sorts things out with Kevin, but she will miss her if she leaves. Her mother has not shut up about her graduation next week. Tia's father has already lined up a job for her at Bankers' Trust. Kate can not wait to start because it is a job in commodities trading. She, too, has spent the whole day with her mother watching the events of Princess Di's death on TV since there was nothing else to watch but the Princess story. They watched as the Royal Air Force plane arrived in England carrying the Princess's body and accompanied by the Prince of Wales himself. It was one of the saddest moments in England because Princess Di was well-loved by the public.

Tia has been on the phone with her mother discussing Princess Di's death, and it brings back the painful memories of the morning Jackson Williams died. Tia was worried about Sarah Williams, so she took Brooke's car and paid her a visit. She was so sick by the time she got there that Sarah insisted she stay and let her take care of her. "I'll call Brooke and let her know where you are in the morning." Tia did not have the energy to argue with her as she discovered Sarah was as bad and as bossy as Brooke. She succumbed to Sarah's attention and spent the night in Brooke's old bedroom.

In the morning, Sarah made breakfast fit for a king, which Tia couldn't eat because of the continued nausea. Concerned, Sarah called Brooke and told her that Tia was staying with her and continued to feel under the weather. Brooke responded, "I'll be there in an hour!" Meanwhile, Jason fumed. He did not want to go to work, but he didn't want Brooke to go home either. Instead, he wanted to drive her to his parents' country home away from her needy friends and the TV media frenzy centered on the death of the Princess of Wales.

"No, hon. I really do have to go to my mother's house today. You can drop me off on your way to work and we can go to the country some other time."

Jason acquiesced, though he wasn't very happy about the change of plans. He could see that pairing up with Brooke meant having her friends in the background all the time. "Hmmm... Jaden said something about that in Holland," he recollected. "I hope it's not going to be like this all the time. I really like Brooke, but her friends are a bit intrusive." Brooke could see he was unhappy as they drove to Sarah's house. She tried her best to make him smile even though she, too, worried about the same things: "I wonder what's up with Jason," Brooke mused. "He was so chipper this morning... and why doesn't Tia see her doctor about this food poisoning? She's been sick a long time." Ironically, neither would share their thoughts with the other despite the physical closeness of the previous night.

Just before he pulled into the drive way, Sarah was taking something from Brooke's car which was parked in front of the garage. Jason came out of the car and opened the door and helped Brooke out. Sarah watched her daughter straightening the man's tie. She kissed him on the lips. They are standing by the car talking or arguing or something, and Sarah doesn't know what to do, so she quickly closes the car door and goes inside the house.

"Don't worry, my sweet," Brooke reassures Jason. "Come and pick me up when you're done at work," an invitation which puts a smile on his face. Brooke unlocks the front door and enters the house with Jason. Of course, Jason has been in the house many times with his mother to have dinner with Sarah, but this time is different. He feels nervous.

"What if your mother hates me?" he says, worrying out loud.

Brooke kisses him to reassure him, while Sarah walks in on them commenting, "Her mother loves everyone who loves B.B."

Jason feels a little embarrassed as Sarah extends her hands in greeting. Sarah Williams is as classy as her daughter; she wears a colorful dress, which loosely drapes around her middle; the higher neckline and lower hemline made the dress more wearable – a dress-up, dress-down kind of garment. She sported eye wear with an angled style that was flattering for her heart-shaped face. She removed the glasses.

"How are your parents, Jason? Are they back from Spain, yet?" Sarah asked.

"Yes." Jason replied. He noticed that she did not hug or kiss Brooke. He didn't let go of her hands. Brooke asked her mother to excuse her while she walked Jason back to his car. Sarah pulled Brooke aside and said "why don't you two join me for dinner tonight?" Brooke did not say anything as she quickly took Jason's hands and guided him to the door. Sarah stood by the window and watched them as they kissed and it looked like they didn't want to let go of each other's hands. When they finally did, Jason was getting in his car but came back to kiss Brooke again. This time, he held her in the air like a light feathery thing and kissed her on her full lips.

"They are in love," Sarah said to herself, "how sweet!" She sat down on the chesterfield near the window and closed her eyes. She thought of Jackson. There was a photo of her and Jack taken in London Green park years ago before Brooke was born. They were not much older than Brooke and Jason are now, and they, too, were so in love. How she missed him so! Sarah has tried to fill in the emotional hole with work, but lately it's not the same anymore. Having Tia staying the night has proved how much she has missed both Jack and Brooke over the years. She wished she could make it up to her for all the time they have missed. She has been thinking about her relationship with Brooke a lot lately. Naana Konadu-Sharp advised her a few weeks ago to try and make an effort to rebuild her relationship as Brooke is growing very fast. She had a lucky escape when her biopsy turned out not to be cancer. She was so worried because she had no one to support her at the time. So, she called the Sharp's and explained to them about the biopsy, asking them to help Brooke deal with what's to come should the results come back with a positive verdict. Bobby Sharp assured her that it would be okay and it has.

Brooke finally came into the house and saw her mother in her study holding some kind of photograph and it looks like she is in her own world full of sadness. Brooke is familiar with this scene. Since her father's death, everyday has had a moment like this – every day. She runs to her mother and puts her head on Sarah's lap and wraps her arms around her. Sarah almost jumps out of the chesterfield she is so surprised to see Brooke. Instead, she slowly puts one hand in Brooke's nicely blow-dried hair and runs it down ever so gently and the other hand rubbing her back. She fought back her own tears. Brooke felt just like she did as a child.

"Oh, B.B. – My sweetheart, whatever is the matter with you?" she whispers.

Brooke is still crying. Sarah continues to rub her back. She can not remember the last time she held her daughter it's been so long, so – so long, she thought.

"My sweetheart, it will be okay. You want to tell me why you are so upset?" she whispered in Brooke's ear.

Initially, Brooke did not respond because she loved her mother rubbing her back and she didn't want her to stop. She turned her face and placed in it on Sarah's lap. She was looking at all the photographs on her mother's desk. There was one from her fashion show last year when Kate, Tia and Brooke were launching Urban Style. She remembered her mother was not at the show. So… who took the picture? It looks like whoever took the picture was very close to get that shot. She thinks back to the night of the launch and of all the photographs that were taken; this one was very different – one of a kind – not like those she and the girls have. Sarah followed her gaze.

"What is it B.B.?" she asked.

Brooke got up and walked to the desk where she picked up two of the photographs and asked, "Who took these?"

"I hired a photographer for the night of your show to take some pictures for me," Sarah admitted.

"Why did you not come, Mother? I needed you there." Brooke asked.

Sarah did not say anything. She got up and went to her desk where she sat down on the chair. She took a deep breath and asked Brooke to have a seat on the chair opposite her desk, but she refused.

"Please, Brooke, sit down so we can talk about this."

"No, Mother. I want to know what was so important that you couldn't attend the launch of my store – I mean, our store."

Sarah stood and took Brooke by the hand and gently sat her down on the chesterfield. Brooke was getting upset with her mother, so much so that she got up and yelled, "Fine! Don't tell me! I am going to get Tia and we are out of here!"

"I had to spend overnight at the hospital the night of your show, B.B.," she said finally.

The word hospital traveled through Brooke like a shock wave. She was frozen all of a sudden, and could not move or think.

The Silent Sisterhood

"B.B., please, I know the loneliness you've felt since Jack's death. I have not been the kind of mother you needed over the years. I am so sorry. Your fashion show was one of the things you've done since college, that I'm so proud of — nothing could have kept me away, B.B. Please, believe that, my sweetheart," she said.

Brooke was in shock. She did not hear a word her mother had said. She sat down on a nearby chair repeating the word hospital over and over again. Sarah watched the changing expressions on her daughter's face.

"B.B... B.B... Are you alright? Talk to me! Say something!" Sarah exclaimed worriedly.

Brooke did not respond. It was like she was not there. Sarah began to shout for her housekeeper when Tia came into the study. "When did you get here?" Tia asked.

Brooke did not respond. Tia turned to Sarah accusing, "what did you do to her *now?*"

"Nothing," she said softly.

Tia took one of the oversized cushions from the chesterfield and hit Brooke on the head with it. Brooke also picked up a cushion and hit Tia back. Sarah shouted at them to stop it. Suddenly, the two girls begin to laugh at the same time. Sarah did not see the funny side so she chose a cushion and hit the two girls on the head. She stalked out of the study in disgust, causing even more gales of laughter from the two girls. Brooke ran after her, "Sorry, Mother! Although, that was funny the way you hit us with the cushion. I must teach you how to hit properly next time. You hit worse than Tia." She was still laughing as she asked why Sarah was in hospital the night of the fashion show.

"You were in the hospital, Mrs. Williams?" Tia exclaimed. "Why didn't you tell me when I dropped off the videotape the next day? I thought you were being a right..." she stopped her self from saying the forbidden word, as they all started to laugh. Sarah asked the girls to come to the study with her. She told them about the biopsy done that night and her stay overnight at the hospital. "I gave the tickets you sent me to a photographer to get me some shots of the show. Naana and Bobby Sharp promised to tape the show for me."

"Mom and Daddy knew? Why didn't they tell us?" Tia asked.

"I asked them not to say anything at the time. I was not sure what the out come of my test would be." Sarah said. Brooke was quiet. She got up and walked to the window. "Why is Tia still in her underwear at ten in the morning?"

Tia replied, "She just woke up. Can you just leave me alone in peace for a sec?"

Brooke yelled at her for not calling her to say that she was sick. "How are you feeling, anyway?"

Sarah could see that the girls are close. For her part, Tia sensed that mother and daughter needed privacy, so she said "I'm going upstairs to take a shower." Brooke turned for a second to acknowledge her. Sarah went and stood by the window with Brooke. She knew Brooke was upset, but she did not know how to explain things to her. "It was so easy when you were a baby, B.B. Please, let me explain. Come and sit with me for a minute, okay? I am sorry I did not tell you sooner," her mother said.

"You could have told me afterward! You wanted me to suffer just like when Daddy died, didn't you?" Brooke spat. She was crying now. "Why do you hate me, mother? It's not my fault Daddy died... You..." Sarah quickly took her daughter into her arms and said, "You silly, silly baby. I don't hate you, B.B. You mean everything to me! Why would you think it's your fault Jackson died?" She let go of her for a second, "Please, come and sit down. I should have had this talk with you many years ago, B.B. I was so lost when Jackson suddenly died.

"I am still lost B.B. – and all this time – I forgot about your pain and loss, my sweetheart. I don't know how, but I did. When I was told that I might have cancer, my whole world came crashing down again." Sarah sighed. "Just like it did the day Jackson died. Only this time," she stopped in mid-sentence as she was crying now. "I had you and all this time I have pushed you away for other people to take care of you, B.B. You are a beautiful woman. You have grown up in front of my eyes without any guidance whatsoever from me. The Sharp's love you. And you love them... I reached out to them out of fear and Naana made me see that it was not too late. She said she couldn't imagine our loss, but we still have one another even though Jackson is gone... and at that moment, B.B. –" Everything became clear to Brooke. "We've grown apart, because I am a selfish mother. It's not your fault, Brooke."

"You are not selfish, Mother," said Brooke.

"Oh, B.B. I am... I am so sorry to say... I am so proud of you, B.B. And although, I never said that I love you, just remember that I swear that I do, and I miss you each day more than you know. Holding you in my arms, having you hug me for the first time in sixteen years, it is like being a kid at Christmas, my sweetheart." her mother said.

Brooke threw her arms around her mother and hugged her again. They spent the morning in the study getting to know each other while Tia was upstairs taking a bath. Afterward, she went back to bed again. Brooke worked from her mother's study since she didn't have much to do in the office or at Urban Style. She wanted to call Jason many times, but she did not. Jason couldn't get any work done since he could only think of Brooke. He missed her, but he couldn't call her because he didn't have Sarah's number. He couldn't concentrate, so he told his assistant that he was taking the rest of the day off.

Chapter 20

Kate decided to go down to Peckham and see Jaden because she was getting worried after so many unanswered phone calls. There was only one parking spot left as she pulled into the lot, but a Mercedes Benz came out of nowhere and took it. The driver, a man, did not make any apologies. He took out his shopping from the trunk as Kate watched him and proceeded into the building.

"What a bastard," Kate said to herself. She saw a lady pulling out, so she quickly parked there. The man in the Mercedes was standing by the lift and when the door opened he went in and pushed the eleven button. Kate has never seen him on the eleventh floor before and she knows most of the people who live on Jaden's floor. The man in the Mercedes was knocking on Jaden's door. Kate felt a little confused because she did not know that Jaden had rich jerk relations. Luke took the shopping and as he was about to close the door, he saw Kate. In a panic, he dropped all the shopping on the floor. His face looked like he had been beaten. Kate wanted to turn back, but Luke had already seen her and he looked very nervous. She helped him pick up the shopping from the floor and asked if Jaden was around. Luke said "no." Kate did not get the chance to say what she was about to say, when she heard Jaden's voice, so she pushed past Luke and went into the flat. Jaden looked a mess. Clearly, something wasn't right. He was in his bed and his body was shaking. He was in and out of sleep, and he looked like he was having some kind of hyperventilation episode. Kate asked what was wrong with him. Luke turned his face and didn't answer. The jerk with the Benz said, "Hypothermia. Jaden has hypothermia. He will be alright in a day or two. I am Edward," he extended his hand to Kate, but she did not shake it. She went to Jaden's room and closed the door behind her. She felt his forehead and saw that he was not that cold; "he is getting better," she thought. She picked up all the laundry on the floor, and brought it into the kitchen and put it in the washing machine and tidied up his room nice and neat. She asked Luke whether there was anything she could do, but Luke said everything was under control. She asked whether Jaden had seen a doctor, and what the doctor had said. Again, Luke did not say anything, but Edward said, "Jaden will be okay in a day or two. The worst is over."

Kate assumed Edward was Jaden's doctor, so she asked "what caused the hypothermia?"

"Prolonged exposure to cold will eventually cause body temperature to fall. It will fall faster if the weather is windy or if you're in cold water for a long time. Alcohol and certain drugs can encourage hypothermia, too," Edward explained. Luke was impressed with Edward's quick thinking.

"Jaden doesn't take drugs!" Kate protested.

Edward was quiet. "Ma'am, I did not at any time imply that he does take drugs. I have been told that he has been drinking a lot more than usual these days," Edward quickly snapped.

"I am sorry," says Kate.

"Alcohol can cause the body to lose heat faster. Typical warning signs are confusion, shivering, weakness or drowsiness. Eventually, the fingers and toes turn purple, muscles stop functioning normally, and breathing slows. Ultimately, the victim loses consciousness. Jaden has passed all those. All he needs now is a lot of sleep," said Edward.

"What can I do to help?" Kate asked.

"Oh, love. It is alright. I have it under control. He didn't want you to see him in pain, that's why I said he was not at home. Please forgive me," says Luke.

"No, it's okay. I know what Jaden is like. I have been worried about him... since I lost the baby he has been drinking 'way too much. I should have called and told you. But he did promise he would stop." She gasps, "I'm sorry; I have not said anything... We've not been coping very well with the loss. We're just getting by." Kate was in tears.

"It's alright love. It will work out, you will see." Luke reassured her.

Kate looked at her watch. It was almost time for her to go and pick up her mother from work. She thanked Edward and told Luke that she would be back tomorrow to see him and if Luke needed anything he should call her. As soon as Kate left, Luke thanked Edward and began to remove all the four by four's bars he had put on the doors and windows.

Jason arrived at Sarah's house at one o'clock. Sarah and Brooke were on the deck having lunch when the housekeeper came and told Brooke that she had a visitor. Brooke excused herself and went to the family room where Jason was waiting. "Jason, darling! Why are you not at work? Is everything alright?"

"I couldn't concentrate, so I packed it in for the day," he said.

She kissed him and said, "let's go have lunch!" She called the housekeeper to set a place for Jason.

Sarah asked Tia how many months pregnant she is and Tia tried to lie.

"I am taking you to the doctor's after lunch!" Sarah asserted.

Tia laughed, "No, you're not! I am not a child."

Just then Brooke returned, walking hand in hand with Jason. Tia's face lit up when she saw Jason. He kissed her on the cheek and asked if she was feeling better. Sarah informed them that Tia was being taken to the doctor's after lunch. Brooke quickly jumped in and said "She doesn't need a doctor!" Sarah sensed Brooke knew about Tia's pregnancy. She gave both girls the disappointed look and said firmly, "I am taking Tia to the doctor's office after lunch. End of discussion!" Brooke tried to protest, but the housekeeper brought her the phone. It was Kate telling her what she had seen at Jaden's flat. Brooke wanted to go to Jaden's flat and find out what was happening since she did not believe the hypothermia story.

"I don't want you to go," said Jason. "I forbid you to go near that junkie, sweetheart."

Sarah looked at Tia as they all hear the words coming out of Jason's mouth. Brooke was upset: "You can't forbid me for anything, sweetheart! You can once we are married and *maybe* I might do as I'm told," she retorted.

Everyone was quiet as they all heard what she had said. Jason's jaw dropped open and he was looking at Brooke in shock. Tia and Sarah were also shocked. Brooke took out her napkin and she saw that all eyes were on her. She dragged Jason from the deck into the living room, Tia and Sarah tried to follow, but she turned and demanded that they stay outside, which they did. She sat Jason down in the sofa. He was still dazed. "I am sorry I yelled at you sweetheart," she said.

"You just said 'when we are married,'" he whispered. Brooke was confused. Jason was smiling.

"Okay... if it turns you on, then I will be rude to you all the time, Jason," she said coyly. Jason took her in his arms and kissed her. "Okay crazy man, let's go and eat." She found Tia and her mother spying on them. They pushed past them hand in hand. Jason was so happy. He couldn't believe that Brooke had been thinking about them getting married.

"Are they getting married?" Sarah asked Tia.

"I have no idea," Tia admitted. They followed Brooke and Jason back to the deck. Brooke sat next to him on the table. Jason picked up his courage to ask, "Did you just say I can forbid you when we are married?"

Brooke dropped her napkin on the table, turned and looked at him. She was somewhat embarrassed that the thought had slipped out. She asked her mother for some more bread and water for Jason while they were all looking at her expectantly. Brooke refused to acknowledge the question. She ate with one hand while her other hand was roaming. She could not think of anything to distract Jason, so she did what she knew would stop him from talking about marriage. She squeezed his knee; she made sure that the table cloth was long enough in front of him, so others couldn't really see what was going on. Sometimes, during lunch, she reached over to unzip his pants while continuing her meal. She kept up the conversation.

Sarah asked Jason, "How long have you been seeing my daughter?"

Brooke wrapped her hands around his penis. Jason almost choked on his food as both Tia and Brooke laughed.

"Mm! Not long," he managed to respond. Brooke kept up her look of innocence and she sensuously stroked him. She continued to talk about silly subjects throughout the entire lunch, while sexually arousing Jason.

Sarah excused herself to make a phone call, and a few minutes later Tia also left. Brooke zipped up his pants and tried to leave him alone on the deck, but Jason grabbed her hands and said, "You are in so much trouble, young lady, when I get you home." She teased him with her fingers on his lips. Tia came back and said, "You two need to get a room. What was the problem with Kate?" Tia asked.

"Some rubbish about Jaden having hypothermia. Who has hypothermia in this weather?" says Brooke. Jason didn't like the conversation but he laughed anyway. "He is trying to kick his drug habit, that's what! I wish he'd get his act together before something bad happens." She poured a glass of water for Jason and turned to Tia and said, "Mother cannot take you to the doctor's, so I will take you."

"No one is taking me to the doctor's. I am fine!" Tia exclaimed.

Sarah returned. "I am sorry, B.B. I will take Tia to the doctor. I have an appointment for her at three."

"I am not going anywhere with you! You are just as bad as Brooke! She tells me what to do all the time and now you. Why can't everyone just leave me be?" Tia cried. Brooke quickly went to her to console her as Jason and Sarah watched them.

"Oh, darling! It's okay... I will take you... when you are ready," Brooke said.

Sarah hugs Tia. "Sorry, girls. It's not up for discussion. Would you rather I take you to the doctor's or should I call Naana and Bobby and tell them what you girls are up to?"

"We are not 'up to' anything, Mother. Please!" Brooke pleaded. Jason was lost and had no idea what they were talking about. Tia yelled, "Stop it! I'm not going to the doctor's. I'm not sick. I am just pregnant. I just want to be left alone. Jason, can you take Brooke home and make sure she stays away from whatever Jaden and Kate are dealing with? We are not kids anymore. And it doesn't matter how much we love each other. We have to solve our own messes. I'm keeping the baby, so there is no need for anyone to lie or to tell the old farts! I will tell them when I'm good and ready. It if makes you happy, Mrs Williams, you can take me to the doctor's because I know you're not going to leave me alone until you do. You're just as bad as Brooke. Everyone gets to boss me about. Well, we will see when I'm in Canada."

"You can't go to bloody Canada with my baby!" Brooke snaps at Tia. "If we are keeping the baby, there is no need for you to go to Canada, Tia."

Jason was confused as he asked whether Brooke was pregnant, too. Tia thought that was so funny... Brooke told her to shut up. She turned to Jason and said she was talking about Tia's baby. Sarah also thought that was funny. She has forgotten how to laugh until today, seeing the girls and their young lives. She has never imagined her daughter's life and friends to be this close.

"I have to come to the doctor's with you. You stop being a brat all the time," Brooke insisted.

"No, you go with Jason. I will call you later. I promise," said Tia. "Please, Brooke?"

"I can't let you do this alone. Tia, I'm coming with you," Brooke glances at her mother and Jason, as she pleaded with Tia.

"You can't be there for me all the time. This is your time with Jason. What are you going to do when I move to Canada?" she asked.

Brooke was upset with Tia and her Canada talk. "You are very stubborn, Tia Sharp, and you are not going to have your way all the time. When you go to wherever you are running off to, you can do what you want. At home you're still the baby, and I am concerned about your health. I am not being bossy."

Sarah promised to look after Tia.

"Okay, we are going home. But you call me and you are not going to Canada with my baby!" Brooke told her.

Sarah asked to have a quiet word with Brooke. Jason took the opportunity to thank Tia. After all, he and Brooke would not be together without her help. Tia tells him not to let her have her way too much, and he must keep her away from Jaden's problems.

"Please make sure you call if you need her and I will bring her home," he promised.

"Thanks, I will be fine, Jason." Tia says appreciatively.

Chapter 21

After Brooke and Jason left, Tia got in Sarah's car and they were at Dr Lomus's office in no time. "Dr Lomus is an obstetrician and gynecologist," Sarah says, "a good friend of mine and your mom's. He is very good. You will like him."

"Why are you doing this?" Tia asked.

" We need to make sure that you and the baby are fine, sweetheart," Sarah says.

The doctor figured Tia was almost nine weeks pregnant. He took her blood pressure and pulse, and a blood sugar test was done. She was fine, but he wanted to go downstairs and do an ultrasound. "It's a painless test done while lying down," he says. A blob of jelly-like lotion was placed on Tia's belly. The technician gently moved a small handle through the lotion and across the skin of Tia's belly. A small screen was attached to the handle. They heard the baby's heartbeat, and the technician told them that the baby has a strong heart beat and that everything appeared to be fine. The ultrasound technician said that she would send her report to the ob-gyn. After the doctor's, there was a pharmacy downstairs where Sarah purchased a package of multi-vitamins. Tia asked to be dropped off at Brooke's apartment, but Sarah said, "No. You are coming home with me, young lady." Tia, at nineteen, reminded Sarah of Brooke at sixteen: very stubborn. She wondered who the father was. She dare not ask as she didn't want to scare her off. By the look of things, the poor kid looks scared. She can't imagine why. Naana and Bobby Sharp are very good parents. On the other hand, Sarah was very happy to see Brooke, in what seems to be, a good relationship with Jason Grey. There is so much she wants for Brooke. It seems that Brooke had carved her own destiny and

Jackson would have been so proud of her. It warms her heart to see her happy. Tia notices Sarah in deep thought. Tia has often thought Sarah Williams is a cold-hearted person until today. Tia is relieved that she didn't fall in love with Kevin. Seeing how much Mrs Williams still loves Brooke's father, Tia doesn't think she could bear falling in love and losing it like Sarah did.

"Thank you, Mrs Williams, but I don't want to impose. I have so much to do at the apartment," Tia says.

"You are not imposing, sweetheart," Sarah says.

"I have to be at the Canadian Embassy in the morning for my landed immigrant interview. I have to get the documents that I need from the apartment," Tia said.

Sarah was tempted to ask Tia why she was going to Canada while still pregnant. "I tell you what: how about we go home, you take some vitamins, and Mary will run you a nice bubble bath? I'll go to the video store to get whatever you need, and on my way back I can collect the documents for you."

"Why do I have a feeling that you are not going to let me out of your sight?" Tia asks, smiling.

Sarah smiled. As they entered the house, Sarah called Mary to run a bath for Tia. "I'll be back in an hour!" said Sarah as she drove off again.

Tia's cell phone has been ringing all morning and every time she sees Kevin's number on the phone's display screen, she ignores it. It was Kevin again for the tenth time! Pouting, Tia turned off the phone and threw it down, almost hitting Mary, the housekeeper. "Miss Tia, it's Miss Brooke on the phone for you," says the housekeeper.

Tia picks up the phone and says "Stop calling every minute! Your mother is holding me under house arrest. She won't let me go back to the apartment."

Brooke laughs. "Poor thing!" Brooke teases. "How is baby Brooke doing?"

"Baby Brooke, my backside! You and Jason better make your own baby. The doctor said the baby is fine, it has a strong heart beat, and is growing well," reports Tia.

"Thank God! Have you told Kevin yet?" She asks.

"No, he came over, we had sex, but by the time I woke up, he was already pissed off and had left. Fuck him! I'm not going to tell him. I don't love him, and I can't be tied to him because of a baby. My true love is out there, I tell you. He may very well be in Canada," Tia informs Brooke.

"Don't you think you are taking this too far with this 'true love that is out there looking for you'? Tia, forget about day-dreamy true love and tell Kevin soon."

Tia falls quiet, and finally she asks, "Have you and Jason done the nasty yet?"

"Stop changing the subject and listen to me!" says Brooke.

"Yes, Mother! Soon… Um, listen Brooke… Don't let Jason get away. He's a good man. I like him. I like the way he looks at you like nothing else matters – kind of like my Dad with my Mum, you know?"

"I am crazy about him, too. Tell Mother I will call later, okay? And Tia? I am so proud of you for keeping baby Brooke. Your true love had better show up soon, before I'm forced to get that Kevin killed." She hangs up the phone.

Back in Peckham, the storm was over for Jaden. He had showered and shaved by the time his father woke up, and was making breakfast like nothing had happened. Luke could not believe the transformation when he saw his son. Jaden made breakfast for his Dad, too. Luke was speechless. There was a knock on the door, and Luke got up to get the door. Jaden said, "it's okay, Dad. I'll get it. It's Kate." Kate was so happy when she saw Jaden, she was almost in tears. "Come on, love. Please, I am sorry. I spoiled our vacation and left you alone. I will make it up to you, alright?" He asked if Kate was ready for her first day at Bankers' Trust, and she said yes.

"One sec' love. I need to get something before we go, love," he said. "See you later, Dad," Jaden said as he closed the door and left with Kate. At Bankers' Trust, Kate had a desk in an open area. Jaden felt proud of her, as he said good bye. The commodities market was open and the commodity traders began trading in no time. Kate was shown around the building by a woman named Joan, who was in her late fifties, the Executive Assistant to the head of Mergers and Acquisitions where Kate was going to work. They went to the seventh floor to the Human Resources Department where there was a very attractive Chinese guy talking in Cantonese on a head set, while signing papers. He seemed upset that he had to leave his office to come to HR to sign some papers. He passed by without even noticing Kate.

Afterward, they came to the lower level where there was a huge restaurant and coffee kiosk. They came back to the fourteenth floor where the Chinese man, who had been in Human Resources, was talking to two of the commodity traders on the floor. He did not look very happy. Kate watched as he went into an office and slammed the door closed. The plaque on the door says "Brendon Chan – Head of Commodities". "That's your boss," says Joan. She gave Kate her log-in code for the computer, and told her other than research, they are not allowed to chat on line or surf the 'net other than work-related reading.

Kate logs on to her computer and begins to work. She is on the phones non-stop for the first two hours and when she turns her chair around, on her screen she notices that Jaden is on line and keeps sending her all kinds of things, so she ignores his messages, but it got so much by lunch time that she blocked him. At two, she was called into Brendon Chan's office. At first she thought she was going get fired for all the messages Jaden has been sending. His office door is wide open and he is putting documents in his brief case. "I have a meeting at Morgan Stanley in Fleet Street. You must come with me. I'm told you speak Cantonese." There was a taxi waiting for them downstairs, and when they came out of the building, Jaden was standing across the road. Kate did not see him, but he was calling and waving as she got into the taxi with Brendon. Jaden was so mad that Kate did not notice him, so he got on the Central line train and returned to his flat. He thinks about sending Kate a "Dear Jane" e-mail, but his good sense tells him not to do it.

Dear Kate,

I hope you enjoy your first day at work. I am so proud of you. Am sorry you couldn't come on line and play. I'll be away for a while... Know that I love you very much. – Jaden.

He hits send and logs off the computer. He looks inside his bedside drawer and takes out his passport and leaves the house.

Sarah returns to the house with two movies: "Face Off" with John Travolta and Nick Cage and "I Know What You Did Last Summer" with Jennifer Love Hewitt. She told Tia the girl at the video store says that this is what all the teenagers are renting these days... "I hope you have not seen them?"

Tia says, "thank you."

"I have to make a few phone calls. Please, excuse me."

Tia told Mary to make popcorn and bring her tea. Tia logs off her laptop with satisfaction. She has rented a two bedroom apartment on St Laurent Boulevard in Ottawa beginning next month. She paid for the first and the last month rent with her credit card. "In three weeks, I will be in Canada," she thinks as she puts "I Know What You Did Last Summer" in the VCR.

Jason plays badminton every Thursday with some of his friends. He calls them up as soon as they get to the loft to cancel. Brooke takes the phone from him and speaks to his friend on the line, "He will be there in forty minutes!" she says and hangs up the phone.

"I can not go out and leave you home alone," he says.

"I'm not home alone. I'm going to be working and will make dinner for us. I have a closing next week, and I have to send everything to my client's solicitor tonight. I will not be able to concentrate with you here. Please darling, you must go and play with the boys. Just don't eat anything," she says.

Jason grabs his gym bag and asks "Are you sure?" She kisses him and pushes him out the door.

When Sarah finishes her phone calls, she goes to the family room where Tia is sleeping. She asks Mary to bring a blanket which she uses to cover Tia. Then the phone rings and it's Brooke calling to thank her mother for looking after Tia. "How is she?"

"She is taking a nap right now. She wanted to go back to the apartment, but I managed to talk her out of it," says Sarah.

"Thank you, Mother, and I'm sorry we did not get the chance to finish our talk," Brooke says.

"We will have plenty of time to talk, my sweetheart. Do you have plans this weekend?" Sarah inquires.

"Jason is taking me to the country tomorrow after work," replies Brooke.

"He's a good boy. I hope he treats you well?" Sarah asks.

"Yes, Mother, he does. I have to finish some paperwork and get dinner ready. I will call you in the morning. Are you coming into the office tomorrow, or will you be working from home?" Brooke asks.

"No, my sweetheart. Tia has an appointment at the Canadian Embassy. I will be taking her there and afterward perhaps we will go to the spa. Do you want to join us?"

"Oh no, I was hoping she was joking about the whole Canada trip. I will join you guys for lunch. I should be done by eleven anyway. Good night, Mother... love you!"

"Good night, B.B. Love you. More." Sarah glances at the sleeping Tia and wonders why she is so determined to go Canada? Poor kid! She looks like the whole world is on her shoulders. Sarah wishes she could help somehow. She has a friend in Canada who might be able to help Tia settle, since she is so determined to go. She wants to call the Sharp's, but she knows Brooke will not forgive her if she does. Sarah decides to help Tia with whatever she needs if Tia will let her. It is nice having her in the house. "It is like a God-send," Sarah thinks. When she came home to the empty house last night, she was not looking forward to another night of TV. It was the paparazzi and the death of the Princess of Wales that caused Sarah to feel so blue. Such a beautiful young woman dead in the prime of her life because of the carelessness of others. "It doesn't seem right," muses Sarah. She finds she doesn't enjoy work anymore… not like she used to do. The cancer really scared her. Sarah thanks God it was not cancer. In a way, it made her think about her life over the years since Jackson's death.

Tia awakes, "Are you sure you don't mind me being here? I don't want to impose." Sarah smiled, and said "No, sweetheart. I'm enjoying your company. The house is too big for me, so it's nice to have you here, Tia. I have a very good friend in Toronto. I'd like to call him and let him know you are coming in case you need anything. What do you say?"

"Sure, that is just what I need! Someone to boss me about. No thanks, I have Brooke and Kate. Canada is my independence, my chance to get away from my family and my bossy big sisters. Everything that I will be is there: I can feel it. My mom and Brooke think I'm spoiled and lazy, and that I'll be back in a week. I'll miss them terribly, but I'm getting suffocated here, Mrs Williams. I believe my Prince Charming is there looking for me. I suppose you think I'm nuts, too, ha! Well! My Dad believes me." Tia gasps and smiles.

Sarah smiled. "I will give you Michael's number, so you can call him if you can't reach your sisters or your Prince Charming." She chuckled and winked at Tia.

It was eight-twenty by the time Jason returned. He opened the loft door and Brooke was standing there barefoot, her hair tied up in a pony tail, wearing underwear and an apron. There were candle lights everywhere in the loft with classical music on the stereo, and she was standing in the dining room holding a glass of wine. Jason wanted her right then and there, but she would not even kiss him.

"I am sorry. I'm late," he apologized.

"You are right on time, darling," says Brooke. She handed him the glass of wine and sat him down. He did not have food on his mind. He was already aroused as soon as he saw her standing there half naked, she looked so sexy. But Brooke sure knows how to turn him on, so she dishes out some food onto a plate for him. She sat on the far end of the dining table and put her glass of wine in between her exposed breasts. Jason wanted to get up and put her on top of the table. She asked him, how was his meal. "It's delicious," he says. She got up to clear the table and Jason stood up to help, but she tells him to sit and relax. She returns with dessert and sits next to him, slowly feeding it to him.

He is so turned on by her. She puts all the dishes in the dishwasher and returning to the dining room, leads him by the hand to the bathroom. By now, his heart rate is elevated. She slowly undresses him. He is as hard as a rock. She slips off her shirt. He makes a move to kiss her. She pulls away. Under the warm shower, he joins her as she bathes him and strokes him. She leans back against the wall, so he tries once again to kiss her. She slips her fingertips in and around his warm mouth. He is burning up with passion, dying for a kiss. Moments later, she dries him all up and leads him into the bedroom. She whispers in his ear to lie down, and he does what he is told as she rubs him down with hot oil. He rolls over and tries to cuddle up to her and steal a kiss. She presses her nipple against his mouth. His tongue feels like velvet. She sits in between his legs and gently rubs hot oil on his testicles. He has been hot before, but this is like a liquid fire. She is searing his senses and melting his passions at the same time. She strokes and rubs his penis. It does not take him very long to climax. As he lays recovering, she explores his mouth with her tongue, lightly licking his eyelids and lashes. Jason is breathless. She whispers in his ear, "How has your evening been?" He frames her face with his hands and whispers, "out of my imagination!" He kisses her softly as she cuddles in his arms.

"Would you like to tell me about yours?" he teases.

"I had a long over-due talk with my mother, and I managed to get three of my pending closings sent out to the buyers' solicitors on schedule. What else... There is this beautiful man that I'm mad about..."

"That beautiful man's name better be Jason Grey!" he says, "or I'm gonna have to hire a hit man!" They giggle together and snuggle closer.

"Listen, Brooke. There is this matter I want to talk to you about. I am sorry for what I said today at your mother's about forbidding you to meddle in Kate's love life. I shouldn't have said that in front of your family like that. Please, don't think I'm one of those cave men types."

"I think that was sexy."

"Are you for real? You almost bit my head off. I thought I was a dead man... until you... until you said, 'you can not forbid me to do anything, when we are married you can and I will listen.'"

"I did not say that!" Jason sat up in the bed laughing. "I am going to call two witnesses who will tell you that you did," he says. Brooke did not find it funny at all. "Ha...Ha!" she remarked.

"I thought that was sweet. But...um... Brooke, I am worried about you and the subject of Jaden and his habit. I don't want him around you until he cleans himself up."

Brooke tried to distract him from the subject. This time Jason did not let her get away like she did on the deck at her mother's house. "I still cannot believe it that I found you, Brooke," he said. "You are everything that has been missing all my life. I am not going to lose you over Jaden and his drug problems." Jason got out of the bed because she was not paying attention to what he was saying. He moved to the end of the bed. "You are one sexy woman and you know how to have me around your fingers, and you know that turns me on out of this world... Right now, I want to do all kinds of sexual things to you, things you can only imagine, but I want you to take this subject seriously, please." Brooke sat up in the bed and said "come and show all the sexual things you want to do to me, Mr. Jason Grey," she teased him.

"Brooke, you can not get caught up in this. We are a couple and I don't want us to be caught up in Jaden's drug habit, or hypothermia as his father calls it. It's obvious his old man knows about his drug habit and is helping him lie to Kate, and you know all this. Why are you not listening? The night I had dinner with you at Kate's mother's house, he was high and you lied and covered for him. I saw it on your face, Brooke. You took over the situation and covered it up." He runs his hands in his hair as he sees he is not getting anywhere with her.

"Please come to me." She says. He stood still. "I share your concern. It's how I feel about Kate. Jason, I don't know how to make her see that Jaden is heading for trouble. She loves him: we all do," she says. She puts her hands out for Jason to come to her but he refuses. She got out of the bed, wrapping the sheet around herself and walked towards him, she dropped the sheet. He resisted reaching for her. "Tia was right this afternoon. I need to concentrate on us and us alone, Jason. I don't like it when we fight," she said. "Jason, I have been waiting all my life for you. Please don't doubt that I am committed to us. I love you and we come first. And like you said… it affects us as a couple. I will not do anything to hurt us darling. Please, let's not fight." He bit the side of his lips, then swept her in his arms and placed her on the bed and did to her what she has done to him earlier, only a lot more. He stopped when she was about to come, but she begged "not yet…" and he said "promise me now that you will not meddle in Kate and Jaden's affair." At that moment, she would have promised him anything.

It's been almost two months since Kate has seen any of her friends. Jaden is off seeing his mother. The only contact they have is through email every now and then and half of the time he doesn't answer her questions. Tia has been staying with Sarah Williams and she has been the only staff member taking care of Urban Style these days. She has not spoken to Brooke in weeks. Kate enjoys her new job. She managed to land an account the first week and after that she has been on fire. Everyone has taken notice of her at the office now. Bobby Sharp has not stopped telling her mother how proud he is of her. In her ninth week, Kate was called to Brendon Chan's office.

"Miss Lee, I was at Routers in Fleet Street this morning. It looks like the Chinese will be cutting interest rates sometime this week. I need you to be on top of your game. First thing in the morning we need to get a head start before the market opens in Wall Street and with the six hours time difference, we will have a head start on the American's on the world market. So please don't be late. Seven o'clock, sharp!" he says. He did not even look up as he spoke. It bothers Kate that Brendon Chan won't look her in the eye, while everyone at the office has been really nice the past two months – except him: it's as if she doesn't exist as far as he is concerned.

"Yes, sir," says Kate.

"Please call me Brendon," he replied. "Oh …Miss Lee. You have done very well, keep up the good work." He did not lift up his head once. Truthfully, Brendon did not like Bobby Sharp forcing Miss Lee on his department. He did his very best to make things very difficult for her, but she has staying power and so far brought in more on the table than all the other commodity traders on his team in the same time period. He is very impressed with her.

Kate's phone rang and it's Brooke calling to remind her about Girls' Night Out.

"Darling, Friday night is girls' night out. Don't forget. I miss you." She said and hung up.

Tia had just finished designing the website for Urban Style. Just before she was about to log off her laptop she saw the Spice Girls. There was nothing special about them, really – just five British girls who can hardly sing, what was all the buzz about them for? She thought their fashion sense was terrible, expect Posh Spice. There is a rumor of romance brewing between her and Manchester United mid-fielder David Beckham. "They look cute together," she thinks. She hardly thinks of Kevin these days. She has not told him about the baby, or about her up-coming departure for Canada. She is not looking forward to the girls' night out. She knows she is going to have to tell the girls what's going on and how she has been dealing with Kevin. She started to cry as she thinks about everything that has been happening to her. She tells herself not to cry. She finally took Sarah's advice and told her parents that she was pregnant and that she was moving to Canada to work for Nortel Networks. They were not happy about it at first, but they have come around since her flight to Ottawa leaves from Amsterdam Scipio airport in two weeks. She will be in Holland to spend time with her grandparents before she leaves.

Chapter 22

Tia went to Brooke's flat to do some laundry, and while she was waiting for the cycle to finish, there was a knock on the door. It was Kevin. He has not called her since they broke up a month ago. Tia wanted to close the door on him, but instead, she smiled and invited him inside. She made some tea.

"How are you?" he asked.

"I'm fine," Tia replied. It was awkward. Finally, Tia couldn't hold in her anger any longer, so she asked Kevin to leave. He did not say anything as he departed. As Tia closed the door, she thought, "I'm not going to cry for him; he is not worthy of it. How could I be so stupid?" Tia asked herself.

In Amsterdam, Jaden has been living an out of control lifestyle. He has smoked copious amount of pot, dropped a lot of E and has been drinking heavily. The girl he came to see is a high class call-girl. Jaden is high most of the time, and does not realize how his life is slipping out of control. His blackouts are more frequent and his nose is always bleeding. He's not been sex-starved, and he always has plenty of money, although he doesn't have a job. Today, Jaden woke up with a huge headache and it looks like someone is having oral sex with him. "Mmm, Kate, you've never done this before. I like it," he said.

There was a voice saying in really bad English, "I want to give you a good fuck."

Upset, Jaden said, "Stop it, Kate! I don't like it when you swear." He opened his eyes to see a girl with bleached-blonde hair, big brown eyes with too much mascara, hourglass figure and the biggest tits he

The Silent Sisterhood

has ever laid his eyes on. The girl kissed him on the full lips and Jaden pushed her away from him.

"What is wrong?" the girl asked.

Jaden immediately got out of the bed. He had no idea where he was or who the hell the girl was. The girl tried to put two pink pills in his mouth, but he took them out. It looks to him like a girlie pill, so he gave them back to her.

"I want to fuck!" the girl said.

"I am a dead man," Jaden says to himself. He is disappointed and disgusted with himself. He quickly puts on his pants. The girl starts to kiss him and tries to get him going, but he isn't having it. He sees the bathroom, so he quickly runs in and locks the door behind him. Suddenly, he realizes he is not in his flat. He sees himself in the mirror: it looks like he has some blond highlights in his hair, his hair is longer than his usual short clean cut, and he does not recognize himself. The girl knocks on the bathroom door and calls him. Jaden ignores her. He sees a tattoo of a hawk on his left upper arm. He frowns, not remembering when he got it. He begins to hyperventilate. He sits on the toilet to relax, but he can not as the girl is still knocking hard on the door. Jaden stands up to open the door, his vision blurs, his heart is racing and his muscles tighten in his hands and feet. He faints as he opens the door. The girl quickly calls an ambulance. She tells the paramedics that Jaden has been taking drugs, but when asked if she knows what he has been taking, she says no. She tells them he is her cousin from England and that he has been partying hard. Jaden is rushed to the hospital as a possible drug overdose. After many tests, the nurse comes to tell the girl that Jaden had some kind of anxiety attack. The nurse tells the girl that it is usually brought on by hyperventilation, stress or hysteria. "Hyperventilation reduces the carbon dioxide level in the blood, causing symptoms that resemble a heart attack. There were traces of a large amount of pot and crack in his blood, and the law requires us to keep him here for forty days. He will be transferred to the second floor of the Mental Health Center in the next building where these kinds of things are dealt with. Are you his only relative?"

The girl sat there with a blank expression on her face. When the nurse finished speaking, she got up and left as the nurse watched in amazement.

Back in England, the girls were partying at Sarah's house. Brooke was the last to arrive, as Jason dropped her off on his way to meet his friends. They have been inseparable since they returned from Holland. She looks more gorgeous than ever. They enter the house hand in hand, holding on to each other's hands as they kiss and hug everyone.

"Yup! David Beckham and Posh Spice," observes Tia. Everyone laughs. Brooke follows Jason into the hallway to say good-bye. They both realize it isn't going to be as easy as they have hoped.

"I don't want to spend the night alone. I cannot spend the weekend alone." Jason fretted.

"We've talked about this, darling," Brooke says. He kisses her on the nose and the neck. Brooke pulls away and says, "Come and pick me up if you miss me." They kiss and she closes the door behind her. She stands there with her eyes closed, and when she finally opens her eyes, her mother is leaning against the wall smiling and watching Brooke. Brooke felt a little embarrassed, so she kissed her mother on the cheek.

"I'm on my way out, sweetheart. I will see you soon." Sarah says. She is wearing an evening dress. Brooke wonders where her mother is going all dressed up. Tia and Kate are sitting on the deck by the enclosed pool. Brooke walks to the hot tub and turns it on. She begins undressing right there and gets into the tub naked and closes her eyes. Her friends watch her with interest. Tia was thinking Brooke has not been in her apartment for months. In fact, she has had Brooke's set of keys along with her car keys since the night Jason came and swept her into his arms and took off with her. She shared this with Kate.

Kate speculates, "Maybe they are living together." The two girlfriends looked at each other and said "no!"

"If you two are going to gossip about me, one of you should tell Mary to bring me a glass of wine." says Brooke.

Tia hands her a glass of wine. "Listen, girls! I'm going to Canada in a week!" Tia pauses to let the information digest. "I have a job at a computer giant in Canada, Nortel Networks. My parents know about the baby and um...Kevin... Kevin and I are done. He's married."

Brooke almost went under the hot tub as she heard the word 'married'. She quickly got out and wrapped a towel around herself. She was fuming. "What the hell were you doing with a married man, Tia?" Brooke shouted.

"Brooke, please!" Kate pleaded.

Tia was quiet. The silence was awkward. "Kevin has been married for the last seven months to some white girl. He told me it was for immigration reasons and as soon as he gets his papers, he plans to get a divorce."

"So, that's why he couldn't travel to Holland with us," snaps Brooke.

"He claims he has not been sleeping with her or nothing romantic going on with them," Tia says defensively.

"Yeah, right! That's the oldest line in the book," Brooke says sarcastically.

"I was not bothered at first. Then, the girl started calling me non-stop about her and Kevin and how they are sleeping together and she wants me to leave her husband alone." She stops to fight back her tears. Her friends listen in shock and disbelief. "He said the girl is telling lies and that he has not touched her. But then... I noticed that he has changed in bed. I mean, he's been doing things we've never done before, all the two years we've been together," Tia sighs.

"Okay, Tia, a man goes out with you for two years and runs off to get married to another woman and you're still sleeping with him? Tia, have you lost your marbles?" Brooke asks, as she pours herself another glass of wine.

"I have not told him about the baby or Canada," she says.

"You are not going to raise this baby by yourself or run off to Canada. I am going to have the son of a bitch deported back to Nigeria," Brooke announces.

Tia laughs heartily. "I am going to miss you, Brooke. It's okay, I'm not in love with him. I just feel a little stupid, that's all. By this time next year, I will be dating a very handsome man whom we all love. And who has a lot of money to spend on me and I will not have to point him in the right direction in bed, okay?" Tia says prophetically.

"Besides, I hear that the average Canadian men our age are such freaks," Brooke adds, "I think it's the cold weather, you know?"

Kate was quiet the whole time. Her relationship with Jaden is in limbo, and she has not received an e-mail from him for weeks now.

"You obviously have thought about this and it sounds like you know what you want, Tia," says Kate softly. "Are you not afraid?"

Tia glances at Brooke for a second and says, "a little, but I am going to be okay. It's time for me to break out… I am not going to be alone. I have the baby with me and I will be on line everyday with you guys and I will call also." She logged onto her laptop and turned it to face the girls. "This is the apartment that I have rented. They didn't have a one bedroom, so I got the two bedroom. Check it out! I can't wait to get there and start my new job. I will be alright."

They eat in silence. Brooke did not eat much as she has not been able to stop thinking about Jason. She called him, and he was watching the F-A Cup between Manchester United and West Harm. "David Beckham has just scored the most amazing goal in British football history," he enthuses, promising to call Brooke after the game.

"How are you at work, Kate? My Dad says you are doing well. He is so proud of you. Brendon is a nice guy to work for," says Tia.

"You know Brendon Chan?" Kate asks.

"Yes, I worked in his department as his assistant the last two summers. He's great!" Tia asked, "Why?"

"He is such a major jerk. Just because he is good looking, he thinks he's all that," says Kate. Kate threw her fork down as Tia glanced at Brooke in surprise. Kate never gets upset about anything except when it comes to Jaden. Brooke did not want to talk about Jaden. She has promised Jason she will not get involved. "Who is this good-looking Brendon person?" Brooke asks. No one responds. "Okay…," she says. "I'm going to come to your office and meet him myself if no one is going to tell me," Brooke threatens.

"My jerk of a boss. He's not once looked at me, since I've been there," says Kate. "It's like, he doesn't want me there or I'm the worse thing that ever came to his department. All I do is work my butt off to please him," she adds.

"Mm! Do tell, darling!" Brooke teases.

"It's not funny, Brooke." Kate changes the subject and turns to Brooke, "Are you and Jason living together?"

Sarah walks in and says, "I'd like to know the answer to that too, sweetheart."

"Mother, please!" Brooke begs.

Tia adds, "You have not been home for ages. Where did you get all these new clothes? You've not been at the store, and I still have your set of keys from when we returned from Holland." Brooke goes and sits in the hot tub and closes her eyes.

"You have fallen in love with him, haven't you?" Tia says.

Brooke opens her eyes and says, "I am so glad you are running off to Canada. You are a pain in my rear end, Tia. I have fallen madly in love with Jason Grey. I want to be with him now. Can you all leave me alone? I need to make a call." Brooke yells. Tia takes away her cell phone, "It's girls' night, Brooke." Brooke was so mad, she got out of the hot tub and was standing stark naked when the housekeeper came and announced, "Mr. Grey is here to pick you up, Miss Brooke." She instructs Mary to send him in. As soon as Jason enters the room and sees Brooke naked, he runs and sweeps her into his arms, not realizing they have audience and they are openly kissing. Sarah Williams clears her throat and throws a towel at Brooke. Everyone is embarrassed. Tia and Kate think that it's the best part of the evening, one they hope to tell her child some day.

Kate and Tia leave the two love birds and go into the family room. Kate is not spending the night because she has to work at the store on the weekends. She says good-night and leaves. Brooke later comes into the family room wearing the towel and asks for Kate. "Kate has gone home and I am going to upstairs to watch TV with Sarah." Tia feels used to Sarah now. In fact, out of everyone she is going to miss Sarah the most when she leaves England. She considers Sarah has been her rock these past few months. "Are you spending the night, Brooke?" Tia asks.

Brooke ponders for a second and replies, "I am spending your last week in England with you, and I don't want to hear anything else. I will see you upstairs."

Sarah is in her bedroom when Tia slips into Sarah's bed and watches her quietly. She picks up the courage to ask, "How did you cope when you lost your husband?"

Sarah sighs and takes a deep breath. "I didn't... I have not got over him. Brooke got me through the loss of her father." It was quiet in the room for a while, and Sarah put her arm around Tia and she cuddled up to her. "Brooke was almost six years old," she says. "I was so much in love with Jackson, as much as I am with him today, even after death. They say forever never dies, Tia. Brooke was my strength. She always has been. She got me through Jackson's death." Sarah reaches for a photograph of herself and Jackson on her bedside table and hands it to Tia. They look so happy.

"How does it feel to be in love, I mean, really in love?"

"Your heart beats faster when you think of him. It's like magic. Only you and he speak a language no one knows."

"How will I know?"

"You'll not be able to get him out of your head. The emotions alone can be overwhelming."

Sarah can sense Tia feels happy. "You know, right now it looks like the whole world is on your shoulders, and you are all alone even though love is gone. Tia, you have love and your child will fill that void as Brooke has filled the void that Jackson left over the years. You will always find the strength in your child. You must not forget those who are still here and who love you. So much time has passed, and I have missed so much of Brooke growing up. For a long time, I forgot Brooke. Don't you forget the people who love you!"

"I know... I am happy that I am not in love with Kevin. It's a lot easier for me to move on. I just feel like an idiot. I should have listened to Brooke's advice. I hate to admit it, but she is always damn right."

Brooke enters the room saying, "you two can't find anything to talk about besides me, I see!"

Tia asks, "Is Jason gone?"

"He is downstairs. I need a bathrobe. I'm cold. Is it okay, Mother, if Jason stays a bit longer?" Brooke asks.

"Of course, sweetheart," her mother says.

She stopped at the door, "Where did you go all dressed up tonight?"

"I had dinner with the Grey's," her mother said.

Brooke came back and kissed her mother and Tia both good-night. Tia fell asleep a few minutes later in Sarah's bed, just like Brooke used to do as a child. Sarah went downstairs to make herself tea. She forgot about her daughter and Jason Grey being in the house. On her way back upstairs, she saw them making out in the hot tub. She stood still for a second watching their happiness before she made her way up to bed.

For the past two and a half months, Jason and Brooke have made love every night. They can't get enough of each other. They get out of the hot tub and head to Sarah's pool house. He presses her against the wall and whispers for her to tell him what she wants. She does not put it in words, but he knows what she wants and he is more than happy to give it to her over and over until they both fall asleep.

The week in Sarah's house passes quickly. Tia is leaving for Holland to spend a week there before she travels to Canada. Brooke told her she and Jason would fly to Holland to see her off on the weekend that she leaves. Naana and Kate came to pick her up for the airport. It was harder saying good-bye than they all thought. She called them every night and the three of them would talk for hours on a three-way line. She never once thought of calling Kevin. It was like he never existed.

Chapter 23

Luke Blake has not seen or heard from his son for close to three months now, and he has been out of his mind with worry. Edward Mercer has advised him to file a missing person report. Today, Luke has decided he will go and do it, but every time the phone rings, he holds his heart in his hands hoping the voice at the end will be his son. The ringing of the phone interrupts his thoughts. He answers it to hear Edward Mercer telling him not to leave his flat, that he is on his way to see Luke and will be there shortly. Luke's heart begins to hammer; his thoughts race through all kind of notions as he wonders what news Edward has for him. "Dear God, don't let my son be banged up in jail," he says aloud. Waiting for Edward was torture, but when the knock finally sounded on the door, his whole body was frozen with fear and Luke could not get up.

"Who... who is it?"

"Luke! It's Ed!"

Luke still could not move, and Edward was getting worried. "I have some good news, sir!" Ed shouted.

Hearing the words "good news", Luke quickly runs to the door. "I am so sorry, for keeping you waiting... the body is not like how it used to be. Please come in. I'll put the kettle on." said Luke apologetically.

Edward can see Luke is very nervous.

"Thank you, Luke, but you don't have that much time. I do hope you have a passport and it's up to date?" asks Edward.

Luke is shaking so much he drops the tea cup on the floor. Edward decides to put the poor man out of his misery and tells him what's up.

"Remember you gave me your permission to have Jaden's computer searched for any clues to his whereabouts?"

Luke could not recall, or understand why that could be good news, but he nods affirmatively anyway. Edward smiles, and Luke wishes his friend would let it out as he was almost about to piss himself with anxiety.

"Well, we learned that the day Jaden disappeared he was on line with Kate Lee."

"Kate... that's his bird, you met her once remember? Anyway, I don't think she knows where Jaden is. Kate has been calling – even this morning – and she sounded pissed – it was the tone of her voice," he said.

Edward continues his long story as Luke listens feeling very agitated, but trying his best not to show it.

"There was another person Jaden was on line with."

Luke could not hold it in any longer, "Edward, please, is my son in jail? If he is, just tell me now, please." Luke interrupts.

"No sir, we found him," he said softly.

Luke sat on the floor crying, "What am I going to tell Joyce," he thought. "Oh, God, no, no. I have to call Joyce and tell her... that her only son is dead."

"No, no! Luke, your boy is not dead! What I mean is we found him, alive and well," Edward says quickly. Luke is still crying, while Edward feels confused now.

"Jaden... my son is alive... and well!" Luke stands up. He runs his hands through his hair, turns around and faces Edward.

"Luke, please, sit and listen to me. He went to Holland to meet with the other girl he was emailing. Anyway, to cut the story short, the girl was arrested two days ago and the police found Jaden's bag."

"Please don't tell me Jaden was arrested again," Luke interrupts.

"No! Jaden has been in a rehab facility for the last three weeks. The police found my card in his personal stuff and they called my office. Come, I have a ticket for you: we must go as you don't wanna miss the plane." Luke threw his arms around Edward and was still crying and saying thank you at the same time as they left the apartment.

Jaden has been going through hell. He is in some kind of locked down facility. Most of the time, he doesn't have a clue what language they are speaking. He is confused and his body feels shivery, weak and drowsy. He has been having all kinds of nightmares that seem so real. He overheard one of the doctors saying in English that he has to be supervised closely to prevent anymore mess ups.

"Mr. Blake," said a nurse, a big black man, over six feet tall, close to two hundred and ninety pounds. Jaden thought his teeth look like white sugar cubes lined up in a row. The white nurse uniform makes the man look blacker. "There is counseling therapy for you this morning, Mr. Blake. I am here to assist you with your bath, so you can be on your way."

Jaden was not sure whether he heard the nurse correctly: he wants to assist *me* with *my* bath. "I ain't a fucking faggot and I don't take IT up the ass from no one," is what Jaden thought he said. Instead, his mouth shaped the words, "Thank you kindly, sir. I can manage myself."

The attendant is impressed: good manners and polite words from a junkie! The nurse assists Jaden to the bathroom anyway. "I have to wait here, Mr Blake, until you are done. I am so sorry," he says apologetically as he stands in the far corner of the bathroom. Jaden feels humiliated at first, but he gets under the shower and it feels so good he doesn't want to come out. He is escorted to the office where the attendant guides him into a chair and the nurse again stands in the far corner of the office. A lady enters dressed casually. She sits down and introduces herself, "I am Dr. Vroom." She looks too young to be a doctor, Jaden thinks. She flips open a file and leans back in her chair while one hand holds her pen. Jaden watches her with great interest.

"You've been here for two weeks now, Mr. Blake. What can you tell me about yourself?" she asks.

Jaden is taken in by how beautiful she looks. He does not hear what she has said. She repeats her question... Jaden is quiet.

"I've been where for weeks...ma'am?" he asks.

The doctor informs him that he is in a rehab facility in Amsterdam. "You were transferred from the Central Hospital for treatment for drug and alcohol abuse." Jaden is having trouble thinking or paying attention. The doctor notices his discomfort. She continues, "You have been here during the withdrawal period, so we can watch you more closely and deal with any possible problems. You have also been given medication to help reduce the withdrawal symptoms. Counseling and support groups are an important part of therapy here." Jaden is still so confused he becomes very nervous and can't think clearly, so he raises his voice.

"Why are you saying these things about me? I don't do drugs! I have been drinking more than my usual since..." He stopped and remembered Kate losing the baby, the tears rolling down on his face.

"The first step to quitting is to admit you have a problem. Be honest and open with family, close friends. Ask for their help," the doctor advises Jaden.

Jaden begins to believe that the doctor is out to get him.

"We need to know exactly how much of the drugs and alcohol you have been taking. Don't hesitate to be honest," she says, pen poised. There is a sneering tone in her voice as if she expects Jaden to underestimate his consumption. Jaden is upset that the doctor thinks he is being dishonest. Because he won't respond, the doctor tells the attendant to take him back to his room. Jaden stops in the middle of the door and turns to look at her again.

"You can not keep me here against my will. I have family back in England. There are laws against this sort of thing." Jaden does not have any energy to defend himself. He puts up a good fight trying to break free from his escort. Sweating and shaking, he suddenly finds himself restrained. He remembers very little of the temper tantrum. It begins to come back to him little by little, all the nightmares he thought he was having were all the things he has been doing over the past three months. "Oh my God! Why I did I do all this?" he asks himself.

Later, the day shift attendant, Philip, came to check on Jaden. "Hey, Philip! Can I see the doc again?" Jaden asked. "Sure, sure," Philip replies. "I'll put you on the list at the nurse's desk."

There was a different doctor at the next session. Jaden admitted that he has been abusing alcohol and drugs and that he needs help to get clean. After that initial assessment, Jaden saw him for twenty minutes every day until he was released. The doctor has advised him to stay away from people who use drugs and who encourage others to use them. "Support-group meetings and counseling can help you quit. Take advantage of both, eat a healthy diet, drink lots of water every day and get plenty of rest." He was also told he must not smoke or drink coffee or alcohol: "They can make you nervous and increase your withdrawal symptoms." The Doctor told Jaden not to dwell on the past. Find new things to do and get out of the house and go for walks. If he needs to take more drugs, call a doctor or a counselor, a friend, or a family member you can trust right away. If he feels his problems are getting harder for him to deal with on his own, call for help. He gave Jaden his card. Jaden shook his hand and thanked him. Philip walked him out of the building and passed him to Luke, who was outside waiting for him. He introduced Philip to Luke, and he hugged and thanked him for looking after his son.

"You stay clean, you hear," Philip said jovially, glad to see his charge going home. Luke could not stop kissing and hugging his son. They went to KFC where, over a bucket of chicken, Luke described the events that lead him to Amsterdam.

"Dad, I'm really, really sorry about all this trouble."

"Aw, son. I'm just glad to have you back."

"I promise I won't go near drugs or alcohol again, Dad."

"Well, now, son, that's music to my ears! But let's just take it one day at a time, okay?"

"Sure, Dad," Jaden agreed, and after a pause, he added, "Can we leave Holland soon, Dad? I just don't want to spend another day here. It's full of bad memories for me."

"Sure, Jaden. We can get a flight to London in a couple of hours. Eat up, son, and let's head to the airport!"

Brooke and Tia were not sure it was him. He has grown his hair long; he is accompanied by an older gentleman, who appears to be in his late fifties. The older man has his arm around him and seems to be more affectionate towards Jaden. Initially, Brooke and Tia were not certain that it was Jaden at all. Jason reminded Brooke of their agreement and Brooke responded by pouting.

Jaden saw the girls and strode across the store to sweep Tia into his arms. "Princess!" he exclaimed as he hugged and kissed her. He let go of her and tried to hug Brooke, but saw that Jason had a tight grip on her hand. "What are you doing here, Tia?"

"I'm going to Canada. I've just spent a few days with my grandparents before I leave. Brooke and Jason have come for the last weekend and to see me off. What about you?"

"Oh, it's a long, sad tale," Jaden said, and then gesturing toward his father, he said, "This is my Dad, Luke Blake." They shook hands all around. "I'm sorry, Princess, but we're going to have to go. My flight to London was just called. Give me a call when you get settled in Canada and keep in touch by email," Jaden said. He hugged Tia again and said, "I'm gonna miss you, Princess."

"Jason, can I have a quick word with you?"

Jason was surprised, but he reluctantly agreed. "Uh, yeah, sure."

"Listen. I want to apologize to you for my behavior the last time we met. I took your advice and... I got help. I love the girls very much and would not do anything ever to hurt them."

Jason interrupted, "You don't owe me any explanation, Mr. Blake."

"I know that. I have always stood up for my responsibilities. I forgot, for a little while. You look after Brooke good, okay?" Jason smiled. "I mean it. If you hurt her..." he stopped. Jason waved his hands signaling acquiescence, "Brooke has missed you terribly and I'm sure she wants to yell at you. You'd better man up and go see her."

"Please, you can scream and call me all the names later. Right now, I could do with a hug. I've missed you," Jaden pleaded with Brooke. "Only if you tell me you are clean and not here buying drugs and your father here is not covering for your habit," Brooke snapped at him.

Luke did not like her already, "how dare you say that about my boy?" he challenged Brooke.

Jaden took her hand and said, "I promise I'm not. I'm so sorry for everything I have put you all through. You can have a go at me later, love. Can I please have a hug?" he begged.

Brooke turned to Luke and said, "You better look after him or I will have your guts for garters if anything should happen to this handsome idiot. I don't want to hear about no hypothermia in summer."

"You better listen to her Dad," said Jaden. "She means business." They watched Jaden and his father as they went inside the gate to board their plane.

Chapter 24

"What are the odds?" Tia said. It has been a good week, and she has enjoyed seeing Brooke so happy with Jason. She told her to try and give Sarah a break and keep her eyes on Kate. Brooke was distracted by a handsome guy who kept looking at Tia. Tia also seemed to be taken in by the stranger and they exchanged a smile. Brooke thought it was interesting to watch the stranger and Tia interacting. Brooke could tell that they have an unspoken connection. Initially, Tia ignored the stranger. Brooke let go of Jason's hands and went to talk to the stranger. She returned with the stranger and introduced him, "This is Nathan Carter. He is a lawyer from Toronto who is taking the same flight as you. I got you a seat next to him." Tia was not impressed at all. She pulled Brooke aside, "My last day and you're still bossing me about, how could you just change my seat without my permission?"

Jason shook hands with Nathan and introduced himself. "Are they always like this?" asked Nathan. Jason chuckled, "Yes, pretty much most of the time."

Nathan said, "Nice meeting you all," and he turned around to go, but Brooke grabbed his hands and said, "Nathan, darling. I am making you responsible for looking after my little sister here for me." She opened her purse and gave him her card. Tia felt a flush of embarrassment. It was time for them to go to the gate and board their plane. Brooke began to cry first and said, "It's not too late to change your mind and come home. I promise I'll stop being the big sister if you come home, darling." Tia held back her tears, hugged and kissed her, kissed Jason, "Thank you. Look after her, okay?"

"I don't want you to go, darling," Brooke cried.

"I'll see you in May. I will call you as soon as the plane touches down," said Tia.

They let go of each other finally and Tia began to walk towards the gate, but then she dropped her handbag on the ground and went back to hug Brooke one more time. Now, they both were crying as Jason came and took Brooke in his arms. Tia instinctively took Nathan's hand and he picked up her fallen handbag as they went into the plane. Jason and Brooke watched the doors close.

"I can't believe she's gone, Jason," said Brooke as he guided her out of the airport.

Nathan guided Tia to her seat as he sat down next to her. They did not talk. He noticed that Tia was deep in her own thoughts for the first two hours of the flight. She did not touch the food on the plane, and she slept throughout the flight to Toronto. He could not take his eyes off her. He wished she would open her eyes so he could talk to her. Nathan Carter was not used to this kind of treatment from women. Usually, he does the ignoring, not the other way around. "Maybe she is a lesbian," he thought. "No, she is way too hot to be a lesbian," he smiled to himself and wondered about the woman sitting next to him. The flight attendant announced that the plane is about to land and they must put on their seat belts. Tia woke up and she took out a mirror from her purse and fixed her hair, adjusted her seat belt and closed her eyes again. Tia's next flight to Ottawa was in three hours. Nathan asked if she wanted to come to his condo and rest up before her flight but Tia declined. He tried his best to break the ice, but Tia was nothing like her sister Brooke. Nathan was tired himself, but he didn't want to leave her. His cell phone was working and it began to ring. "Hey, Nicole!" he answered. Nicole replied, "Hey, yourself! I'm stuck in traffic downtown, I'll be there shortly."

"Listen, my ride is stuck in traffic in down town Toronto. How about I buy you an ice cap?" he pointed to the Tim Horton's concession stand. Tia said no. He sat down with her, but she had her eyes closed the whole time.

Nicole was a white girl in her mid-twenties with bright red hair and blue eyes, very beautiful, pale ivory skin. She wore a dark gray pants suit with her hair tied up in a pony tail.

"Sorry, I'm late, Nate. Traffic was a bitch," she said.

Nathan got up and kissed her on the cheek. He turned and saw that Tia's eyes were open. "This is Tia Sharp," he says to Nicole. "Tia is going to Ottawa. She works for Nortel."

"Nate always brings home beautiful girls," Nicole observes as she extends her hand to greet Tia.

Nathan's cell phone rings again and it's Brooke calling. He hands the phone to Tia, "It's your sister." Tia was wondering how Brooke got Nathan's number as she took the phone.

"When is your girlfriend's flight leaving?" Nicole asked.

"In three hours," Nathan whispered.

Tia came back and handed the phone to Nathan. "Thanks, but you don't have to wait with me. I'm going to check in at the flight desk and go upstairs." Nathan knew he was not going to get anywhere with her, so he gave her his card and said, "Please call me if you need anything."

He got to the parking lot and put his bags in the trunk of the car. "Hey, Nicole. Go on without me. I'll see you later" and he was gone before Nicole could ask where he was going. Nathan went to the upstairs waiting area first. He did not see her, and he was about to go downstairs when he heard her saying, "Are you stalking me? I am sure it is illegal to stalk people in Canada." Nathan was relieved that he was able to hear more than two syllable words from her.

"I see you're not going to leave me alone."

Nathan sighed and smiled as he sat down next to her.

"Why are you so sad?" he asked.

Tia ignored him. "I just want to be left alone and tens of thousands of miles away and you find a way to bother me. Thank you, Brooke," she said to herself. "Where is your girlfriend?" Tia asked.

"She's gone home." Nathan replied.

Tia thought that was strange because there is no way she would leave him alone with another woman at the airport, or anywhere else if he was her boyfriend. The ground crew began calling for the passengers going to Ottawa to board the plane.

"Well, that's me. Thank you, Nathan, for waiting with me. That was very sweet of you," Tia said.

"My pleasure, Tia. Please let me know how you are, okay? or if you need anything," Nathan offered. Tia smiled. "I mean it," he said. He watched her check in and she turned and waved at him with a smile. "She is so beautiful," he thought.

Before Tia knew it she was at Ottawa International Airport. She got in a taxi and told the driver that she was going to the Airport Inn at Hunt Club. In less than five minutes she was there. She checked in and ran a bubble bath, and afterward, feeling refreshed, she jumped straight into bed. As she got comfortable, she felt the baby kick for the first time and for some reason all her fears went away as she slept rubbing her belly. The next day, as she went and got the keys to her apartment, she found the weather to be a lot colder compared to Europe. Her apartment was on the tenth floor. Gazing down from her window, she saw a small mall nearby, so she decided to go and have a look around. She discovered a furniture shop and bought a queen size bed, asking them to deliver it today. She went to Sobeys supermarket and did her grocery. With too much stuff to carry, she paid five dollars for delivery. She felt so happy that everything was working out so well already, she light-heartedly went back to her apartment to unpack her belongings. Her groceries were delivered first and the bed followed shortly after. A little while later, there was a knock on the door. "Who could that be?" she wondered. It was another delivery. Tia was confused because she had not bought anything else. The delivery guy asked for Miss Tia Sharp. "I'm Tia," she said as she signed the delivery note and they brought the stuff in, one thing after another. The last item was a small box, which she opened first. It contained a cell phone that suddenly began to ring. Mystified, she answered the phone and found Nathan Carter on the phone. Tia was not pleased to hear from him, as she asked rudely, "what is your game, Mr Carter?" She told him, "I cannot be bought."

"Get over yourself, Miss Sharp! I didn't send you the stuff. Your sister gave me money and your address along with a list. She wanted you to get these things today," Nathan told her.

"Oh, Nathan, I am so sorry. I'm not normally this rude. It's just…," she stopped breathlessly.

Nathan tried to ease up some of the tensions, "if it's any consolation, I'd like to say I would have loved to have sent you those things myself, for you to start off your new life in Canada. But the truth is I am a broke lawyer who is living with his best friend and her boyfriend at the moment."

"You're just saying that to make me laugh," Tia teased.

"No, I'm not. I was thinking, if you were in Toronto right now, I was going to ask you to buy me dinner," he said.

"You are crazy! Thank you. And again, I am sorry," Tia said.

"I'm not joking. You see, I figure my line will be you are by far the most beautiful woman I have ever laid my eyes on in a long time. I mean you and your sister, but she is already taken. Right?"

Tia could not stop laughing. Nathan continued, "Well, I guess you don't want to hear it, right? What the hell! I am going to tell you, anyway," he said.

"You know, you are a lot worse than Brooke. Do you know that?" Tia commented.

"Ha…ha… so does that mean that if you're ever in Toronto, you will buy me dinner? Or better… you could send me twenty dollars to buy myself dinner. I like to give a tip so maybe add five more dollars."

"Stop it, you are too much, you know that?"

"I have a hearing in the morning, can I call you tomorrow? I have to prepare or I'm not going to eat, if I lose," he joked.

"Sure, crazy man. Thank you, again," said Tia as she ended the call. Then, she thought, "I am going to kill Brooke," though she missed her already, and then she called her parents and Kate. Next, she and Sarah talked for a long time; she told her that the baby had been kicking and how good it felt. Her phone rang and it was Brooke."

"Nathan just called and gave me the number. I have been worried sick about you. I don't know why Bobby and Naana let you go off like that, you brat!" she shouted.

"I miss you, too," Tia teased.

"You can still come home, you know."

"I am at home, and I love it! Thanks for the house warming gift. You didn't have to do that. I almost bit Nate's head off when the things were delivered. I thought he had sent them to me."

"He is hot! Like you said… by this time next year, you could be dating a handsome rich man we all love. That's Nathan right there," Brooke wagered. No time to tell her that he's just barely making ends meet.

"He says the same about you," Tia adds.

"That is the kind of man I'd like to see you dating. I have something to tell you… Jason and I are getting married!" she said excitedly.

"What took him so long to ask?"

"You knew he was going to propose?" Brooke asked, surprised that Tia knew.

"Everyone knew. He went to mom and dad, Sarah, Lola, Kate and me to see whether we would make him a part of the family," Tia told her. Brooke was crying because she did not know how much effort had gone into Jason's proposal. "How sweet!" she thought.

"The wedding is going to be in September, so you and baby Brooke can come home," she said.

"And if the baby is a boy?" Tia asked.

They talk and laugh as if they were in the same country. Tia loves everything about Canada: her job and the people. She has never been in a country so diverse, and yet everyone is so kind. She had her ultrasound the other day and it confirmed that she's expecting a girl just like Brooke predicted. She has not thought of Kevin in a long time. The pain of his betrayal is getting better each day, and it doesn't hurt as much as it used to do. She has shared her feelings about him with Nathan. She and Nathan have become good friends. He knows how to make her laugh. Recently, he asked whether she would spend the

Thanksgiving weekend with him and his family, who live in a suburb of Ottawa. His father is a doctor and his mother is a professor at Ottawa University. Tia has declined the invitation because she is looking forward to spending Thanksgiving alone. She has four days off, so she wants to start getting things ready for the baby and look for a car now that she knows the city well. But Nathan is still hoping she will change her mind. He knows she is not ready for a relationship after her "Kevin experience", but he still hopes that Tia will give him a chance to prove that not all men are like Kevin.

He would love to to get to know Tia a lot better, if she will let him. He called her to say he had just arrived in Ottawa. "Can you buy me dinner? ... You promised! Remember? I'd like to collect, if I may!" He hangs up before Tia can say she's got plans.

Tia lives in two bedroom apartment on St Laurent Blvd. The open concept apartment is painted white. The living and dining rooms are separated by two beams; the walls are decorated with some contemporary paintings as well as some African art objects. White furniture and a glass Connor desk with Tia's laptop complete the design. The bleached oak dining table is set up for a dinner party. The apartment is very clean. Hearing a knock at the door, Tia peeps out the peep hole, but no one is there. Seconds later she finds a sketch of two people having dinner pushed under the door. She laughs and opens the door. Brooke is right: he is one sexy man! Nathan has a silly grin on his face. Tia doesn't know whether to hug him or shake his hand. She decides to hug him. "God, he smelled even sexier," she thought. He has brought dinner and a big box for the baby.

"A broke lawyer bought dinner? Wow!" She teased.

"Not to worry, I'm going to have to ask for a check afterward!" He joked as he winked at her. "I also brought movies. A client of mine gave me a box of African movies that he collected during a trip to Africa, and I thought of you. It is so nice to see you smile. I like that it makes you way too sexy. He winked at her as he put a spoonful in his mouth. They talked about his work and Tia's. He was impressed how much Tia knew about the law. She looked so sexy in her gym clothes. After dinner she asked if Nathan would mind watching some of the movies that he brought her.

By the time the movie was done, Nathan had fallen asleep on her sofa. She did not wake him up. Instead, she went to the hall closet and got a blanket to cover him. Then, she went on-line with Jason and Brooke for about three hours. When she logged off her laptop and swiveled her chair around, she noticed that he was awake and was looking at her.

"I am so proud of you…" he said softly. "You've been though a lot, Tia, yet you still keep it all together. How do you cope?" he asked.

Tia rubbed her stomach. "She helps me cope. She is kicking right now," Tia says as she goes and sits next to Nathan, taking his hands and placing them on her belly. Nathan felt the baby kick really hard. The feeling was unreal. He didn't want to take his hands away from her belly.

"Wow! That is a hard kick. How do you feel when she does that?" he asks.

Tia takes a deep breathe and says, "I can't put it in words. It is fantastic!"

It was almost midnight when Nathan glanced at his watch and said, "Thank you for having dinner with me. I must be on my way." He asks if Tia wants to do something tomorrow, but Tia seems so far away, gazing off in space, so Nathan says, "Why don't we go to Paris and get married?" Tia jerked back to the moment, "Say what?" Nathan chuckled, "Tia, honey, where were you just now?" He touches her gently on the shoulders. "Oh, nowhere special. Where are you staying in Ottawa?" Tia asks.

"I will be staying at my parents. They are in the Virgin Islands for Thanksgiving, a trip I found out about at the last minute. They have a condo on Riverside Drive about five minutes from here. That's where I'll be most of the time. I should be on my way. It's getting late. I was hoping you and I could spend some time together while I'm in Ottawa. What do you say?"

"I was thinking… you should stay with me while you're in town." Tia pauses, unsure how to proceed. "I mean, I do have a second bed room, and it beats being in a beautiful condo all alone."

Nathan grins broadly, and pausing for effect, he says, "Um... Tia, honey, you do know that I have a huge crush on you. I was not kidding about the marriage proposal. I'm already in love with pretty Princess here." He pats Tia's bulging stomach.

Tia is quiet and does not respond right away. She's pregnant and the most beautiful man she has ever laid eyes on just told her he has a crush on her. "Is this guy for real?" she wonders. Aloud, she says, "You are full of it, Nathan. It's raining and you've told me you're not the best driver. Besides, you're only going to spend the whole night on the phone with me, anyway, unless you have a date?"

"Hey! I thought I was on a date with you and Pretty Princess. I am crazy about you and the baby, too. I think when she kicked me my whole word changed and I know you are not ready for anything right now," he stopped to get his breathe and then he said, "I'm going to get my bags from the car, okay?" He runs out of the apartment, not wanting to go back, but also realizing how much power she has over him, and he doesn't want anyone to have that kind of power over him. He takes out his bags and locks the car doors. "You are making a huge mistake, Carter," he tells himself. Nathan has not gone a day in his adult life without waking up beside a beautiful woman. Since he met Tia, things have changed: his friends have noticed he goes to work, often staying late, and then spending the rest of the evening talking to this Tia no one knows.

Back in Tia's apartment, he took a shower and wrapped a bath towel around his waist. Tia noticed he was in good shape and not an ounce of fat on him. He knew Tia was checking him out and loved it. He went into Tia's guest bedroom and put on his bath robe. Tia asked if he felt cold.

"No. Actually, I'm hot. I am always hot." He had his eyes closed and he knew she was watching him. He finally opened his eyes and said, "Thank you Tia for having me as your guest. I am going to get some sleep now."

"Do you want anything before you go to bed?" asks Tia.

"I would love a Tim Horton's ice cap," he said.

"You know, you got me hooked on those things when you bought me one at the airport," she says, laughing.

Nathan remembered and was laughing as Tia threw a cushion at him and went to the kitchen. Nathan followed her, and watched her put all kind of fruits in a blender.

"What are you making? You can not be still hungry, are you?" he asked.

"Very funny! I'm making a milkshake for you, Mr. I-am-hot-all-the-time!" she teased.

"You are making a smoothie? For me?" he asked.

She handed it to him and he drank some. "This is good. Thank you. Are you not going to have some?"

"No, I have my tea," she pointed to her tea.

Nathan slept in the morning soundly, while Tia studied media law. When he awoke, Tia was in the kitchen making tea.

"Good morning, Mr. Hot!" She teased. "How was your sleep?" she asked.

Nathan liked it when she teased him. "I was in this beautiful apartment with this sexy woman, but strangely, I slept too much," he said. He knelt on the kitchen floor beside Tia, rubbing her belly and talking to the baby, which Tia thought was so sexy. She was almost in tears as she listened to him and watched him being silly. He finally got up and kissed her on the cheek. "He smells so sexy," Tia thought, but aloud she said, "Sit down, please. I am making us breakfast."

He grabbed her and said "No. I am taking you to the gym for a workout, and afterward we will go to Tim Horton's for an ice cap, and later you can help me do some shopping. Bring your credit cards. I may need to borrow money from you!" Nathan says. "And stay awake! Don't you pregnant women sleep all the time?"

Tia laughs, "What makes you think that?"

"Oh! Well, when two of my friends were pregnant, all they did was vomit and sleep."

"Well, yes, that's true. Lots of women have morning sickness and feel tired all the time at the beginning of the pregnancy, but I'm past that stage. I feel pretty good these days!"

Nathan thought Tia has so much energy to go university and to be working at the same time. After the gym, they went the spa where they both got a massage, and Tia gets her nails done. They stop by his parents' condo on Lees Avenue, where he orders lunch for them. The went to the Farmers' Market and buy what they needed for Thanksgiving dinner. Tia refuses to let him pay. Tia asks him what he wants for dinner and he says that he is taking her out to see the Ottawa Senators play the LA Kings and that after the game they will have dinner at the Yak Yak comedy club.

"That sounds good. I have not watched any hockey since I've been in Canada."

"You like hockey?"

"Oh, yes! I'm mad about sports, basketball, football, motor racing... you name it, I love it."

"Not many women like sports."

"My grandfather and my dad both like sports. My sister, Lisa, and I often go motor-racing with my grandfather."

Nathan enjoyed the Thanksgiving weekend with Tia. He got to know more about her than what Brooke had been telling him. The more time he spent with Tia, the more he feels she is the one. He loved how Tia is so well organized.

Chapter 25

Nathan Carter returned to Toronto well over the hills in love with Tia. A month ago, he hired a private investigator to find out about the Sharps and their family tree, discovered Kevin Peters and had the PI gather information on him, too. Tia's ex-boy friend: the report was on his desk. He couldn't be happier when he read about Tia's family. Nathan has no doubts about the kind of a woman Tia is; his only problem has been the same since they met, that Tia may not be equally attracted to him. The long weekend was the most incredible weekend he has ever spent with any woman in his entire life. He has been hoping to talk to his parents about her, but they never seem to be available these days. He told his brother Steven that he used the Thanksgiving weekend to get to know the woman he had met only two months ago at the Amsterdam airport. Steven's response was, "You're crazy, man!" and then pointed out that Tia may never have any feelings for Nathan. "Tia is a woman who has everything; yet, she leaves it all behind to move to a country where she knows no one and doesn't have any family support."

"Yeah, that has puzzled me, too. But don't you think coming to Canada all alone like that is an independent thing to do? That's what really attracts me to her."

"Yeah, since when do you love any woman other than Mother?"

"Well, Steven, Tia just might be the Mrs Nathan Carter I've been wanting all my life!"

"Too bad your charms did not work on her, eh?" Steven teases.

"No… she sees the real me. I think she is afraid of getting hurt. Anyway, I learned today that her mother is going to be in New York next week. I was thinking of meeting with her. What do you think?"

"I think you're crazy, but I was discussing this very same topic with one of the actors on my new movie. He seems to think that you may have the right idea to win Tia's heart."

"I do love, respect and trust her. I know she is very stubborn, strong headed and is probably going to have my head when she learns that I'm not broke and I've been lying to her."

"What do you mean, Nate?"

"It was the only way to get close to her. Her sister wanted me to send her some things when she first arrived in Canada, so I figured I would try to romance her with gifts. She almost bit my head off. So, I played the broke lawyer card and it broke the ice between us. She thinks that it's romantic. I've been sending the baby flowers and stuffed animals since I came home. She says that I'm crazy, but I held her at the airport and the feeling was incredible, Steven. I put my hands on her belly and the baby kicked. It was like a wave of energy flowing through me, it's crazy. I knew that moment that I couldn't let Tia go. I'm in love with her and it scares the hell out of me. Something tells me even if I do win her love and trust, it will only take one mistake for her to destroy me. Does that make any sense, Steven?"

"Please tell me this is not one of your games. I don't want to go with you to meet this lady if you are planning just to sleep with her daughter and move on to the next beautiful woman. Tia's mother sounds like a very powerful woman, and she may not want to meet with us, Nate."

"No, no. This is not about sex. Steven, I want to marry Tia before the baby is born. I haven't been thinking about sex. Come on; just put my past out of your mind. Tia is going to be your sister-in-law, soon. Just make sure that Mrs Sharp doesn't see me as an arrogant jerk. Mrs Sharp will meet with us… besides, I'm told that she is hoping Tia will return to Europe. I've got to go, Tia is on the line. I'll see you in two days, Steven."

Nathan gasps as he answers the phone. He tells Tia that he was about to call and thank her for her hospitality. "Oh, anytime, Nathan!" Tia replies.

"Well, in that case, what about next weekend? One of my associates is getting married in Toronto. Will you come to the wedding with me?"

"Yeah, sure! I was planning to come down to Toronto next weekend, anyway. Yes, I'll accompany you to your friend's wedding."

"Is there any chance you'll stay with me?"

Tia laughs. "What? stay with a broke lawyer living with his friends? No thanks! I've reserved a room at the Nova Hotel." Nathan was disappointed, but he understood. Truth be told, Tia Sharp has also got it bad for Nathan Carter, and she is happy about how their friendship is developing.

Nathan could hardly wait until the weekend so he could see Tia again. On Friday, he took a taxi to the airport to meet Tia, but was late arriving because of the heavy traffic, and consequently missed her. He didn't want to meet her with his usual means of transportation, a Porsche 911, so he jumped into a taxi and headed back in his office. Retrieving his messages from his assistant, there was nothing from Tia. Nicole comes into his office and tells him that it looks like their Ottawa office is on the go, and if everything goes well, their new office there will be ready to open as Nathan wished. She asks if all the sudden move to Ottawa has anything to do with Tia. Nathan didn't say. "Are you upset about something, Nathan?" Nicole asks.

"Tia is in town, and she has refused to stay with me while she's here," he sighs.

Nicole has tried to be nothing but supportive when it comes to Nathan and this Tia Sharp, and their budding relationship. She knows very well how Nathan feels about Tia. She did the only she could do: she said something supportive.

"Nate, good things are worth waiting for. If you love this girl as you claim, you have to learn to communicate with her well and not get upset all the time," Nicole smiles.

The Silent Sisterhood

"Thank you, Nikkie. You're right." He chuckles. "The Lakers are at the Air Canada Centre on Sunday, I have tickets. I was hoping you and Ian would go with us to the game… maybe afterward we can go to dinner. What do you say, Nikkie?"

"We will meet you at the wedding. Ian is out of town," Nicole says.

Nathan always feels better with Nicole around because she has a calming influence on him. His assistant buzzes and says that Miss Sharp is here to see him. He flashes Nicole a smile and says to the assistant to send Miss Sharp in. Nathan pulls his chair back, stands, and walks to the door, his heart pounding as he opens the door for Tia. Tia's hair is swept over one shoulder; she wears diamond stud earrings, a black pants suit with high-heels and carries a Channel handbag on one shoulder. Nicole thinks Tia looks even more beautiful than their first meeting at the airport. Tia smiles and kisses Nathan on the cheek, and Nathan takes her hand. Tia fixes Nathan's tie as Nicole clears her throat. "Oh, I'm sorry, I wanted to surprise you. I should have called first, Nathan," Tia says.

"No. I missed you at the airport. I'm hoping Nicole and her husband will joins us on Sunday. Please come in. You remember Nicole?" Nathan says softly.

"Of course! Hello," Tia says with a smile as she extends her hand and shakes Nicole's hand. Nicole stands up and says, "It's good to see you again, Tia. I have to go now, but I'll see you two later." As Nicole closes the door behind herself, Nathan pulls a chair closer for Tia. "You look beautiful," Nathan says. Tia didn't expect Nathan's law firm to be this big, and she was impressed. She also realized that he has lied to her about just starting out, unless they have suddenly grown very rapidly. Nathan grabs his jacket and says, "Let's get out of here, so I can show you around Toronto."

"Oh, I know Toronto very well."

"Well, then. How about lunch?"

"Hmm. No. I've just lunched with an old friend of my family."

Nathan sits on the edge of his desk and pulls Tia on his lap, who goes willingly. "Would I be out of line to ask who is this old family friend that you had lunch with?" Tia chuckled, "It's okay. He is old enough to be my father."

"Mmm, I'm not gonna worry about old guys taking you to lunch, then." He smiles. "I have missed you."

"Me too. I like your office. It is very sophisticated." Tia smiles. She loves being in his arms. Tia looks very tired, and pretty Princess is not kicking when Nathan places his hands on her belly. "There it is." The baby kicked. He sits Tia on the desk and puts his head on her stomach, wrapping his hands around her waist. It warms Tia heart when he does that. "Oh I have missed you and mummy so much! Please tell mummy, she can't go and stay in that hotel while we are all in the same town. I would be very sad and you will not want me to be sad will you, Pretty Princess?" Tia rubs his back and says, "My God, you are very manipulative; you must be a very good lawyer! Talking of hotels, I was thinking you and I could have dinner at my hotel." Nathan stands and puts his forehead against Tia's and says that he will have dinner with her anywhere she wants. "Since you will not come home with me, can I come and stay with you?"

"You want to leave your comfortable home and stay in a hotel room?"

"No, no, that's not what I had in mind, but yes, I'd like to come and stay in a hotel room and order room service, and get a massage. Why not? I'll not be able to think knowing you and Pretty Princess are less than a five minute drive from me. There is a second option: we can get out of here and go home. I will rub your feet with lotion; we will spend the rest of the afternoon doing whatever you want, except making love because I promised my mother that when I meet the girl of my dreams, I'll wait until we are married."

Tia is laughing hysterically at him. "You are way too much, you know? Besides, I think the foot rub sounds good. Can we pick up food first?"

"No need! Everything you need is at home. Let's go check you out of that hotel now!" Nathan exclaims.

"I haven't checked in the hotel yet; my stuff is still in my car."

"Good! You can drive us home; I don't own a vehicle. Shall we?"

"You don't own a vehicle? Yeah, right! I don't buy your broke act for a second.... You don't own a vehicle? Well! Today, you can ride in my car," she smiles.

They walk hand-in-hand and Nathan introduces Tia to some of his associates before they leave the building. They drive to a luxury condominium on Lakeshore Blvd, and take the elevator to the twenty-second floor. Nathan opens the door and finds a woman there, whom he introduces to Tia as Peggy. "Peggy looks after me," he says to Tia. "You mean, Peggy is your housekeeper, who spoils you rotten and picks up after you?"

"Um ... Tia, sweetie, let me show you to the spare room, so that I can give you a foot massage."

"Oh... I'm loving this just fine, Mr. Hot... Maybe Peggy can show me to the spare room," Tia winks.

Peggy asks whether she can get anything for Nathan before she leaves. Nathan nervously looks at Tia. He asks Tia to excuse him while he discusses with Peggy his housekeeping needs for the weekend. Nathan's condo is richly decorated with French furniture, modern art, and a replica stamped tin ceiling covered the high ceiling from the hallway to the den. The den is warm with a gas fireplace, over-sized sofas with big cushions, a handcrafted eagle with an oval glass topper in the middle of the room as his coffee table. The dining room has the same handcrafted French furniture with a fireplace. There were photographs of his family when he was a little boy, playing football. Tia smiles when she sees him standing by her with his hands in his pockets. He points to a photograph of his mother and father; he tells Tia that it was taken the night his father proposed to his mother at a charity event in Ottawa. He also showed her his very favorite photo of the day at college when his team won the NCAA championship, with all his team mates. For a moment, Nathan disappears and comes back with his jacket off, carrying a glass of milk for Tia. Tia is in the den with Peggy. "Do you want Peggy to fix you a snack?" Nathan offers. Tia says, "No. I know where the kitchen is. I might fix something later." After a pause, Tia asks "What is college like in America?" His experience was the same as Tia's when she attended school in America. He drinks some of Tia's milk, and Tia asks if he wants her to go and fix a snack for him. "No, I don't want you running after me like you did when I came to Ottawa. I want to see you relax, Tia, before I'm forced to check us into a hotel with room service for the whole weekend."

"So tell me, what snacks did Peggy prepare for you?" Tia chuckles. Nathan retorts, "You are not going to let this go, are you? She made fruit salad and your favorite cinnamon rolls. You'll love my father's pasta. He makes the best pasta in the world!"

"Mmm... A man who can cook? I love Peggy and your father already. I love your place." Tia leans her head back on the sofa and closes her eyes. She wants to tell Nathan to give Peggy the weekend off, but then she felt it's a good thing that Peggy is there to ease the sexual tension between them. Nathan looks sexy sitting behind his desk in his office, very sophisticated. Where has he been all her life? Nathan sits down next to Tia, lifts her feet and gently places them on his lap. He asks Tia what she's thinking. "Me? Oh, I'm just happy to be here." Nathan takes her hand and kisses the back of it. He wants to tell her about his meeting with her mother last week in New York. "So, are you going to tell me about your meeting with my mother?" She asks pointedly.

"I figure, she should know who you are spending your time with. She is one beautiful and very powerful woman. She broke my heart, you know? I thought since I wasn't getting anywhere with you, I'd go see her and plead my case. I called her office in England today and I was told she's in a meeting. I'm giving her a week before I call her and ask for your hand in marriage, or she's gonna have to adopt me just so I can be close to you."

Tia laughs. "Are you always this strangely charming? I mean, what makes you so sure there will more than this between you and I? We are not compatible, Nathan."

"I am very sure about us. We are more compatible than we both know. Besides, we are both very sexy. I think you are just being cautious, me too, in a way. I see the three of us being a beautiful family, um... your mother thinks that I'm crazy."

"Yep! Absolutely! She thinks you're nuts, too. You just got out of a relationship with your Dutch girlfriend. Why rush into one so soon with a huge responsibility attached?"

"It was not like this, not even close to this. Life is a responsibility. A child that I love makes me feel whole and warm. What you and I share is a lot more – it's hard to explain. Pretty Princess knows my heart. I think she and I do share a bond already. Have you noticed how she moves around when I rub your belly? I'm happy to have you both here with me. It's nice to see you relax. What are your plans for the holidays? Are you going to Europe?"

"No, I planned to spend it alone and study for my exams, and maybe fix up a nursery for the baby. Why do you ask?"

"I will be Ottawa the second week of December. I was hoping we could spend more time together, maybe spend the holidays with my parents. I love being with you! I think it would be fun! My sister Jackie will be there as well as Steven and his girlfriend." Their eyes meet and hold for a moment. Tia asks if she can think about it. He says "No… you should say 'yes'." She tells Nathan that she may be working for CTV in Ottawa after the holidays. Nathan likes the way she sets her mind on something and goes for it. He hopes that she does fall in love with him. He tells her that she has a lot confidence and he loves that about her. Steven rings while they are talking, so Nathan puts the phone on speaker, and they converse in French. Tia clears her throat and says in French, "*Ah, cherie, je parle français parfaitment!*" She winks at him and excuses herself. "Wow! If you don't marry her, can I?" Steven asks.

"You have caused enough trouble already with your loud mouth. You can say a quick hello and go back to doing whatever it is you are doing," Nathan tells his brother who is still laughing when Nathan passes the phone to Tia. He puts the television on in his office while Tia finishes talking to Steven. Tia has taken off her shoes and her suit jacket. She has made him a smoothie, and Nathan gently pulls her onto his lap, saying, "I want to take care of your every need this weekend not the other way around. I love the smoothies that you make, but you must let me give it a try." Peggy knocks on the door and says dinner has arrived. Doing a little pre-planning, Nathan asked Peggy earlier to order fish and chips, as well as some roti from the African and Caribbean restaurant downtown. Peggy has ordered all kinds of rice, goat, beef, yams, fried fish and plantain dishes. Nathan didn't want to let go of Tia long enough to let her cook a meal because he enjoys holding her and having her sitting on his lap so much. It feels to him that they are in love and in their own world where nothing matters.

"Have you been able to reach your parents yet?" Tia asks.

"Yes! Actually, Dad called today. They are both fine, but you know, I haven't talked directly to my Mom for a while now."

Tia senses that he and his mother are very close; she likes that in a man. Before they sit down to eat, Nathan sends Peggy home. Tia didn't eat much, so he fills the huge tub up with bubble bath and oil for Tia. She loves Nathan's idea of taking care of her.

Nathan Carter is her idea of perfection in a man, but the last thing that Tia wants now is a man. She is able to do for herself things that she didn't think she could do four months ago. Romance is not what she is looking for, yet everything that Tia and Nathan do is romantic. A knock on the door disrupts her thoughts. "Are you all dressed? Tia, may I come in?"

"Yes, Nathan. Please do come in." Tia sports a white towel bath robe with her hair up. "I was trying to make tea for you," he says apologetically as he holds out a Tim Horton's tray with teas and ice caps. Tia could not help but laugh. "What am I going to do with you?" Nathan shrugs his shoulders.

"You can invite me in... we can watch a movie, while I hold you until you sleep," he suggests.

"You have it all planned, haven't you?"

"Yep! Is that a yes? Or good-night?" He makes a sad puppy face. Tia sits on the bed and smiles, "yes." She is not really watching the movie. She feels so relaxed that she easily falls asleep. Nathan slips out of her bed, covers her up and turns off the television. He stands by the door and smiles before he closes the door.

Nathan's condo building has a gym where he takes Tia the next morning before breakfast. Afterward, Tia makes oatmeal and fruit salad for them for breakfast. The wedding is at eleven at St Joe's Church in North York. Nathan tells Tia that the limo will be by to pick them up at ten. He kisses her on the cheek and runs to take a shower. In no time Nathan is dressed and in his study talking to Brooke on the phone. He swings his chair around and his jaw drops when he sees Tia in a black sexy halo daring dress with a long hemline and flirty pumps. She looks fabulous. She is trying to put on her earrings and has no idea that Nathan is standing behind her. When Tia turns and sees his face, her heart skip a beat and she smiles. "God! He looks so sexy in a pinstripe suit." She turns and fixes his tie. Both of them are speechless. "Sorry, to keep you waiting, sweetie. I'm going to grab the gift so we can go," Tia says. "Oh the gift… I forgot to ask Peggy to pick up a gift for me," he says sheepishly to Tia. "Well, why don't we give them this from the both of us, hey?" She smiles, "you look hot, Mr. Hot!" Nathan is suddenly nervous.

At the wedding reception, they were seated at the same table as Nicole and her husband, Ian. Nicole introduces Tia to Ian as Nathan's girlfriend. Ian asks if Tia wants some champagne, but Nathan quickly says Tia can't. Nicole asks why not. He puts his hands on Tia's stomach and smiles.

"You dog!" Ian exclaims. He turns to Nicole and says "why didn't you tell me that Nate was going to be a father?" Nicole smiles and says, "Because I didn't know, sweetie," and turning toward Tia, she asks, "How far along are you?" Tia was not paying attention because she has seen someone she knows. Nicole repeats the question. "Oh! I'm sorry for my rudeness, I'm almost five months," Tia tells them.

"It's a baby girl." Nathan says proudly. Tia asks to be excused. Nathan mistakenly thinks she is upset until he sees her hugging one of the guests, a middle-aged white man followed by a younger man. Tia is laughing with them. Nicole follows Nathan's gaze. "What's wrong, Nate?" she asks. He frowns slightly, smiles and says nothing. Tia returns to their table with the man; she is laughing and introduces the men as Nick and his son Patrick Collins. They are friends of her family from Holland. Ian says, "I thought Nicole said you were from England?"

"I grew up in London, but I also spent a lot of time in Amsterdam with my grandparents," Tia explains.

"Did you ever visit the red light district?" Ian asks.

"Of course! One of my favorite night clubs is near there. I love the place! It's a great place to party." Nathan is chuckling as Tia winks.

Looking at Tia with Nathan is like seeing a different woman from the one Nicole met at the airport. Today, Tia seems more fun and very compatible with Nathan. Ian is also taken in by Tia's charm and says he loves Tia's sense of humor.

Both Nicole and Nathan say simultaneously, "Since when do you love anything other than the stock market?"

As a reply, Ian asks, "Do you mind, Nathan, if I dance with Tia?"

Nathan smiles at him, "Sure! If the lady will have you!" Nathan and Nicole watch Ian and Tia dancing and laughing. "I'm sorry, Nate. Tia is either a freak or a saint. How can she laugh with Ian? The man's jokes are not funny. I should know," Nicole says, rolling her eyes.

"Come on! Let's go show them how it's done," Nathan stands and puts his hands out for Nicole to take.

By the time Nathan and Nicole return, Ian is sitting on Nathan's chair. He and Tia are talking about the stock market. Tia also has the same hand-held PDA as Ian. She pushes a few buttons on Ian's and gives it back to him to try. Ian beams and gives Tia a high five. Nicole and Nathan are more puzzled. Nicole says to Tia, "You *are* a geek!" Nathan and Ian are offended by what Nicole has said, but Tia laughs and says, "Totally! When it comes to computers, I am total a geek. I also love the stock market. Since both my parents are in that field, it's hard to get away from it. It's relaxing! You should try it sometime." Nicole looks at Nathan and they both say at the same time, "a geek!" They are all laughing. Tia shakes her head and says, "You two are lawyers." Tia chuckles.

Nicole didn't want to spend Sunday with them, but she is now looking forward to the game tomorrow. They ride together in the same limo on the homeward journey. Nicole admits to Nathan the next day at the game that she didn't really like Tia at first when they met because she seemed like a snob, but she is all right. Nathan and Ian want to take them somewhere to dinner, but Tia insists that they have dinner at the condo and will not let them order out. Nicole wants to help her in the kitchen, but Tia says, "Why don't you go and talk law with Nate? Ian can give me some stock market tips." Nathan plans to go back to Ottawa with Tia the next day after his pre-trial hearing to see his new offices there. With Brooke's input of what Tia likes and dislikes, he has also found a home in Ottawa that he will view while he's there. He is still trying to find the right time to talk to Tia about his plans. Tia looks up and smiles at him from the kitchen. He sighs with pleasure.

"I'm sorry, Nikkie, that I didn't tell you about the baby," says Nathan apologetically.

"I'm happy for you, Nate. I think Tia is perfect for you. Just don't go and fuck it up like you do with your other relationships."

"Thank you very much, Nikkie. I don't know why I bother sharing things with you and Steven," Nathan spat. Nathan says to himself "whatever it takes to make Tia my wife… I will do anything to make that happen." He sighs and takes another sip of his drink.

Chapter 26

When Jaden returned to England, he had lost his job and missed the whole term of school. He remembered the doctor's advice and made sure that he sought all the help he could get to stay clean. He told his mother what he had been doing and promised her that he would change. He was up at five in the morning to run and he went to the gym every evening. When his father saw him, he was angry because he thought Jaden was taking drugs again because his body had changed so much. Luke saw Jaden taking some vitamins and freaked out. Jaden had to show his dad the label on the bottle just to reassure him.

"What is going on with you and Kate?" Luke asks.

Jaden does not immediately reply. He remembers the night he returned from Amsterdam. He wants to see Kate so badly and apologize to her, but it looks like Kate is seeing that Chinese guy he saw her with on her first day at work. Seeing Kate with another man triggers Jaden's desire to drink. Testing himself, he goes to a nearby pub and orders a beer. He sits there looking at the beer for an hour and decides to leave without touching it. He begins running from Kate's workplace in Central London to his flat in New Cross Gate. When he gets home, Jaden gets under the shower and has a good cry. Afterward, he surfed the internet and found support with a group which he now attends three times a week. They have a gym there, too. One of the guys shows him how to use the machines, which he hates at first because his whole body feels sore the first few days, but now he really enjoys working out.

"Son, what about Kate? Poor love has been worried about you," says Luke.

Someone knocks on the door. Luke opens the door to Brooke and Kate. Kate seems unhappy when Luke opens the door. Jaden has only a towel wrapped around himself as she steps into the flat. Kate notices the tattoo on his upper left shoulder and sees that he is in good shape and that he has grown his hair long. He does not smile either and looks as upset as Kate feels.

"Hello," he says casually.

"You look alright," Brooke observes caustically.

"I'm fine. I've been busy since I got back. I should have called and asked how Tia is doing," he says.

Kate notices that Jaden avoids looking at her, like he is going out of his way to ignore her. Brooke notices it, too.

"You look okay. Well, I am going home. I just wanted to see how you are doing," Brooke says matter-of-factly.

"I will walk you to the lift," he offers.

He pushes past Kate without looking at her and opens the door for Brooke, "Thank you, Brooke; you've always been a friend."

"Call me, okay? I don't want to come to this dump again," Brooke commands.

"Don't worry. You'll soon be looking for a flat for me. I promise." Returning to the flat, Jaden goes straight to his room and closes the door. Kate opens the door without knocking. Tearfully, she asks, "What's going on?" Jaden ignores her. Kate feels so frustrated after about ten minutes because she can not make Jaden even look at her or say a friendly word. "If you want to dump me, be a man and speak up for yourself," she demands.

Jaden finally laughs. Kate is not impressed with him at all. It is like looking at someone new; he doesn't look like Jaden at all, so cold and mean. The Jaden Kate knows doesn't have a mean bone in his body. He has always been so kind and sweet. "Okay, I got the message loud and clear. I have been a fool all this time, no phone calls, no emails. Brooke told me an hour ago that she and Jason saw you in Holland three months ago when you were coming home with your dad. It's been five months of worry and not knowing whether you were dead or alive! This how you treat someone you plan to marry?" she asked. Kate is crying now. Jaden feels ashamed as Kate's words pass through his whole body like electricity. He still loves her so much, but he has let his anger and fear overtake him. He is crying, too. Kate sees the tears rolling down Jaden's face and knows deep in her heart she loves him still. She stops for a minute, watching him cry.

"Jaden, love, please… Whatever is the matter? Please, tell me." Kate sits down by him and lifts his head up, but he can not stop crying. She hugs him and rubs his back. She notices he has become all muscle, his body is more toned and sexier than ever.

"Please, forgive me, love," he says softly.

Relief washes over Kate as she hears his sweet voice. "Oh, love, I love you," she says as she begins to kiss him, but Jaden does not return her kisses. In fact, he gently pushes her away from him. He stands facing the window with his back turned on her. "I am sorry, Kate." He stopped speaking because he couldn't bring himself to tell her all that he had done. "But I must!" he says to himself.

"You don't fancy me anymore?" she whispers.

"I do Kate. I have not stopped loving you… but you will stop loving me when I tell you… what I've been doing," he predicts.

Kate does not want to hear it. "I love you Jaden and I've missed you. The last few months have been crazy without you. Please!" Jaden turns and faces her. He wants to take her in his arms, but he restrains himself. "I know. It's been like that for me, too, but you need to know this, Kate. Please listen to me!"

Kate is not making it easy for him. He really would prefer that she didn't have to know about his escapades in Holland, but he does want to marry Kate, and Jaden feels there ought to be complete honesty between them. Bravely, he gets to his knees in front of her and takes her hand to help her up, wiping her tears with the back of his hand. She misses his touch. She doesn't want him to stop, and truthfully, he didn't want to stop either. It feels good to hold her hands again. He kisses the back of her hands and places them on his face to wiped his own tears. "Kate, love," he whispers softly. "I love you more than you know. I don't want to break up with you." Kate doesn't let him finish before she presses her lips against his and he responds wholeheartedly. Jaden realizes he has missed her a lot more than he thought. As they make love, Kate notices that Jaden is a lot stronger. She loves his body, so muscular, so sexy, she could not keep her hands off him, she wants him more and more. Holding her afterward Jaden says, "I got tell you something, Kate," but she is not really paying attention. She is so turned on by him, re-discovering him and thinking of him like having a new man because the love making is different, changed by Jaden's experiences in Holland. Jaden realizes he isn't getting anywhere with her, so he lays her down on the bed and gets on top of her.

"I've been doing drugs, and I cheated on you with a girl in Holland," he blurts out.

Kate's whole body freezes, as she hears "cheated". Jaden continues, "I've been doing all sorts of drugs. I went back to Holland and I moved in with a girl that I met when I was there with you." Feeling her blood pressure rise, Kate pushes forcefully against Jaden, "Get off me! You bastard!"

He does as she asks, but keeps talking. "Kate! I got really messed up in Holland…"

Kate scrambles into her clothes and looks around for her purse.

"Kate! Please listen!" Jaden cried out, sensing his last chance to resolve things with Kate was this very moment. "Kate, my love, I was hospitalized and for weeks I didn't really know where I was. It was the best thing that could have happened to me."

Finding her purse, Kate hit him on the face with it. Jaden grabbed her wrist and pulled Kate toward him. "Kate, dear, I needed help to get clean – a lot of help. I spent a couple of months in the hospital going to group therapy and getting in touch with my issues." Kate struggled in his arms and Jaden felt his nose was bleeding from the well-aimed purse. He gently sat Kate on the bed and wiped the blood off his face. He put on his pants and stood leaning against the door.

"Kate… losing the baby was my fault. You don't drink or do drugs… You did not fall during your pregnancy…" he paused to gather his thoughts. "…it was because of me. I am the reason why we lost our child." Kate hears Jaden's words, but does not understand them. She is so enraged by his cheating that she just wants to run away from him. She can not deal with what he is saying.

"Why are you doing this to us," she screams. "You want to break up? Let's break up now! Please don't do this, Jaden, please!" She tries to leave, but he will not let her go.

"Everything, I've been telling you is true... and more," he says.

"Well, thanks for telling me," she replies sarcastically as she hits him again. "I just don't want to hear it!"

" I been a prat."

Jaden has never seen Kate this upset, and he wants so much to take her in his arms and hold her, beg her to forgive him. Instead, he takes the coward's way and he opens the bedroom door for her, which Kate is too happy to exit. He follows her to the living room and makes an attempt to grab her hands, but just then Luke opens the front door. Kate notices that the jerk from the Benz is stepping into the flat. She recalls meeting him in Jaden's flat months ago. She pushes past the men as Jaden makes one more attempt to stop her.

"Son, let her go. I will go after her," Luke says as Jaden goes into the bathroom to wash his face. In frustration, Jaden begins to kick his door. A few minutes later, Luke returns, "Sorry, son. I couldn't stop Kate before she drove off."

Jaden dresses, not knowing what to do about Kate and wishes he could know where she was heading. He thinks, "she will not go home. But she might go to Brooke's place." Telling his mother was not this difficult.

Don't dwell on your problem and find new things to do: the doctor's advice for moving on with life. As Jaden kept reminding himself of those words, he snaps and punches the walls. Thinking something is dreadfully wrong, Luke and Edward came running into the room.

"Son, you have to take it easy," says Luke. "Um. Son, Ed, Mr. Mercer here came by to see you. He would like a quick word with you."

"Why the hell would he want to talk to me?" Jaden wonders. He joins them in the living room and sits down in his favorite chair, his jaw as tight as ever. Both men can see the anger in his face, so Edward comes straight to the point.

"I am looking for a legal assistant to help at my law office. The position is only part-time. I thought of you…" Edward pauses… "If you are interested, you can stop by the office and see Kim and she will sort you out." Edward gets up to leave.

"Mr. Mercer. Sir, thank you. I'm chuffed, but I'm afraid I cannot accept your offer. I thank you." Jaden says.

Angered, Luke stares in amazement at his son, but Edward tells Jaden to sleep on it and Jaden thanks him again for the offer. Jaden thinks long and hard about Mr. Mercer's offer and about Kate as well. He decides to go to Brooke's apartment to see whether Kate is there. Jaden doesn't really want Kate to be alone right now, so he calls Brooke's apartment not expecting anyone to answer the phone. They don't answer, but that doesn't really mean anything. Jaden doesn't want to call Kate's cellphone, though. He compulsively paces the living room. Luke says Jaden will soon wear out the floor and Jaden smiles in response. Suddenly, Jaden sits next to his father.

"Dad, how did you get through it all?" he asks.

Luke knows what his son means, so to order his thoughts, he goes into the kitchen to make tea for the two of them. When he returns, Luke says, "It was not easy. I had a lot of help. Still getting a lot of help."

"Still?" Jaden asks.

Luke didn't say anything. Jaden was confused by his father's response. Jaden assumes Luke can not still be an addict after everything that has passed. How could he be? It's been over twenty years now. "I cannot go the same path," he says to himself.

When Jaden returned to England after so many months in Holland, he found a lot of cash in his overnight bag that he doesn't remember accumulating. When the police returned his belongings to his father in Holland, they made no comment on the large amount of cash. Superstitiously, Jaden refuses to touch that money even though there certainly is enough there to re-start his life. "No," he thinks. "There has to be another way." Back in his room, Jaden takes the only suit he owns out of the closet and hangs it over the back of a chair, he polishes his black dress shoes and goes to bed. He does not sleep the whole night for worrying about the task he has set himself for the next day. In his heart of hearts, Jaden wants to send Kate an email to tell her about his plans, but he fears her rejection. In the morning, Jaden is dressed and out of the house by eight o'clock. He gets a hair cut and takes the train to Liverpool Street, where he sees a woman selling flowers. Jaden stops to look at the selection of flowers. He looks so intently that the flower vendor expects him to buy a big bouquet. She notices his profound sadness and wonders how one so young could have so much sorrow.

Mercer Law Office: Jaden sees the building, takes a deep breath and enters the building. A middle-aged woman sits behind a desk, talking on the phone. Jaden waits politely until she finishes her conversation.

"Good morning, young man!" the woman says as she replaces the phone on its cradle. "How can I help you today?"

"I am Jaden Blake. I'm here to see Kim, ma'am."

The woman rose from her desk and walked toward the hallway. Turning to look at him, she remarks, "don't stand there, Mr. Blake. We got work to do!"

Jaden follows her to a desk in the back room. The desk is laden with files and the lady points to them saying, "We are transferring all these files onto our computer. They need to be filed under the right section of the law. Don't file the corporate and tax law together! I need your social security number, so I can get you a password for the computer system." Kim White is middle-aged, Jamaican woman with a strong English accent. She stands only five foot one inches tall, not more than one hundred and twenty pounds. Kim is very organized and able to multi-task. She is also intimidating despite her diminutive size.

"Mr. Blake, would you like a coffee?"

"No, thank you, ma'am."

"Please, Mr. Blake, my name is Kim. Call me Kim."

He blushes, but manages to stammer, "Call me Jaden, Kim."

The first day, Jaden spent most of his time in the file room. On the second day, when Jaden came to the reception area and told Kim, "The files are sorted," Kim could not believe it and needed to see the filing room for herself. When she came to the file room, all of the files were gone from the desk. Jaden went on the computer and showed her all the documents. She noticed that Jaden has also filed each document under the right code.

"How did you know which codes to use?" Kim asks.

"Hm… well, you see, I'm about a year shy of becoming a lawyer myself," Jaden replies.

Kim was impressed. "The partners have afternoon meetings at three. You can take an early lunch, Jaden, when you come. I will show you, after lunch, how the phone system works." When Jaden left the office, he returned to Liverpool Street Station and bought two bunches of flowers. He took one bunch to Banker's Trust and asked the receptionist to deliver them to "Miss Lee. Miss Kate Lee." Next, he took a taxi to Brooke's office and told the taxi driver to wait. As Jaden entered the building, he met Jason and Brooke at the door about to go out to lunch. He gave the flowers to a surprised Brooke. Jason did not recognize him and felt jealous until he realized who it was. They asked if he would join them for lunch, but he said he had to get back to the office.

"Oh! Where are you working, Jaden?" Brooke asked as she hugged him. "I'm so proud of you, you know."

Side-stepping the question, Jaden told Brooke that he was ready to move out of his dump of a flat. "I want to buy, instead of renting. I'll call you soon, okay?" He picked up some donuts from Upper Crust and went back to the office. He told Kim the donuts were for everyone. Kim introduced Jaden to the other two partners and their assistants, Gabriel Goodwin, who does the tax law, and Abby Evans, his assistant. Wendy Mercer is Ed's wife and her assistant is Peter Hilton. " Pete here is also a law student," Kim tells Jaden. Quickly, Kim shows him how the phone system works and they return to work for the afternoon.

The flowers are given to Kate on her way out of the building that afternoon. Her mother is going to Hong Kong, and Kate is running late to pick her up to drive her to the airport. Kate reads the card from Jaden and throws the flowers in the nearest bin she can find. She makes it just in time to drive her mother to the airport. Seeing a nearby Thomas Cook Travel Agency, Kate enters the kiosk and asks about flights to Ottawa that weekend. The agent says, "There is only Air Canada leaving from London Heathrow Airport on Boxing Day morning." Spontaneously, Kate decides to buy the ticket right there. She gets on her cell phone and leaves a message for Bobby Sharp that she plans to go to Canada for the New Year to see Tia and that she leaves in two days. Returning to the office, she completes the tasks in her work load. Finally, Brendon Chan tries to initiate some small talk with her about the office Christmas party. Kate cuts him off with a curt reply, "I will not be attending, sir. I leave in two days for Christmas vacation."

"Going somewhere warm, I hope?"

"No, I am off to Canada."

"I will not be in the office tomorrow. I am going to get you your gift, Ms Lee." In a few minutes he returns with a beautifully wrapped gift and a card for Kate.

"I'm sorry, Mr. Chan, um… I did not get you anything, sir, since I did not know the common practice in the office."

Brendon is laughing as he turns and walks back to his office. A moment later, he stops by Kate's desk to say, "You cannot open it until Christmas Day, and… Oh, yes… Give my love to Tia." Kate remembers that Tia once described the experience of being Brendon Chan's assistant.

"I will sir, thank you," she replies.

Before leaving the office, Kate sends Brooke an email.

Brooke,

I have two weeks off. I am going to go and surprise Tia on Boxing Day. Meet you at your mom's house tonight.

Love, Kate.

Kate finishes her work and tidies her desk before leaving at the end of the day. On her way out of the bank, she notices Jaden, dressed in a dark navy blue suit with a blue Oxford shirt and no tie. His hair has been cut short with the top part spiked up with gel, very sexy. She does not want to make a scene, so she jumps into her car and drives off, while Jaden stands on the sidewalk watching her. Through her rear view mirror, she can see him looking at her. She can not stop the tears as she drives on. Part of her wants her to go and throw her arms around him. How could he cheat on me repeatedly? She remembers him making love to her in Amsterdam the same night he cheated. "I should have known," she thinks, feeling humiliated by his actions. It's all coming back to her now. "Was Jaden's drug use the reason they lost the baby?" she wonders. "Why did he turn to drugs? After everything he and his mother went through with his father... Damn it! Brooke was right. Damn!"

Chapter 27

Nathan has spent the last ten weeks romancing Tia. The more time they spend together, the more he falls for her. Tia is warmhearted like his mother, and she looks adorable to him. Nathan goes to Tim Horton's every morning to get her a cinnibun and ice cappuccino before she wakes. It is like they are a couple. Then, they work out at the gym. Tia is a part-time broadcasting student at Carlton University. She studies while Nathan works on his up-coming hearing. Tia's kitchen is very organized because she hates eating out. After their evening meal, they watch African movies. Tia makes him a smoothie every night before she goes to bed. Nathan is not a good cook like his father, but he enjoys watching Tia cook. It is now two days before Christmas and Nathan has still not been able to speak to his mother because she is always sleeping whenever he calls during the day. "Tia, I'm going to the cottage to see my parents. I'd love it if you could come with me." Tia tries to think of an excuse for not going, but then she thinks, "why not?" Inexplicably, she is also worried about Nathan's mother sleeping all day and night. Instinctively, she suspects there must be some explanation for the mystery.

"I'd love to," Tia replies with a smile.

Nathan is more than surprised. He really did not expect she would go with him.

"Are you sure?" he queries.

"Yes, Mr. Hot. I would love to spend the Christmas holidays with you and your family. We have to leave early," she says. "I want to stop at St Laurent Fruit Market before it closes. I need to pick up a few things. How about after gym, I buy us lunch and we can head off?"

"A beautiful woman wants to buy me lunch? I won't say no." Nathan teases. Tia wants to say she has enjoyed his company. She loves how relaxed she feels with him. It's like nothing matters when she thinks of him. She will miss him when he goes back to Toronto. She smiles. The town of Cassleman is not more then forty minutes from Ottawa. They arrive a little after three in the midst of some blustery, snowy weather. There is a storm warning in the towns of Orleans and Cumberland as well as the surrounding area, which includes the Casselman district. Nathan and Tia arrive at the Carter cottage just before the storm begins in earnest. Tia has not seen this much snow before, and already five centimeters of snow has fallen. She loves it, it looks so beautiful.

Nathan's father is out salting the driveway as they pull up. He wears a hat that covers much of his face. Nathan calls out a greeting to him, and he almost loses his balance when he sees how beautiful Tia is and slips on the slippery driveway. Tia quickly goes to him and asks if he is all right. Nathan is too busy getting things out of the trunk of the car. He sees his father holding hands with Tia, talking like old friends as they go into the cottage. Tia admires the cottage, a 1920s house with some modern upgrades. The first thing that draws her attention is the huge stone fire place. Anthony Carter steers her straight to the fire, and pulls over a chair for her to sit in as he helps with her coat.

"I will make you a hot chocolate," he offers.

"It's okay, show me the kitchen, Daddy. I will make it myself."

Anthony likes this girl already. She is not like Nathan's usual girlfriends he normally brings home. "Kitchen is right here, honey." Anthony Carter stands about six feet tall, one hundred and sixty pounds with a touch of gray in his hair; he still has a touch of a West Indies accent as well as the traditional West Indian sense of humor.

The kitchen is a big country kitchen with oak cupboards and granite counter tops, and a rectangular island in the middle. A huge stone fireplace just like the one in the living room adds to the cozy atmosphere as do enormously large windows providing a view of the woodlands behind the cottage. Tia quickly switches on the kettle. "You have a lovely home. I adore the fireplace."

"It's double sided," Anthony says. "Come, I will show you, honey." He takes Tia's hand. Nathan has come inside, and with some amusement watches his father holding Tia's hands again. Talking and laughing like they are like old friends, Nathan is jealous. He has known Tia longer than his father and it took him six weeks before he held her hands. "Never mind me!" he says out loud. "I am only your son, who brings home the beautiful girl."

Tia and Anthony both laugh. He comes over and shakes his father's hands.

"Nate, my boy!" Anthony says. "Good to see you! Your mother misses you very much, nice of you to come home and bring Tia, son. Mother is sleeping. Come, let's go make hot chocolate."

"Nathan, I need the groceries from the car, sweetie, please." Nathan likes it when Tia call him sweetie, beautiful, and Mr. Hot. It makes him feel warm inside. He asks his father to give him a hand. Anthony asks why they brought so many groceries. Nathan tells his father he has no idea. "Tia wanted to get them on the way here. She felt Mother maybe tired. I told her you do all our cooking, but she would not listen to me, Dad."

Anthony laughs. "A woman who can stand up to Nate? I love this girl, Nathan." His father winks.

"Me too, Dad. Me too."

"She is a keeper! This one, son… don't let her go," his father advises him.

By the time they bring in all the groceries, Tia has already made the hot chocolate and she has the blender out on the counter top. She takes out some fruit and puts them in a bowl and washes them, then gets the milk out of the fridge as the two Carter men watch her. She gives Nathan a smoothie and the hot drink to his father.

"How is your hot chocolate, Daddy, good?"

Anthony glances at his son when Tia calls him Daddy and smiles. He is so proud of Nathan. He asks why Tia brought the grocery items. Tia tells them she wants to cook dinner for them. Anthony smiles at his son again. Anthony says he will help Tia cook dinner. As they prepare dinner, Anthony learns where she went to school and all about her parents and why she took the job at Nortel Networks. They talk and laugh like they have known each long time. Nathan sits on the island working on his laptop, listening to them and watching them every now and then. He realizes that in an hour Tia has shared her whole life with his father. Likewise, his father has shared stories with her that Nathan didn't know. Anthony and Tia are very comfortable with each other. Nathan knows his father thinks Tia is his girlfriend, but he does not correct him that Tia only sees him as a good friend.

"Does Mother always sleep this long in the afternoons?" Nathan asks.

"Most of the time, she does. I will go now and check on her," his father says.

Heather Carter has been doing chemo-therapy for the past six months. The treatment takes a lot out of her. She has not been sleeping much, and she has had almost two days of vomiting. Anthony has hired a private nurse, who comes in each day to help him, but he has not told his children about Heather's illness. He knows Nate will take it the hardest. Nate and Heather are as close as a mother and son could be. Anthony doesn't know how he is going to break the news of his wife's illness to Nathan, Stephen, and Jackie. Heather is awake and the nurse helps her sit in an easy chair next to the bed. Anthony quickly closes the door before his wife sees him. He comes back to the kitchen and asks Tia whether he can borrow Nate for a second. They go into his small office and he breaks the news to Nate. Initially, Nate does not say anything; he just runs out of the room upset. Tia notices Nathan is upset, so she puts on her coat and grabs Nate's jacket. He is outside kicking the snow his father has cleared out of the drive way and crying. Tia doesn't know what to do. Tia helps Nathan put on his jacket, but he does not say anything and she does not ask. He tries to hide his feelings, as he always does by throwing a snowball at Tia. Tia knows him so well now that she recognizes the avoidance behavior. She doesn't really want to play. The storm has not stopped and there is more snow on the ground now. "Will you take a walk with me, Nathan, please?" Tia puts her hands out to him. He shows her where his mother has her vegetable garden during the summer and the tree house he and his brother Steven built when they were nine years old to hide from their younger sister Jackie. Tia can see Nate's vulnerability when he talks about his family: they all mean a lot to him. Perhaps that is why she is attracted to him. "My first kiss, I had my first kiss right there." His voice is full of romanticism as points out the spot to Tia. They walk back to the house and he says. "I don't want to go in." Tia asks why. "I will have to let go of your hands and I don't want to," he says. She takes his other hand and says, "Please tell me why you are so upset." He tries to change the subject by distracting her, but she will not let him. "What is wrong with your mother, Nathan?" He takes a deep breath and lets go of her hands. He has tears in his eyes. "Mother has cancer," Nathan says softly. Tia did not know what to say, other than to hug him. They draw apart and Tia tells him, "Cancer is not as dangerous as it used to be. With love and support, your mother will beat it in no time, sweetie. In the meantime," she murmurs, "you cannot run out like you did before... your father needs you and your mother cannot see you upset this much." She wipes his tears with her warm hands and hugged him again. "I'm guessing... you did not know until now?"

"My mother has been going through something horrendous, Tia. My father just kept telling me lies every time I called home. She has been essentially alone. Why would he do this to me? I want us to leave now, Tia! I don't want to be here. Everything seems... suddenly unbearably sad," he says as the tears roll down his face. "Please don't say that. We can't leave, Nathan. Daddy needs you... I can't leave."

"Tia, please!" He runs back into the house.

Anthony is in the kitchen when Tia comes inside. Tia's heart goes out to him, and as she stands by him, without even thinking she asks Anthony, "how are you coping with everything?" There is a reason why Anthony Carter likes this girl. "She has a good heart," he thinks. His eyes linger on the fire. "Not too good," he says, his voice filled with emotion.

As Nathan was getting his stuff together so he and Tia could leave, he thought of what Tia had said when he told her about his mother's prospects filled his mind with joy, but the anger for not being informed about Heather's illness gurgled like water boiling in a pot, and then, also like water boiling in a pot and he felt enraged, so he throws down the bags. Walking into the kitchen, Nathan lashes out at his father, "If you want to keep things from me, that's fine! I am going to be on the outside looking in while Mother dies." There is a silence. A long silence. Tia grows increasingly puzzled and alarmed by Nathan's rude behavior. Usually, Tia finds Nathan charming, marvelous, just the ideal boyfriend she has always wanted. Even though she denies having any feelings for Nathan, she can see his dark side also surfacing. He does not want Tia to see his sudden anger towards his father this way. He tells her so, and says, "Tia, honey, please let's go before the storm hits." Anthony knows his son's temper. He turns to Tia and says, his voice full of tenderness, "It was an honor to make your acquaintance, honey." Tia wants to stop Nathan from leaving but does not know how. She wishes that Brooke were here because she is always good at situations like this. She walks over to Nathan, and touching his face says, "I know you are upset, but we are not leaving. Sweetie, take a time out and put yourself in Daddy's shoes." Nathan can not believe he is being told what to do. He tries to contain his anger as his father watches them. "Tia, please let's not do this here," he says firmly. Tia walks away from him and says, "I need you and Daddy to set the table. You two boys should play nice now. I will go and see if Mother needs anything."

"Tia! We are going now!" Nathan demands with a touch of exasperation in his tone.

"I want you to lower your voice, Nathan, please. Stop being a prick!" Tia goes back to where he is standing.

Nathan starts to speak, but she silences him with a look. She speaks in a small voice: "Family means everything to me, Nathan. We are not leaving just because you are angry with Daddy. Baby, think about what Daddy has been going through all the time, watching the woman he loves more than life itself slip away from him."

Nathan is not listening to her. For a second, he thinks of grabbing her by force and leaving anyway, but then he restrains himself. "Tia don't make this harder for me than it is," he pleads. Tia fights back the tears as she takes his hands and says, "if we leave now, it will be a lot harder for us." She places his hands on her stomach. The baby was kicking like crazy. The baby's kicks always make Nathan think. His father watches them not knowing what was going on. Nathan got to his knees as he has been doing every morning talking to the baby. He says, " Oh... Pretty Princess, I am so sorry. I'm so afraid of losing my mother." Tia gently rubs his back. It breaks Tia's heart to see Nathan this way. "You won't baby, you won't. You don't have to be afraid because we are here with you," Tia assures him.

Nathan heart is beating a lot faster now as his father moves toward him with a conciliatory gesture, "Nate, please, son. Don't leave. Mother wanted you to know. I'm a selfish old man for keeping it all to myself." Nathan got up and hugged his father with a willingness that showed he felt more himself since he and Tia had arrived at the cottage. Tia's heart was unprepared. She has fallen head over heels in love with Nathan Carter. It was just like Sarah Williams has told her about true love. Her heart is beating more quickly than usual. She watches the father and son embrace and she begins to breathe easier. Nathan also knows that Tia has fallen in love with him from that very moment, even though he has reservations about Kevin and how Tia quickly ended their relationship. Like his father said, Tia is a keeper, just like he has always known. Thanks to Brooke, he knows more about Miss Sharp and her family, and he knows without a doubt that she is the one for him. Anthony feels the love Tia has for his son too, so he hugs Tia and says, "Angel, you are going to be all right with Nate. I thought you were going to be like Heather. His mother has spoiled him just like you do, but you also know his heart."

Tia smiles. "Is it okay if I go and check on Heather?"

"Oh, yeah, sure," replies Anthony. "Mother is awake now. Why don't we all go and introduce Angel here, Nate?"

"Sure, Dad. You go ahead. We will be right there," Nathan nods to his father. Nathan takes Tia's hand and he sits her down on his lap, his head buried between her warm breasts. She likes that and so does he. "Thank you. I'm scared of losing her, Tia," he mumbles.

"I know, sweetie. You won't. You can not let fear take you away from your loved ones, baby."

"How did you get to be so smart?" He wants so desperately to kiss her that moment, but he reminds himself that he will not because he wants to wait for her to kiss him. Although, it has not happened – yet, he is very happy to have gotten this close to her. He likes the fact that she will stand up to him. Tia is very familiar with his needs and the relationship feels comfortable. He and Nicole have been friends for a long time, but not this close. Even though they have sex every now and then, they are still not this close. He is comfortable around Tia as she is around him. He does not want to force her to endure his mother's illness. The home care nurse interrupts his thoughts which he thinks is irritating and Tia sees it. "Mrs Carter will see you now," says the nurse. Nathan nods at the nurse, and lifting up his head Nathan asks whether Tia is ready. "Nathan, sweetie. I don't want you to endure sadness. You hide behind your charm. Promise me you won't?" He smiles. "I was thinking about you being forced to endure this... Tia, I wanted you to be here so you wouldn't miss your family so much at the holidays," he stops. "I am so sorry, Tia." Tia does not let him finish and she kisses him. He is unprepared for the kiss. He has kissed many women in his time, but this kiss was nothing he has ever experienced. Her mouth fits perfectly with his, warm and relaxed. As he, too, kisses her back with soft and wet passion, he holds her in his arms and slips his tongue into her mouth slowly, while she caresses the back of his neck. He pulls away so gently from her. It was impossible for Tia to be certain of anything except the heat in his eyes. As he stops and looks into her eyes, he asks in a whisper, "What was that for? ... I mean ... I enjoyed it... but I don't like taking things that are not mine, Tia." Tia is confused, and a little embarrassed. It was incredibly exhilarating kissing him like that. "Are you mad at me for kissing you?" she asks, intrigued.

"I am a ferociously jealous man when it comes to my relationships... I don't like to get hurt by my loved ones. You saw how I tore up my Dad... I cannot be a replacement for your ex. I want it all or nothing, Tia. I don't want to date you... I want us to be a family."

"Your ego is bigger than Canada, Nathan. You are the perfect partner for Brooke," Tia spat. "Did you stop and think that I may feel like that too? And for your information, I have never kissed any man the way that I kissed you." This is not the reaction he is hoping for. Nathan knows by now when Tia gets upset she can go on and on. He gently places his lips on hers and this time with more passion than the first time. As his heart beats faster, he can feel Tia's beating just as fast, too. He kisses her gently on her forehead: "I'm a jerk. I've been wanting to kiss you like that forever, Tia."

"Well, I don't intend to encourage your bad behavior if – I can be very unforgiving when I'm hurt." She reminds him. That much he knows about her. "I will be the best man I can be and you will always set me straight when I'm wrong, that much I know. I cannot ask for more." He pulls her close and hugs her. The baby is kicking again. It is like she knows her mother is in love. Nathan doesn't want to let go of her because he knows that she is what he has been searching for all his life. It is evident to him now that he is in love with Tia. He can also feel that the way the baby kicks is different now; it warms his heart and brings happy tears to his eyes, new emotions that he did not know until the night he placed his hands on Tia's belly and felt the baby kicking. It was a lovely feeling, one that he will never forget.

Heather Carter is in her early fifties – blue eyes, dark hair with waves on the ends. She is wearing her trademark diamond earrings and her husband is planting a kiss on her when Nathan and Tia walk into the room. She sits on the sofa with a white blanket covering half of her body. "She looks radiant for a sick person," Tia thinks. The family room is filled with red poinsettias, there is a Christmas tree nicely decorated with gifts underneath. Nathan quickly releases Tia's hands and kisses his mother on her cheek. She touches his face and is still holding onto his hands when Nathan turns and looks at Tia. He reaches for Tia's hands and says, "this is Tia Sharp, Mother." Gazing at the young woman, Heather Carter says, "My, isn't she a sweetheart?" and turning to Nathan, she remarks, "Way more beautiful than your previous girlfriends, sweetie," his mother exclaims. Nathan is blushing furiously. "She can cook, too, honey," Anthony adds. Heather beams. "I am so sorry, sweetie, when did you arrive?"

"A while ago, Mother." Nathan hates seeing his mother like this. Although, for someone who has been having chemo-therapy, she has long beautiful hair. It is darker than his mother's usual hair color, he muses. "I love the color of your hair, Mother. It's different," he says. Everyone starts to laugh.

"What is so funny?" Nate asks. "It's a wig, sweetie. My nurse brought it for me today," Heather explains to Nathan. Tia asks to be excused and comes back a few minutes later with tea for Heather. "The nurse was making your tea. I sent her home. I hope you don't mind? She explained the assistance Mother will need. I think between the four of us we should manage well over the holidays, hmm?" She turns to Nathan and says, "what do you think, baby?"

"When is the wedding, sweetie?" Heather asks.

Nathan is laughing hysterically. Tia can see where Nathan gets his humor.

"Oh, Mother! I would have married her before our visit, but she won't marry me. Maybe you can tell her what a good boy I am, Mother," he winks at his mother.

"I told you, honey, she is a smart one," Anthony is laughing. He hopes Nathan will marry Tia because there is something so natural about her. "She is an angel," he thinks to himself. They all enjoy their dinner. The conversation over dinner is all about how Nathan and Tia met. After dinner, Tia insists on doing Heather's care, and Nathan and his father offer to clean up the mess in the kitchen. Nathan couldn't remember the last time he brought a girl home that his father liked as much as Tia. Tia helps Heather with her bath and rubs her feet with oil and lotion. "The chemo makes my skin very dry," she tells Tia, and privately, Heather thinks, "Tia just seems to know what I need."

Later, Heather tells her husband that he has lost his crown as the best masseur in the world. "Tia did range of motion exercises with me. I felt no pain, honey," Heather says as she is almost falling asleep while she's talking. Anthony is overwhelmed with Tia's generosity, and he is almost in tears as he says good night and thanks Tia. Nathan has been very quiet. He has left Tia and disappeared somewhere in the house. He comes back with a smile on his face. He leans against her chair, and when Tia looks up, she thinks "he's so handsome."

"You must be very tired. I have drawn a bath for you," he puts his hands out. "Come on. I will show you to your room, Miss Sharp."

"I want to talk to you about Mother," Tia pulls him close to her.

He put his forehead against hers. "We will in the morning. Right now I want to take you upstairs and give you a bath, if you will let me."

"Thank you, Nathan. I can give myself a bath. I'm worried about your state of mind of everything."

"I'm okay. I have you and Pretty Princess with me. I love you, Tia Sharp." His voice is soft and he is in tears as he speaks his love. Tia put her arms around him and says she knows.

Tia slept right after her bath. Nathan spent half the night learning about cancer. Nathan learns about what is mother is facing, and he feels a pain like he has not felt before. He is so angry that he picks up his laptop and throws it against the wall. The loud crashing sound wakes Tia and she rushes to Nathan's room. He is crying openly in his bed. She goes to him and tries to console him. She comes down to the kitchen to make a smoothie for him. She holds him the rest of the night while he sleeps in her arms. Every time she tries to let go of him he holds on tighter. It feels good holding him. She has missed that kind of closeness in a relationship. The realization that she has fallen in love with Nathan has hit her hard. She doesn't want him going back to Toronto. She didn't know how to tell him just how nice it has been spending their weekends together since Thanksgiving, but she wants more than a weekend relationship with Nathan, though not a married relationship. She kisses him softly and closes her eyes to sleep.

Chapter 28

It is Christmas Eve in England already, cold and dry. Sarah Williams has decided to enjoy the holidays this year. After seventeen years of ignoring Christmas, her house is nicely decorated for the season inside and out. She has invited the Sharp's and their girls as well as Jason Grey and his parents to celebrate. The past few months she has been very close to her daughter and to Kate, especially now that Tia lives in Canada. Kate has been staying at the house for the last three days helping Sarah put everything together. She has been a little out of touch, but she has gifts under the big tree in her living room for all her guests. They all sat down to eat. Jason and Brooke are the last guests to arrive. Right after dinner, Brooke calls Nathan. "It's lunch in Canada now," she says to Kate. "Hello beautiful," says the voice on the other end with a vaguely American accent. Brooke puts on the speaker phone. "Happy holidays, beautiful," he adds.

"Merry Christmas, my darling. How are you, Nathan?" Brooke asks.

"I'm good. How is Jason?"

"Merry Christmas, Nathan. How is Tia?" Jason asks.

"I will get her for you, one second. Thanks man, I took your advice about the matter we discussed last month. Tia is with my parents in the family room." Bobby looks at Naana and asks, "Who is Nathan? I thought the boy's name was Kevin?" He is bewildered. Naana gently squeezes her husband's hand. Nathan Carter flew to New York City a month ago when Jason and Brooke told him that Naana Konadu-Sharp would be in NYC for business. He made his intentions about Tia and the baby clear to Tia's mother, but Naana Konadu-Sharp didn't really give him much of a thought as she thought kids these days fall in love as quickly as they fall out of love. He has called and left messages for her. Soon after, she called Tia and told her that her new boyfriend was nuts. He called again this morning to ask for Tia's hand in marriage, so Tia's mother hung up on him. "Baby, I have your sister on the phone." Nathan hands the phone to Tia.

"Happy holidays, sweetie," Tia says. They all thought she sounded so different on the phone, but Bobby's and Naana's faces light up when they hear their daughter's voice. "Merry Christmas, Tia!" everyone says at once. Tia is in tears and can not respond because she misses them so much. She speaks to everyone and gives the phone back to Nathan. Afterward, he is on the phone for a long time with Brooke. Then he speaks to Tia's parents in private for a very long time. He does not stop thinking about his mother and Tia. He knows for sure that he will not be going back to Toronto when the holidays are over. He has sent an email to his partners in Toronto about his mother's condition and has asked Nicole to take over his up-coming hearing which she is only too happy to do. He has no idea what to do next.

"I adore you, Mr. Carter. You're are full of surprises." Tia has been thinking about the whole Carter family. Nathan has been distant the whole day, but right now he is standing by the fireplace looking so intense he could melt an iceberg.

"I hate seeing you unhappy, Nathan. Please talk to me," Tia says. She looks at him with concern. He sits down on a nearby chair and gently pulls Tia into his lap. Nathan Carter has always protected his heart when it comes to relationships. With Tia, she sees through him, and it is difficult to hide part of himself from her. She knows things before he tells her. "Mother is going to be okay, Nathan. I am more worried about you."

"I'm fine. I know mother is going to be okay."

"Then what has rattled your cage all day, Nathan? Please talk to me."

"It's you, Ms Sharp!" He brushes her hair away from her face and smiles. "You know how to take my pain away. I wonder how?"

"You wonder how, what?"

"It's Christmas Eve in two hours. I had planned to ask you on the most romantic date ever."

"I thought I was on a romantic date already?" Tia raises her eye brows and smiles. "What more can a girl ask for? You made me so happy calling Brooke. I talked with everyone and didn't feel home sick, Nathan. I want to see you happy just like you made me," she murmurs. Nathan's heart melts when he sees her happy. "I'm very happy. After all these months, I finally got to kiss you, Tia. It was a lot sexier than in my dreams. You see, in my dreams our first kiss was more like this." He kisses her gently on the lips. Tia smiles. He is so sexy without even trying to be. She found herself feeling things she has not felt before. She stands and brushes her hair over one shoulder. "I want you to tell me how you feel about..." she pauses. "Please, tell me how you feel about, mother's illness?"

"I don't want to leave and go back to Toronto. I wasn't going to go back anyway, Tia, mainly because I don't want to leave you and the baby." He puts his head on her lap and closes his eyes. Tia searches her mind trying to figure out what to say to him. She doesn't want him to go back to Toronto either, but she has to be realistic. She has no doubt about how she feels about him, but she is afraid of getting hurt. Tia takes his hand and kisses the back of it. "Can I make a suggestion? Nathan... um..." Nathan opens his eyes and smiles. "Why don't you sit down and talk to Daddy about Mother's condition? This way you can... um... decide what is best."

"I will, but it will not make any difference. I want be to close to home. I have already made arrangements for office space and a home nearby here. After the Thanksgiving weekend I decided to move here. I've been meaning to discuss it with you. I enjoy our weekends together, Tia. I just don't think... Well, I want more... I want to wake up holding you... I'm in love with you... and also with Pretty Princess. Please tell me what you want. Tia, please, even if it's not the same as me. Please?" Nathan is panting even though he is not running. He feels like he has been waiting for Tia's response for a long time. "I want you to stay if you can. I enjoy our weekends together, too. Having you living in the same town will be terrific," Tia says softly. Nathan hugs her and kisses her on the forehead. He says something but Tia isn't sure what it is. Anthony comes in before Tia can ask what Nathan means. Tia tells them she is going to spend some time with Heather before she sleeps. It is evident that Nathan is still upset. His father puts his arms around him and asks what is wrong.

"I need to know about mother's condition and what I can do. Please, don't lie to me, Dad," he says. "I have spent half of the night worried out of my mind. Tia is almost five-months pregnant. I cannot have her worried like this, too, Dad." Nathan doesn't realize that he has just told his father that Tia is pregnant. His father's face lights up and he hugs his son, but the reaction is not what Nathan is hoping for. Anthony quickly drags Nathan into the family room where Tia is reading to Heather. "Oh honey," he says to his wife. "I told you that Christmas is a miracle day. We are going to be grandparents!" Heather Carter is so happy. She asks who is having the baby. Her husband replies, "Nathan and Tia are going to have a baby."

"What are you talking about, Dad?" Nathan asks.

"You, the baby, Tia being almost five months pregnant?" his father says as he hugs Tia. He turns to Nathan and says, "That is why you were on your knees yesterday when you were upset! You were talking to your baby! This is wonderful news, Nate." Anthony looks so happy. Nathan puts both his hands on his head as he takes one step forward towards Tia. He can see Tia turning red with embarrassment. He gropes for something intelligent to say. He tries to come up with a smart, sophisticated way to break the news that the baby is not his, but his brain refuses to engage. "Um..." is all Tia can manage, then she gasps, "I think there is a misunderstanding here." Nathan asks his parents to excuse them. Something in Nathan's expression intrigues his parents. Every nerve in Tia's body is shimmering with tension, unlike anything she had ever experienced before. Nathan puts his hands on her shoulders. He flexes his fingers, tightening his grip to see if she will try to run away. He draws her slowly toward him. He does not want to make a complete fool out of himself.

"I told father about... um... Pretty Princess, and he just... um..." He stopped and sighed.

"Daddy thought it was yours and mine," she finished his sentence for him. Nathan is losing his grip on her. "I will go and tell them the truth. I need to know that you are... okay? I cannot have you stressed, Tia." He spoke very softly.

Tia was quiet as Nathan sat her down and held her hands. "I don't like to lie to people that I love, just like you, Nathan. This may sound crazy, but I do love your parents. I don't like my loved ones hurt or getting hurt. This will hurt them. I have to tell the truth about the baby. Daddy knows about my relationship with Kevin anyway," she says.

"Do you love me, too?" he asked in a child-like, tiny, muffled whisper.

"I do Nathan. How could I not? I just don't want to get hurt, and most of all, I cannot hurt you. I have shared more with you than I have shared with any guy that I have dated in the past and I'm not even dating you, in a way. You have been my rock. Today I saw a man with whom I may have fallen in love, even though I wasn't impressed with how rude you were to Daddy yesterday. If Daddy had not been standing there, I would have probably hit you. Nathan, I have never felt this way about any guy. I don't think I'm ready for what you want."

Nathan did not let her finish. His response was immediate and electric. Excitement crashed through him. He was literally shaking with joy and Tia saw that. He wrapped his arms around her neck and put his forehead against hers. "I don't want to date you. I don't want to be anything like the men in your past," he said. Tia got up and walked away from him. "Tia, I'm in love with you, and I want us all – Pretty Princess and you – to be a family. When I met with your mother in New York City six weeks ago with my brother Steven, I told her how I felt about you and the baby. She and Steven thought I was nuts since you and I were not even dating. She told me good luck and told me to get out of her hotel suite before she had me arrested." Nathan said, chuckling at the memory.

Tia turned and faced him. She could just see her mother getting the best of Nathan Carter, and she was laughing, "I know you're all about romance, but let's be serious here."

"I am, Tia... Tia, I'd rather lose you now than... later... I will not be returning to Toronto. I called a realtor to find us a home near here in Orleans. He has sent me information about five homes by email. I was trying to find out more about mother's condition when I got pissed off at Dad and let it slip about the baby. Tia, this is what I want for us. You cannot think about it... I need to know right now... What is it you want? I know you said you want me to stay close by... I want us to live as man and wife. I can't be just your friend," he said.

"I want to be with you, Nathan, but marriage and an instant family is a huge commitment, sweetie. I don't want you to feel I am – we are – a burden to you. I have come to love you in the last few months. The past six weeks that we have been living together... I didn't want it to end ... but not like this. Marriage means a lot to me, probably more than most people my age. You want to be near your mother. There is no reason why we have to get married and buy a house. You can buy a house or rent a condo and still be near your mother as well as near me without us getting married. We've been playing house all this time, but getting married is... huge." Nathan was very quiet as he listened to her.

"There is also the financial aspect of it. I have money saved up, but not enough for a down payment on a property in Orleans, so buying a house right away is probably not a good idea. We need to rethink things," she said thickly.

"Probably not buy a house? Tia, I can not be apart from you and the baby. Can't you see that ? ... Probably not?"

"But I can't seem to think of a better plan." She could hardly catch her breath, but breathing was the last thing on her mind, she was so caught up in this moment. "You can't think of a better plan?" Nathan said with a smile. "Tell me you want this, Tia!"

"I want you, all of this, but marriage is not a child's play. I can not get a divorce like other people do. What I have with you is wonderful."

Nathan assured her that he doesn't plan to get a divorce, or be a part-time father to a child that he feels is his. "I can't be without you and Pretty Princess. Tia, you have been with me since your very first day in Canada. I told your mother today that we kissed." Tia hit him on the head. "You gonna take an ad when we make love and tell the whole world, too? What is wrong with you, Nathan? You're too much!" Nathan said that he wasn't thinking about making love, at least not until the Doctor said they could make love. "What do you mean?" Tia asked incredulously.

"Ha! I meant us making love – while you're pregnant – Tia, what did you think I meant?"

"Are you some kind of a freak, Nathan?" Tia asks with one eye open.

"What are you talking about?" he grins. "Of course, I'm a freak! Why else do you think I made a point of telling your mother that we kissed today? I also asked your father's permission to marry you, or I'm going to keep calling him and your mother until they agree. And of course, I'm gonna take an ad when we make love!" He winks and kisses her.

Tia jumps up, "I am going to find out about mother's condition, Sweetie, before I kill you!" Frustrated with not being able to get her own way, Tia strides across the room to talk to Heather and Anthony. Before Nathan can respond, she is in the family room talking to his parents. He sits down in the nearest chair and listens to what his father has to say about his mother's condition.

"Did she say she would marry me?" He asks himself. "Hey! Tia, did you just agree to marry me?" he wonders out loud. They are all looking at her. She stands up, walks over to Nathan and kisses him on the forehead. His mother and father are still holding their hearts in their hands as Tia winks at them. "No, sweetie. I did not agree to marry you."

"I love you Tia, but I will not date you." His father and mother both chuckle and begin to smile at their son. "Well! Mother don't you think a man should propose in a fashionable, romantic manner before a girl can say…yes or no?" Tia asks. Nathan's parents are both laughing and Nathan is not too pleased with Tia.

"See, honey? I told you. Angel can handle Nate," his father said with admiration. "She will soon get him out of his spoiled ways. You will see, honey."

"We are thinking of buying a home in Orleans," Tia informs them. "That is if the bank gives us a mortgage. Apparently Nathan doesn't believe in living together before marriage." His parents looked at him very proudly. "Wow!" his mother said with a smile. Nathan has not told Tia that he has money. "Baby...um."

"Okay, what lies have you told me... um baby... Nathan Carter? Let's hear it!" Tia demands.

"Um...you know? When I said I was broke, I was ...um... only joking."

"You mean you lied! Just to get close to me, Nathan, huh?"

Anthony and Heather looked at each other with worried expressions.

"No, baby, I didn't lie. Well, not exactly," he pauses. Tia waits expectantly. "Um... well, as a matter of fact, well, yes, I did."

"Oh... um baby... guess what? I knew you lied, Nathan Carter. Marriage is about honesty, respect and commitment. If you think for once that I will put up with lies from you and with your disobedience with Daddy, then you are sadly mistaken, babe!" She hit him on the head and sat down by his mother, crossing her legs. "You can't bring your job home. You may not know this, but every time you tell lies, I know it before you open your mouth. I don't plan to get a divorce either!" Anthony said, "Congratulations, son! I could not have picked Angel for you myself." Nathan's father and mother chuckled. "Thanks a lot, Dad!" Nathan says. "I see you two are on her side now, ha! As you all can see I am a man who doesn't wear the pants in this relationship. What was I supposed to do? She would not talk to me until I told her that I didn't have money. One would think having money is a bad thing in Tia's world." He spat at them.

"That's is a good argument, sweetie, in court, but not in a lifetime relationship. You had plenty of time to tell Tia the truth. Let it be a lesson to you," his mother says wisely. "Yes, Mother," Nathan says softly. Tia and his parents begin laughing again. His father shakes Nathan's hands. "That's how marriage is, son. So when is the big day?" they asked.

"Next year." Tia said.

"No, no, no! You can't have your way all the time. We have discussed this, Tia, please."

"No, we didn't."

"Tia, baby, can we discuss this in private?"

"Why? So you can tell more lies? We are family. There is no need to be overly private. We will get married next year."

"Fine! I promised my mother that I," he paused and without warning picked up Tia and said, "Please, excuse me. It looks like of all the women in the world, I had to fall in love with the most stubborn one!"

His mother's face lights up. Nathan turns and says, "Mother, we are getting married before my daughter is born! We are getting married next week, so please start planning a wedding for us, Mother."

"Tony, sweetie, did you hear that?" Heather said excitedly. "Nathan is going to have a baby girl!"

Heather asks Anthony to pass her the phone even though it was already evening – and Christmas Eve, too – and too late in the day to call a caterer. Tia is still laughing as Nathan kicks open the bedroom door and places her gently on the bed. He kisses her on the cheek and says, " I promised my mother that we are getting married before Pretty Princess is born. Tia, you can overrule any decision that we make as man and wife over the next sixty years, but not this one! We are getting married soon!"

"You are so sexy!" Nathan looks behind himself and asks, "Who is so sexy?"

"You are! I wanna thank you for a wonderful Christmas Eve, Nathan." Nathan smiles as she plants a kiss on his full lips before she pulls away from him gasping. She smiles at him. Nathan thinks she is an incredible woman, and he can't believe she has agreed to be his wife. Nathan gently kisses Tia goodnight on the cheek and leaves the room.

Chapter 29

About midnight, Nathan was in the living room putting wood on the fire when he saw her, looking so beautiful with her hair up. "You can't sleep either, eh?" He sits next to her on the sofa and runs his hands through her hair. He wants so badly to make love to her by the fire. He rests his head on her stomach, slips his hands under her bathrobe and gently rubs her belly as the baby kicks. "I'll be going to Ottawa in the morning. Would you like to come?" Tia suggests that he take his father with him, so the two of them can spend time together. That is not what Nathan has in mind. He wants to spend the day alone with Tia, away from his parents so that they can do something romantic.

Tia assures him that they will have a lifetime of being alone together. "I want to be home alone with Mother so we can gossip about you. She can tell me how to spoil you. Please, sweetie? I want Daddy to take his mind off Mother. Do something fun with him for me." Nathan loves how Tia puts everyone's need before her own. He kisses her fully on the lips. Tia has known desire in the past, but never like this. She could feel herself growing much more in love with him and told him so. It pleases him to hear it. He slides his warm palm up the inside of her bare legs until he touches her already dampened panties.

"We shouldn't until we are married," he says softly.

"I want to wake up in your arms. Nathan, it's been so long. I can't wait until we are married," Tia replies. Nathan knows what she wants.

"That is one thing I cannot give you right now, Tia. We're gonna have to wait until we are married. We have to check with the doctor first before we can make love. I don't want the baby to get hurt," he insists. Tia asks whether she turns him on. He smiles and lifts her into his arms. Nathan carries Tia up the stairs, down the hall, into his room and lays her down on his bed. He kisses her on the nose and says, "Ever since I met you, I have wanted you and only you. Of course, you turn me on!" He places her hands on the crotch of his trousers. Underneath the fine wool fabric, he is so hard. Tia begins to relax. As she caresses his hard-on, Nathan emits a husky groan and wrenches himself away from her, getting to his feet. She watches him strip off his shirt, trousers and boxers and race to the bathroom where he douses himself under the cold shower. When he steps out of the shower, Tia is standing there with a towel which she throws at him and leaves. For spite, she locks him out of the room. Nathan threatens to break the door down if she doesn't let him in. Not wanting to upset the Carters, she opens the door.

"Damn it, Tia! We have discussed this. We agreed to wait until we are married."

"No!" she shouts. "You agreed to wait. I did not agree to anything of the sort," she spat at him.

"The whole country can hear you, Tia. Please lower your voice," he begs her. He briefly presses his hands against her belly, but she pushes away his hands. He gets into bed next to her and reluctantly pulls himself close to her. He rolls her on top of him, but she does not respond to his attention. He whispers in her ear... incredibly sexy things. No man has ever talked to her in such a sexy, intimate way like that. She feels him fumbling with her night gown. He gets it off her body, and next her bra vanishes. His palm rasps lightly over her nipple. She drags her nails along his back as she shivers with anticipation. She puts her mouth very close to his, fierce and demanding. With a tiny, muffled moan, she wraps her arms around his neck and clings to him. He kisses her and the more he kisses her the more she wants him.

Tia is breathless, the excitement crashing through her like thunder. She has never before known this kind of desire. Nathan massages her breasts, and he enjoys pinching and sucking the nipples. He rips off her panties and explores her clitoris with his tongue, stimulating her G-spot. Finding her deliciously wet, Nathan slides his fingers inside her vagina. Nathan himself is one very hot and highly aroused man. He is so hard and she is so wet that his penis easily parts her vaginal lips as he sits her on top of him. Tia tickles his balls, strokes his thighs. As she slides up and down his cock, she pleasures herself by massaging her breasts and rubbing her clitoris. She also intensifies his response by lightly pressing the base of his penis. Tia feels wanted, needed, sexy, and desirable. She can't help crying despite the high of several orgasms. Nathan stops. Whispering tearfully, he says, "I'm sorry I hurt you. That's why I wanted us to wait until... we see a Doctor, honey, but you will not listen to me." Tia bubbles up with laughter and starts kissing Nathan's face. As he slides into her, his belly rubs against hers, adding to the excitement. "I do not understand women," he says with exasperation. "Are you okay? ... did you come?" She nods and smiles. He kisses her nose, unable to think clearly and certain she has awakened something within him. He gasps with a sudden realization, "If the doctor says we can't make love, please don't be mad at me," he says softly. "We can make love, Nathan. There is no risk to the baby. I read about it in my pregnancy book," she re-assures him.

"I still want to make sure the baby is going to be okay, Tia. Please don't frighten me. I want to make love to you every day, every chance that we get… but you cannot have your way every time, honey. You gonna have to meet me halfway sometimes." Tia stopped his mouth with kisses and they made love again.

And so, in such fashion, Tia and Nathan celebrated Christmas, their flowering love, and their promise to marry throughout the night until they slept the sleep of the sated like spoons in a drawer. Nathan cradled Tia in his arms; Tia unconsciously rubbed her belly; and the baby kicked contentedly.

In the morning, Nathan wakes with a huge hard-on. Tia is not in bed, so he walks to the bathroom where she is about to get under the shower. She says, "good morning, Sweetie." Nathan picks her up and sits her on the vanity top. Roughly raising her legs and parting her thighs, Nathan thrusts his rock-hard penis into her. It was the wildest, roughest sex ever, and she loved it. Tia likes that Nathan knows when to be naughty. Under the shower she surprises him by holding his hands against the shower wall and taking him in her mouth, teasing his cock into an encore. Laughing, Tia dashes into the bedroom, still damp from the shower.

He makes love to her on the bedroom floor, taking her from behind. Afterward, as they lay panting on the floor, Nathan very gently rolls his tongue around Tia's, as she pulls his tongue deep into her mouth. Tia gave him a playful approval. Nathan Carter has slept with all kinds of women, but Tia Sharp is, by far, the sexiest of them all and she is one naughty girl in the bedroom. And out of bed, he can't believe that she is real. The way she kisses with her tongue is incredible. He loves making love to her, and the last thing he wants to do is let go of her. They are both breathless. She gasps and smiles, "How are you feeling?" He responds by sliding his tongue in her mouth before they draw apart. They press their foreheads together as they catch their breath. Tia realizes that her relationship with Nathan has not only changed, but also she has also begun to imagine herself with him. Even so, Tia is cautious: every time something wonderful happens to her, something is wrong with the relationship. Maybe she's dreaming, and this past night has all been a spark of imagination. Again, she feels his hardness inside her, the softness of the carpet against her back and she closes her eyes and caresses his back as she wraps her legs around his waist, tilting her pelvis to meet his urgency. Their hearts beat faster as Nathan thrusts deeply into Tia's wetness. He, too, can't believe that he has been making to love to Tia finally after all this time. It is more than he has imagined and everything about their sex games exceeds his expectations.

On their way downstairs, he pulls her against the wall and kisses behind her ears and whispers, "I loved making to you… you're so versatile… Mm… you excite me. I want to take you back to bed."

"Oh, no, baby. We're not making love until we're married…. We are not making love until we see the doctor," she teases. He smiles slightly. "You are in so much trouble later, Miss Sharp!"

Kate's flight arrived on time. When she came out of the baggage claim area, she saw Nathan standing there talking to an older black man. When Nathan saw Kate, he touched his father's shoulder and said, "there she is." He quickly went and took her luggage, hugging and kissing her in greeting. "This is my father Anthony Carter. Dad, this is Kate Lee." Nathan lead the way to the car in the parking lot and on the drive home, he explained that Tia was in the country with his mother.

"She has no idea of the surprise I have for her!" Nathan exclaims enthusiastically.

"Has Tia agreed to marry you yet?" Kate inquires.

"Oh, yes! But she has no idea I'm planning the wedding for New Year's Eve!" he adds with a chuckle. "My mom is trying to find out Tia's idea of a dream wedding so I can make it all happen." Nathan pauses to negotiate his way through an intersection. "I will take you to the apartment to freshen up and then we can go pick up the tuxedos. The caterer already has the menu list that Mrs Sharp sent me. The spa is booked and a deposit paid for fifteen people. I have the ring," he handed Kate a small velvet box. "Well, here we are: Tia's apartment!"

Kate loves Tia's apartment, so different from those she has seen in England. The apartment reveals Tia's good taste in every room. The phone rings: it is Brooke calling to make sure Kate has arrived safely. Nathan passes the phone over to Kate. He goes and stands by the window with his father, watching Kate chat on the phone with Brooke. He taps his father's shoulder to get his attention. Last night he informed his parents that the baby Tia is carrying is not his. In fact, he has known her less than five months. His parents listen. Back in the present moment, Nathan tells his father, "I fell in love with her the moment I laid my eyes on her, Dad." There is a great emotion in his voice when he talks about her that his parents have never witnessed before. "She and the baby mean to me like you all do. I cannot imagine my life without them. I just can't. She doesn't even know – oh, there's lots she doesn't know – she thinks I'm a poor lawyer starting out. She pays when we go shopping and she takes very good care of me. She doesn't put up with my..." His father finished his sentence for him, "she doesn't put with your spoiled ways." He and his mother both laughed. "I kissed her for the first time yesterday. I hope you are not disappointed, Dad." Anthony turns to his son, "I am so proud of the man you have become. Tia is a sweetheart, and she has suddenly brought out the romantic side of you. You need that in a marriage. Communication is everything, even when you screw up, son." Kate overhears Anthony's advice for his son, and she thinks about Jaden.

She has shut him out and refused to talk to him even though she still loves him very much.

Tia is spending the day with Heather Carter. Heather is feeling rather well today by the time Tia and Nathan come down for breakfast. She is in the kitchen in her husband's arms. It is so sweet the way they are with one another. Heather has a different wig on today that makes her look perky. They order out lunch and sit together by the fire in the family room. A girl from a spa comes and does her nails and gives her a massage after lunch. Heather tells the girl that she is going to be a grandmother soon and introduces Tia. "Tia has a good hands, too, honey," she says. She describes how she and Anthony met in the Virgin Islands. "Almost forty years ago, I was on vacation with my parents. Tony had just returned from the U.S. where he was studying at the time. He had the biggest Afro I've ever seen! Some kids were playing beach volley ball, and they needed two girls, so he came and asked my parents if my sister and I could join their team. My father was a doctor and was reading a medical journal that caught Tony's attention. He forgot about the game and spent the whole afternoon talking medicine with my father. He invited us all to his family barbecue that same evening. His father was in politics and they owned a big part of the island. Father thought he was a fine young man, and he never stopped talking about him when we returned to Canada.

"They kept in touch and Tony landed a job in Toronto as an intern at the Children's Hospital. He liked to spend most of his weekends with mother and father at the cottage. They loved him and he loved them. I won a scholarship to UCLA, so I was away studying while this relationship was developing. When I came home for Thanksgiving weekend, Tony was already there and had prepared the whole Thanksgiving meal by the time mother woke up. All that was left to do was to put the meal in the oven. I was very impressed. He would not date me because he thought of me as a little sister. Even father told him once that I had had a crush on him since we met, but he still wouldn't date me. Two years went by and I returned to Ottawa University by that time. He was a resident at the Ottawa Children's Hospital. We did not see much of each other until one day at a benefit event, a familiar voice asked if I wanted to dance. We saw each other every day for seven months. I said to myself, Heather, he is not going to kiss you, so honey, you are going to plant one on him!" Tia was laughing because that was exactly what she did to Nathan. She told Heather about her experience. Heather replied, "Well, the kiss must have worked: we've been married almost thirty-three years." Tia thought it was a wonderful love story.

Love story aside, Heather is more interested in what kind of a wedding Tia wants. Tia has not thought about getting married. She would love to get married to someone like Nathan, but she doesn't want to end up divorced a few years down the road. Tia says, "marriage for me is for better or worse like my parents, or like you and Daddy. These days, young people, we walk away from relationships so easily. I don't want that for me or Nathan, you know, Mother? I feel Nathan and I should wait and get to know each other a lot more. An instant family is just too much pressure for anyone. Nathan is a lot like me, very stubborn and determined." Heather listens and watches her. "You have fallen in love with my son, but you see something in him that scares you," Heather observes.

That is exactly how Tia feels. She smiles. She thinks for a moment. "I see the good in Nathan, even though he tries to hide it deep within himself. I often tell him to trust himself and let people see who he is. He is very romantic, too. Yes! I have fallen in love, not just with Nathan but also with you, too." Tia is almost in tears. "A wedding for me will be a family affair. You know? With my husband's family and mine, maybe a few close friends just enjoying the whole day. A low key event," says Tia. Heather can't help asking, "Have you and Nathan set a date yet?"

Tia laughs, "Nathan wants us to be married before the baby comes. I don't mind waiting until this time next year so all my family can be a part of it, but Nathan will not hear of it. You know? After Thanksgiving, he flew to New York with Steven to meet my mom. He told her then that he plans to marry me and be the baby's father. Mother threw him out, of course, but he has been calling her non-stop telling her how much he loves me and the baby and he just won't leave her alone." Tia chuckles. "He wants to wait until we are married before we make love. He can be an old funny daddy sometimes."

Astonished, Heather comments, "My son wants to wait until he is married to sleep with you? Wow! You have changed him, Tia!"

"Nathan is a gentleman. You have done a wonderful job raising him. He loves with his whole heart, a little spoiled, but I can handle him. I do adore him." Just then the door opened and he was standing there looking so sexy.

"You too lovely ladies still gossiping about how handsome I am? I see!" he said, so full of himself. He is carrying a lot of shopping bags. Tia asks, "Did you get the stuff I need from the Body Shop?" Laughing, teasing, Nathan replies, "Oh, yes! Daddy bought the whole shop for his, Angel."

"Oh... no!" Tia exclaims. "You shouldn't have let him."

"I'm not talking about father. I am talking about this Daddy," he points to himself. Tia goes and kisses him. Then she hits him when she sees Kate standing there. "Oh, Mr. Carter! I do love you big, Daddy," she says. Nathan bends to kiss his mother, and he says playfully "she called me, Big Daddy." His mother is so pleased. Originally, Heather thought her son was rushing in to a marriage with a girl he hardly knew, and even though she adores Tia, she is concerned about the huge responsibilities her son has assumed. Nathan notices his mother's face light up, and she looks at him like she used to whenever he brought home an 'A' from school. "Okay, Mother. I have not brought an 'A' from school. What is it? Are you okay?" Nathan says with concern. "She loves you, sweetie," Heather whispers. "She really is the one." Heather Carter has always been the romantic kind. "I know, Mother. She called me Big Daddy," he repeats, savoring the moniker. "Big Daddy."

Like Tia, Kate loves the Carter's home. She couldn't believe how cold it is in Canada and how much snow piles up. "When did you arrive," Tia asks and Kate replies, "This morning."

"Where have you been all this time?" Tia wants to know.

"Nathan and his father had things to do, so I accompanied them," Kate admits. She can not wait to see Tia's face when she finds out that in four days everyone is going to be here for her wedding.

"I have missed you," Tia says as she hugs Kate. This is the longest time the two girls have been apart since they were six years old. It has felt like forever to them. She introduces Kate to Heather. Heather tells Nate to take Kate's luggage upstairs and asks her husband to make hot chocolate, but the girls say they will do that. Heather has a dazed expression. Anthony can see that she is still so beautiful. He can not believe how much he still loves her after all this time. He thanks God that the cancer is in remission as it has been very difficult over the past year seeing his Heather enduring so much pain. In private moments, he has broken down and cried many times, and he does his best to keep his grief away from his children. He knows they will not forgive him, but he has promised her not to let the children see her in pain and has always kept his promise. He bends to kiss her on the cheek, and she smiles as she takes his hands.

She shivers again, and then she seems to come back to herself. He wonders where she has been. "She is in love with him, Tony," she murmurs. "They are going to be alright." They both gaze into the kitchen and they both think, "Tia is the perfect girl for Nathan." Understandably, they are worried about the baby's natural father. Nate has assured them that he will not be a problem or come between them. Still... babies have a way of bringing couples together.

After supper, Kate and Tia take a long walk around the Carter's cottage. When they return Nathan's parents have gone to bed. Nathan is on his cell phone and his laptop at same time. He stops his work to say good night to the girls, but he won't take Tia away from Kate. Upstairs in Tia's room, Kate takes a bath and updates Tia on everything that has been going on with Jaden. Tia advises Kate to sit and talk to him and if she can't forgive him then that is okay. Kate wants to ask about Kevin, but she does not. Instead, she says, "I like Nathan. He seems nice and he loves you. I'm very happy for you."

"I will be going to town with him in the morning, would you like to come?" Tia asks. Kate knows what she will be doing with Nathan. She has seen the houses today with him and his father. Kate replies, "Why don't you two go and do your stuff? I will spend the day with his parents and answer some emails." Soon afterward, Kate slept, so Tia goes downstairs where she finds Nathan still on the phone and computer. She makes him a smoothie and a tea for herself. She wants to leave him alone, but he takes her hands and says, "Come to daddy and tell him about your day. My Ottawa office will be finalized by

Monday, but I want to show you something tonight," he says. Tia notices that Nathan seems very quiet. He puts on his jacket and helps Tia with her coat. She insists that he tell her where they are going. He says, "I'm taking you out for dessert! Stop worrying! You'll love it." A few minutes later, he pulls up in front of a house and pushes a remote control device so that the garage door opens and he drives in. He opens the connecting door for Tia and they enter in the house. Surprisingly, Nicole is there. Tia did not know she lived in Orleans. "I thought Nicole and Ian lived in Toronto?" Tia asks.

"They do, baby. I needed her here today."

"I was about to leave, what took you too so long? I hope everything is to your liking. I'd love to stay, but I've got to run. I'll see you at the office in the afternoon, Nate. Happy holidays, Tia! Ian sends his love," she adds. Since the wedding in Toronto, Ian and Tia have become good friends. Nathan follows Nicole to the door and Tia is left alone in the house. It is a beautiful house, of the type that would appeal to Sarah Williams, but much bigger, and the kitchen is a lot bigger, too. There is no furniture in the house that Tia could see. Nathan returns holding some papers Nicole has given him. "Do you like the house, Tia?" Tia smiles. Nathan couldn't read her expression, so he took her hand and showed her the main floor. Tia pulls him towards her and asks "Why was Nicole here waiting for us at this time of night?" Evasively, Nathan says, "I just needed her to do something for me."

Suspicious, Tia asks, "Does Nicole always leave her husband and run around doing errands for you in the middle of the night?"

"We are business partners, Tia. Ian knows how his wife works. She likes to be hands-on with everything," Nathan explains.

Tia walks down to the end of the house and Nathan follows her, adding, "Nicole does real estate law, one of the areas of law that I don't do." He senses that Tia wants answers. He also wants everything to be right. So far, everything seems to be going the way he wants. He shows Tia the main floor of the house. They couldn't explore the back yard because the snow has covered the deck. Tia notices candle lights on the stairs. "Before I show you upstairs," he says, taking a ring box out of his pants pocket and getting down on one knee. Tia thought he was going to do his talking to the baby thing that he does all the time, so she did not pay much attention, she was looking at the beautiful ceiling. When she finally looked down, the diamond sparkled and it was huge. Her whole body began to shake, her knees felt weak, and she was in tears when Nathan finally said, "Miss Tia Sharp!" His voice was soft. Tia could see his hands shaking. He was not himself, spoiled with big ego. He looked like a little boy unwrapping a birthday gift, not knowing the content in the box. "Will you please do me the honor of being my wife?" He was so nervous he kept talking as Tia bent to kiss him. "I don't want a kiss, Tia," he says. "I want you to say you will be my wife and you will marry me on New Year's Eve. I have all your family arriving in two days." He was crying, overwhelmed with emotion. Tia kissed him again. Suddenly, Nathan was angry. Feeling a fool, he stood and said, "Tia, what is it going to be before I walk out of this house?" Tia was so overwhelmed by Nathan's proposal that she suddenly realized she has not given him a response. She took a step back from him. Nathan turned and was heading for the front door, tears running down his cheeks.

She said, "You know? ... For a very smart man and a lawyer ....you are so stupid sometimes." He was enraged. How dare she make such fool of him! He is stupid! He stopped and took a deep breath, turned and looked at her. He looked in shock. Tia has the ring on her finger and is waving her hands in the air. Nathan still does not know what she means.

"Tia, please," he said. "I cannot handle this emotional roller coaster. I need to know where I stand right now!" he demands. Tia is still holding her hands in the air, this time smiling. Nathan leans against the wall and closed his eyes. He doesn't like losing at anything. He is boiling with anger and frustration. He feels her hands around him and he flinches, "Please don't touch me," he says. He feels an exquisite restraint. Tia realizes that she has to put him out of his misery. "I will be your wife. I will marry you on New Year's Eve," she says. Her hands are caressing the back of his neck. Still leaning against the wall, Nathan bites his lips as he hears the words he been waiting for. His body feels like thunder storm is hitting him. He is still shaking when he turns to face Tia. She looks more beautiful than she has ever looked. He raises his hands to touch her face, but drops them. "What did you just say?" Tia kisses him on the eyelids and wipes the tears off his face. He likes that. "I want very much to be your wife, your lover, and the mother of your children." He pauses, then whispers, "The mother of my children?" She whispers in his ears "yes," and she kisses him behind the ears. He picks her up and takes her up the stairs, kicking a door open. There are candle lights everywhere in the master bedroom. He gently lays her on the bed, and brushing her hair off her face, he lays beside her. "I love you so much, and whatever it is that your heart desires is what I want and will always want, Tia." She reaches into his pants and discovers he is as hard as a rock. He immediately got out of bed and was himself again. Firmly, he says, "No! Not that! For the love of God, Tia, you almost gave me a heart attack a while ago. I forgave you, of course, because you've made me the happiest man alive."

"You forgave me?" Tia asked. She sits up in the bed and straightens herself. "You have been lying to me after we have agreed that is not what we both want or need in our life." She screams, "… and you and your red-haired, hot girlfriend…," she stops, shocked she has expressed what her heart has always known. Nathan's heart rate accelerates as soon as Tia refers to Nicole as his girlfriend.

"Listen: Ian may not know, or may choose not to want to know or care, but I do! Are you sleeping with Nicole?"

"Oh… no, no! She is not my girlfriend! I have not laid a finger on her since college, Tia."

Tia's jaw drops. As she hears those words, it was like she was back in Brooke's apartment with Kevin the day his wife called and told her to stay away from him. She could not believe that she has made the same mistake again. This is a nightmare! Nathan sees the anger in her face as she gets up from the bed and heads down the stairs. She throws the ring at him. Tia is waiting in the car by the time Nathan comes downstairs. He has no idea what has just happened. "Tia, please come out of the car and talk to me." He pleads and begs. She would not even look at him. He is terrified. Millions of things pass through his head as he gets in the car and drives back to his parent's cottage. By the time they both got inside the house, they both could not hold in their anger any longer, at least Tia couldn't. She spat accusations at him.

"I have not slept with anyone since I met you. We were friends with benefits," he admitted. Everyone in the house heard them as they lay still in their beds listening to Tia and Nathan screaming at each other. They have forgotten where they are. "I will not go through this again, no matter how much I love you!" Tia shouts. "I will not share you, Nathan."

Nathan knows he is telling the truth. "I have not done that. I never will do that, Tia. You know I will not do that. Tia, please! I just want us to wait until we are married. I've not been doing what you think I've been doing."

Tia does not believe him. There is a dead silence in the house as his parents and Kate no longer hear them screaming at each other. "Tia! Please, say you believe me," he insists. "You've lived constantly in the center of my thoughts."

"I don't believe you. You've been sleeping with her, and I think you are still sleeping with her!" Tia screams.

Nathan is upset about what she has just said. He punches the wall so hard everyone jumps out of their beds fearing the worst. He is crying as he begins defending himself as if he were in the court room. "Let's look at the evidence, shall we?" He walks towards her. "I have not thought of anything since I saw you at the airport in Holland. I have not had any of my usual wild sex – I am a man with a very high sex drive – yet I have..." He stops. Tia is sitting down now looking into the fireplace. Nathan's father has had enough of his son's antics. He is in the family room now attempting to intervene.

"Nathan, what the hell did you do now? I will not have your spoiled ways do this to Tia, son. Nate, you need to grow up; you're about to become a father and a husband," he says firmly.

"I swear on my life, Dad. I am telling the truth. Tia's accusations are unproven. I don't understand why this has happened." He explains tearfully to his father that he took Tia to show her their new home, he officially proposed to her, and "after almost giving me a heart attack she told me she would be my wife and marry me on New Year's Eve." He stops to catch his breath. "Dad, she said... she said she wants to be the mother of my children," he was pointing to himself. Tia's heart melts as she listens to Nathan's telling his father about their evening together. She could not see his face. "Daddy, I have just lost my future before it's begun. I have not been with any woman since I met Tia. I will not, Daddy, you know I will not lie. It goes against everything you've taught me. Daddy, please, I can't have you doubt me, too." His father's heart broke for him. Antony believes his son is telling the truth, but he has no idea how to help him.

"I don't want to live in the house you and your ex-lover picked for us," Tia hollers. "I just won't!" Anthony gestures that Nathan should go to her, comfort her. He does as his father has instructed. "That's okay. I will call the realtor to find us another home, I promise," he says. "Tia, please, believe me: I have not been sleeping around with anyone." He kneels before her trying still to reassure her. She wipes the tears off his face, as his father and Kate watch them. He puts his head down on her lap and looks up at her, whispering, "Tell me you believe me."

"I do. I'm sorry, sweetie," Tia says. Nathan feels able to breathe now. He has almost lost it all. He is determined not to let anything or anyone cost her. Tia is happy again. She concludes that Nathan is nothing like Kevin. She has been scared, but she is not frightened anymore. And she is looking forward to being his wife. Later, Kate found them sleeping on the sofa together.

"That was a close one," she thinks with relief. Kate is not able to go back to sleep after the argument, but with the time difference she decides to call Brooke and tell her all about the big blow-up. The two girls conclude that the whole incident with Nathan and Tia is a good sign that they are meant to be together. Kate tells Brooke he really loves her and his parents love Tia, too. Hanging up the phone, she turns down the lights and thinks of Jaden. She decides to see whether Jaden is online. She turns on her laptop and sees that Jaden is indeed online. She plays with her fingertips and begins to type.

Hey J!.

I hope u had a good Xmas.

She hits the send button. Five minutes go by with no reply. Then she sees it.

He has sent a rose. Another five minutes go by...

K.K. ... Have I Lost u?

Jaden writes back.

Good night, J

Kate quickly sends him and logs off the computer.

Over the last few months, Kate has felt humiliated by Jaden's actions. The drugs did not bother her as much as the girl he shagged. Kate can't stop herself from wondering whether the girl was more beautiful than herself. Needing to hear a sympathetic voice, she calls her mother in Hong Kong after she goes downstairs to the kitchen. Anthony has baked and made all kinds of food for breakfast. Kate feels bad; she had intended to bake, but she spent too much time on the phone with her mother. She offers to help.

"Everything is done. Nate came down to help and he has just gone to get Tia, honey. Sit! I'll make some tea." There was cinnamon oatmeal, scrambled eggs, sausages, sautéed mushrooms, turkey roll-ups, cheese omelettes, yogurt… all ready on the island. Nathan and Tia come downstairs holding hands. Anthony remarks, "Now, that's what I like to see!"

Tia is blushing as she leans forward to kiss him on both checks. "I'm so sorry for last night, Daddy." Anthony puts his hands around her lovingly and says, "You two are going to have many fights. As long you don't go to bed angry, you will be fine, Angel."

Kate feels a little envious of what Tia has found. Tia has just finished making a raspberry smoothie for Nathan, when Nicole walks in and says she needs some papers signed, so she can take it to the land registrar's office at City Hall. As she says "good morning" to everyone, all eyes are on her. Nathan quickly stands up. Tia asks Nicole to join them for breakfast. Anthony excuses himself to go and check on his wife. Kate says she will go with him. Nathan pulls a chair up to the table for Nicole as Tia hands her a plate. "I trust you love the house, Tia?" Nicole inquires.

"Yes, very much so, but we will not be living in that house," Tia replies.

"May I ask why?"

Nathan does not like the direction of the conversation.

"We will be looking at new homes this morning," says Nathan non-committally.

Nicole reminds them that they own that house already. She asks how they plan to find another house with such short notice. Nathan says, "We will. Don't worry about that. Can you just tell the seller that the offer is off the table?" That's when Nicole exploded. "That house is yours and Tia's. You've paid for it, Nate. You don't buy a quarter of a million dollar home, pay cash, and change your minds twenty-four hours after closing!"

Nathan stands up and says, "Now, I'm telling you, we don't want it! You do your job and fix it!" He yells at Nicole.

"Enough of this, Nathan. You know that legally the house is yours and Tia's whether you two like or not. You drag me here to close in twenty-four hours, and now all of a sudden, you don't want it? Well, too bad!" she yells back. She turns to Tia and says, "Are you going to let him do this? Tia, honey, he said the house has everything that you wanted. What happened?"

Tia has had it with Nicole, so she bluntly replies, "I don't want to live in a house that Nathan picked for us with the help of his ex-lover." Nicole stood up and said, "Please, Nate tell me you didn't do that?" She does not let Nathan respond before she begins laying into him. Tia feels confused, and Kate and Anthony who are in the family room eaves-dropping feel confused, too. "Nate, for months you've been telling everyone how in love you are with Tia. It has not been three days since you told me you were going to be a father and how much you are looking forward to all this and you go and fuck it up? You are not in college anymore! Grow up!"

Nathan yells, "Stop it! Just stop it, will you?"

"No woman will live in a home that her husband's ex-lover helped to pick," Nicole finishes.

"Enough!" Nathan said. "I did not do that. I am getting fed up with this matter." Nathan raises his voice and blurted out, "Brooke helped me pick the damn house."

Shocked, Tia turned and shouted "Brooke!"

Nathan was quiet. "Why did you not say so last night?" Tia asks.

He is still quiet when Tia asks Nicole if she could excuse them so they can talk privately. Nicole joins the others in the living room eaves-dropping with shocked expressions on their faces. Nathan has had it with the whole issue of the house. He grabs his keys and says to Tia "I'm leaving." Tia begs him not to go. "I love the house, baby. Please don't leave." Nathan throws his keys down in anger and puts his hands in his face. He feels exasperated. "Tia, you have a tendency not to listen to me when you get upset. Baby, all I have been trying to do is what is best for us. Tia, I'm out of here before I lose it." He frowns. "I feel absolutely awful, sweetie," Tia cries. "I appreciate all that you are doing. I just wish you had discussed it with me before you went ahead and bought the house. It would have saved us all this unpleasantness last night... Nathan, I love all the effort you're making... but don't you think you and I should discuss all this without Brooke or Nicole first?"

Nicole returns to the kitchen, "What is going on with you two? Nate, you can not upset Tia in her condition. You need to grow up. Marriage is hard work. She loves the house, the house is yours whether you two want to live in it or not. I hope you did not invite this Brooke person to your wedding?"

"God damn it! Be quiet, Nicole! Brooke is my soon-to-be sister-in-law. Stop meddling in my family and go make sure the office is ready. You don't need me to remind you that I have a family now. You need to pull your weight instead of meddling! Tell all the associates that I will stop by with Tia this afternoon. I don't want to hear anymore about this house! This is between me and Tia." Nathan snaps back at Nicole, and hugs Tia. Nicole could not believe that Nathan Carter is really in love with Tia. Nathan holds Tia by the waist, and Nicole couldn't take her eyes off them. Kate and Anthony enter the room to witness Tia and Nathan finally sign the papers for Nicole.

As a parting shot, Nicole remarks, "You know, communication is the key to a good marriage. Ian and I have a good marriage because we communicate with each other. I like her, Nate. Don't go and screw up this one like you do with everything else, Nate," she adds. Nathan sighs and as he takes Tia's hand in his, he asks whether she is sure about the house. Tia whispers that she will show him how much she loves the house when they go back there later.

Chapter 30

Kate helps Nathan and Tia shop for furniture for their new home. Afterward, Nathan and Kate skate on the Ottawa Canal, while Tia sits and enjoys hot chocolate. It has been a long day, but they got a lot done. Nathan insists that all the furniture be delivered the next day. His in-laws are coming and he wants them all under one roof. Tia feels tired by the time they return to the cottage, so Nathan gives her a bath and a full-body massage. Of course, Tia wants more, but he tells her that Kate will be spending the night with her as he has a lot of work to finish for Nicole for the up-coming hearing. Luckily for him, Kate comes in and saves him before Tia can seduce him. "Is he sexy or what?" Kate teases.

"Oh… it's so unreal. He is like the man of my dreams, Kate," Tia says. "I was meant to come to Canada, I think. My life is so perfect here." Kate can tell. Tia seems a lot happier than she was during her last months in England. Of course, everyone misses her and Kate knows everyone will be happy for her when they see her. They discuss Urban Style and Kate reports that they have three people working in each store and the enterprise is doing well. "The web site you built helped increase sales," Kate says happily.

"Good! That was one of my main worries when I was leaving," Tia says.

"Any thought of what you are going to do about Jaden?"

"Uh –um… I don't know. I still love him… I can't forgive him for cheating," Kate says. "Also, I can't get him out of my head. He has changed. Tia, you would not recognize him if you saw him. He even has a tattoo and his body is like Nathan's. I swear!"

"No, no way!" Tia screams. "Since when?"

"I swear he has been body-building his body is so well-toned," Kate says.

"Do you remember when you guys came to my mom's gym and he couldn't even lift ten pounds of weight?"

"Yep! Well, he has done it somehow." Kate says. "So what is sex like with Mr Hot?" Kate asks, changing the subject.

Tia smiles, "He wanted to wait until we were married."

"No! No way! Does he really?" Kate asks.

Tia is laughing, "Of course, I had my way with him and now he can't keep his hands off me." She falls quiet for a bit and Kate asks, "What's wrong?"

Tia said "last night I felt I could have lost him. It all became clear how much I love him and I was not going to lose him. My whole body went cold when he said he had slept with Nicole. I thought that's it: they're the best of friends, they have so much in common."

Kate begins to laugh, "You and Nathan have a lot more in common than you know."

"You think?"

Kate tells Tia not to be too hard on Nathan. She does not want to mention Kevin. "I don't think he will do anything to hurt you. His father will probably murder him if he tries." They both laughed at the idea. There is a knock on the door. It was Nathan bringing Tia a glass of warm milk. Kate notices that he kisses and talks to the baby and then kisses Tia good-night. He asks if he can get anything for Kate, but she says she is okay. He whispers something in Tia's ear and Tia's face lights up as she tells him, "You are in so much trouble!" Turning at the door to blow a kiss, Nathan leaves the room.

The next day Nathan is very nervous because Tia's family is arriving that evening and he wants everything to be just right. He has rented a limousine to pick up everyone from the airport. They have already decided that Tia's parents and sisters will stay at their new home. Brooke, Sarah and Jason will stay in Tia's apartment. Kate is going to stay at the cottage with them. The wedding is going to be held at the

Fairmont Hotel & Resort, where they've all been staying since the 30th. There is a club in the hotel, which Nicole has booked for Tia's hen night. Steven asked if Nathan wanted a bachelor party. "I don't want any bachelor party," he tells his brother, who is his best man. "I just want to get married and look forward to my daughter's birth."

Tia knows where she wants to put everything in the house. Their new house has five bedrooms. There are also two finished rooms and a rec room in the basement with a full bathroom, that Tia did not see during her previous visit. She tells Nathan that they can all fit in the house. They each will have their own office. There is a small space for a gym near the enclosed sun-room where the hot tub is located. There are three gas fireplaces: one in the family room, one in the master bedroom, and one in the sun-room. The house has three bathrooms and an *en suite* bathroom. Nathan hires extra help to get the house decorated before the new year. By lunch time, all of the furniture is placed where Tia wants it. Nathan is impressed with her. He returns to the cottage where they are all having supper together. His father and sister have spent the day cooking, insisting that all the meals should be prepared before Tia's family arrives. "This way," Jackie says, "we just pop something in the microwave or into the oven, and we can enjoy each other's company!" Anthony agrees.

At the last minute, Nathan says he is not going to the airport. At one o'clock, the limousine is going to pick up Tia and Kate at the cottage and take them to meet the plane at Ottawa International Airport due to arrive at two. Supper will be at six o'clock at the cottage. "Nope! I can't do it! I've changed my shirt four times today, and my hands are shaking so bad, I can't calm down," Nathan exclaims frantically. Heather takes his hands in hers and strokes the palms until he calms down. Steven is the first to arrive with his actress girl friend. Steven is a rising Hollywood film director, who at the age of twenty-five has four blockbusters under his belt. His new girlfriend, Kelly Powers, is in his new movie. The movie opens in Toronto two days after Nathan's and Tia's wedding.

The conversation in the limousine with Tia's family is all about the Carter family. The limousine glides into the Carter's cottage driveway and Anthony and Steven Carter are both outside to welcome Tia's family. Tia's parents watch as Tia embraces Anthony. Tia introduces her family to Anthony as Steven guides all of them inside. The huge stone fireplace gets everyone's attention. Nathan holds his mother's hands, and his heart rate escalates when he hears all the voices in the house. He whispers to his mother, "I don't want to meet them." He hears Brooke asking about him and finally he stands up still holding his mother's hands. Tia can see how nervous he feels, so she quickly goes to him and gives him a kiss. Tia grasps Heather's other hand and introduces her parents to her and Nathan. Both Naana and Bobby kiss Mrs Carter on the cheek and hug her. Bobby shakes Nathan's hands. Naana gives Nathan a kiss and a hug, tells him to relax in French. He smiles. He tells Tia's mother it was easier when he and Steven came to NYC to see her. Naana agrees, "It was a bold move." He lets go of his mother's hands as he picks up Brooke in the air to embrace her. He says to Jason, "You are one lucky man." They hug and shake hands. Nathan kisses Tia's two sisters and Sarah Williams. They all sit down to supper. Naana feels a little relieved when she sees how attentive Nathan behaves toward Tia and how comfortable the whole Carter family is with everyone. Bobby thinks Nathan is a fine young man. Sarah Williams hits it right off with Heather Carter. Both women share the same taste in art. Naana is amazed when she learns Anthony cooked all the food. She told him the next time they must all come to England, so he can teach Bobby how to cook. They laugh.

In their own vehicle, Nathan is very quiet on the drive back. Every now and then, Tia would take one hand off the steering wheel and rub his shoulders. She knows him so well now. They arrive before the limousine. Tia goes inside, Nathan stays to help Sarah, Naana and the girls out of the limousine. He gives the limo driver a big tip as he watches the car drive off. As Nathan stands outdoors watching the receding taillights of the limousine, Bobby joins him, and putting an arm around his shoulders observes, "Looking at you brings back the memories of twenty years ago when I met Tia's grandparents for the first time." Nathan smiles as he hears Naana bubbling with laughter, "Yeah, Bobby changed his clothes four times that evening."

Meanwhile, the three girls have disappeared into the house just like they always do when they are together. Tia finally comes downstairs and takes Nathan by the hand to the sun-room. She sits on his lap and asks how he is doing. "A lot better" he confesses. He asks, "Do you still want to marry me?" Brooke comes into the room and says, "Of course, darling! I didn't travel to Canada just to see your gorgeous faces. I can see your handsome face everyday on the web cam. It's so cold here! You two better get married before I have a bloody cow," says Brooke. Tia didn't know Brooke and Nathan have been talking over the Internet all this time. She wonders why neither of them have never once said anything? Brooke says she loves the chic furniture. She asks whether the furniture has been delivered already. Nathan reports that Kate and Tia brought all the pieces only yesterday. "I think they are exquisite, baby," he says. He notices that Tia seems far away when Brooke is talking. He kisses the back of her neck and whispers something in her ear that makes her smile. Brooke is a little jealous of Tia and Nathan. Life with Jason has become a routine these days, no excitement. She looks at Nathan and Tia and knows her relationship with Jason needs some romance to keep the fire burning.

"Baby, I have to run now. I will come and have breakfast with you before my date with the ladies." Nathan will be taking his mother, Naana and Sarah out to some kind of pre-New Year's extravaganza in downtown Ottawa. Tia doesn't want him to go to back to the cottage, but she gives in anyway. Brooke watches with fascination as Nathan says good night to Tia. After he's gone, Tia hugs Brooke, "Thank you, darling."

"Thank you for what, darling?" she asks.

"You know? None of this would be possible without you, and don't think I don't know what you've been up to!" Tia says with a warning tone. Brooke could not stop laughing. How she has missed her! "You know, darling. It has not been the same without you."

"Yeah, of course! You don't have anyone to boss around anymore." Tia observes.

Everyone is asleep. Kate is working on the computer in Tia's office. She never stops working. Brooke drinks wine while she watches Tia still on the phone with Nathan. She wonders what they could possibly have to talk about all this time? She kisses her on the cheek and goes upstairs to their room. Jason is already asleep. She takes a shower and goes to her mother's room. Sarah is still awake reading because she could not sleep. She has not been outside the U.K. or on a plane since the death of Brooke's father. She felt a little nervous on the plane, so she took a sleeping pill and she slept until they reached Canada. There is a knock on the door and Sarah answers. It's Tia with a mug in her hands. "It's okay to eat for two, darling, but not two days before your wedding," joked Brooke. Tia passes the mug to Sarah, and hits Brooke with a pillow.

"I see nothing has changed," Sarah says with amusement. She drinks some of her tea. Pointing to Tia, she says, "You are about to get married in two days," and pointing to Brooke, "and you are engaged to be married soon and you're still behaving like children!" The two girls watch Sarah puts her mug down on the bedside table. They look at each other and smile as they begin hitting Sarah with a pillow. She joins them.

Before they know it, Naana Konadu-Sharp is standing in the door wondering why Sarah Williams is engaging in such foolishness with the girls. They all put away the pillows when they see her and straighten up themselves. Just like the girls, she is thinking of Sarah and wants to see if she is alright. Sarah turns to Naana and says, "Darling, this is a unique way to relax." Naana smiles and asks, "Can I borrow Tia?" Brooke spends the rest of the night with her mother. They both fall asleep right about the same time. Tia has not had a private moment with her mother since she arrived. She has been trying to avoid her and her private talks. She wonders where her father is as those two are like teenagers. They like to tag-team her with their talks. The two women sit down on the sofa. Tia wishes Nathan could be there with her. "You look well, Tia." Naana says. "You've taken very good care of yourself. I'm so proud of you."

"Did the old fart just say she was proud of me?" Tia asks herself quietly. Tia fixes one of the cushions behind her to support her back. She pulls up both knees and rests her cheek on her knees. Naana Kanadu glances at her daughter and asks whether Tia is alright.

"Mm mm...huh.. mum, I'm okay. My back is a little sore," she complains. Naana knows too well about pregnancy and a sore back. She asks if there is anything she can do for Tia. When Tia doesn't immediately respond, Naana realizes that she is beginning to fall asleep. Naana goes into the hall closet and takes out a blanket to cover her.

Nathan was called out to the Ottawa police station in the morning to see a client who was arrested and charged with over seventy counts of felony theft, fraud and senior abuse. The young lady's story appears in every newspaper in Ottawa and even in the *Toronto Sun*. In addition to the Internet news sites, she makes both the six o'clock and the late evening news. Nathan spent the whole night listening to reports as the media essentially tried and convicted the poor girl before she even entered a courtroom. She was twenty-three years old, a landed immigrant from the Philippines, working as a Personal Support Worker. She owned a town house in the west end of the town of Kanata. Most of the evidence was in her house. She also had a young child. Her boyfriend, an African man, was arrested, too. The media did not mention much about his background. They focused entirely on the girl because the victims were all seniors and in her care. This case centered on two concerns of the Canadian justice system: the abuse of seniors and the rights of the disabled. Nathan called Nicole right away when the call came through, and Nicole advised him not to take the case because the media has already convicted the girl; the police have a mountain of video evidence against her; and the public has already heard a lot of secondhand speculation, which might set the precedents for the case, making it a very difficult case to defend.

"There's a potential for very serious punishment here, Nate," said Nicole, but Nathan laughed aloud, saying "We will see about that!"

Steven drove him to the Ottawa court house where the front steps seemed to be occupied by members of the press, all clamoring for a sound byte. Nathan met with the Crown Attorney and they agreed on terms before he went and met his client. Nicole was still trying to convince Nathan to let this one go.

"Come on, Nathan. Our firm is new in Ottawa. This is the kind of publicity we don't need! You're not used to the media. They will eat you alive," worried Nicole.

Nathan just smiled. The girl's name was Esperanza Lou. She was brought into the interview room. Nathan introduced himself and Nicole and asked if she was okay. Nathan did not waste time.

Concerned about surprise details, Nathan asked about her boyfriend, where he was from, how long they had been together and whether he was the father of her child. He informed Esperanza that he had arrange for her bail. A five thousand dollar lean has been put on her property to assure her bail.

"You will be going home soon, Miss Lou." Esperanza begin to cry and thanked Nathan. "You must follow the judge's rules; otherwise, you will be back in jail without bail! You must end your relationship with your boyfriend, if you want to stay out of prison, Miss Lou. The police will escort you to court number nine in front of the judge in an hour. Do not say a word, and just let me do all the talking."

The police officer escorted Esperanza back to the holding cell. Nathan called Tia to say that he would not be home for breakfast. He did not offer any explanation and hung up. He called the limousine company to have him picked up by the court house in two hours. He told Nicole to have his assistants find out about Esperanza's boyfriend. "I need to know where he's from, where he works or goes to school, how he got to Canada, whether he has a criminal record… I'd like to know everything about this individual within the next half hour," he demanded. The lead police detective was a woman, well respected for her work on elder abuse cases. She and her team have put together a good case for the Crown Attorney. "It's a slam dunk," says the Crown Attorney. In response, Nathan studied the evidence carefully and smiled to himself. The judge agreed to the terms and the conditions of Esperanza's bail. She was told to surrender her passport within twenty-four hours of her release to Detective Roberts at the Ottawa police station. She was to report to Detective Roberts if she needs to leave Ottawa for any reason. She was not to leave Ottawa without the Detective's permission and she must maintain good behavior. No contact with the victims or their families, no contact with the co-accused. She must appear in court when she is expected or she will be back in jail. She was set to appear back in court room number six in three weeks at nine in the morning. Nathan took her aside and explained to her again everything the judge has said. He thanked the judge and shook hands with the Crown Attorney and the detective and left with his client.

Nicole was waiting outside the court room, "The press are outside. Perhaps we should use the back door." Nathan puts on the sunglasses that Tia has bought him for Christmas and says to Nicole, "Let's go play the press game." Nicole's jaw dropped in surprise. There were cameras and photographers everywhere just like Nicole had said. As soon as they came out of the door, the cameras flashed on them like Hollywood movie stars. Nicole quickly rushed Esperanza to Nathan's limousine. The press are no longer interested in her as one of them asks why Nathan took the case? He replied, "why not take this case?" He flashed them a sexy smile and they went nuts as Nathan walked to his limousine. They were still snapping photos as the limousine drove off. Tia's sisters were watching TV with Jackie, Nathan's little sister, in the family room. When they started screaming out loud, everyone in the house rushed to the family room thinking something horrible had happened.

There he was in his dark navy-blue suit with a pink shirt and tie, eyes hidden behind shades. Tia's heart skipped a beat as she listened to the news and saw Nathan on the screen. Nathan used an intelligent, plain-spoken approach to the press and the questions they asked. He was asked about the victims' rights and all the evidence piling up against an already very high-profile case. Nathan did not hold anything back as he addressed the most critical issues at the heart of the case and the criminal justice system. He came across to most of the TV viewers as a passionate victim's rights advocate, even though he was the defense lawyer in this case.

The viewers and the media were fascinated with this young defense Lawyer. It was intriguing to watch him on television because he had a great personality for the small screen, Tia thought. The reporter said that Nathan was getting married to a Nortel Networks executive tomorrow, which made Nathan look like a movie star. Everyone turned and looked at Tia. Not long after the broadcast, Nathan arrived at the house with his mother and Nicole in the limo. He was not aware that he had been on TV already. He played it cool and said, "I can't discuss the case because of lawyer-client confidentiality." Nicole raised an eyebrow and smirked. Tia was in the kitchen with Sarah and Nathan was on his knees talking to the baby before he swept Tia into his arms. The whole household was watching them. Heather told them that Nate does that with his baby each and every day. They all thought it was sweet. He spent the afternoon with all of the mums: Heather, Sarah and Naana. He took his seventeen-year-old sister, Jackie, and Tia's sister, Claire, to ice skate with Kate and they went to St Laurent Shopping Center where he bought all kinds of DVDs, posters and CDs for the girls. Next, they went to *Toys-R-Us* and again they bought all kinds of toys and stuffed animals. Jackie was like a child in the toy store – she didn't want to leave until Nathan picked her up and said that she is always like that at the toy store. The three girls laughed, seeing Jackie and Nathan argue all the way home until their mother stepped in and told the two of them to stop their bickering. Tia's mother liked that side of Nathan. His father and Steven with Kelly Powers joined them in their new house for supper. Nathan has told his assistants to order all kinds of take-out food to be sent to his home by five. Tia had a special night planned for her and Nathan in her apartment. Tia knew that Nathan would insist that he has work to do and Tia must wait until they are married to make love again. Nathan told her all their family were having dinner together at their home in Orleans. "I know, sweetie, but tonight is just going to be the two of us, no cell phones and no family." She has candle lights everywhere in her apartment with an Enrique Iglesias CD playing.

Nathan did his best to protest, but in the end he was smitten with her and he gave in to Tia's plans. He had no idea how romantic Tia could be: they ate in bed, he wanted to massage Tia to sleep, but she had other ideas. She massaged hot oil on" his whole body with her hands and her tongue. He has never been aroused by a woman like this before, and he moans and gasps as Tia kisses and nibbles his ears, whispers in a sexy tone, "do you still want us to wait until we are married to make love?" Before Nathan could respond she was out of the bed and in the living room by the fireplace. Her hair was down, and she stared at him as she dropped to the floor the pink silk robe that she was wearing. Seeing her naked body, Nathan walks slowly towards her, his heart beating faster and faster until his lip finally touches Tia's. It is exhilarating making love to her, and he confesses that he missed her last night and he didn't want to go back to the cottage. "I love the way you kiss me. You are so sexy, Tia," he whispers. Tia says that she loves how he kisses, too, then she sits up and sucks on his fingers, the passion between them was incredible. They made love again before she went to the kitchen to make him a smoothie. "I must say this is the first time a woman has seduced me and made smoothie for me naked." Tia smiled and kissed him on the nose.

Chapter 31

The next day, they all moved to one whole floor in the Fairmont Hotel & Resort, where Nathan and Tia had requested a whole floor for three days for their wedding party. The ladies went to the spa and the men just played pool at the hotel bar. They had the rehearsal dinner and the girls departed with Nicole for Tia's hen night. It was nothing the three British girls have ever done and it proved to be a wild night. "All men under the ages of twenty seven," Nicole informed them, "with well-toned bodies half naked." Tia feels embarrassed and wants to go back to the hotel room as soon as she sees the young men, but Nicole, Kelly, Brooke and Kate collectively say, "no way!" The ladies dance and drink while Tia sits down with her sore back. After a few dances, she slips away quietly and goes back to the hotel. Once in her room, she takes a bath and gets into her bed and sleeps. She couldn't believe she would be getting married the next day. By the time the girls realized Tia had left, they were drunk out of their minds. Brooke offered to go and see if Tia was okay. Kate was out of control dancing and making out with one of the strippers in the private room. The stripper was a well-built black man, apparently adept at oral sex to judge by Kate's responses. Brooke knocks on Nathan's door, but there is no answer, so she turns the door handle and opens the door. Someone plants a kiss on her and soon clothes are coming off, and he has her pushed up against the door as he takes his time kissing every inch of her body. She returns the favor by rubbing and digging her fingers in his back; he slips his fingers between her legs and discovers she is very wet and ready. He penetrated her roughly, riding and trashing her so thoroughly that she cried out for more. As soon as it was all over, he brusquely said, "Get dressed."

Brooke realizes with shock that she and Nathan have just had sex. She has no idea how it all began. Nathan walked into the bathroom. Brooke could hear the running of shower. She was still naked as she went into the bathroom, hoping for some action in the shower. However, Nathan stepped out of the shower, wrapped a towel around his waist and grabbed another one. He did not look at her as he began to brush his teeth. Brooke walked slowly towards him, and as she was about to touch him, he grabbed her hands and said, "You got what came for, get dressed and get out." He pushed her hands gently away from him. Her knees begin to shake. What had just happened? She picked up her humiliation from the floor and got dressed. "Don't you think we should talk about this?" Brooke asked, feeling a lump in her throat. "Good night Brooke!" Nathan called out.

Brooke was so enraged. "You twisted bastard! What kind of sick game are you playing? How dare you treat me like this?" Brooke was not able to fight her tears. Nathan threw the towel on the floor, lifted her up in the air, and leaned her against the door and kissed her as she responded. He whispered in her ear, "It never happened! I assumed it was Tia at the door, though I did enjoy every bit of it." He chuckled as he set her on her feet. Brooke tried to talk, but Nathan interrupted in a soft voice, "I am getting married to your sister tomorrow night. There is nothing to talk about." His green eyes were bright, but Brooke could see evil behind all his charm. He kissed her and let go of her. Brooke tried her best not cry, but could not hold it in any longer. What just happened? And what kind of a man is Tia marrying? Her whole body trembled and shivered. "What have I done? How could I do this with you," she said aloud. Nathan laughed heartily. "You wanted this Brooke, as much as I did. Let's go now and tell Tia that we just had sex," he suggested. "She will marry me still, but you will not be there, and you will lose her and Jason. Come on, let's go tell right now!" He added, "we might as well tell Jason that you and I did it in a way you two have never done before." He chuckled. Brooke tried to slap him. He took her hand and begin to stroke her breast. She was flustered and blushing when Nathan lead her to the bed. He undressed her, kissed and nibbled and sucked her breast. "It never happened... Brooke," as he began kissing her. He stopped and said, "I will not lose the woman

I love and my child... and you are not going to lose Jason... You know we both wanted this, it was inevitable, Brooke," he whispered.

He helped her get dressed and walked her to the door. Before he opened the door for her, Nathan asked her to tell him what she wanted. She did not respond right away. Nathan brushed her hair back from her face and kissed her on the neck. "You are so sexy, tell me, please. Don't be afraid," he said. "Tell me what you desire, Brooke."

"I want... I want you to make love to me," she found herself saying.

"I would love to make love to you... Just not tonight, Brooke... I don't want anyone to know about this or any other night you and I will share in the future."

"I can't have an affair with you, Nathan," Brooke said quietly. Nathan kissed her, and then he took her hand and slipped it under her panties making her feel herself. He whispered in her ear, "you want to Brooke. I want to." There was a knock on the door, but he did not stop what he was doing to her as he opens the door. Brooke knees felt weak and she almost fainted with fear. There were two sexy white girls at the door. Nathan invited them into the room and closed the door behind them. He took his hands out of Brooke's panties. He sat down on a chair and said to the girls, "I want you to undress her for me." One of the girls began undressing Brooke as she stood still. The other girl was giving Nathan a blow job right in front of Brooke. He told Brooke to go and sit on the bed facing him, while she looked at him. Brooke was in a new world of sex games. The other girl wasted no time going down on her, as Brooke had the most powerful, explosive orgasm she has ever experienced in her life. Nathan put on a condom and told the girls to leave as he locked the door behind them. He bends over Brooke and rides hard and low until he comes.

Nathan spent the morning in his room working on his case because he didn't want to think about his wedding. Several times, he picked up the phone to call Tia, but hung up instead. He called room service and when they showed up he gave the lady a huge tip and asked her to take what he had ordered to Tia's parents room. The lady was too happy to do it after that kind of a tip.

Naana called Tia when she realized that the room service had made a mistake. There was a box of jewelry, two of them and a hand-written card. Tia read the card and the tears began rolling down her face. Brooke's heart rate went up as she thought Nathan has revealed to Tia what happened last night. She had no idea how she was going to explain this one. Tia put the card down and lifted one of the jewelery boxes and handed it to her mother. "This one is for you, from Nathan," Tia said. Naana opened the box, "It is exquisite," she said. The card read:

I thank you, Mrs. Sharp, for giving me an opportunity to be a part of your family. I promise you that I will be the son-in-law you always wanted for Tia.

You have my word as a gentleman and a new son that I will always love and respect Tia and our children, and that nothing will ever come before them.

This much... I promise you, Mother, when I marry your beautiful baby girl tonight.

Love, Nate.

"I'm going to see Nathan. Do you want me to thank him for you?" Naana asked Tia. Naana noticed that he had been working. Nathan guided her into a chair, still holding Naana's hand. She could tell he was very nervous. She sat down on a chair near his.

"I wanted to stop by and thank you for the exquisite gift you sent me. That was very lovely," Mrs Sharp said.

Nathan smiled. She continued, "Everyone can see how much you adore each other. Don't spoil her too much like we have, Nathan." She added, "You must have the balance of your needs first sometimes, darling." Nathan's heart warmed up when she said that. "Bobby and I have no doubt that you are a wonderful man. It makes us happy that Anthony and Heather are nearby to support and guide you and Tia when we leave. We are not so much concerned about her as we are about you." Nathan did not like the comment. "Tia likes to have her way all the time, and we can see that already not only have you but also the whole Carter family has spoiled her in a short time." Nathan was a little more relaxed and smiled. "Bobby and I have told her that a man is always the head of his family. The woman may think she wears the pants, but it is not so. You must communicate with one another, darling. Don't be too afraid to stand up to Tia when need be."

Nathan likes his mother-in-law already. He enjoys their talks, and for the first time, he feels relaxed and ready for tonight. Naana speaks very passionately about Tia and their up-coming marriage, and Nathan is impressed with how thoughtful and in-touch she is to their relationship. She assures him that all will be well before she leaves and that Nathan should try and relax.

Tia was reading Nathan's note and was very quiet. Brooke glanced at her unable to read Tia's expression. The events of last night shocked her deeply, and there was no way to share her experience with anyone. How could she have done that? She was not drunk. Tia can't marry a man like Nathan Carter... The walls are closing in on her, but she needs to keep it together. This is worse than what Jaden did to Kate. Tia saw the look on Brooke's face. She knows that look as she glances at Kate. Kate also has the same look on her face. The girls go into Tia's room with her, and as soon as she closes the door, Tia exclaims, "Okay, girls. Dish! I want to know what happened last night!"

Unable to hide it any longer, Kate confesses, "I hooked up with one of the strippers last night." She begins to giggle silly.

Tia glanced at Brooke who did not hear what Kate had said. Both Kate and Tia noticed she looked kind of dazed. It's not like Brooke to be this distant. She realized that Tia and Kate were looking at her, so she straightened up.

"Did you hear what Kate just said," Tia asked. For emphasis, Kate repeated what she did the night before.

Brooke laughed and said, "Well, since we're all coming clean about what we did last night," she paused, "I cheated on Jason, too. I feel just sick about it."

Tia quietly contemplated her friends' confessions. They seem to have changed quite a bit in the short time they have all been apart. Tia didn't know what to say to them.

"I thought things were going well between you and Jason?" Kate asked.

Brooke replied, "They are... it is like a routine with us now, no excitement anymore."

"So what do you plan to do about it?" Kate inquired.

"I'm not sure... It made me see how much I love Jason. I can't tell him what I got up to last night." Brooke was in tears now, "I have been trying to justify what I did, but I can't." She wiped her face and asked Kate, "Is it over between you and Jaden for good, or did you want to hurt him?" Brooke asked.

Kate said, "We did not have sex!"

Tia began to laugh. "What did you do, Kate?" Tia asked.

"Well!.. You know? ... Um... He said he always wanted to have ... um ... oral sex with an Asian girl. Before I knew it, he was under the table getting my knickers off and going right at it. I don't know if anyone saw us in the club," said Kate with a silly grin on her face.

"I have always thought Canadians are freaks. It must be the the cold weather." Brooke told them.

"Nathan is not like that," Kate asserted.

"You have no idea," Brooke thought.

"Here is a very sexy man who wants to wait until he is married to have sex with his wife. I think that is so romantic, Tia. You hold on to this one, you hear me?"

"You mean, you and Mr Hot have not done it yet?!" Brooke asked, surprised.

Tia ignored her. She was so nervous, and the baby was kicking all over the place. Her cell phone rang: it was Jaden calling to wish her a Happy New Year. She told him she was getting married in less than two hours and Jaden couldn't believe it. He said he had often thought he and Kate would be the first among their friends to get married. When Kate heard him say that, she was in tears but still refused to talk to him. Tia did not want to butt in, but felt she must. "Listen!" she said. "We have been friends for a long time. We are sisters, and you two know how much I love you and always looked up to you."

Brooke was very ashamed after what Tia had just said. She tried to hide it, so she walked to the window as she listened to Tia talk.

"We have always carried ourselves in a certain manner. Kate, we all know how much Jaden has hurt you. I feel partly to blame because I thought I was protecting you. Please, sweetie, don't lose who you are over this." Kate was in tears as Tia's words went to her heart. She turned to Brooke, who was still looking out the windows. "Brooke you are so beautiful and intelligent. You waited your whole life for Jason. He is a good man and loves and respects you, Brooke. Don't hurt him. It's not easy being hurt and betrayed by someone you love and trust. Kate and I know that very well." Brooke wanted to come clean right there, but how could she? The wedding was in less than three hours. If she told them, how would the friends and family members react? No one would believe her. Nathan is a purely evil man hiding behind the veneer of his high profile law practice and his media image. Her heart ached with fear and pain, knowing what she knows about him. He is a master manipulator. How could she not have known? This is all her fault. She has got to find a way to stop this wedding, but how? She searched her mind, but no plan formed itself. She even thought of calling that low life Kevin and telling him that Tia was carrying his child, but what would that serve?

Chapter 32

They were all dressed up and looking like they were going to a fashion magazine photo shoot. Naana and Bobby were ready first, so Naana went to check on Nathan while Bobby waited for Tia and the girls. Nathan looked even more handsome as he hugged and kissed Naana. She noticed he seemed nervous as she took his other hand and said he looked adorable, relaxed. Tia's sisters joined them, followed by Kate and Brooke. Kate had designed and stitched Tia's gown for her: a lime silk wrap gown, very sexy unlike the traditional wedding grown. Her hair was put up in a French twist. They had written their own vows and Nathan kissed her gently on the lips. He turned and hugged his father and brother, who were both standing right by him. There were a few tears in his eyes, when he made his little speech about his new bride and thanked everyone who was there. He left with Tia to freshen up in their suite. Tia noticed that it was not on the same floor as they been staying the night before. He carried her to the suite. There were candle lights every where and it looked so romantic. He turned to Tia and said, "I love this suite, but I'd rather spend my wedding night in our own home in our own bed so I can share this experience with my children someday. Can we please go home?" He asked. Tia took a deep breath and said, "I'd love to." They stopped by Tia's parents' room on their way out and Nathan pressed the keys to the honeymoon suite in Bobby's hands and winked at him. Bobby was a little bit embarrassed, but he was pleased nevertheless. Nathan carried Tia into the house, up the stairs, and into their bedroom. He turned on the fire. There were no lights, only the glow from the fireplace as he sat her down on the bed. He put some classical music on the stereo and then he went to the bathroom, coming out with his jacket off and tie loosened. He asked if she wanted anything to drink and she declined.

He undressed her, took her to the bathroom and gently placed her in the big whirlpool bath.

"I've been wishing for something like this the whole day. How did you know?" Tia asked. He smiles as he takes off his pants and gets in behind her. He strokes her back. "You, Mrs. Carter, have made me the happiest man in the world." He kissed her hands, and she relaxed. Later, after a soothing bath, Nathan rubbed cocoa butter lotion on Tia's whole body as she quietly slips off to sleep. They made love over and over again the next morning. It was New Year's Day. The rest of their family and friends spent it at the hotel.

The whole week went by so quickly. Before everyone knew it, they were at the airport heading back to England. Kate had left two days after the wedding because she wanted to make an attempt to meet Jaden and try to sort things out or move on with her life as the whole situation was getting out of hand. They met up at Brooke's apartment. Initially, it was very uncomfortable for both of them. Jaden tried to break the ice by asking about the man Tia had just married. Kate's reply made him feel even worse than he was feeling already. He said, "I did not come here to ask or beg you to forgive me. I have done that. It's up to you if wish to or not." He took a deep breath, "I have always loved, and always will love, you no matter what. I am so sorry that I hurt you. I can see how uncomfortable you are with me now, so I will go and give you your space." Before leaving, he wrote down his new address for her. "I have moved out of the flat and I'm back in law school starting from tomorrow." He left and closed the door behind him. Kate was sitting down crying as Jaden could hear her. Unable to leave right away, Jaden stood outside the apartment door, leaning his forehead against the front door. He couldn't stand to hear his beloved cry. Fighting the urge to drink, he ran down the stairs and drove to the gym to take out his frustration on the gym equipment. He was so overwrought that the management told him to can it or get out.

When Jaden got home, he sent Kate a lengthy e-mail before he went to sleep explaining his feelings and bringing her up to date on the efforts he was making to turn around his life. It was different at the college this time for him because he felt less stress. He had also learned how much he loved the law and everyday at Edward's law office he learned something new. Edward and his partners have come to trust and respect him as a developing young lawyer.

Meanwhile, Kevin Peters has finally got his immigration papers and is able to get into university. He is still married to the white girl and he thinks of Tia everyday, especially when his brothers and sisters always ask about her. They all loved Tia very much and they felt she was perfect for him. During an argument that morning, Kevin's younger brother, Paul, asks "Why are you still married to *that girl*?" – referring to Kevin's wife. "I just don't like her, none of us do," he said. Kevin was quiet and did not respond. His lectures finished early that morning, so he decided to drive to Brooke's apartment to see Tia. Jason opened the door as Kevin extended his hand to say "hello." Seeing Kevin Peters in the doorway, Jason suddenly said, "Why don't you fucking piss off before I call the police? I know all about your fake marriage!" Kevin was torn apart as Jason closed the door on him. Brooke was getting some things from her bedroom and asked Jason who it was at the door. "Oh, it was just that low-life Kevin Peters. I told him where to go."

Brooke wanted to go after him, but she dare not as Jason was upset. "Darling, I don't like to see you upset," she said. She has been looking for ways to make it up to him for what she did with Nathan since they got back from Canada and it's been almost three months now since they last made love. All Brooke can think about is Nathan and Tia. She has been hiding at work most of the time, so she doesn't have to deal with Jason. "I was thinking," she said. "Today it's our holiday, we are not going back to the office."

"I have a lot of things to finish up. You've been so busy lately that I took up more work load to occupy my time," Jason explained.

"It's okay, darling. You can drop me off at the loft. I'm taking a day off," she said. Jason knew Brooke was making an effort for them to spend time together, and he felt badly that he couldn't take the day off to spend it with her. He misses her. He has been uncertain of their relationship lately, but isn't sure why. She leaned forward and kissed him before she left the car. Jason was a little relieved as he watched her go inside the loft. A few minutes later found Jason outside his office building, and suddenly he turned the car around, almost hitting a passing vehicle as he was not looking when he turned. He parked the car and loosened his tie before running up to the loft. He could hear the music. His heart was pounding as he opened the door and saw her taking her shoes off. Without warning, he picked her up and carried Brooke into the bedroom kissing her endlessly. "God! I've missed you," he moans. They made love the whole afternoon, and afterward Jason ordered take-out for their supper. He confessed that he thought she'd gone off him and that he had been scared since Tia's wedding that they might break up. Brooke immediately ran into the bathroom and locked the door. She began sobbing thinking, perhaps he knew that she had slept with Nathan. Poor Jason was beside himself, not understanding the reason for Brooke's tears. He stood behind the bathroom door and could hear Brooke crying.

"Sweetheart... Please come out and talk to me," he said, anxiously. Brooke is sitting on the floor when her whole body begins to shake. She needs to think fast: "maybe I can beg and promise... I will not do that again," she thought. "I can't lose him." Frantic, she opens the door and goes to him. "I am sorry, Brooke. I don't like to keep things inside," he says. "I didn't mean to upset you. I don't want to lose what I have with you."

Brooke realized that Jason didn't know that she had slept with Nathan. How could he have known? No one knew. She smiled at Jason and his mood lightened. "I love you, sweetheart," he says.

"Oh... I love you, too. I have been afraid you'd gone off me," she blurted out.

"Oh, my God, Brooke! Never! You are my world. I thought you were bored with us," he replied. "I've been trying to be as charming... in a way to be more like Nathan."

Brooke pulled away from him, feeling angry now. "Do you think if I wanted Nathan Carter, I would be here with you?" she spat at him. She went on to say, "I am not Tia and I know all about that man *she's* in love with." Jason was happy to hear her say it. She stops and turns to him, "Jason, you promise that you will get any ideas you have about becoming Nathan Carter out of your mind. That is not a man I plan to spend my lifetime with," she demands. Jason has often thought that Brooke fancies Nathan and even felt jealous of Tia. He was so sure of it. He wanted to tell Nathan to stop making passes at his woman in

Canada, but he thanked God now he hadn't. She goes on to say it's easy for an outsider to say maybe Nathan and I fancy each other, but the same can be said about me and Jaden because we're so close. "I am sorry. I had a feeling you might fancy him," Jason says. Brooke feels calmer now. She lied and said, "Darling, I fancy every good-looking guy that I meet, but I have the only man that I have ever been with. The only man that I will ever be with in my whole life. If you leave me tomorrow, Jason, I will not enter into another relationship." Jason quickly runs to her as Brooke manages to turn around on him, her heart was beating faster now, more than just the night before Tia's wedding, she felt like that night as she began kissing Jason.

Married life is a lot better than Nathan Carter expects. Tia is a perfect wife in every way. Tia loves spending her weekends with her in-laws and Nathan's new associates. Everyone they meet falls in love with her. Nathan has been a good husband, a romantic one, and he hates the fact that Tia will not give up her job. At eight and half months pregnant, she is still working; she likes taking him on dates and still pays. Tia loves to send him dirty emails during the day when he is in the office. Nathan won his senior abuse case, and he has kept the young mother out of jail with six months' house arrest and two years probation. The word got out after that, and as a result, both of his law offices are doing very well. He wins one high profile case after another, and Nathan is loving his life and his work, and he feels he could not have asked for a more perfect life, he tells his brother Steven.

It is May 1997. Tia is due to give birth in less than two weeks. Brooke is arriving in Canada. Tia has an exam to write at the university, so she can not meet her at airport, but the driver has just given Brooke the note to meet Tia at the house in Orleans. He opens the limo door for Brooke to get in and to Brooke's surprise Nathan is in the limo. Brooke sits opposite him. Nathan gives her a white rose, which Brooke takes and smells, her heart skipping a beat as Nathan hands her glass of champagne. They do not talk, but he never takes his eyes off her. Brooke wishes he would say something. This is the first time the two of them have been alone together since their wild night before his wedding to Tia. The limo stops. Nathan gets out of the limo first, and Brooke notices they are not at their house nor at Tia's apartment. They are at Chateau Laurier in downtown Ottawa. Nathan does not go to the front desk, so Brooke assumes that he and Tia have been staying there. You can see the back of Parliament Hill and Rock Cliff Park from the view: "it is beautiful," Brooke thinks. Brooke is standing by the window looking at the view. When she feels his hands rubbing her breasts, kissing her neck so sensuously, Brooke's whole demeanor changes the moment he brushes his lips against hers. She wants desperately to stop, push him away even, but she finds herself sliding her hands inside his trousers and giving him a quick squeeze: he has a huge erection. His cell phone rings and rings, but he does not stop to answer it. They have sex in every position known to mankind: on the floor, on the table by the window, and on the bed, Brooke on top, Nathan behind, both supine, both standing. He calls room service afterward and has them send up some food, but they do not talk while they wait. When they return to the limo, the driver tells Nathan that his assistant wants him to call her back ASAP.

Henry is Nathan's trusted driver. He could not get the message to Nathan because he did not pick up his cell phone. Nathan tells the driver to take them to Ottawa Civic Hospital. "Tia is in labor," Nathan mutters to Brooke. Brooke tries to hold his hand, but Nathan pushes her hands away. His cell phone rings.

"Where the hell were you, Nate? Tia is in labor. Your father is with her. Tia needs you…" Nicole sees the limo pull up to the front door of the hospital and Nathan steps out and helps Brooke out. Suddenly, it makes sense to Nicole why Nathan did not answer his cell phone. She informs Nathan that Tia's contractions are less than a minute apart now. Nicole pulls Brooke aside and says, "you are going to get hurt." Brooke tries to protest her innocence, but Nicole tells her "to bag her lies."

Brooke stands outside the labor ward door feeling ashamed. Brooke is on the phone in the hospital corridor informing the Sharp's that Tia is having the baby and she will call them as soon as she hears anything. Tia is in so much pain by the time Nathan gets to the labor ward that he does not know how to console Tia. He is broken up by the amount of pain Tia is in, he begins to cry himself and yells at the nurse and the doctor to do something to take his wife's pain away. His father assures him that everything is being done that can be done. "The baby is crowning. It will not be long now," his father says. Nathan has no idea what that means. He steps out of the room and begins to kick the walls like a football. Nicole tells him to keep himself together and get back in there with his wife. He sits in the corner with his face in his palms while Tia screams as the nurse keeps telling her to push, push, Tia. Nathan has had enough of hearing the nurse telling Tia to push. Nathan tells the nurse to leave his wife alone, and that Tia is doing her best. The doctor says he can see the baby's head. Nathan stands up and goes to Tia and says, "Please, baby, one more time, baby, push." Tia cries out loud in pain that she can't do it. Nathan feeds her ice chips as she pushes and pushes, and the next thing they hear is the baby's cry. It's a baby girl, six pounds four ounces, and the doctor hands her over to Nathan. Nathan is shaking as he cries and kisses the baby and hands her to Tia and kisses her, too. Nathan tells Tia that he is so proud of her, and Tia gives the baby to Anthony while Nathan goes outside and tells Brooke. "Your sister wants to see you." Brooke watches Nathan hug Nicole as he smiles. Nicole wipes his face with her handkerchief. Brooke is certain that Nathan and Nicole are sleeping together as she watches them together she can tell. Brooke leans over to kiss Tia. Tia feels a little warm. The baby is small and she has jet black hair, she is almost white. Brooke cries when she holds the baby. Tia is sweating and the nurse notices the rise in temperature and brings it to the doctor's attention. The doctor asks that baby to be moved to the nursery immediately. Nathan's father asks if everything is okay with the baby. The doctor directs his eye on Tia. She is really hot now and complains of a headache and a stiff neck. She has a fever of 101° F. There is some confusion as Nathan enters the room and asks why they are moving the baby to the nursery. "The baby stays with my wife," he demands. "We have a private room. I don't want my baby in the nursery."

The doctor explains, "The baby has to go the nursery for now because Tia may have some kind of infection and we don't want the baby to get it, too."

Nathan demands to know "what kind of infection and how is it possible? My wife was in perfect condition a while ago," he looks accusingly at the doctor. Tia begins vomiting. The nurse asks everyone to leave, but Nathan refuses. His father taps his shoulder and leads him out of the door. Nathan's cell phone is ringing again, and he irritably turns it off. Tia is immediately moved to isolation where she can receive round-the-clock care. The family wait and wait, none of them know what is happening with Tia. Nathan is panting, and begins quivering with fear of not knowing what is going on with his wife.

Chapter 33

After what seems like forever, the doctor comes to the waiting area and says that Tia has bacterial meningitis. Nicole, Brooke, Nathan and his father are all in shock. They ask how it could happen? Nathan stands there like a broken man. He has no idea what the doctor is saying and his face is expressionless. Brooke asks if she can see Tia. Anthony nods to the doctor, "This is my daughter-in-law's sister. She arrived from the UK a short time ago. Please let her go see her sister."

Brooke puts on a gown and the nurse takes her to the isolation unit where Tia is asleep. Brooke asks the nurse, "Is my sister in pain?" The nurse replies, "Yes, a little. She has been given antibiotic medication that will help." Anthony and Nicole try to console Nathan and advise him to pull himself together, to little effect. Brooke returns from seeing Tia and says, "She is sleeping. I need to let my family know what's happening, so I will know what to do with the baby." As soon as Nathan hears her say that, he stands up and shouts, "You will do no such thing!" He grabs Brooke right in front of everyone and pushes her against the wall where she almost falls. Brooke stands her ground and she fires back at Nathan, "That is my sister and her baby in there, and you don't get to tell me what to do!" Nathan tries to talk, but she silences him by reminding him, "Tia may be your wife, but the baby has a father and it's not you!" Everyone hears the exchange. "How dare you, Nathan Carter, put your bloody hands on me! I don't give a damn who you are. Don't you ever put your hands on me again." Brooke is well-spoken and assertive with an even-toned voice. Nicole glances at Anthony, who is visibly embarrassed by his son's actions. Nicole empathizes with him. Nathan is angry and panting like a caged animal. Anthony quickly takes Nathan's hands and tells him to restrain himself. Brooke walks away from them and calls everyone in England.

She calls her assistant to book a hotel for her in Ottawa, speaking loud enough that both the Carter men and Nicole hear her. She also tells her to try and locate Kevin Peters ASAP! She hangs up the phone and walks past them. She goes back to the nursery to see the sleeping baby. She puts on her gown and heads back to the isolation unit. She tells the nurse that when the baby wakes up they should come and get her right away.

Nathan angrily leaves the hospital and goes home. Later, when Brooke comes back from the isolation unit, she sees that Nicole and Anthony are still there. "Tia is still sleeping," she informs them. Anthony asks her to come to his condo, which is located on Lees Avenue, not far from the hospital, but she declines. "I am going to stay here in case the baby or Tia needs me. There is nothing I can do for Tia right now, but my niece may need me when she wakes up." Brooke fights back her tears.

Nicole tells Anthony to go home and that she will stay and let him know if there is a change. He really does not want to leave Tia or the baby, but he knows there is nothing he can do. Three hours later, the nurse comes and says the baby is awake and crying. Both Nicole and Brooke glance at each other as their hearts skip beats at the same time. Brooke asks the nurse to get a bottle for the baby, and tells her she will be right there. A few minutes later, when Brooke goes into the nursery, Nicole can see through the nursery window from where she is standing. Nicole watches as Brooke picks up the baby and kisses her, she feeds and rubs her back to sleep. Nicole invites Brooke to come back to her place for some rest, but Brooke says no.

"This may be a bad time to say this, but if I were you, I would be careful with Nathan," Nicole warns her.

Brooke laughs and says, "I know all about Mr. Carter. Unfortunately, I learned about him after he had married my sister."

Nicole is confused, "Oh, but I thought you were sleeping with Nathan."

Brooke snaps back, "Well, you would think that, wouldn't you? Nathan Carter maybe our Tia's cup of tea, but not mine!" Brooke adds, "I will protect Tia and the baby any way I can from Nathan."

Nicole likes this girl, but she is going to need some help if she is going take on Nathan. She takes Brooke by the hand and goes to Tia's private room in the hospital. As she closes the door behind them, Nicole says, "We never had this conversation." Brooke can hear the fear in her voice as she speaks. Nicole writes a name on her business card and presses it into the hand in which Brooke holds her cell phone. "Please call her now, Brooke, and tell her about your sister and the baby, and the fact that..." Nicole stops, "and the fact that Nathan Carter is not the biological father, and tell her about your sister's condition." She leaves Brooke in the room feeling confused about why she should call a lawyer.

"Why should I trust her?" Brooke wonders, but she dials the number anyway. "This is Christine," the voice on the phone says. "Miss Freeman," Brooke gasps. "I was hoping I could retain you to assist my sister with some legal issues." Christine is about to tell her to call her office in the morning, but as soon as Brooke mentions that her sister is married to Nathan Carter, Christine tells her to stay put and that she is on her way. Brooke asks, "Don't you need to know the situation at hand?"

Christine assures Brooke, "Oh, I will know soon enough. I'll be at the Civic Hospital in ten minutes."

Brooke comes out of Tia's room and says to Nicole that the lawyer is on her way to meet with her at the hospital. Nicole breathes a sigh of relief, "I am going to keep Nathan away while you and Chris talk. I will call you on your sister's cell later."

Brooke wonders what Nicole's interest in all this might be, "what is she up to?" She is Nathan's friend and his business partner, so her role is automatically suspect. Brooke doesn't really want to know her game, but she does want to teach Nathan a lesson about trying to push her about.

Meanwhile, at home, Nathan is sitting in the hot tub with his eyes closed. The front door is unlocked so Nicole lets herself in. "How are you holding up?" Nicole asks. Nathan smiles. Nicole has always been there for him no matter what. Despite everything he did to her when they were in college, she is still willing to run his errands. He recalls the first day they met. She would do anything for him back then.

Nathan was a quarterback at high school. He was just as good-looking then as he is today, and by the time he was ten years old, he was an all-star in every sports team the school had. Of all the sports, he loved football the most, so when he won a scholarship to go to Stanford and play football, it was a dream come true, especially since both his mother and father went to university in America. He was an outsider as his team mates constantly made Canadian jokes at his expense. He had to try out to be on the Stanford elite football team regardless of his scholarship, and the fact that he had three national Canadian high school championships under his belt seemed to help his chances. The Americans were stronger, but then he was strong and faster, too. He was often alone until the day before Thanksgiving. Everyone was going home for the long weekend except him. The coach has always had a soft side for him, as he found Nathan to be more respectful than the other boys on the team. He was always the first one to come to practice and the last to leave. Coach invited Nathan to join his family for Thanksgiving. At first Nathan didn't want to go, but his dorm was so quiet, the silence was killing him. He thought he was the only one in the law library, when he decided to play his usual Perry Mason imitation, only out loud, forgetting about the no talking rules. Naturally, the staff told him to leave.

"You can't make me leave," he protested.

"Yes, I can!" said the young lady. "I work here and I take my job seriously." She whispered, "You dumb jock." Nathan heard what the girl had called him, so he quickly packed up his stuff and left. The girl could tell that he was upset, but she could care less. She was fed up with people getting a free ride on education. Nathan was in such rush that he left his book of hand-written poetry behind. The girl saw the book, and tried to get his attention. Nathan had run out and she felt kind of bad for what she had said. She opened the book to see what was in it and read the first page. She could not put it down because it was so well written.

The girl realized that it was late as she rushed through the campus. She saw Nathan walking with Stacy James, her roommate. Stacy was holding hands with Nathan, which was odd because she thought Stacy was seeing Eric Ross. "Hey! Hey… Nikita," Stacy called out to her.

Nicole joined Stacy, who said "Meet my friend, Nathan. I am trying to get him to come have Thanksgiving dinner with us, but he will not. Help me convince him to come. Eric is joining us," she said. "He loves the law just like you," Stacy added. "Nathan Carter meet Nicole Bright."

Nathan extended his hand and said, "very nice to meet you, Miss Bright. As I was saying to Stacy, I have a lot to do this weekend. Thank you both kindly for the invitation." Nicole was a little embarrassed. She called after him, "You left this behind earlier." She tried to take out his book from her backpack and everything dropped to the ground. He helped her pick up her things and he noticed how heavy her backpack was. He carried the book bag for Nicole, walking hand-in-hand with both girls, who lived just a twenty-minute walk from campus. They walked Stacy to her car first, where Nathan kissed her on the cheek; then he turned to Nicole and asked which one was her car. Nicole got in her car and before she drove off, she called out to him, "Nathan, I'm sorry for what I said. I mean before."

"It's forgotten," he waved at her.

Later, he went to the gym and as he was leaving the gym he saw Nicole looking kind of lost. "What are you doing back here this late?" Nathan asked.

She knew what she was going to say because she had it all prepared. "I have my brother in the car and we are going to this Pre-Thanksgiving Party... there's going to be a lot of girls... and food and you are coming with us."

Nathan thought that she had a lot of nerve assuming that he wants to go on a date with her. "Thank you, but no thank you," Nathan said politely.

There was a voice that Nathan recognized calling out to him, but he could not tell whose it was. The guy came out of the dark, one of the seniors from his team – Bright. He came and patted Nathan on the back, "Come! You can ride with me." Nathan was a little reluctant, so Bright dragged him to his car. The party was in a big house off campus. There was food and drinks everywhere, and the students were openly making out everywhere Nathan looked. Nathan did not know many people at Stanford, but they knew who he was. The girls all loved him, but his father has told him to be careful with the girls, and he was not about to disappoint his parents. He grabbed a plate and filled it with as much food as he could and sat in the empty dining room to eat.

Later, he saw Nicole with her boyfriend. The boyfriend was trying to make out with her right in front of Nathan. Nicole told the guy to stop, but he wouldn't. Nathan recognized him as one of the college's basketball players. Nathan told him to leave the lady alone, but the young fellow got angry with Nathan. He wanted Nathan to come outside and fight, and everyone was egging them on to fight. Nathan offered to take Nicole home. Nicole was crying and unable to respond, so Nathan picked up Nicole in his arms and began to walk towards the front door. One of the seniors at the party yelled out, "Oh Canada! You cannot just come to our town and steal our women." All the students thought the remark was funny. Nathan kept on walking and he put Nicole by her car as all the students at the party began making the chicken sound. Nathan turned and said, "Okay... Let's do it!" All the students went wild as one of the big guys on his team came and pushed Nicole's boyfriend aside and said, "You and me, Canada." Bright observed, "Dude, that's not a fair match!" The big guy said, " I see Canada is doing both the brother and the sister. Whoa!"

The students thought that was funny, too. "What are we waiting for?" Nathan yelled. The big guy took a swing at Nathan and almost got him on the side of his face. Nathan turned and punched him right up in his groin, flip-kicked his face, and stood back to survey the damage. The students went wild as they began chanting "Finish him Canada! Finish him Canada!" Nathan looked back at Nicole. She looked displeased with him. He helped the guy up and said, "I'm sorry, man. We guys shouldn't fight over pussy like this. It's not cool." The big guy lifted Nathan up in the air and shouted, "The championship is coming home to Stanford!!!" He put Nathan down and the students were still going nuts as the young man told Nathan not to leave. Nathan said he had to take Nicole home. The rival put his arms around Nathan and gave him some condoms and said "You stay safe 'lil dog'!!" He walked Nathan to Nicole's car and said, "I'm keeping my eyes on you, too."

Nicole drove Nathan back to the campus. They did not talk until just before Nathan got out of the car. He apologized to Nicole for fighting, and Nicole finally began to laugh. "I'm so happy you that you think getting my face kicked in on your behalf was funny. You have a good night now, Miss Bright!" Nathan said. He got out of the car. Nicole was still laughing as she ran after him. Nathan told her to go home as girls are not allowed in his dorm. Nicole asked him to come back to her place and he said no. "Are you a fag?" Nicole asked.

Nathan stopped walking and turned to walk back to Nicole's car. She could not see his face to know whether he was angry or what. Nathan slapped his lips against hers and began kissing her; before she knew it, they were in the back seat of her car having sex. It was wild, not only because Nathan was a good kisser, but also because he was a good fuck. He sent her flowers thanking her for a good Thanksgiving two days later. Nicole was pissed when Nathan told her that he has too many lovers to be going with one girl. She soon forgave him, though. A week after their sex in the car was Nathan's first game against UCLA. The starting quarterback got hurt in the first half and Nathan was told to warm up and go in to substitute. It was a home game and the crowd went nuts even though Stanford was down ten points. Nathan was ready; his parents had come to visit and they went to the game with Nicole, but they didn't know he was going to play until his name was announced.

He ran to the field with his helmet under his arms and the camera zoomed in on him; they put his profile on the big screen, and the UCLA coach started to kick the water cooler when he saw Nathan. He remembered going to Canada to recruit Nathan a year ago. At that time, Nathan had told him flat out that he was not interested in a career as a ball player and he was going to be a lawyer. Stanford had the ball, Nathan threw it and the running back was none other than Nicole's brother Bright, who had fumbled the last two Stanford balls. Only this time, Bright caught Nathan's forty yard pass. He jumped in the air, caught the ball, and ran all the way to touch down. The Stanford crowd watched the freshman from Canada throw a record-breaking four more touch downs. In the last four minutes of the game, the UCLA coach told his guys to be all over Carter or else!

UCLA had the ball for the last forty-five seconds of the game. When they threw the ball, Carter came out of nowhere and intercepted the ball. He ran forty yards to touch down and broke yet another school record. The commentator hardly knew what to say. After the game, in the Stanford locker room, the players went wild! Nathan took his shower and was gone before any of his team mates noticed. He joined his parents and Nicole. As he took his mother's hand, he saw the coach from UCLA, standing by the bus so pissed off at his boys.

Nathan quickly went over and greeted the coach. He remembered how well-mannered Nathan was when he met him in Canada. It looks like the kid has not changed much. The coach asked if he was okay at Stanford and Nathan replied, "Yes, sir." Turning to Mrs Carter, the UCLA coach said, "You have yourself one good boy here, ma'am." He got on the bus and waved at them. Nathan went on to break more records during his first year, although Stanford lost in the final four to the University of Ohio. During his sophomore year, they were again in the final four: this time Stanford beat University of North Carolina, becoming the conference champions. Nathan announced that he would not be playing football in his junior year. He wants to be a lawyer. He and Nicole have been the best of friends. He asked if she wants to come to the Virgin Islands with him. She accepted his invitation and while they were there, they made love for the very first time since that night in the back seat of Nicole's car two years ago. Their relationship became strange and they broke up. Throughout college, every now and then they end in bed. When they graduated, Nathan returned to Canada and went to law school.

Nathan and Nicole were reunited when they were both taking the California bar exams, which they both passed. They worked at the same law firm for two years and they were roommates. Nathan got fed up working for other firms, so he returned to Canada after three years and settled in Toronto. Six months later, Nicole joined him and Carter, Bright and Associates was formed. They have been friends and business partners ever since. Over the years, Nicole has witnessed Nathan's bad behavior with woman after woman. Nicole knows he loves Tia, but with Nathan one must always take precautions since you don't know what he may do next. Right now, he looks torn. "I am being punished by God," he says. "And my wife is paying the price of all my sins."

"Nate, she is going to be okay." Nicole assures him.

"I should have been there. Tia and I should be sleeping with our baby right now," Nathan protests.

Nicole does not know what to say to him. "Nathan, she is getting the best medical care this country has to offer, right now. You need to stay strong for her. I am going to call Brooke and find out how Tia is doing. Okay?" Nicole speaks to Brooke who reports that Tia is sleeping still, baby Jayzel is awake and has been crying for awhile. "Nathan, you've got to go and see Jayzel. She will not stop crying." Nicole tells him.

"I will not go to that hospital again! Tia is going to die and Brooke is going to take Jayzel away from me. It's better to let them all go, now." Nicole has had it with Nathan's self-pity. She tells him, "If you stay away and your wife dies, you have as good as lost that baby you already love so much. And if she doesn't die, you are going to lose them. As a lawyer, you know that baby is as good as yours. If you stay away, your sister-in-law will turn all your in-laws against you. You go to the hospital. Don't start anything that will push her over the edge. Show her kindness, suck it up and be there for your wife at the time she needs you. This will either make or break your marriage. Don't open the door for people to hurt you, Nathan. We have been friends for a long time, and I am telling you as a friend, you are making a grave mistake." Nicole left him to ponder her words.

Chapter 34

Nathan calls Brooke a little after Nicole's departure. "How are you?" Nathan asks.

Brooke has been advised by Christine not to get on his bad side and she must keep him close. She sighs. "They need you, Nathan. I am not your concern: your wife and child need you, if you care." Brooke restrains herself. She would like to say something biting, sarcastic, or worse, but she holds back the words.

"I am so sorry for before, Brooke. I felt lost when Tia fell sick, I felt helpless," Nathan mutters. "I am on my way. What can I bring for you?"

"Nothing. I am fine," she hangs up the phone. The baby fell asleep a little after midnight. Brooke tried to sleep in Tia's private room, but found she could not sleep. Naana has assured her that Tia will be fine, that she is not in any real danger, that Naana herself intends to come to Canada in two days' time. Brooke calls her mother, even though it is five in the morning in England. Sarah has been out of her mind with worry as soon as Bobby called her with news. She asks if the doctors know how Tia got the infection, but Brooke told her mother no.

There is a knock on the door. Nicole has brought some take out, but food is the last thing on Brooke's mind. The baby wakes up every four hours, she notices. She thanks Nicole and tells her to go home. If anything changes, she will let her know, she promises. Brooke removes her shoes and reclines on the hospital bed. Closing her eyes, she begins to cry. The nurse knocks on the door as she steps into the room. Brooke sits up, thinking the baby is awake. Apologizing, the nurse says, "I'm off duty now. Is there anything I can get for you before I leave?" Brooke thanks her and wishes her good night.

Nathan has returned to the hospital and is talking to the doctor when Brooke returns to check on Tia. The doctor explains that the lights are bothering Tia's eyes, so they have been turned down. There are patches on Tia's chest which connect to a kind of TV screen to monitor her heart. An IV tube has been inserted and taped onto her left hand for giving medicine and liquids. "Mrs Carter has been given antibiotics to help fight the bacterial infection. Acetaminophen also has been given to bring down her fever," the doctor said. Brooke asks whether Tia's nausea has stopped and when are they going to do the CT Scan?

"Anti-nausea medication has been given to get rid of the nausea. We have not done a CAT scan yet," the doctor replies.

"Dr. Michael Doyle will be here in the morning to take over my sister's care," says Brooke. She has not been impressed with this idiot of a doctor. She goes into the room to see Tia. The doctor tells Nathan that they are doing everything they can for Tia and Nathan thanks him and follows Brooke into Tia's private room.

"I came to take you to my parents' condo, so you can rest," Nathan offers. Brooke ignores him. "Brooke, please!" he begs. "Tia and the baby both need you now, I cannot have you falling sick as well. I am begging you now, please don't do this. I let my fear get in the way. I don't know what we are up against here. I am trying my hardest here, my wife's life is at risk and I'm useless to her, Brooke. I cannot have you sick, too. Tia, Jayzel and I need you."

"I will not leave Jayzel or Tia alone in a strange hospital!" Brooke cries. Nathan picks her up and places her on the bed and taking off her shoes, he covers her with a blanket. He sits down in a chair and tells Brooke to get some sleep. Brooke tosses and turns, but cannot get comfortable enough to nap.

"That's it! I'm taking you home!" Nathan says assertively.

Brooke feels too tired to fight with him. He should take her to his parents, but since it is almost two in the morning, he opts to take her to the house in Orleans. Upon arrival, Nathan quickly turns on the hot tub and tells Brooke to get comfortable while he goes and fixes her something to eat. The hot tub sure is inviting, and Brooke feels she needs to be surrounded in its warmth and feel the jets massage her aching muscles. She strips off right there and jumps in naked. While relaxing in the hot tub, Brooke can hear Nathan pottering in the kitchen. Clearly, he is not as accomplished in the kitchen as his father. She hears a mild curse as a plate shatters on the floor. Chuckling to herself, Brooke gets out of the hot tub, wraps a towel around herself and goes to the kitchen to investigate.

Brooke only wants a cup of tea, but Nathan does not know how to do that. Laughing, she makes tea for both of them. "I don't usually drink tea," Nathan admits. "Tia usually makes me a smoothie." He angrily throws the mug of tea in the sink. "This all my fault! I should have picked her up like I said I would. She would've been all right if I did." Brooke saw Nathan expressing real emotions for once. She hugs him and says, "Tia is going to be okay. She knows I'm here. She'd better be okay!" Nathan smiles. "I like how you always make a fuss of her. Thank you, Brooke. I don't deal with emotions as well as you do."

They were sitting in the family room when Nathan suddenly left the room. When he came back, he had a bottle of scented oil in his hands. At first, Brooke did not see what it was, but she enjoyed its fragrance as Nathan massaged it into her shoulders. She wants to tell him to stop, but she finds herself relaxing almost to the point of sleep. "Do you want me to stop?" Nathan asks. Brooke moans "no." Nathan stretches out on the sofa and pulls Brooke on top of him. He, then, covers them both with a blanket and massages her whole body with the rich, hot oil until she falls asleep. Beginning to relax, too, Nathan watches the glow of the light in the fireplace. "She looks so beautiful," he thinks. "How can I do this at a time like this?" He admonishes himself, "I will not lose my wife and child! I need to keep my eye on Brooke. She's crafty! And who is this Dr Michael Doyle she's got coming to take over Tia's care?" With a million and one questions on his mind, Nathan also fell asleep.

At six in the morning, Nathan opens his eyes, rolls Brooke over gently and goes to Tia's office to work on her computer. He notices her email box is open, so he reads every single message. He learns his wife really does indeed love him. There is no Kevin Peters on her contact list, and even though he looks through her private list too, she only has Nathan down with pink love hearts. He signs her out.

Dr. Michael Doyle, a specialist in bacterial infections, is the leading neurologist in Ontario. Nathan remembers reading about him, but wonders how Brooke got in touch with him in such a short time. He steps into the hallway to see if she's awake yet. Brooke is still sleeping, so Nathan quickly accesses his email box and responds to all the emails. Next, he calls his father and mother to give them an update on Tia and the baby. He informs them he'll be at the hospital once Brooke wakes up. His father is pleased that they are not fighting any more. Then, Nathan goes to the Tim Horton's to buy coffee and some muffins. When he returns, Brooke is still sleeping. He calls his in-laws in England and is told that Tia's mother will arrive in Canada tomorrow evening. He feels pissed that Brooke has not mentioned Naana's imminent arrival; nevertheless, he goes upstairs, takes a shower, and slips back into the sofa next to her.

Brooke feels him move next to her, and without thinking she moans "Jason" and feels for his crotch. Nathan, between the legs, is aroused. Brooke wastes no time to go down and give him a blow job, but Nathan gently pulls her up as he slips on the condom and sits her up to ride him; she opens her eyes to see Nathan nibbling her neck; she stops riding him, and as he begs her not to stop, he rolls them both on the floor and gets on top of her. He holds her afterward, and she has no idea how it all began, but a lot of ideas are going through her mind.

Nathan rubs her back and kisses her while she tries to talk. He moans, "No... let's not talk. Please, let's enjoy this time together." Nathan sits Brooke on top of him and brushes back her hair. He takes her hand and kisses it. "I'm so sorry I took out my anger on you last night at the hospital. I can not get through all of this without you." He puts his fingers in her mouth for her to suck.

"I've never known anyone as beautiful as you," Nathan says. He pulls himself up since Brooke is still sitting on him. "I promise that you will not see that side of me again, Brooke. Please say you believe that. I have thought about nothing but the night we shared four months ago. I did not want to call and confuse you, that's why I have not called you. This doesn't feel wrong to me." Brooke tried to respond, but he kisses her lips, instead. "Please tell me... you want us to be there for each other... when we can, Brooke." Nathan kisses her gently between her breasts.

"I've thought of you, too. I'm not sure about this. Tia will get hurt and we could both lose her," Brooke whispers.

"No, don't say that. Everyone knows you hate my bullying ways. My father and Nicole saw me physically grab you. They have also seen the hateful way we are toward each other... no one will ever think of a love affair between us. I know I come across as this is just sex between us... but there is more than that. Please don't say it's over. It cannot be over for us. You are all I think about." She kisses him on the mouth.

"We need to get back to the hospital," she murmurs. "We will, but not yet," and then Nathan whispers something naughty in her ear and she smiles. He takes her to the shower and washes and massages her hair. By the time they leave the house, it is almost lunch time. Brooke is angry with herself because she has not been able to keep to her own schedule, and also because Nathan can be *so* distracting. As they get into the limo, Nathan tells the driver to take the long way to Civic Hospital. He slips off her panties in the back of the limo and eats her up until they reach the hospital. Nathan is a very different lover than Jason. Oh, Jason... she has not spoken to him since she arrived in Canada. She begins to worry. "I have Jason on the line," Nathan whispers. Surprised, Brooke says, "Oh...no! I can't talk to him right now!" Nathan nods to her to take phone, but she refuses. He puts the cell phone against her ear and whispers something into her left ear as she talks with Jason. Nathan steps out of the limo, leaving Brooke talking to Jason. Nicole is in the hospital already with Nathan's father. They feel bad for him and for what he is going through: they both hug him. A few minutes later, Brooke is at the nurses' station holding a couple of boxes from Tim Horton's.

"She stopped at Tim Horton's to buy donuts and muffins for the nurses?" Nicole comments, "British people are very strange." Anthony is impressed. He thinks, "That's just like what Tia would do." Aloud, Anthony observes, "They are very thoughtful young ladies, and at a time like this Brooke thinks of other people first. I don't want your foolishness like last night, Nate. You are not the only one who loves Tia and the baby, son."

"I will not let Brooke walk all over me, Dad. They are my family! I will not put up with her. She dislikes me and the feeling is mutual," Nathan spat. Nicole joins the conversation. Brooke has coffee for all of them. She asks Anthony about Heather's health. "My mother has a gift for her. I must bring it to her soon. Do extend my apologizes to her for me. I should have at least called her this morning myself," Brooke says.

Anthony responds, "only if you come and have dinner with us tonight. Nathan will bring you, and you two must get along. Tia will be very upset to know you two are constantly at each other's throats. Please, honey, we are all worried about Angel. Nicole gave the baby her bath and I fed her bottle, so she is sleeping now. Any ideas about when Tia wants baby home?" Anthony asks.

"She was in and out of sleep, and I was hoping to talk to you and Nathan about that after my meeting with Dr. Doyle. Do you care to join us?" Brooke asks. "If we all meet together, then we can have all our questions answered. I need you all here, if you don't mind... and I am sorry for my rude outburst last night. It was really uncalled for."

Nathan says, "it's okay, Brooke. We're all stressed."

"No, it isn't okay. It was an added stress none of you deserved," Brooke adds. "I was unprepared for this. Tia is my little sister, and I'm usually telling people what to do, not the other way around."

"Really? We had not noticed," Nathan says sarcastically.

"You know? It's too bad your son doesn't have your charm. Are you sure Nathan is your child?" Anthony and Nicole laugh. "Trust me, honey, he is our child." Anthony assures Brooke.

Nathan gives her a hug. Seeing peaceful relations established, Anthony and Nicole feel very proud of Nathan. Dr Doyle is an older doctor. He remembers Anthony from Toronto years ago when they were both interns at Toronto Children's Hospital. They have not seen each other for years. "Seeing them re-connect is like watching a pair of teenage boys," Brooke thinks. The family has gathered with Dr Doyle in Tia's private room. Brooke is not happy with Dr. Doyle. "Dr Michael Doyle, I trust." Brooke cuts in. Everyone becomes very still and quiet as they knew her well by now. "My sister is in here with tubes all over her body." Dr Doyle tries to say something, but Brooke immediately snaps at the doctor, "I'm not finished! Don't interrupt me when I'm speaking!" Nathan has had it with her rudeness towards the doctor and Nicole taps his shoulders to relax. "As I was saying... I need for you to give me your expert opinion on my sister's illness." The doctor tries to say something and again, Brooke silences him one more time: "She is in isolation right now, all the necessary medication been given to her to control her nausea and fever. I want you to perform a CAT scan on Tia right now, doctor. Let me know if the infection has been spreading to her brain. I need you to tell me how the infection is, and what we need to do to contain it!" Everyone in the room is staring at Brooke. "You must be Jackson and Sarah Williams' kid," Dr Doyle says with a smile on his face. Nathan feels relieved. "She knows him, so that's why she was able to get him in such short notice," he says to himself. "Dr. Doyle, may I remind you that you have been retained as my sister's doctor? This is not a social call!" Brooke reminded the doctor. Everyone in the room expresses shock at Brooke's pushy demeanor except Dr. Doyle. "You, honey, are as beautiful as your mother was at your age. You have Jackson's spirit." Dr .Doyle adds, "Come here, honey, and give your dear old uncle a hug." Nathan and his father were able to breathe. Brooke is a little embarrassed, but she hugs Doyle anyway. He lets go of her and says in soft voice, "You know? Jack would have been so proud if he was here today. The way you had a go at me just now... that was old Jack." Dr Doyle is a little tearful.

"Tia..." he continues. "I am way ahead of you. Sarah told me a little about Tia's condition this morning." He takes an X-ray out of its protective sleeve and holds it in the air. "This is a picture of Tia's lungs and heart. It shows how well they are handling the illness, but she's not out of danger yet."

"Is the illness present or is she still in danger?" Brooke asks.

"I am waiting on her blood work. I will know more when I get the results from the lab," he comments.

"That's not acceptable to me Doctor. I have family at home sitting on pins and needles right now, waiting and worrying about Tia's condition."

Nathan interrupts, "Brooke. A word in private? Right now, please."

"Dr. Doyle, please excuse me. I want you to think about something while I have a quiet word with my brother-in-law here." She points to Anthony Carter, "you see your old chum here is Tia's father-in-law. The poor darling has been here half the night not knowing what his daughter-in-law faces, or when he can take his baby granddaughter home. I need to know about Tia blood work in the next ten minutes or I will be forced to throw a British fit!" She points to Nathan and says, "Tia's jerk of a husband and his girl pal over there," she points to Nicole whose mouth is open in shock and surprise, "will be filing some kind of a lawsuit against me to prevent me from taking the baby back to England. Dr. Doyle, I must say, I am not impressed at all!" She made a hand gesture and left the room. Dr. Doyle turns to Anthony and exclaims, "Wow! Isn't she adorable! I hope your boy can hold his own, Tony?" Dr Doyle and Anthony both laugh.

Chapter 35

Nathan broods, thinking over what has just happened in Tia's room. When he finally speaks, Brooke is surprised. "Are you sure you sell houses for living? You sure sound like an attorney in there, Brooke." He hugs her and whispers. "I am so proud of you. I want to get you out of here and have my way with you." Nicole walks in on them hugging and says, "Thank God, you two are not fighting." She turns to Brooke and says, "Are you sure you're not an attorney?"

"That was what I just asked," Nathan says. "I've been so worried. I just don't know what to ask. Thank you, Brooke, for everything." He continues, "I mean it, Brooke. Nicole told me how you comforted the baby last night and now this, too. Thank you." He knows Nicole is standing there, but doesn't care if she hears it. "I love you, Brooke." He murmurs again, "I love you." Brooke returns to the room. Nathan goes to Nicole, hugs her and thanks her for her support. "Thank you, Nikkie." He has not called her that pet name for a long time. Since he met Tia, their under the table love affair, as they both call it, has been almost non-existent these days. She misses him. Her affair with Nathan has helped with her loveless marriage to Ian. The man has no spontaneity in the lovemaking department. It is always the same, and even after five years of marriage, nothing has changed. "Nate, I'm going to head back to my hotel; call if you need me. I leave a day after tomorrow for Toronto." Nicole reminds Nathan.

"Wait! I will come with you now," he says. She knows that tone; her heart feels warm. Nathan tells Brooke and his father he has to leave, something needs his attention at the court house. His father is not very happy with him at all, and voices his displeasure: "That's what assistants are for, son." Brooke adds, "There is no point all of us waiting at the hospital. Anthony, you should go home, too, and spend time with Heather. If anything changes, I will let you all know." Turning to Nathan, she winks, "Don't be in a rush to come back!" Nathan grins in reply as he and Anthony go in search of the limo. As they get into the vehicle, Nathan tells the driver to drop them off at Tia's old apartment. Nicole is sub-letting the place until August when Tia's lease runs out. Nathan tips the limo driver and tells him to take Anthony home and to return to the apartment for him at six. It is now twenty after one. The chauffeur loves driving Nathan because he gives more tips than the driver makes in a month.

"Yes, sir, Mr. Carter!" the driver responds as he pulls away from the curb. Meanwhile, Nicole is in the dining room sorting files – which to take to Toronto and which to leave in Ottawa – when Nathan takes off her panties, bends her over and presses his hardness against her bare buttocks. She moans softly as she rests her head on the table and feels his warmth inside her. He sleeps afterward. Nicole didn't want the afternoon to end. They have not shared an afternoon like this for a long time. Since Nathan met Tia, it has been nothing but work between them. Nathan wakes and sees Nicole deep in thought. "Nikkie, what are you thinking about?" he asks.

Nicole smiles: "We've not made love..." she stops and he finishes her sentence for her, "Since I met Tia. We don't have to do this anymore if you don't want to. You never wanted to be my wife. This is what you wanted, remember? I will not leave my wife for you Nikkie." He murmurs, "I have a family now."

Nicole is visibly upset. "I was not thinking of that! The thought has never crossed my mind, Nate. We have not been together for a long time. I just figure things have changed or maybe we are finished! That's all."

Nathan sits up, "Do you want us to be done? I don't want us to be over, Nikkie," he says softly.

Nicole does not respond. Nathan gets out of the bed and begins to get dressed. "So you're just gonna fuck me and run?" Nicole yells at him.

"I will never apologize for my marriage. I have sucked it up for the past five years as your sex slave. I am in love with my wife. Nikkie,

I don't want to lose her and my child. What I have with her is more than your wild sex games," replies Nathan.

"Your ego is bigger than the whole country. You made me get rid of our child, Nathan, and here you are fighting for a baby that isn't even yours!" Nicole screams, in tears now.

"We promised never to mention this matter again. I am leaving now," he screeches. As he closes the apartment door behind himself, Nathan calls a taxi and then calls his office. There are no messages for him, so he tells his assistant to call his wife's cell and let his sister-in-law know where he is. He also asks her to call Henry, his driver, to pick him up from the office at five, instead. Nicole calls Brooke and asks, "What did Christine advise you to do?"

Brooke guardedly replies, "Oh, all that's under control. Don't worry, Nicole."

Nicole responds, "I understand you don't trust me, and it's okay. I am concerned about Tia and the baby. In case Christine did not advise you to register the baby's birth and keep Nathan's name off the birth records as the baby's father, you should be doing that before the baby leaves that hospital if you wish your sister to be able to leave Canada with her child one day."

Brooke couldn't help feeling suspicious of Nicole, "May I ask what is your interest in all this?"

"I leave for Toronto tonight; you have my number if you ever need me. The man is my business partner, so I cannot assist you in any legal matters, but I have the best lawyer to help when the time comes and Tia needs it. I know Nate better than you and your sister," Nicole reveals, avoiding the real question.

Tia will be in the hospital for another three weeks. Brooke calls Bobby Sharp and tells him there is no more danger; she will take the baby home tomorrow once Tia's mother arrives. The baby's name is Jayzel-Gertrude Sharp. Bobby asks why the baby's surname is Sharp instead of Carter. Brooke tells him to read his email now. He does as Brooke suggests. As he comes to the end of the message, Bobby thinks about what he has read for a minute and says, "well done, Sweetheart! If there is anything that you need help with, let me know, okay? I love you!" and he hangs up the phone. Bobby asks his assistant to retrieve as much information as she can find about Canada's family law. He calls Kate and leaves a message for her to get Jaden to call him. It's been almost two weeks since Tia gave birth. Her health is improving though she is still in isolation. The baby has been at home since the arrival of Tia's mother in Canada. Nathan hires a nurse for the baby, and Jayzel spends her first weekend at the cottage with the Carter's and Mrs Sharp. Nathan tells his parents and his mother-in-law that he has to be in Toronto over the weekend and will return on Monday afternoon. He wastes no time meeting Brooke in Chateau Laurier where he keeps a penthouse suite. He calls Jason their first night, while he makes love to Brooke and insists that she have phone sex with Jason. He gives her no choice as he whispers the words she should say to Jason while he makes love to her. They both enjoyed the evening the next day across the river in Hull. Nathan takes Brooke to Casino de Hull, where they spend the night at the Ramada Hotel nearby. They win a lot of money playing card games at the casino. At one o'clock in the morning, as they leave the casino, Nathan remarks, "I have a surprise for you, Brooke" as he slips a blindfold over her eyes. He leads her into the hotel and up the elevator to their room.

"I want to know whether you still remember this," he says as he pulls up a chair and tells Brooke to sit down. A moment later, Nathan lets two women into the room. Brooke feels frozen with fear, but Nathan reassures her that everything is okay. He speaks in French to the women, telling them what to do, and gives them all his winnings from the casino in payment. Brooke has a strong sense of déjà-vu: the sex games are reminiscent of the night before Nathan's wedding day. Later, he walks the women out of the room. As he stands against the door leaning his head on it, he says, "Tell me your wildest sexual fantasy and it's yours." Brooke has never imagined people like Nathan really existed and yet some how she has let herself become part of his twisted sexual games. She enjoys every moment and every element of surprise. She feels she has let his best friend's horny husband take over her sexually... She has reached a point of no return because she is getting married to Jason in two months. How is she going to explain herself if news of this affair ever comes out?

"Thanks to you, I have lived all my fantasies. What about you?" Brooke asks. Nathan simply winks and smiles.

Tia is home with her baby, and her mother is still in Canada. A week before her mother leaves, Tia goes to the British Embassy in Ottawa to obtain a passport for Jayzel, accompanied by her mother and Nathan. While at the embassy, Nathan is surprised to learn what Brooke has done: his name is not listed on the child's birth records as the child's father. Angry, he tells Tia that he needs to be at the office, and he will see them at home later. Nicole is in Ottawa on business, so Nathan asks to meet her in the apartment.

"No, Nate. Call one of your other whores. I don't have time for your games!"

Dissatisfied with her response, Nathan walks down the hall to Nicole's office. Even though she is on the phone, he takes the phone away from her and disconnects the call. He slams the baby's birth certificate on the desk. Nicole does not blink an eye. Screaming, Nathan accuses, "You knew about this?" Nicole does not flinch.

"Look at me, Nicole! Please tell me you did not know about this? ... Tell me now!" he demands. Nicole still refuses to respond. Nathan leaves the building in a flurry of slammed doors and muttered curses.

Chapter 36

In the afternoon, it is hotter than when Nathan left the house in the morning. He jumps into a taxi and goes to the gym. He feels broken up inside and needs to let off some steam. By the time he gets home, it is late and Tia is asleep. He spends the night downstairs in his office finding out what he can do to have his name put on the baby's birth record. The phone rings, Jason Grey is calling from London. "I know you played American football at college, but do you like soccer?" Jason asks. He sounds excited. Nathan does not know how to respond. "Um, no, sorry Jason. Why do you ask?"

"I have two tickets to the FIFA World Cup Finals in France and I thought we could have a boys' night out when you and your family come down next week for our wedding." Nathan didn't have to think about it: "It sounds good. I will take care of the flight and the hotel from my end," Nathan says. He has a big smile on his face when he hangs up the phone.

Brooke and Jason's wedding is very lovely, certainly less stressful than Tia's, she found. Tia notices a lot of things in England have changed. She didn't like being there as much as she thought she would. She took the train to Oxford Street to do some shopping with Kate two days before returning to Canada. Someone taps her on the shoulders and she turns to see who it is, and her heart skips a beat as she hugs and kisses the man. Kate watches them, puzzled. Tia reveals to the man that she has a baby and is married and living in Canada, where she is returning on the day after tomorrow. The man looks surprised. He asks Tia for her number and Kate gives it to him.

"Who was that guy?" Kate asks.

"Oh! That's Aaron, Kevin's younger brother," Tia replies.

Kate wishes now that she hadn't given him her number. "Perhaps, he will not mention it to Kevin after all. He always knew where we all lived and not once has he come by and said a simple hello," Kate thinks. As soon as Kate and Tia return to the Sharp's home, the phone rings. It is Aaron calling to ask Tia whether he can come by and see the baby before Tia leaves for Canada. Tia says, "Of course, anytime you want." Tia does not give the call a second thought. It is her last night in England.

They are leaving in the morning to drive to Holland. Nathan has gone with his father-in-law to rent a car for the trip. The door bell rings and Kate answers the door. To her surprise, Kevin and his brother are on the doorstep. Tia is just coming downstairs with the baby and asks, "Kate, who is at the door?" as Kate swings the door wide to reveal the Peters brothers.

Tia gasps when she sees him. Smiling, Tia invites the men to come into the house. "Can I hold the baby?" Aaron asks. "Sure!" Tia says as she passes the child to him and goes to the kitchen to prepare some snacks. When she returns, Kevin is holding the baby, smiling. "Are you really married?" asks Kevin. Tia replies, "Yes, to a wonderful man!" She returns to the kitchen and on her way back to the living room, she meets her father and her husband at the door. "We are all set, baby!" Nathan says happily. He sees a guy he doesn't know holding and kissing the baby. He has met all of Tia's relatives in the past two weeks, apart from the her grandparents, so these strangers take him by surprise. Tia takes Nathan's hands and she introduces him to Aaron and Kevin.

"This is my husband, Nathan." Nathan takes the baby in his arms and asks to be excused. He goes to their room with the baby. Kevin and his brother wish Tia a safe trip back to Canada. Before they leave, they give her some cards from their other brothers and sisters wishing her love. Once the Peters brothers are gone, Tia finds Nathan putting the baby to bed. She finishes packing all their stuff, and asks Nathan to put it all by the door. Kate notices that he looks a little bit uncomfortable and asks, "Are you okay, Nathan?"

He tells her good night and retreats up the stairs. Kate feels anxious about Kevin's visit and the look on Nathan's face when he learns about Kevin. It sends strong chills down her spine. It is hard saying good-bye to them in the morning.

Tia sits in the back of the vehicle with the baby. Before too much time has passed, they are in France. Just before they arrive at the border between France and Belgium, their car spins out of control and crashes on the barriers of the bridge. There is smoke in the car as Nathan manages to get out of the vehicle. He looks at the car hanging half-way tilted over the bridge, as he stands there cleaning himself up. A passing car sees the accident and stops. The stranger asks whether he is okay, in French and English, but Nathan does not respond. He sees Tia holding the baby out as she tries to open the car the door.

The stranger quickly takes the baby and places her on the ground and manages, just in time, to get Tia out of the car before it flips over the bridge. Tia cries out, "my husband is still in the car!" She buries her face in her hands as she cries out in pain. Nathan quickly goes to her and wraps his arms around her, "Baby- baby, I'm not in the car," he says softly. Tia is still in shock and crying as Nathan holds her close. Tia pushes him back thinking he is the stranger. She screams, "Why did you not save him? He is the only man that I truly loved and he loved me." She wipes her face and sees Nathan. He looks unchanged. She touches his face and drops her hands. And then touches his face again. She says, "You look so handsome, even in death." Confused, Nathan looks at the stranger holding the baby. Speaking in French, he asks the man if he knows what is the matter with his wife. The man replies, "She is in shock. All of you probably are in shock." Nathan asked if he knows where the nearest hospital is. The man says that Tia will be fine. He asks where they were going.

Nathan says, "Amsterdam." The stranger calls the insurance company for them, puts the baby in his car and tells Nathan to help Tia into the vehicle. The police arrive before the tow truck, and they inquire whether Nathan and Tia need any further assistance. Nathan says no. Coming out of her shock, Tia could not stop kissing and hugging Nathan and the baby. She hugs the stranger, too, thanking him for rescuing them. The stranger wants to drop them off at the nearest car rental place, but Tia asks how far it is to the nearest airport. The man replies that an airport is not far, closer, in fact, than the car rental place.

He drops them off at the airport and both Tia and Nathan give him their cards. Nathan wants to give him money for gas, but he refuses. There is a KLM flight going to Amsterdam in an hour. Nathan manages to get them a seat on it. The baby is awake. Miraculously, she has slept through the whole ordeal. As Nathan hands Tia a cup of tea, she notices his hands are shaking, so she immediately hugs him. She calls her grandfather to send Guntar to meet them at Shcipol Airport in Amsterdam. Guntar and Osei Kofi are both at the airport waiting for Tia and her family. As soon as he sees them he calls Gertrude and asks her to call Naana and Bobby to let them know that they are okay. Osei Kofi tearfully hugs and kisses Tia. Tia takes the baby from Nathan while he hugs Osei. When they arrive at the grandparents home, a doctor is waiting to see them. Tia claims she is okay, but Nathan insists that the doctor examine his wife and the baby. "They are all fine," he affirms upon concluding his examinations. Gertrude could not put the baby down, "She is so pretty, my dear," she whispers to Tia. The baby is now three months old. "She sleeps through the night, now" Nathan says proudly.

Gertrude calls Rose, her maid, "Will you get my camera, please, Rose?" A proud great-grandmother, Gertrude takes many photographs. "Come here, Nathan! Come and sit with me and have your picture taken with us – baby and me!" Turning to Tia, Gertrude announces, "Tomorrow I have a photographer coming here to take formal photos of all of us. Is she not the most adorable baby?" Gertrude's eyes beam. "She has grown since the last photograph that we have of her," she pointed to a table in the corner where all kinds of photographs of the baby were proudly displayed, even some which Nathan had not seen before.

They had lunch and Tia slept afterward. Nathan could not get the accident out of his head. He was trying to recall how the whole thing happened. He was sure it was all his fault. Why did Tia bring *him* to see the baby? He trusted her. Did she sleep with *him* while we were there? The thought of Kevin holding the baby haunted him so that he had no sleep that night just thinking about it. Finally, Nathan was able to lay down and sleep. He had a nightmare so real that when he woke up his whole body was soaking wet, his body was shaking so badly he could not stop. Tia held him and said that it was okay and it was just a dream. She held him while he sobbed. Nathan held on tight to her, but his own thoughts felt God was punishing him for all the wrongful things he has done. He wants to tell Tia everything, but he feels it is best to wait until they are home in Canada. At least there he stood a better chance of her forgiving him.

When Kate was told about the accident, she was relieved that Tia, Nathan and the baby were all safe. It was Saturday, and Kate found herself at her mother's by herself again. Brooke was on her honeymoon in Italy. Tia was in Amsterdam, so Kate decided to call Jaden and say she was ready to talk. She didn't want to talk to him at her mother's or at his place, so they decided to meet in the middle, at a small coffee shop they both knew well. Jaden got there first. He waited for three hours, but Kate did not show. He was disappointed, but not surprised considering how strained the relationship has been. He went to the gym for a workout and then to Aldie Mart near his place and bought some milk. When he got close to his house, he saw Kate waiting by his door. He began to panic, thinking they were meant to meet up here. Kate smiled when she saw him. "I was be beginning to wonder where you were." Jaden did not know if he should kiss her or tell her that she looked nice. He opened the door and asked her to come in. There was no furniture in the place.

It was nicely painted in earth tone colors. Kate could smell the paint. She asked if Jaden been painting. "Yeah. The bathroom and the bedrooms were painted just a few hours ago. I was hoping the smell would be gone by now. I left all the windows open on my way out. I'd better close them before the rain gets in." The kitchen was a lot larger and cleaner than the kitchen in his old flat. Everything looked new. "I like the place," said Kate.

"Yeah, me too. It was a fixer-upper. Brooke warned me not buy it. I think once I'm done, it will look a lot more like a home." Jaden smiles. "I will get you a chair. Just one second." He came back with an office chair for her, then he dashed off to the kitchen and made tea. It tasted different. "What kind of a tea is this?" asked Kate.

Jaden told her, "Honey lemon tea." There was silence between them.

"I thought we were meant to meet at the coffee shop. I sort of stood you up," they both said at the same time. They both laughed. Kate said, "I couldn't find my keys, and then on the way out, my cell phone died so I couldn't call. The lady at the coffee shop said you came and waited a long time. She remembered because you were alone," she smiled.

"I went to the gym and then did some shopping," said Jaden.

"I am sorry I have not returned any of your calls, Jaden," Kate said.

"I do understand," he murmured. He looked more relaxed and at peace with himself. He was laying down on the floor looking out of the window. "You said you wanted to talk… What do you want to talk about, Kate?" he smiled encouragingly.

"I miss you..." she paused, " and I let things spin out of control. I can't pretend that I'm happy with you," she said softly.

"I cry all the time when I think about how much I have hurt you, Kate," Jaden confessed. There was a box of tissues beside him. He took one and wiped her tears off her cheeks. He continued, "I know that what I have done can not be changed. That's what hurts the most. I want you to be happy with whoever you are seeing. I hope he treats you with much more respect than I did. I really did not mean to embarrass you the way that I did. I am so very sorry, Kate."

"I cheated on you," she blurted out.

Shocked, Jaden exclaimed, "So you were sleeping with him! I was right!"

Kate, confused, asks, "Who are we talking about? I am not sleeping with anyone. Why would you even think that?"

"You just admitted it," he said.

Kate was upset, so she spilled the beans. "I was minding my own business at Tia's hen night... The next thing that I knew, one of the strippers I had been dancing with earlier was under the table giving me..." she paused.

"What was he giving you? Did he drug you?" Jaden asked, frowning.

Kate, red-faced, blurted it out: "oral sex."

Jaden ran to the bathroom and slammed the door shut, out of his mind with laughter. Kate didn't know what to think. A few minutes later, he returned and said, "Sorry, Kate. But that was so funny. You should have seen the look on your face!"

"I am leaving! I should have kept it to myself and lied just like everyone else," she snapped at him.

"Kate, love, I'm sorry. I'm glad you told me. I thought you were seeing someone from work. That's why I was jealous," he said. "Kate, I'm still very much in love with you, but I cannot make you forgive or forget what's in the past. You have to know what you want, okay? I will support whatever you want as long as you are happy. Kate! I will! Please, don't leave unless you want to." She stopped. "Come, I want to show you the rest of this place," he said, taking her by the hand. Later, they came back to the living room to watch TV. "So… tell me: Did this stripper eat you up better than I used to, or what?" Jaden asked with a silly grin on his face. Kate had forgotten what a tease he could be. "You must admit it *is* hilarious," Jaden added. "It's not your average hen party wild sex story."

"You are not going to let this go are you?" Kate asked playfully. She was glad they were talking. It was nice, and it wasn't as bad as she thought it would be. Later, Kate said, "I want us to try again."

Jaden kissed her on the cheek and said, "I would like that very much." They spent the weekend together. She helped him study for his finals, which he passed, and was later offered a job at Edwards Law Office. Just two weeks before Christmas, they eloped in Scotland. Only their mothers were in attendance. When she heard the news, Tia was very happy for them. Brooke was not as delighted as one might expect, but she came around when Jaden hired her to find them a home to buy as Kate was pregnant and this time he wanted everything to be done right for them.

Chapter 37

It is almost Christmas. Anthony and Heather Carter have already left for the Virgin Islands for the Christmas holidays. It is Nathan's and Tia's first Christmas with the baby. Tia has noticed since the birth of the baby she and Nathan have not made love. He seems to be very distant when he is home, often in his own thoughts. He still has nightmares about their car crash in France and will not talk about it. She has given him his space, perhaps too much space as her mother-in-law has advised her. It is the day of the Santa Claus Parade and he wants Tia to come with him and the baby, but Tia told him she has to study as she is using her maternity leave from Nortel to finish her degree. She tells him to go with the baby's nanny and promises she will fix something nice for them for supper. She kisses him and returns to her books. The afternoon passes quickly as Nathan, enjoying the time alone with the baby, realizes that he has let his jealousy and anger affect his marriage. He needs to fix it quick, but he has no ideas how. He loves the baby very much and he knows that she could not be taken away from him as easily as he has been thinking. He laughs out loud and the baby does, too. She is seven months old and already crawling. She loves climbing on top of him, and he often lays down on the nursery floor so she can crawl all over him. It is relaxing playing with her. She is getting bigger every day and looking more adorable each day, too. On their way back from Santa's parade, they stop at the Orleans Mall and visit Toys-R-Us. He notices that the baby is a baby magnet, too. Everyone is looking at them as he buys as many toys as he and the nanny can carry.

When they return home, Tia is done studying for the day and talking on the phone with Sarah Williams. As she watches Nathan and Jayzel play, she thinks they look like two kids playing. Tia loves that side of Nathan. He gives the baby a bath every night and sings all kinds of songs to her: mind you, he can not carry a tune to save his life! Tia makes supper as she planned. As usual, they eat in silence as no conversation flows between them. Tia is making a smoothie for him later that evening as she normally does at the end of the day, when she told him she was planning a pre-Christmas party for him and his associates in Ottawa. She thought it would be a nice way to thank them for making the transition to Ottawa easy, and at the same time thank them personally for their support when the baby was born. It warms his heart as he listens to her about her plans; it was just like last year when he took her to his parents' cottage. As soon as she learned about his mother's illness, she made everything better for him and that was when he fell madly in love with her. Tia interrupted his thoughts.

"Sweetie! Are you listening to me?" She stops what she is doing. "Nathan!" She sits down next to him. There is a great silence for about a minute. Tia says, "I don't know what is going on with you, but I want my husband back."

"What are you talking about, Tia?" Nathan says defensively.

"Baby, you have been distant from me since.... well, at least since I returned from the hospital. I thought maybe..." she stops.

"You thought what?" he asks nervously.

Encouraged, Tia continues, "I know how much you hate it when someone you love gets sick, Nathan. I am sorry I put you through that." Nathan tried to hug her and tell her that it was not her fault, but she moved away from the sofa and stood up. "I did not want to be sick and leave you with our child." Nathan's heart spiked a beat when Tia said that. "I know my mom being here put a lot of stress on us." Nathan tried to grab her hands, but again, she moved away from him. He pleaded with her to stop, claiming that what she said about her mother was just not true. "I love Brooke. I know what a pain and a bossy pants she can be." Nathan did not like where this was heading at all. "Nathan... I wanted to have the baby with the man that I love by my side and come home and enjoy being a parent... being in love with the most wonderful man that I know, besides my Dad and my father-in-law." Nathan could not hold it in any longer. He exhaled and bit the side of his mouth as he wiped the tears off his face. Tia was in tears, too, as she continued and said that she had not wanted to return to England for Brooke's wedding. "I told Brooke that a marriage should be based on love, respect, and trust, and I could not be a part of her wedding knowing she had cheated on Jason the night before our wedding."

Nathan almost had a heart attack: he could not breathe as soon as Tia mentioned Brooke and the night before their wedding. Tia had her back turned on him when she said it. She did not see the expression on her husband's face. "I only agreed to go because you wanted to see the football in France and my mother thought it would be nice for us to spend the summer there, so she can show you and the baby off to everyone. I wanted to show you and the baby off, too." Nathan was still breathless. He was panting...

"Who did Brooke cheat with on the night of our wedding?" he mumbled. Tia turned and said, "I know that you and Jason have formed a friendship, so this is not our business. I don't know who she slept with, Nathan, and I don't want to get involved in that subject as it makes me very uncomfortable. I fear the consequence when the truth of that night comes out. I somehow feel Brooke's foolish act has tarnished everything we all believed about a relationship."

Nathan did not know his wife as much as he thought he did. He finally took her in his arms and he had this serious look on his face when he said, "Tia, we have a good marriage. I thank God everyday for you, and now the beautiful baby girl upstairs. Baby, I am so sorry that I have abandoned you as your husband. I let my jealousy get to me, and I almost killed us."

Tia asked, "What do you mean kill us?"

He had his face in his hands, sobbing. "Tia, the car crash was all my fault! I wasn't paying attention as I should have."

Tia rushed to him and said, "No, sweetie, it was not your fault." She kissed him on the check. "Sweetie, please, you need to get that out of your head. Baby, you have not had a good night's sleep since the crash. I don't know how to help you deal with the nightmares as you won't talk to me about it. I thought I should leave you be. I am so sorry for all of this."

The Silent Sisterhood

Nathan was angry and he shouted, "No! Kevin is the one who should be sorry!" Tia was confused. "Who the hell is Kevin?" she asked.

"Jayzel's father!"

Tia was angry, too. "Kevin Peters is not Jayzel's father! The hell with you!" She ran upstairs. Nathan ran after her and found her in the baby's room. He has never before seen this much anger in his wife. She pushed past him on her way to the kitchen, where she took out a bottle wine from the fridge and went to her office. Nathan followed her.

"Tia, please! We can't leave things the way they are." Nathan said softly. "We need to discuss this."

"I am done discussing." She raised her glass and drank some of the wine. "Please hear me out, Tia, if not for the sake of our marriage then for our baby girl's sake." She threw the wine glass and almost hit him. "Our baby girl!" she screamed. "A minute ago she was some idiot's child. Is that why you did not put your name on her birth record?" She spat accusation at him. Nathan was equally angry now. "How could you say that?" he responded. "I've loved Jayzel from the moment she kicked my hands, only to be told in front of strangers in a hospital when she was born that she was not mine and will never be by Brooke Williams. What was I supposed to do, Tia?" Tia threw the book right at him and said, "You're supposed to be my husband!" She was throwing at him everything and anything she could get her hands on. "What's mine is yours and what's yours is mine." She threw more things at him. "Isn't that what it's supposed to be?" She screamed, "or it does it not apply to your wife's bastard child!" Nathan Carter could not believe those words came out of his sweet, sweet wife's mouth. "Tia, restrain yourself. I will not have you refer to my daughter in that manner. I will not have my wife..." he paused. He sat on the edge of her desk listening to the baby crying. Tia got up to go see to the baby, and he grabbed her hands gently and walked up to the baby's room with her. By the time Nathan and Tia got there, she had stopped crying and gone back to sleep. He picked Tia up and swung her body out of the baby's room onto their bed and lay down next to her. He held her tightly, fearful she might run off. "Tia, I want you to listen to me, please," he said in a soft spoken voice. "Everything you said was true. I should have stood up and been your husband when Jayzel was born. It was never the reasons you've been thinking. I have been really insecure, more so when I saw Kevin holding Jayzel in your parents' living room." He let go of her and sat up on the bed. "Tia, I don't want a marriage that has no trust. You and I have always had that. I love you and Jayzel very much, especially since I could have lost you both in the accident has some how changed me. Not how ... much you girls mean to me, but..." he paused and got back in bed next to her again. "I have everything that a man could want with you and our daughter, a complete desire." He sighed. Tia said she was sorry for starting the argument. They were in their own thoughts as they slept.

Tia made good on her promise: she wanted Nathan's three associates and their wives to join them for dinner on Christmas Eve. She was told by Nathan's assistant that the office would be closed on the tenth, that most of them would be out of town with their families. She arranged to have a drink up and a small dinner party for them in the conference room, instead. Tia turned the conference room into a Christmas oasis. She hired a caterer for the food and drinks. The afternoon of the party she got her nails and hair done; at five, Nathan's driver was there to pick her up, and she looked simply stunning as she walked into her husband's private office unannounced. Nathan was in his own world after talking to his sister. She was spending the Christmas with them, and she was the only family member who had not yet seen the baby. He lifted his head up as the door opened. His heart skipped a beat as Tia seldom came to the office. "It's everything alright?" he asked.

"I need a date for a party I'm going to," Tia said casually. Nathan looked at his watch, saw it was five o'clock in the afternoon, and thought "why would his wife be going to a party in the middle of the week? She has an exam to write in the morning... what the hell is she playing at?" He has had enough of her little games and he is going to put a stop to it now. He cannot have her behaving like one of his whores, he thought. He came out from behind his desk ready to lay down the law to her. Tia took off her coat. She looked fabulous, and he told her so as their eyes met and held until his assistant came in and said, "Mrs Carter, everyone is down in the conference room as you requested, ma'am."

Tia thanked her and asked her to tell Henry the driver to join them. Nathan was lost. Tia walked slowly to him and kissed him softly on the lips. She has not done that for ages. Then, she fixed his tie.

"So... is my sexy husband going to be my date or what?" she asked playfully.

Nathan was aroused. He wanted to rip off her clothes right there. He took a deep breath and grabbed his jacket. She asked again, "Do I get my sexy, very hot husband to take me to this party or what?" Nathan smiled: she always knew how to ignite the passion in their relationship. "Is that a yes?" she asked. He took her hand without asking where they were going. The office looked empty and quiet as they walked past the elevator. He pulled her gently towards him and asked if she wanted to walk down the stairs. She told him that she has something in the conference room. The door opened and everyone was there eating and drinking, all the staff were there, Henry his driver came and said "thanks, boss" and that he can't drink. Tia said she would make sure there would be plenty of drinks for him to take home. All the associates were there with their wives and girlfriends. The conference room was big enough to have all the people there. There was classical Christmas music playing. Nathan was speechless as he looked at his wife. She was full of surprises. Tia put her arms around him, whispered in his ear to relax, and they ate and danced. There was a big Christmas tree in the corner with gifts underneath. Tia told Nathan to get them and hand them out to each of the associates for her, while she helped the caterers clean up. One of the senior associates said that this was the first time that he had worked for a lawyer who truly cared about his staff. He complimented Nathan on his selflessness and Tia on her generosity toward the staff. Nathan overheard the comment and it warmed his heart to hear people say things like that about him. It reminded him of the respect his college coach and team mates had for him: Nathan thinks he has changed since then. He sometime wonders who he is, and he doesn't like the man he has become. Although, since returning from Europe, he has changed most of his ways, but it has not much helped his marriage.

He and Tia are still very much apart since they had that talk about the baby's birth records. He managed to put his name on the birth record as the father after the fact. He has come to love and respect his wife much more, and he wishes he could go back and do things very differently. They sleep in the same bed, but they have not made love since the baby's birth. He has not slept with anyone since Brooke left, either. Tia watches him as he stands with his hands on his chest. She misses him. She walks over to him and asks whether he is ready to go home. They do not talk much on the way home, but just before they reach the turn-off to their house, without warning Tia unzips Nathan's pants and tells the driver they are not in a rush to get home. Henry knows what she means. She slowly takes him in her mouth as he leans back his head and closes his eyes; his body shakes as she climbs onto him, riding him gently; he is afraid to touch her and spoil the moment. She softly kisses him and wipes the tears off his face. He is still inside her when the car stops in front of their house. Tia opens the door and gives Henry a big tip and a kiss good-night on his cheek. Nathan is still sitting in the car. Henry asks, "Do you want to go somewhere, boss?"

Nathan shakes his head no and as he climbs out of the limo, he gives Henry a hug, "Good-night, my man." Nathan watches Henry drive away. Entering the house, Nathan could not find Tia right away. He goes to the baby's room where Jayzel is sound sleep. Tia isn't in their room either. He takes off his jacket and tie, making his way downstairs, but she isn't in her office or in the kitchen. He hears music coming from the sun-room where Nathan discovers Tia in the hot tub. Her hair is up in a pony tail, she has a glass of wine in her hands, and Nathan notices she is moving her wedding rings around on her fingers. He stands still and stares with surprise as she comes out of the tub naked. Her body is well toned, but he has not seen her naked since she gave birth to Jayzel. She takes off his shirt and raises her lips to kiss him, then pauses, and going back into the tub, Tia says in her sexiest voice, "Are you going to join me, or do you want me to beg?" Nathan didn't need more invitation that: he quickly joined her in the tub. She passed a smoothie to him, and he loves how she never forgets to make a smoothie for him every night. He wants to tell her that and also to thank her for the party, but she is spread-eagled in the tub, her back leaning against the wall of the tub, muscled arms spread along the rim of the tub, and her legs up on his shoulders. She looks very fit and strong. He tries to talk, to express his feelings, but Tia rubs her big toe against his lips, saying, "I don't want to talk, Nathan. All we do now is talk and fight."

Inexplicably, Tia's attitude made Nathan nervous. He begins to think that perhaps she knows what he has been up to with Brooke and this is Tia's way of pay back before she leaves him. He has stopped all the emails between himself and Brooke, since the day at the British Embassy when he learned that his name was not on the baby's records, and that the baby's last name was Sharp not Carter. Tia pulls him towards her as she wraps her legs around him, kissing him; he responds this time and holds her tightly as he kisses her neck and rubs her back.

"Okay, Mrs Nathan Carter. Why don't you tell me what you desire?" Nathan pulls away from his wife's embrace.

She drinks some of her wine and smiles. "What's so funny," Nathan asks.

"I was just thinking about the handsome lawyer that I met at Amsterdam airport. He took away all my fears. I knew you then... I mean ..." she gasps. "I told Kate and Brooke at Mrs Williams' house that by this time I would be madly in love with a man we all loved. I knew you before I met you and you made me laugh," she said softly. Tia closes her eyes. It's strange, but Nathan has also believed since he was in college that he would meet and fall in love with someone just like her. He and Nicole have been very close, but he has known all along that she was not the one for him, even though out of desperation he asked her to marry him when she was going to get married to Ian. He thanks God that he waited. He asks Tia, "What kind of a man was the man you hoped to fall in with that all your sisters would love, too?"

She replies, "It's you, Nathan, but in my head I can only see the sweet and the romantic side of you." He asks whether Tia regrets marrying him.

"I do have many regrets in my life, but never with you, Nathan. You are everything that I want in a man, a good father, a romantic man. I don't like your jealousy much. I dislike like how you talk back to Daddy, every time he tries to help us. I wish you could trust yourself and the people who love you more." Her comments made Nathan sad.

Tia had her left hands on his face, softly stroking down his cheeks. He likes that, his mother used to do that while they talked when he was a little boy. He asks what he can do to make her laugh again, almost in tears. Tia sets down her wine glass and puts both arms around him, "I am very happy, and I want to see my husband happy again. I want to put some romance back into our marriage. I want the sex to be sweet and dirty!"

Embarrassed, Nathan smiles sheepishly. He wants to tell her that he has been thinking the same thing, but his wife has him going crazy with her kisses. He couldn't think or get his words out. Later, they retreat to their bedroom and make love and talk through the night. It feels good after such a long time apart. In the morning, Tia is gone by the time Nathan wakes. There is a note for him to pick her up from the university at two and a reminder to meet Jackie at the airport. Nathan and Jayzel pick up Tia after her exam and together they go to the airport to meet Jackie. "We are going to the airport to meet Auntie Jackie," Tia says to the baby. It is nice just the three of them. This is what Nathan has envisioned all the time as a family. Jackie arrives with her boyfriend. She immediately takes the baby in her arms. On the homeward drive, she and Tia sit in the back with the baby and talk excitedly about "the baby this" and "the baby that". The two men listen in on the conversation until they get home. Jackie and the boyfriend leave on Boxing Day to travel to Montreal to spend the rest of the holidays with his family. Nathan does not have much to do during the holidays. Ever since the party at his office, Tia will spontaneously, shamelessly seduce him. The sexual tension is nothing like he has ever experienced and he has had some wild ones, too. On their first wedding anniversary Tia sent him out of the house after lunch on some ridiculous task. On his way back, he received a text message from her that made him almost crash the car. He replies with a text message that he will be home soon. Jayzel is asleep already by the time he returns home. He lights some candles. Tia is coming out of the bathroom with only a towel wrapped around her. She is on the phone with her mother since it is the New Year already in Europe. She kisses him lightly on the lips and hands him the phone. He talks to his in-laws while his wife sucks his fingers. Tia knows how to be naughty and how to turn him on. He tells her that he has something for her and that it is on the bed. Tia drops her towel on the floor and flips her hair back, saying she wants him right here. Nathan smiles and says she can have him any where she wants, so he lifts her up onto the bed. Tia is still kissing him when he places the nicely gift-wrapped box in between her breasts and gets out of the bed. He sits by the window, hands folded in his lap. "Open it, Mrs Carter." Tia doesn't want more jewelery, but when she opens the box, she discovers Nathan's hand-written poems, the most romantic ones, too. Tears roll down her cheeks as she reads them. Some of them were written when Nathan was in college as Tia can tell from the dates. She looks up at him and flips the pages forward to September 1996, the day they met. She reads it aloud:

I have found her at last,
God has kept his promise to me...
My heart feels whole...
She would not look at me...
The earth has moved and I feel my love's pain...
She's been hurt...
Only I can kiss the pain and the hurt away...
My sleeping beauty...
Oh God, let my love look at me and forget the pain...
My heart feels whole....
She will not look at me...
God you have kept your promise to me...
She is just like in my dreams...
I am sure... It's my love. A gift from God.

Tia loves the gift. "When you told me you wrote poems, when we met, I thought you were just saying that to make me laugh. Nathan, you have given me all kinds of gifts, but this, by far, is the most adorable of all. This is a part of you, sweetie. I love it! I love it! Nathan, this is you," she holds up the book and walks toward the window where he is sitting.

He tries to hide himself again by saying, "Looking at you sitting next to me with no clothes is making me hornier than I am. Do I get to make love to my wife on my wedding anniversary or what?" Tia laughs and grabs her bath robe to slip it on.

"Damn baby! You can kill a man," he teases. She stands between his legs with her head on his shoulders, "You know how much I miss my real husband, the real Nathan Carter, not that high profile lawyer with no heart that I've been having an affair with!"

"Should I be jealous that my sweet wife has been having an affair with an impostor?" he asks in a sexy voice.

Tia kisses him, "No. He is not as loving as my husband." Nathan smiles. "Why don't I remind you of the man you fell in love with right there," he points to the bed.

Nathan's parents are back from the Virgin Islands and are staying at the cottage. His mother catches a glimpse of her son and his wife when they arrive for a visit. She notices an unconscious essence of unique sexuality about the couple. They seem a lot more affectionate with each other, and looking at them is exhilarating. Heather wonders if perhaps Tia might be pregnant. She shares her thoughts with her husband and he agrees that something has transformed their relationship. "It could be Jayzel," he says.

Anthony Carter knows all about his son's bad behavior. He thanks God that Nathan has come to his senses and didn't lose his family. Anthony was worried for a while and he didn't like the man his son was becoming even though he's a doting father to Jayzel and a good husband.

Nathan was domineering at the beginning of their relationship. He and Tia have expressed different emotions. Sometimes it's a tender lovemaking; at other times, its an almost expression of angry feelings, where the only feeling is unalloyed lust; and sometimes for both of them, it is mainly pleasure and simply being in love as they shared some soft moans and words of endearment. This is all Nathan has been looking for and now he has it with his wife. They talk about their feelings and share their fears with one another often. Their home is a happy one, even though Brooke Williams' interference with his family has not been forgotten.

Chapter 38

Back in England, Jason, drunk at a friend's party, confessed to Brooke that he cheated on her while he was in Paris with Nathan Carter during the FIFA World Cup Finals between Brazil and France. Brooke was so distraught by her husband's one-night stand in France, she thought of leaving him, but then decided to hear him tell her again in the morning. She hardly slept the whole night, thinking about what Jason had told her. Perhaps he's cheating on her still. How could he? It was only days before they got married. She never wanted him to go to that stupid football game with Nathan Carter in the first place and look what he went and did! Jason was sleeping soundly after throwing up and breaking her heart. Tia was right: when it's done to you, you feel it worse. She felt humiliated that Jason could just go with some stranger he had just met, whereas she knew Nathan, and there was an attraction there, she tried to tell herself. By the time she woke up, Jason was gone to his parents'. She didn't know what to think: maybe she dreamed about the whole thing, she thought. Dream or not, Brooke reached for the phone by her bedside to call him to insist he come home to talk it over. She picked up the phone and threw it. Jason appeared in the door of their bedroom and asked what was upsetting her. Brooke was startled because she thought she was home alone. He had a coffee mug in his hands, which he handed to her as he leaned in to kiss her, but she moved away. She raised the mug with both hands and took a tentative taste, swallowed and closed her eyes.

Upon waking, Jason recalled last night's confession, so he decided not to go to his parents' until he had sorted things out with Brook. He was relieved to find her in bed with him when he woke up. He assumed it was a good sign, and he could tell she was not inclined to talk to him, but he must say his piece.

"I suppose you remember what I said last night?" She nodded, "Of course." She drank some more of the coffee.

"I wanted to tell you what happened," he said after a long pause.

"No!" she said quickly. "I'd rather not talk about it."

"You don't care that a few days before we get married I was unfaithful?" he asked cautiously.

"Well... While we're caught up in this nightmare..." she paused. Then taking a deep breath, she plunged into the morass of emotions, "I may as well tell you that I also cheated on you." She could feel his eyes on her, pensive and uneasy, but she did not speak. She drank more of her coffee. Jason's knees buckled as he sat on the floor. "Yeah? When?" He spoke gently this time, but he made the words a command, and delivered them the way he would have in any other type of emergency: coldly, demanding a response. "Tell me why. Now!"

Brooke, silent, suddenly felt trapped in the rumpled bedding. She was on her feet, but Jason grabbed the pink satin robe away from her as she tried to snatch it from the bedside chair. "I want to know who you cheated with, and when you cheated," he demanded. She refused. Suddenly an incredible rage washed over Jason as he hauled Brooke onto the bed. Her body shivered under her husband, as she stared at him with a shocked expression. It was a pure brutal fuck, nothing more. Even with Nathan, Brooke has never experienced this level of hatred. She did not recognize him. She draped the sheets around herself as she ran out of the loft.

Sarah Williams was still in her bed at eleven o'clock in the morning. She has been hooked on on-line chatting. She was on-line with Tia and they have been chatting all morning about her marriage, the baby and Nortel Network's sudden job losses that may affect her. She heard a sudden scream from downstairs as she logged off. Sarah grabbed her robe and answered the phone at the same time. It was Nathan Carter. "What a pleasant surprise, Nathan! I just got off-line with our Tia," she said.

Nathan went straight to the point. "Miss Williams, ma'am. This is not a social call."

Sarah Williams thought how rude of him. "Miss Williams, it's imperative that you listen and pay attention to me, ma'am, as at any moment your daughter's life is about to...," he paused as his wife came into the room. Sarah heard the maid scream again. "I am sorry, Nathan. I do have to attend to something downstairs." She was now running down the stairs as Nathan anxiously asked her not to hang up on him. The maid pointed to Sarah's study as she could not speak. Sarah wondered why she looked so afraid. She dropped the cordless phone on the grand piano.

Nathan slammed his hands on his bed as he heard the phone go dead. He asked Tia to excuse him as he went into his office and dialed Sarah Williams' number again. He told the maid to give the phone to Miss Williams. The maid did as she was told.

"Miss Williams, I trust Brooke has arrived?" Nathan asked.

Sarah was sobbing as she replied to him.

"I have a lawyer on her way now to see to you and your daughter's every need. Miss Williams, I am Tia's husband, Nathan Carter. I have a mother and a sister. I have a daughter. I care very much for you and your daughter. For the love and trust you have for my wife, I am begging you to listen and follow my advice, ma'am. Please tell me how is Brooke?" Nathan asked. Sarah was confused. "Please tell me what is going on, Nathan?" Mrs Williams begged. She tried to touch her daughter, but she looked scared and frightened. Sarah wanted to hold her and tell that she was safe. She called out to the maid to run a bath for Brooke. Nathan overheard it on the phone and said "no."

"But Brooke looks like she has been attacked by a vicious animal. She needs to be cleaned up. I should call Jason."

"No," said Nathan. "You must not call anyone." Just then, the door bell rang. The maid came in to say that a Miss Jennifer Haywood is here to see Mrs Williams. She told the maid that she was not seeing anyone right now.

"Miss Williams… Who is at the door?" Nathan asked.

"Um … Haywood. Jennifer," she said.

"Please give the phone to her, Miss Williams," Nathan demanded.

"Miss Haywood, please come in. Nathan Carter would like to speak to you." She handed over the phone to her. Sarah tried one more time to hug her daughter, but it was no use. Brooke's whole world was spinning around and she didn't know what was happening. Jennifer Haywood was still on the phone when the maid announced that the doctor was here. Sarah had not called a doctor. A minute later two police constables arrived. Miss Haywood talked to them while she was still on the phone with Nathan.

There was another stranger in the house. Miss Haywood asked that Miss Williams excuse them as she closed the door on her in her own home. Using her cell phone, Sarah quickly called Kate and Jaden and told them the news. Jaden asked her to stay calm that he and Kate were on their way. Jennifer Haywood came out of the study and said the police would like to take your statement now. She noticed that the other man had a camera and was taking photographs of Brooke and filming her at the same time. The police woman asked if she knew what had happened to her daughter.

"I can not say," Sarah was sobbing. Meanwhile, on the police walkie-talkie Sarah Williams overheard that Jason Grey was arrested and was being questioned for spousal battery and for raping his wife. Sarah Williams collapsed. The man with the camera was still filming. As Brooke refused to give them a DNA sample, she told them that her husband did not rape or beat her. Jaden knew Jennifer Haywood.

"What's going on?" asked Jaden, but Ms Haywood would not say. Turning to Sarah, Jaden asked, "Who called the police?"

Sarah replied, "I have no idea. They just showed up – all of them did."

Jaden asked them all to leave and that if Brooke wished to press charges, he would bring her down to the police station himself. Sarah told herself that she has to be strong, and that she can not let her daughter down like she did when she lost her father. Nathan has been on the phone talking to her for the past hour assuring and comforting her. She could not believe Jason Grey would do something like that. Brooke has cleaned herself up and has retreated to her old bedroom. She heard her mother talking and sauntered into her mother's study.

"Mom, why did you called the police?"

"But I didn't, sweetie. I thought you had called them."

"So who let them in the house?" asked Jaden.

"I believe Miss Haywood did," Sarah says.

Brooke asks, "Who is Jennifer Haywood?"

"Tia's husband sent her," Sarah replies. Brooke looked horrified.

Jaden asked Brooke, "Why would Tia's husband send a lawyer and the police to the house, assuming that you have been raped by Jason?" Suddenly, the puzzle pieces fell into place: the answer to Jaden's question was written all over Brooke's face. It was Tia's husband that she had slept with the night before Tia's wedding. Brooke asked her mother to excuse them, so Sarah stepped out.

"Mmm, I don't like this," Kate said. "Jaden, will you please take me home?"

"Come on, Kate. Let me explain, please," begged Brooke. "It's not what you think."

"Yeah, sure. That's what everyone says," responded Kate sarcastically. "There's really no use. I confided in you, Brooke. I told you that Nathan looked too smooth and that he could not be trusted, and all this time you've been sleeping with him anyway! And then you let Tia go ahead and marry him! Now I know, and when Tia learns the truth, I will lose her because of you. How can you do that, Brooke? We've always looked out for one another."

Brooke was speechless.

"This is not something I want to be a part of, Brooke."

"I am sorry, darling. I will fix it." Brooke mumbled, shame-faced.

Kate spoke gently, "You cannot fix it. Look at what has just happened to you! You and Jason had a strange fight and he was almost charge with... with..." she paused thinking over recent events. "Tia and Jayzel are in danger! The car crash in France last summer... He left them in the car to die! Tia thought he was in shock, but I am not so sure now."

Brooke protested, "No! Darling, Nathan would not do that. He loves Tia and Jayzel."

Kate was on her feet enraged with Brooke's response.

"He did do that," she said. "I saw the look on his face when he walked in and found Jayzel in Kevin Peters' arms. I saw the same look the morning they drove off to France, just before the car crash. Of course, he wouldn't do that! Because he gave you a good shagging the night before his wedding to your best pal?" Brooke was shamefully shaken. She could not comprehend what Kate had revealed. She wondered how Nathan Carter could have known of the events in their loft?

"I have to ask… Did you make a phone call to him while you were in shock?" Jaden asked.

Brooke shook her head no. "Please don't contact him, until we know what he's after. He will make a mistake," instructed Jaden.

Kate was sobbing, "You two can do whatever you want. I am going let Tia know the man she is married to, and Bobby and Naana are going to hear this from me."

"Please, don't do that just now," Brooke pleaded with Kate. "Sleep on it for a day or two. Let things sort themselves out."

"Yes, but Tia needs to know…" objected Kate.

"You're right, love," agreed Jaden. "But we also need to determine what Nathan's plotting." They all agreed to wait a few days before Jaden and Kate left.

Brooke wrote a lengthy e-mail to Tia. She did not mention that she has been having an affair with Nathan Carter. Instead, she wrote:

Tia, darling, Nathan has been seeking revenge on me because I tried to protect your rights and Jayzel's rights when you fell sick after giving birth. I wanted to be certain that you could return to England with the baby. That is why I didn't put Nathan's name on the birth record. I know he keeps a room in the Chateau Laurier in Ottawa. Christine Freeman is a lawyer that I hired to help protect your rights when I was in Canada. I asked her to have Nathan followed to gather information on any wrong doings because I was leaving Canada to come home. Ms Freeman has everything you might need, Tia. I need to make things right with my marriage. I will call you at work next week. Please be careful, my darling, as I feel all this is my fault. Tia, I do love you and Jayzel very much.

Two days later, the whole thing was in the British Sun's News of the World papers and on the Internet. It was Tia's first day at the CTV/Global Media Group as a Production Assistant on the early and late evening news. When she saw Brooke appear briefly on London ITV news, Tia could not hold back her tears as her producer said, "I hope Jason Grey gets put away for life!" Tia protests, "No, he could never do that to Brooke. Jason loves her. He is not that kind of a man." The producer said that Jason has said that "his wife liked it rough and he was giving her what she wanted. It was reported that his wife had suffered scratches and bruises on her arms, hip and face during an altercation which resulted in violently raping his wife. I don't know about the U.K., but in Canada misdemeanor battery violence and rape requires a mandatory detention period before being released. He could face a lot of years in jail." Tia still did not believe it. She decided to call England when she got home tonight. The British press has lit their own fire under the story: a middle class English man admitted to brutally raping and assaulting his young newlywed bride and saying that's how she liked it. During the Prime Minister's Question Time at the House of Commons, the members were even talking about it. They have never seen or heard anything of the sort in British history. One person said, "This sort thing only happens in the U.S of A., not England." The tape made at Sarah Williams' home was leaked to the press and it became one of the most frequent downloads of all time, not just in Britain, but around the world.

Sarah Williams did not know how to protect her daughter. Jaden filed a law suit against the British Sun News of the World. The judge granted his request for the Williams' and Grey's family privacy as they have suffered enough. Jason Grey confided in Jaden that it was not his idea to cheat on his wife. He was in France with Tia's husband; apparently he had been drinking when the girls begin to undress him and Nathan. He told Jaden that he had no idea how the whole orgy began with them. He later learned that it was a pre-wedding gift from

Nathan to him. He could not keep it to himself and when he confessed to Brooke, she revealed that she also had slept with someone. "When she would not say who, I lost it, but not the way everyone is saying. She is my wife; I would never do that to any woman. I called Tia afterward, but she was not at home. I talked to Nathan and he said not to worry. Why did this happen?"

Jaden told Brooke, "It was Nathan Carter behind all of the nastiness between you and Jason. I think Tia and the baby may be in danger. There is red flag around this guy. I just don't know what I can do to help at this point."

Brooke assured Jaden that Tia and the baby are safe and that she has someone looking out for them, though she did not say who.

Tia has been very busy at her new job at the TV station. Working at the TV studio is not as glamorous as most people seem to think. She misses her old job at Nortel Networks. It was a lot more stressful and you get yelled at by everyone a lot at the studio. She has not spent much time with her family since she began working at the studio. She leaves for work at two in the afternoon and returns at two in the morning. It's been four months now of twelve-hour days. It was eight in the morning in England when she called Brooke, happy to hear her voice finally. She told Brooke how busy she has been with work and that the time has just slipped by. Brooke asked her where she was.

"I'm at home in my office," Tia says.

"Well, read your email and I'll call you tonight at work, and we can talk then," Brooke says. She hangs up before Tia can tell her that she will be home the next few days as she would be working on a day-time show. Tia puts her coffee mug down and logs on to her laptop. She is not upset after she reads what Brooke had sent her a month ago. Instead, she rings Sarah Williams and seeks her advice on her marriage. Not only did Sarah gave good advice, but she also told her how comforting Nathan was during the ordeal between Brooke and Jason. As Tia listened, she put everything together that her husband was, in fact, behind all that mess. Tia couldn't figure out why Nathan would go to that extent to hurt Brooke and Jason. It was five in the morning and she was still up looking at the glow of the fireplace when Nathan found his wife in the family room drinking tea. He hardly sees her in the morning anymore. Tia drinks some more of her tea and smiles at him she wonders who he really is? She puts the mug down to hug and kiss him. "I've missed you," he says. She rubs his cheeks and replies, "me, too, baby. Me, too." He plays with his wife's hair and says, "I've been meaning to talk to you about something. There never seems to be enough time in the day for us these days." Tia agrees. "Come on. I have not had any sleep yet." She pauses. "I sleep a lot better when you hold me." She pulls his hands. Tia is so torn apart by her husband's actions. She cries herself to sleep as Nathan holds her in his arms. He has no idea about the pain his wife is experiencing, or how upset she is with him right that moment. Tia thinks that she has passed through the worst night of her marriage with Nathan. Little did she know that there were more nightmares to come, a lot more!

Chapter 39

Christine Freeman has been waiting for this phone call close to two years now and when the call comes through, she raises her coffee mug in the air and says to herself, "Touch down!" She has never met Mrs. Nathan Carter in person before. She does not have a strong British accent like her sister. She sounds more American, or maybe Canadian, she thinks. The anticipation of their meeting is too much for the usually calm young lawyer to contain herself. A black Mercedes SUV backs up and parks in between two parked cars near Christine's building. Christine stands by the window watching with interest. It was the year 2000. At the MTV award show one night earlier, Chris Rock said that the Latinos have invaded both the music industry and Hollywood. Puff Daddy, as he was called at the time, is dating the very hot, sexy, Latino singer-actor Jennifer Lopez. "J- Lo", as the press has nicked named her, is the trendsetter of how every young woman wants to dress. The woman who has just stepped out of the black Mercedes SUV is all "bling up" as they say in Hollywood. Her hair is neatly swept over one shoulder, she wears over-sized sunglasses, and she carries a take-out Tim Horton's tray. Christine could not see where she went. "She looks better than J-Lo," Christine muses.

Tia went to the building, removed her sunglasses, and scanned the notice board to see where Miss Freeman's office was located. She took the elevator up to the fifth floor. Miss Freeman's office was on the left. Christine Freeman opened the door to Tia's knock and was surprised to see the woman from the black Mercedes. She had more "bling, blings" on her than Christine had seen earlier. She was wearing a diamond stud earring and many chain necklaces as well as a bracelet as the woman extended her hands to greet Christine. "Mrs Tia Carter here to see Miss Freeman," Tia said. The woman at the door appeared anxious and nervous to Tia, so Tia asked again whether Miss Freeman was around. Christine pulled herself together and said, "I'm Christine, Mrs. Carter. Please do come in." It was a small office. Jayzel's room was even bigger than the office, Tia thought. She sat down and handed Christine one of the teas she had brought. Tia put her at ease saying, "Miss Freeman, I am not here to seek a divorce." Christine smile nervously, and asked, "So what does bring you by my office today, Mrs. Carter?"

"Please call me Tia. I believe my sister retained your services eighteen months ago?"

"Yes, ma'am. She did," Christine replies.

"Miss Freeman, my husband is a high profile defense attorney. I work in television. I know firsthand how the media works. I don't want my visit here in the spotlight. I would like to stress that the celebrity factor could very well imperil what I seek," says Tia. Christine is fascinated with Tia: she finds her intelligent and articulate. Tia reaches into her bag and takes out an envelope, which she hands to Christine. She drank her tea while Christine read the contents of the envelope.

"Mrs. Carter.... Tia, this is not necessary as we are bound by client confidentiality," says Christine.

Tia replies, "I know. This is a contract between you and I, until the day I will file for a divorce from Mr. Nathan Carter." Tia puts her Tim Horton's cup down and hands Christine a pen. Christine's face lights up, and her heart begins beating faster. Tia studies her body language as she signs and hands a copy back to her. Tia asks for any surveillance evidence she may have accumulated over the past eighteen months from watching her husband. Tia writes a cheque, thanks Christine and says she will be in touch. Tia leaves. Christine stands in her office wondering what has just happened. When she glances out her window, the black Mercedes is gone.

Later, at home, Tia reviews all of the evidence provided by Miss Freeman. She is more shocked than she anticipated. Feeling dirty, she sits under the shower, crying and crying for what seems like ages. She has no one to share this travesty. She has just learned that the man to whom she is married is not quite who she thinks he is. Needing to cleanse herself, Tia writes a script about the whole mess. Each day, she writes her feelings and her thoughts on her laptop, creating a character based on her husband's behavior, a very powerful, sexy woman who breaks all the rules. What she has written has all the ingredients to make a hit television show, the kind viewers sit on their lazy-boys, eyes glued to the television. One of her producers on the morning show that she works on often sees her writing. One day, the woman asks Tia what she's writing about.

"Oh… this is just for fun!"

"Can I read it, then?"

"Mmmm… it's not that great. It's not, you know, polished." The producer wanted to read it anyway, so Tia asks her to make sure that it is saved and logged off when she is done.

Amy Hall is a hard nosed news producer. She can play the television game better than the boys in the industry. Amy knows the television industry very well, not just in Canada, but in England and the U.S., too. Amy has worked in the industry since she was sixteen and has worked in every department. Although the television industry has changed in the twenty-five years since she started out, it is still a man's world while women still have to give television executives and producers a blow job. Amy prides herself in getting where she is in the television game with her merit. Mind you, she wasn't the prettiest girl in school, but she would like to think she was. She was pretty much out there with rest of the not-so-popular girls at the school. She joined the small media class at her high school and found her place where she truly belonged. Amy Hall knows talent when sees it. She reads Tia's story and she could not get enough of it; the more she reads the more she loves it. Amy thinks her young production assistant has written a blockbuster prime time show. It has passion, romance, intrigue and scandal with sexy young characters. Amy smiles to herself and says, "This is it!" She has been looking for a story like this to produce for the last twenty years. Growing up, Amy loved the prime time shows. In the eighties, there were the Ewings in Dallas and the Carringtons in Denver. *Dynasty* and *Dallas* were the biggest prime time shows at the time, and viewers loved J.R. Ewing and his cheating ways – both in business and with his wife, Sue Ellen. Alexis Carrington Colby was no different in *Dynasty*. Amy often had a dream to one day produce a

Canadian show just like *Dallas* and *Dynasty*. That is what Tia Carter has written.

Tia left the CTV studio and drove to Ottawa's Chateau Laurier Hotel. Henry stood by Nathan's car. Tia tapped his shoulder and handed him what looks like lunch. He was grateful and thanked her profusely. Tia told him to take the rest of the day off since she and Nathan planned to spend the day at the hotel away from the baby. The driver did not think to call and warn his boss. He took off smiling.

At the check-in desk, Tia told the clerk that she was there to see someone in this suite. She has studied her husband's routine in the hotel, and when the clerk pointed her to the elevator, Tia was taken to the penthouse suite. She gave the bell-boy a big tip as she opened the door and sat down in the nearest chair she could find, her knees suddenly weak. Nathan called out, "You may come in! I'm getting a massage in the bedroom." Tia sauntered into the bedroom and stood by the window with her back to Nathan while he enjoyed his massage. A little while later, he walked towards her and grabbed her breast from behind. To his surprise, the woman who sounded very much like his wife said, "That feels good, sweetie, but I prefer to fuck you in our own home, not where you take all your whores!"

Nathan almost had a heart attack. When Tia turned to face him, he was speechless. She left him in the bedroom and to the living room while Nathan stood still, not knowing what to do or say. He has never before felt this much shock. As he dresses, he feels like he is three steps behind himself. Tia calls the front desk and asks them to prepare Mr. Carter's bill as he will no longer need the penthouse suite. "Oh, baby, I have sent Henry home for the day," she said apologetically. Entering the living room, Nathan could not see his wife's expression as she was looking at the view. "Please get dressed," Tia said. "I don't want to keep Daddy and Mother waiting!" Her voice was level, expressionless, without inflection. Nathan reached out and touched her shoulders. She fought back her tears, "Please get dressed and let's go." Nathan took her hands, quivering with fear. There were tears in his eyes as Tia said that she was heading down to pay the bills, so they wouldn't get caught in the traffic back to the cottage. She left. Stunned, Nathan wondered why his wife was not more upset. He has just been caught red-handed. He threw the towel down in anger speculating on how she could have known. "And why didn't Henry call and warn me?" He had millions of questions. As he walked out of the hotel and the doorman opened the door for him, he almost lost his balance as he got into the car. Again, Tia showed concern and asked if he was all right.

He asked, "Can we go home instead and let Jayzel spend the weekend alone with Mom and Dad?"

Tia said firmly, "Mother is not feeling well. This is the only weekend we both have to spend with them. Did you forget we are going to the Virgin Islands on Monday?" Nathan could not understand Tia's attitude. Any woman in her position would be calling a lawyer by now, he would be out of the house with a restraining order against him, and now she still wants to go on a vacation with him? It was a torturous experience watching Tia driving and singing along to the songs on the radio all the way to the cottage.

He was still in the car as Tia opened the door and got out of the car. She could not hold in her anger any longer, but she refused to give Nathan the satisfaction of a hissy fit, so restraining herself, she told him to snap out of it! Inexplicably, Nathan felt piqued that Tia was not angrier with him. His father was standing behind him as he asked his wife, "Tia, you just caught me in a hotel room cheating on you. Are you not mad at all? Don't you care?"

"Keep your voice down!" Tia reminded him, "This isn't the place for it." Tia was embarrassed and she quickly kissed her father-in-law and ran into the house. She could see the two Carter men outside the house arguing. Tia went back outside and told the two men to stop it. Her father-in-law was equally stunned that Tia was so relaxed about what his son had done.

"Daddy, you know as well as I do that marriage is hard work…" She paused and wiped her tears away. "I cannot let Nathan's infidelity destroy our family."

"Tia, Angel, once a cheater always a cheater," her father-in-law said prophetically. Nathan thought his father's comment was disparaging: "Why are you trying to drive a wedge between me and my wife, Dad?" Nathan asked his father. Tia could see the distress this was causing. Hearing Nathan sassing his father was intolerable.

"I am very much upset with Nathan for putting himself in this kind of position. Not just our marriage, but everything that makes us a family has been tarnished by his actions. Please, I am not encouraging him, but perhaps if I was a good wife, my husband would not feel the need to seek other women." Tia said simply. Anthony Carter raised an eye brow. He was considerably alarmed by his daughter-in-law's attitude towards his son's infidelity.

Tia pleaded; "For the sake of …" she looked back in the house. "For the sake of all of us, please let's not fight about this now. Daddy, I promised you that I am not blinded by my love for him, but we will discuss this once we go home and if Nathan wishes to have mistresses and see other women, I will have no other choice but to leave him. This is not the place to confront this matter, Daddy. Please, this is Jayzel's and mother's weekend. I don't want to spoil it for them."

Nathan quickly took his wife hands and said that he was sorry. His enraged father watched Nathan as he walked into the house holding hands with that sweet girl. Anthony wished that Nathan was a little boy so he could take his belt to him. Tia pulled him against the wall and said firmly, "Don't think for one minute that I don't know what you've been up to with Brooke and Jason. You attempted to have the poor man put in jail for your so-called rape! Your thoughtless behavior, Nathan, ends here. Next time, you stop and think of everyone, and remember that everything we do in our lives affects everyone. Some people are not as forgiving as others, and remember, too, that you are a husband and a father." She let go of his hands and went inside the cottage. His father was a little relieved when he heard what Tia had said to his son. Nathan stood there with his hands on his head panting like a naughty school boy who has been called to the headmaster's office. He turned and faced his father and sighed deeply.

Chapter 40

At the resort in the Virgin Islands, everyone loved Nathan's wife and the baby. Steven was shooting a film there, so he put the little toddler in the movie. "This is Jayzel, my beautiful niece. I'm going to make her a big Hollywood movie star one day," he told the crew. He told Nathan that he would trade everything to have what he and Tia have. As they both glance at Tia writing on her laptop, Nathan confessed to his brother what he has done and how he got caught by his wife. "I think she is going to kill me once we get home, Steven. I'm not joking." Nathan blurted out. Steven hit him on the head and said, "You should let that be a good lesson to you. There are not many women like Tia out there," he told his brother. "I should know... I've slept with them all!"

Amy Hall, Tia's loud mouth news producer, who fancies herself as a television producer, was waiting on Nathan and Tia's driveway upon their return from the Virgin Islands. "Oh, no! No! No!" Tia exclaimed.

Nathan asked, "What's the matter?"

"That's my crazy producer. What is she doing in our driveway?" Tia cried. Nathan kissed her on the cheek and said, "I'm sure whatever it is, it will be alright."

Amy did not let Tia out of the car before she began her pitch: "Honey, you are the next big thing. I tell you! Your father-in-law told me you were arriving today, so I figured I would stop by with the news myself."

Tia asks, "What? Am I fired?" Amy has now turned her attention to Jayzel, and is holding the little girl and kissing her on the cheeks.

Tia know Amy well and can see that she's not getting anywhere with her. Amy invites herself into the house. For just a second, she forgot why she was there. Tia brought her back to the present moment.

"Honey, they loved your script!" she said as she opened their cupboards and closed and opened another one and pours them a glass of wine that she has brought. Nathan grins broadly, enjoying the manic disposition of Tia's crazy producer. By the time she leaves, Tia won't have time to deal with his indiscretion in the hotel room two weeks ago. Feeling like he has a get-out-of-jail-free card, Nathan pulls a chair out for Amy to sit down and begins asking questions about the script.

"Your beautiful wife, here, has written a juicy script that I want to produce as a television show."

Before Tia knew it Nathan was swinging her in the air, kissing her, congratulating her. Amy watched the young couple and said, "I can see why there's so much romance in your writing." Tia asks "what script?" She still did not know what Amy was talking about.

"Baby, I didn't know you were working on a script!" Nathan takes his wife's hands and puts his arm around her. Tia has been using her anger about her life to write, and most of the time, she has no one to turn to about secrets of her husband's extra-marital affairs. Her marriage seems idyllic to everyone they know. Her writing has given her the strength to cope with Nathan's unfaithfulness, even when she doesn't know who to talk to, and writing helps her deal with things. She doesn't deserve this much humiliation. This will cause more embarrassment for her and the rest of her family. She cannot bear to tell anyone about her life and now her crazy producer wants to put it on a television for everyone to see.

"Miss Hall, I was not writing a television script," Tia says as politely as she can.

Amy replies, "I know your brother-in-law is a movie maker, Tia, but he will not do your script the justice it needs. I can see the characters growing and the television audience drawn to it. A movie director will not do the script justice! Honey, tell her!" she points to Nathan. "This is better than *Dallas* or *Dynasty*. Tia, the good thing is it's Canadian grown. I did not have to fight the network on this. Everyone who read it said the same thing. This will give *The OC* a run for its money on Monday evening prime time. Honey, trust me! Looking at you and your sexy husband, the love and the romance you two obviously translate into your writing, this is the beginning of a romantic epic saga, Tia."

"I am going to get Jayzel ready for her bath. Please, listen to her. She knows the business well." Nathan says as he excuses himself.

Tia sits down and listens to Amy describe her negotiations with the network. Tia has no idea what it all means, but she feels very happy to see Amy leave. Tia was sleeping on the sofa by the time Nathan came downstairs. "My wife is full of surprises," he thought. He carried her upstairs to bed as he does most of the time. Tia awakens.

"I meant what I said Nathan. If you keep doing what you have done in the past and do things that hurt me, I will leave you. And our daughter will grow up with a part-time father. I don't want to hear your sanitized version of your betrayal, Nathan," and with that she kissed him and lay down to sleep. Nathan cuddled behind her and rubbed her back, feeling ashamed of himself.

It was Nathan's twenty-ninth birthday a week after they came back home. Jayzel was spending the weekend alone with her grandparents as she does most weekends. Tia begins to work on her marriage. First, she sends Nathan a birthday gift at work. He opens the big envelope with Tia's handwriting on it. An attached note reads "for your eyes only!" Enclosed, he finds some almost nude photographs of Tia, several of them are very daring, too. He has an instant hard-on. Preparing to leave the office, Nathan is reluctant to answer the phone when it rings, but he sees his home number in the caller ID window and decides to pick up the phone. Tia sounds so sexy over the phone, asking him about his day. She has not asked in weeks. She tells him that she misses him and she wants him home. He looks at his watch. It is only one o'clock in the afternoon. "Jayzel is gone for the weekend and I'm walking around the house naked, looking for something to do." Nathan hangs up the phone and runs to the car, telling Henry to take him home fast. Just as he was getting out of the car, his cell phone rang – Tia again. He did not answer, but instead he told Henry that he would not need him for the weekend. "I'm sorry, baby, how are you?" He asked as he opened the front door and stepped into the house. He asked where Tia was and she replied, "I'm in my office." He headed straight there and found her sitting on the edge of the desk facing the chair with her back towards him. She wore one of his shirts. He leaned down and kissed her on the neck. She pointed him to the chair and told him to sit. He noticed that she had no panties on and the shirt was un-buttoned. There was a large basket of fruit on the desk, a bottle of white wine and a cake. Tia poured some wine into a glass and handed to him. She uncrossed and re-crossed her legs like Sharon Stone did in the film *Basic Instinct*. It was like the gates of heaven had just opened. She sat on his lap, slowly took off his jacket and tie, leaned to kiss him, but at the last moment said in a low sexy voice, "Happy birthday, Daddy!"

Nathan has forgotten that it is his birthday. Nathan was hoping for a slow, soft kiss like she used to give him, right before she gives him a blow job and rides him until he comes. Instead, she tied both of his hands behind the chair with his tie and dipped a strawberry in the wine and fed it to him. She fed him all kinds of fruits and cake while her other hand is in his pants rubbing his manhood, torturing him the whole afternoon until he could not hold it in any longer and he came.

He's not come like that in a while, so it felt good. He murmured, "Although, I would have preferred to make love to you, Tia, I have missed you and I promise..." Tia shushes him with a kiss on the lips.

The next day Tia has some tickets to the Ottawa Senators game. After the hockey game, she took Nathan to the spa. She told the massage therapist to leave them alone, giving the woman a huge tip to take a break. Tia removed Nathan's towel and poured some oil on his back, whispering to him that she wants him right there. "Are you trying to send me to jail?" Nathan asks. Nathan has always thought that he was a freak, but he had no idea what a wild freak Tia could be until that afternoon. He has never experienced this kind of seduction in a public place before. Nathan has done it all when it comes to sex and foreplay. They left the Spa as if they had been there for a simple massage. Nathan Carter has just learned that weekend that his wife is his perfect match. He has died and gone to heaven he tells his brother when they talk next, tattling about his wife and her endless romantic ways and he says that he is done cheating on her.

Brooke went back to the loft. She and Jason tried to put their marriage together but it was a lot harder than they both expected. They have been staying at Brooke's apartment, but still there is a distance between them. Jason has been wondering whether Brooke cheated with Nathan, but he dare not ask her.

Kate and Jaden welcomed a baby boy weighing almost nine pounds. Kate still has not forgiven Brooke, though the new baby has reunited them once again.

Gertrude suffered a stroke at the beginning of the summer of 2001. Brooke flew to Holland to visit her. While she was there Tia arrived with Jayzel, who has grown and is now walking and talking. They have not spoken about the incident. The little girl loved Brooke, and can't seem to stop kissing and hugging her all the time, although Brooke has not seen the baby since her birth. Brooke remembers how Jayzel felt and smelled when she was a baby, and the little girl still smells that way. Brooke was wearing a white skirt suit as she emerged downstairs for lunch, strings of pearls on her wrist with make-up on and her hair combed straight down her back. Her hair looked more golden than her usual blonde, Tia thought. Tia finally asked her why she did not put Nathan down as the baby's father. Without thinking Brooke replied, "Nathan Carter is an evil man. He does not deserve to be your husband or Jayzel's father. I was not going to lose Jayzel to him like I lost you to him. If he hurts you, I will personally kill him!" Because Jayzel was sleeping, Brooke took the opportunity to say, "There is something I must tell you. You are going to hate me, but I must tell you anyway."

"A lot of people have been hurt already," Tia said. "We've all been hurt. It's time we all moved on. Unfortunately, some people will have to be left behind." Brooke did not understand what Tia meant.

Tia looks at Jayzel and says, "I think about him everyday. There has never been a day that I don't think about Kevin and what we shared. My marriage to Nathan has been one mess after another. I cannot cope anymore. I should not have gone from one situation to the next. I fell madly in love with Nathan's parents and also with him. I'm very much in love with him still. I can't live with things that Nathan has done."

Brooke sits up. "You have filed for divorce already?" Brooke asks, her enthusiasm is sparked again.

"No, I was about to serve him the divorce papers before I found out that I was expecting his child. Your mother has been advising me and helping me cope. She is aware of everything I have been dealing with Nathan. I have tried to recuperate the marriage, but he is not going to change." Tia says sadly.

Brooke asks, "Why have you kept this to yourself, daring? What are you going to do?"

"I have tried and tried with Nathan's infidelity and his spoiled ways. Right now, I don't know what to do. I don't know how to deal with him. It's lonely sometimes, and I'm more in love with him now... I was... um."

Brooke understood Tia's situation and tried to find some common ground: "Jason and I live in the same apartment; we share a bed, go to out together to business dinners, and see friends and family occasionally. Most of the time, we don't have much to say to each other any more. I am still very much in love with him. Our life has changed. It's like we fell in love too quickly with our husbands. Life with Jason is lonely all the time, too, Tia. We've kind of lost it, and hanging out together on the weekends is the hardest."

"That sounds lonely," Tia remarks, although her own life is no better than Brooke's. The two friends sit in silence with tears in their eyes. Tia says, "Jayzel will not return to Canada with me. I will be writing and working as an Executive Producer on a new prime time show for CTV, which will air beginning in the fall on Monday nights. I'm hoping to discuss my marriage with my parents. I know my Dad will support me, but my mother, I am not so sure. My mother was born into a life of privilege, and I don't think she has any idea of the grief other marriages face, including mine.

Nathan is the son-in-law she always wanted, and in a way, a husband that I always wanted. How am I going to survive? And there is my mother and father-in-law..." Tia gasps and wipes away her tears. Brooke suddenly thinks about her affair with Nathan, seeing how much pain Tia is bearing, and she wonders how she could have done it. Kate was right: this is one scandal that is going rip them all apart.

"I almost lost you," Tia pauses to blow her nose. "Poor Jason could have ended up in prison for five years because of Nathan."

"By leaving Jayzel here for the rest of the summer maybe things will change between you and Nathan. You will have more time to spend together and get to know each other and work through some things. Marriage to Nathan is a challenge. You must try and save your marriage, Tia." Brooke advised her. Brooke feels protective of Tia, and in some ways, Tia feels the same about her, too.

Nicole and Nathan have not spoken to each other since the day they went to British Embassy for Jayzel's passport. Today, Nicole is in Ottawa with documents for Nathan to sign. To expedite matters, he just signs them without even reading the contents, returns the documents to her, "Now, just leave me alone, will you?" She can see he is upset. She can always tell. She closes the door and sits down. Nathan asks, "Is there something else for me to sign?"

"No," Nicole says. "I just wanted to know why you thought I had something to do with your name not being on the Jayzel's birth certificate." Nathan does not respond, so Nicole leaves.

He begins to think that he has been wrong about Nicole, that she would never do anything to hurt him. He needs her; she has always been a loyal business partner to him; and they used to have an under-the-table romance going on too that his wife didn't know. Any woman would have told on him by now, but not Nikkie. He instructs his assistant to call Miss Bright and find out whether she is free for lunch.

"Miss Bright has gone to the court house to file some papers, sir," the assistant replies. Nicole has always been a hands-on lawyer. She still does most of the work herself that legal assistants typically do. He calls her on the cell phone, but her cell phone seems to be turned off. He calls Tia in Holland and the maid says, "Tia has gone to England with Brooke and the baby." He is upset that Tia has not called to say she's going to England. It is one way for her and another for him. He throws the phone onto the desk loud enough that the whole building seems to hear his frustration.

Having returned from the court house, Nicole enters Nathan's office, "I'm taking you home now," and she tells his assistant "Mr Carter won't be back in the office today." Nathan is glad that he doesn't have to go and beg her. She takes Nathan's hands in her own warm, soft hands and leads him to the waiting limo outside. They are still holding hands in the car. Meanwhile, Christine could not believe her eyes, with a document that the UPS guy has just delivered to her. She calls and leaves a message for Tia to call her back.

Bobby and Naana express the hope to Tia that what ever Nathan has done she should try to forgive him and give him another chance. They remind her that marriage is about couples working things out and growing together. They encourage her to go back to Canada and work things out. With renewed hope for her marriage, Tia leaves several messages for Nathan that she is coming home, but Nathan is not at the airport; instead, his father meets her.

Giving Anthony a big hug, Tia asks, "Is everything okay with Nathan? I haven't been able to reach him for a few days. We seem to miss each other whenever we call."

"Oh, yes," says Anthony. "I think everything is fine. I got a message this morning from Nathan asking me to meet you at the airport. I guess he's just really busy at work." Anthony took Jayzel from Tia's arms. She has grown in a short time. "Heather and I miss you both very much," her father-in-law says.

"I wanted to leave her behind with her other grandparents, but I couldn't," says Tia ruefully.

The little girl was asleep by the time they got home. Oddly, Nicole's car was parked outside the drive way. Tia opened the door for her father-in-law and Jayzel to go in. Her father-in-law quickly came back out with the baby. He looked like he has seen a ghost. Tia drops the suitcases on the ground and enters the house to discover Nathan and Nicole naked on the family room floor. They have no idea that she has been watching them for several minutes. Nathan rolls Nicole off him as he sees his wife in tears standing in the entrance to the room. He tries to grab her hands, but she runs upstairs to the bathroom to vomit.

"Get dressed, Nicole, and get out!" commands Nathan. He runs upstairs as he puts on his pants. He meets Tia at the top of the stairs. No one knows how it happened, but in the blink of an eye, Tia is at the bottom of the stairs.

Half naked, Nicole screams loudly. Nathan is standing at the top of the stairs with his hands in his pockets. Anthony Carter is outside talking with Christine Freeman when they hear Nicole's scream. Christine Freeman was just locking her car door, but drops her keys and quickly runs past Anthony into the house where she finds Tia on the floor. Hardly conscious of her own actions, Christine takes out her cell phone and dials 911. She sees Nathan at the top of the stairs half-naked, Nicole a few feet away from Tia, and she feels confused by the scene. Anthony Carter comes in with Jayzel, now awake and asking for her mother. He covers the little girl's face, but she quickly runs to Tia. Christine picks up the little girl while Anthony checks Tia for a pulse. Thinking the ambulance should be here by now, Anthony calls 911 again and the dispatcher says that EMS is on its way. When the paramedics arrive, Anthony Carter tells them that Tia has sustained a concussion due to a fall and lost consciousness.

They inquire about any current medical problems. Christine tells them Tia is pregnant but she's not sure how far along. She looks meaningfully at Nathan who is talking heatedly to his father. The paramedic asks, "Who is the husband?" and Nathan comes downstairs to talk to them as they are about to transfer Tia to the ambulance. Momentarily, Tia regains consciousness and says she has a headache. She is asked how many months pregnant and she responds about three months. Nathan is crying openly now. He is holding Jayzel when the police arrive and the ambulance drives off with Tia and Christine inside. Nathan refuses to answer the police's questions and tells them to get off his property. He dresses quickly, takes Jayzel away from his father, and drives off, following the ambulance. Nicole, now dressed, tries to explain to Anthony, but he is not interested. He puts Tia's suitcases in the house and leaves. By the time he arrives at the hospital, technicians have done ultra sound and X-ray tests. Tia and the baby are both fine, though they are being kept overnight for routine observation. Tia sleeps while Nathan and Jayzel wait in the room with her.

Seeing Christine in the waiting room, Anthony asks, "And who might you be?"

"I am the lawyer handling Tia Sharp's divorce from Mr. Nathan Carter," she replies.

Anthony is stunned but has no time to ask further questions. The police have returned to the hospital, and they want to question Anthony to verify Christine's version of events. Anthony calmly asserts, "Mrs Carter lost her balance and fell. Now, if you boys come in the morning, Mrs Carter herself will tell you the same thing. Now, beat it!"

Nathan comes out into the hallway, overhearing the conversation between Anthony, Christine and the police. As the police depart, Nathan asks Christine, "Who are you? Have we met?" Nathan couldn't see her face, but her voice sounded very familiar, sending chills down his spine. Christine did not say anything and kept her head down as she walks away. He tries to think how he knows her, but his father interrupts his thoughts. Anthony is still in shock over everything that has happened in the last four hours or so. He goes into Tia's room and comes out with Jayzel. Nathan tries to talk to him, but he ignores his son and takes the little girl home to his condo. Nathan couldn't believe Tia was pregnant and did not tell him. He wonders why she has not told him.

Chapter 41

Anthony arrives at his condo with Jayzel. He quickly changes the girl into pyjamas and puts her to bed. He looks in on Heather, who is sleeping soundly. He has no idea how he will break the news to his wife. "How could Nate behave this way," Anthony asks himself. Wanting a cup of tea, he goes to the kitchen.

"Penny for your thoughts, Daddy," says Tia.

"You left the hospital, Angel?"

Tia smiles and nods. "I didn't want you staying up worrying about me." She goes to check on Jayzel, glances at the clock, and sees it is almost midnight. She is in a great deal of pain. She drinks some of the tea her father-in-law has made.

"Are you okay, Angel?"

"I'm not too sure of the word 'okay' anymore, Daddy."

Anthony smiles encouragingly. Tia continues, "Why did this happen? And in our home, too. He knew I was coming home."

Anthony wants to ask about the divorce, but can't bring himself to ask about such a painful subject. After all he has witnessed, he wonders whether Nathan pushed Tia. Tia kisses her father-in-law good-night and retreats to the guest bedroom. She can't sleep for thinking about everything: this morning, when she left London, she had been looking forward to sleeping in her own bed with Nathan. Now, she doesn't even know whether she wants to set foot in that house again. Deciding to be productive instead of tossing and turning, Tia goes to Anthony's office and logs onto his computer. Finding the MLS site, she begins to look for homes in Ontario. She finds a home in Stoney Creek, Ontario, not far from Toronto. She smiles and googles it to see whether there is an airport nearby. She checks her emails and responds to most of them. She sends an email to Amy Hall and asks her if she knows Stoney Creek at all. She knows Amy is originally from Hamilton. Having solved one problem, Tia is able to sleep.

Tia was sleeping when Nathan kissed her on the cheek and left the hospital. He had a meeting today with his private investigator, but for some reason forgot all about it until now. He should feel miserable, but for some unknown reason he feels excited about his life. He left the police station at three in the morning and it was almost four before he reached home. The house was so cold and empty without his wife and child. He wondered why Tia didn't call to tell him they were coming back today. He is going to be a father. He did not think about the earlier events; instead, he thought his future with Tia was set, especially with the baby on the way. There was nothing his father or anyone could say that would make his wife leave him. He is going to be a changed man. "God took pity on me for my sins today," he thought. "I could've lost it all." His marriage to Tia is a gift from God, Nathan believes, and nothing can take away what God has blessed. He drank some water and threw the bottle in the trash. He decided to part ways with Nicole and their firm to prove to Tia that he is all about her and the children now. He did not want to sleep with Nicole, not after the incident in the hotel room. He had learned his lesson. He still remembers the look on Tia's face that day and it has been haunting him. He promises himself never again. Oddly, he has no idea how he ended up in the family room making love to Nicole for Tia to come and find them like that. Tia has a big heart and knows his needs better than any woman. She will forgive him just like she has in the past. Tomorrow will be a new beginning for them, a better one, he thinks as he dozes off to sleep.

Jason overheard Brooke's phone call from Canada, and by the time she got off the phone, he had booked a flight to Canada for her in two days' time. "I'm sorry, honey, but it was the only one I could find on such short notice," Jason said apologetically. Tears rolled down her eyes as she listened to him telling her about the flight. "Can you ever forgive me?" she asked. "I never really did say I was sorry, Jason," she murmured.

"I'm the one that ought to be sorry, not you, sweetheart."

It has been almost six months since that fateful morning. Their friends and family all think they have put the past and the public humiliation behind them, but Jason and Brooke live with it every day. They don't sleep in the bedroom anymore, and their once-loved loft is now their living nightmare. They have been staying in the apartment most of the time. Despite the late morning hour, Brooke is still in her white satin pyjamas sitting in bed. Jason removes his blazer to sit and cuddle her. They both have their own side of the bed, so the middle of the bed looks puffed up. When Jayzel and Tia visit, the little girl will climb into their bed in the morning and sleep in between them, and she will look higher than everyone else.

They both miss the little darling in the mornings. "Please come with me to Canada," says Brooke. "It would be our second honeymoon. I missed you when I was in Holland. I don't want to go without you, Jason," Brooke whispers. He kisses her on the forehead and reaches for the phone. Brooke does not mention to anyone that Tia is in hospital, the result of a fall that Nathan may have pushed her down the stairs. Tia and the baby are okay.

It is five in the morning in England, when Brooke opens her eyes to find her husband holding her. They make love, and it feels like the very first time, sweet and warm. They both cry and made love again. There is a new respect and a much stronger bond between them now. They are both very thankful to have each other still. Not many couples could survive what they have been through all because of one man.

"I am going to make sure that Nathan Carter pays for his sins," Brooke thinks to herself. She quickly puts on the kettle and takes a bath. Coffee has always been her drug in the morning as Jason hands her a mug while he zips up her dress. He asks her if she thinks that Nathan may have pushed Tia down the stairs.

She replies, "only Tia can really say what happened. My husband will never push me and our unborn child down a flight of stairs and stand there and watch me in pain. You will never do that to me, Jay. I hope Nathan was a man enough like you. I just hope, sweetheart."

"Did you love him?" he asks finally. Brooke has been dreading this topic for months, but she is not going to lie. She can't let her husband know about her affair with Nathan. That will kill everything he feels for her. She puts the mug down, "Did I love who?"

"The person you cheated on me with." In response, Brooke frowns, "I did not plan to kiss any other man, other than yourself. I had it all with you. The night before Tia's wedding, Tia left the party. I got worried and left as Kate seemed to be enjoying herself with one of the dancers. I was coming back to our hotel room to do a little striptease dance for you and have my way with you after. The next thing I know someone kisses me and I kiss the person back. I felt sick about it. I didn't even tell the girls about it as I was so ashamed of myself. I thought maybe it was one of the strippers who had kissed me. I have no idea how Nathan knew.

"When I returned to Canada for the birth of the baby, he felt mistreated because I wasn't going to back down to him when Jayzel was born and Tia became sick. I stayed in Tia's private room while she was in isolation. Mr. Carter asked me to come and stay with them, but I wanted to be close to the baby and to Tia at the hospital. I hired a lawyer to help me protect Tia and the baby's interest in case Tia didn't make it. I did not want the Sharp's to lose their blood granddaughter to the Carter's. I never thought Nathan would seek this kind of revenge. When you told me you have cheated on me, I was hurt. I stayed up all night crying while you were asleep in a drunken state. Part of me didn't want to believe it." Jason was in tears now, as Brooke continued, "When you repeated it in the morning, it hit me all over again like a tone of bricks."

"I couldn't keep it to myself anymore... I didn't intend to hurt you." Jason said softly. "I wanted to be the one to tell you rather than you hear it from someone else."

Gathering his courage, Jason asks, "Did Nathan ever want to sleep with you?"

"Holy shit!" Brooke thought. She knew she had to say something, if not the whole truth. She hated lying to him. She was about to say yes and shook her head no as she cried more and blew her nose. Jason put an arm around her. She lied again and said, "No, he knew that I had kissed someone the night before his wedding. He tried to use it against me by threatening to tell you. That's why," she paused again.

"That's why, what?" Jason prompted.

"That's why when Jaden told me what really happened with you two in France, I knew that you would never have done it. Nathan did it to get back at me for not putting his name on the baby's birth certificate."

"I can not believe he would try and have me put in jail for that!" Jason got out of bed and went into the kitchen with his cup.

Brooke said, "In Canada, being married does not automatically make you the father of a child." Jason did not want to hear any more, though he found the twists and turns of Nathan's life strangely titillating. Brooke rattled on, "Nicole, his law partner, is his lover, the same Nicole that Tia found him with in their home having sex last night. She told me how to use the details of Canadian family law when the baby was born." Jason sat down and started to believe that his wife was telling the truth.

"Jason, it was Nicole's idea to call a lawyer while she went and kept Nathan away from us in the hospital. The attorney told me not to trust her." Brooke took out a file from a drawer in her bedside table and handed it to Jason. "Read it," Brooke commanded. Jason did not want particularly to read it.

"Jason, I'm your wife. You obviously think I slept with Tia's husband and I'm trying to cover it up. You must read what's in that file and ask yourself why I would sleep with Nathan, and you tell me if Nicole did not set up Nathan for Tia to find them in their home last night. There is also a copy of their divorce papers that was faxed to me last night to read the content."

He read through the report half way, and then he reached out and touched Brooke. He was cuddled up to her by the time he got to read the divorce papers. He ran his finger through his hair and said, "Uh-oh my God! No, it cannot be true!" Jason looked terrified.

"Brooke, you should tell the Sharp's. You cannot sit on this!" Jason insisted. "Tia is going to need all the help she can get, and you cannot protect them from so far away. Brooke, please!"

Brooke went and stood by the windows. She sipped her coffee. Jason could not understand his wife's actions. What he had read in that file was like the plot of the soap operas his mother liked so much. He was mystified why Brooke could be so relaxed about it.

Jason seldom spoke to Brooke in this manner since the incident in the loft. He rarely barked orders at her. He felt Brooke's history with Tia and the Sharp family has made his wife determined to be overly protective of Tia and Jayzel. To top it all off, Nathan Carter is a man who enjoys playing games with human lives, and Jason did not want his wife traveling to Canada. He wished Brooke would understand that this is Tia's problem and she should sort it out herself.

"I want my wife back," he said to her. "I am afraid to say that Mr. Nathan Carter is an evil man. I don't want you caught up in his affairs with Tia. There is a new life here, sweetheart, and I fear the man is going to fight to the death no matter what the divorce papers say. It's all power and control with men like him. Please, sweetheart, you promise me…"

The phone was ringing and wouldn't stop ringing. Brooke answered the phone as Jason left for his morning run.

Chapter 42

Tia awakens with a huge headache. It takes her awhile to remember the events of the previous night and why she is in the guest room of her in-law's condo. The pain is more than she could bear. She could hear her in-laws and Jayzel talking and laughing like they usually do. How is she going to get through all this? She wishes Brooke were here. She sits up in the bed and sees her reflection in the mirror. Half of her face is bruised and swollen. She tells herself that she needs to be brave, but she finds herself crying. She didn't lose the baby, which is a huge consolation for Tia. She sighs and pulls herself together.

"Good morning!" Tia says.

"Oh, honey, Tony tells me you fell last night. Are you okay?" Her mother-in-law asks solicitously.

Tia leans over to kiss her and Jayzel, "I'm good, Mother. I hope I did not worry you too much last night? No more wearing high-heeled pumps in the house, eh?"

Heather was wearing a black dress, with her blonde hair swept back – she looked beautiful.

"Poor Nate must be out of his mind with worry... where is he?" Heather asks.

"He's at work by now, Mother. I left the hospital last night. I could smell Daddy's pancakes from there, you know?" Tia teases.

Anthony Carter thinks that Tia looks tired. Slowly the agonizing memories of last night all come back to him now. He looks lovingly at her, but Anthony has been increasingly worried since last night about Tia, and with Nate's betrayal once again he wonders how Tia finds the strength to deal with his son.

Tia listens to the CNN news report on Sean "P. Diddy" Coombs, also known as "Puff Daddy." Mr. Coombs is the president of Bad Boy Records, turned clothing designer. He is charged with criminal possession of a firearm after a shooting in a Manhattan nightclub. Several people suffered injuries as a result. Mr Coombs is facing fifteen years in jail. He hires none other than Johnnie Cochran, the man who defended O.J. Simpson. Mr Coombs, of course, vehemently denies all the charges, even though witnesses say they saw him and his girlfriend, Jennifer Lopez, flee the club after the incident with two other men in Coombs' car. A not guilty verdict is announced. Tia wonders whether Nathan is watching as this is his type of case. The door bell rings and Anthony hopes to God that it's not his son. It is, however, Tia's lawyer, Christine Freeman. "Why can't she leave her alone?" Anthony thinks. He invites her into the house and guides her to the kitchen. There is something open and kind about the lawyer's face. She thinks Tia looks sedate, subdued, dignified and beautiful despite the bruises and the swelling on her face. Tia smiles at her and offers her a seat. Christine asks, "Can we talk in private?" Tia leans back and notices that her mother-in-law and Jayzel are sleeping together on the sofa in the living room.

"I believe you met my father-in-law last night?" Tia asks. She hands Christine a mug of coffee and tells the lawyer to talk. "Mrs Carter, I must insist on speaking in private," Christine says.

Tia moves to stand by her father-in-law and asks again, "What brings you by?"

The lawyer raises her eye-brows, takes a deep breath and says, "Your husband's office has requested that we return the divorce papers no later than noon this afternoon."

Anthony is about to talk, but Tia shushes him by tapping his shoulder. "What divorce papers? The last time we spoke, I asked you to wait. I will let you know if and when and where I will ask my husband for a divorce."

"Yes, ma'am. You did." The lawyer glances at Anthony Carter again. This time Tia says pointedly, "Miss Freeman, this is my father-in-law's condo. He is not going anywhere, and as I don't have time to explain myself over and over, anything you have to say you can say in front of him."

"I called you a week ago in Holland, when I received the papers from your husband's office. He has asked for a divorce from you." Anthony is about to speak. Again Tia taps his shoulders, and tells the Lawyer to continue.

Tia asks, "What are the terms and custody agreement with regards to Jayzel?"

"Em... There is no custody agreement. You get full custody of Jayzel-Gertrude Sharp." Christine pauses for effect, "He has also given up his parental rights on your unborn child." Heather is not as asleep as Tia, Anthony and the lawyer expect. She is listening attentively to the lawyer as her heart races fast and faster.

"Mr. Carter has asked that his name should not be associated with yours or with the children in any way." Anthony Carter has heard just about enough. Tia asks him to relax. She leans back to check that Heather and Jayzel are still sleeping. She asks, "What else?"

Anthony says, "Please don't tell me there's more?"

The lawyer looks nervous, but Tia says, "No, no... It's alright. Go ahead. Let's hear it."

" There will be no support payments. All the marriage assets belong to him. You can not take anything from the home you two shared. He has asked that your wedding and engagement rings should be returned with the papers this afternoon."

Heather Carter had just suffered a heart attack and died as she listens to the details of Nathan's divorce from Tia. Anthony couldn't listen anymore. He got up to check on his sleeping wife and granddaughter. As he stands by the windows, with tears running down his cheeks, Anthony asks himself why would his son go to this extent to hurt his wife. What kind of a man is he?

The lawyer asks if she should petition the court for child support and if she should contest the divorce.

Tia replies, "No." Anthony returns to the kitchen and pleads with Tia to reconsider her position. "You can't let him abandon his responsibilities like that," Anthony insists. Tia smiles, closes her eyes as she kisses her wedding rings and hands them over to the lawyer along with a diamond charm bracelet on her wrist. When her cell phone rings, she sees it is Lyden calling, an employee of Nathan's law practice. Tia talks and laughs with Lyden over the phone as if nothing is happening. Christine and Anthony watch her with amazement. Tia looks so relaxed as if her world is not falling apart. Whatever pain or sorrow Tia has does not appear on her face. Tia asks the lawyer to leave the papers and that she will have them to her before noon.

The lawyer looks nervous and anxious when she insists that Tia should sign the papers now since she will be in court all day. Tia says, "Oh, it's okay. I'll have these papers to you well before noon." But just when Christine is about to leave, Tia suddenly signs the papers and hands them to her. "Remember, Tia," Christine says, "Nathan has taken out a restraining order against you, so you cannot call him or go near him."

Tia chuckles, "Oh, that won't be a problem. By the way, what were you doing at my house last night?"

"I received a message from Nicole that you were coming and that you wanted to see me at your home," Christine explains. Tia glances meaningfully at her father-in-law.

"Mmm… Well, thanks for coming by," Tia says. "I suppose I should congratulate you and Nicole on a job well done then. Or perhaps I should begin plotting my own revenge," Tia says gleefully.

Both Anthony and Christine are confused in response to Tia's remark. Tia walks Miss Freeman to the door. Once Christine Freeman has departed, Tia sits on a kitchen stool and smiles. Anthony asks why Tia does not call another lawyer to look at the papers before she signed them. Tia says that she believes if something is yours, it will always be yours no matter what. She also tells her father-in-law that she fears the worst is yet to come. Anthony asks what she means. "I'm not sure, Daddy. I'm madly in love with my husband: that is one thing that I'm sure of, Daddy." Anthony is concerned about Tia. The old man has witnessed the lawyer describing the terms of the divorce not ten minutes ago, and yet the divorce papers are still there on the kitchen counter. Since Tia has nothing to wear, she asks if she can go to Rideau

Centre and do some shopping for herself and Jayzel. Anthony is not sure of Tia's mental state. He asks again if Tia is alright and she says yes. Anthony is still standing by the window, mulling over his own thoughts about how he will break his son's despicable actions to his sweet, sweet wife. When Jayzel begins to cry, Anthony goes to her right away. It looks to him that Heather is sleeping through the little girl's cry. She looks so peaceful with a smile on her face, but he knew it as he bent down to kiss her. Her face is still warm as Anthony calls 911. He fixes Jayzel a snack, and covers Heather with a blanket. He is still holding her hands when the ambulance and the police arrive to transfer Heather's body to the morgue.

Nathan has just awakened. He calls his assistant to say that he will not be coming in today. He calls Molly Maid Service to send him a cleaner right away; he orders some food from a caterer that Tia uses some times, and buys some flowers. He shaves, takes a shower, and he thinks about calling his parents to see how Jayzel is, but decides no... "I will let my father tell me how disappointed he is with me. When I go pick up my daughter, I will then offer some meaningless apologies and a cry," he thinks with a laugh.

Tia calls the condo from downtown where she is busy shopping, but the phone is unusually busy. She calls Amy Hall and tells her that she has arrived home and asks whether Amy has read her email about Stoney Creek yet? She is happy to learn that, in fact, Amy's mother lives in Stoney Creek. Tia takes a taxi and returns to the condo. Anthony is reading to Jayzel when Tia enters the condo. Tia asks, "Is mother still sleeping, Daddy?" Anthony kisses Jayzel on the forehead as he takes Tia's hand to the living room. Tia assures him that she is okay about everything and that he must not worry. "I am going to find out what mother wants for lunch."

"You don't have to, Angel," Anthony says softly. Tia asks if they have had lunch already. Anthony breaks down in tears and says, "I miss her already, Tia." Tia realizes that her mother-in-law is not there. A wave of dizziness washes over Tia as she sits down. The condo feels cold all of a sudden. The phone is ringing and without hesitation Tia answers it: it is her mother, just in the door from her shopping and has heard Anthony's message about Heather. She, too, is crying as she tells

Tia they will be in Ottawa on the weekend and that Tia and Nathan should look after Anthony. Tia cries, "I have to go and see if Nathan is okay, Daddy."

Anthony says, "No, Angel. You can't: he has a restraining order against you. You can go to jail, Angel, please don't go near him."

Tia cries, "Mother will not want him by himself. I need him, and he will need me, Daddy." She pauses wondering why everything is falling apart? She picks up her daughter as she asks who she should call. Anthony says that everyone has been told. Tia asks if Nathan has been told. "I have left messages for him to call me, but he is not answering his cell phone." Tia calls Lyden and tells him to tell Nathan that she is on her way to the cottage with her father-in-law and she needs him. Before she hangs up the phone she also tells Lyden that she wants the package at her father-in-law's condo before four o'clock.

In the morning, Nathan is busy with the police and his private investigator, Lyden. He tells Henry to take him to his father's condo. It is a gated community, so the security guard asks them to wait while he calls Dr. Carter. Nathan gets out of the car and walks into the condo. He is met by his father by the door. "I am here for my family, father. Save the speech for later," Nathan snaps. He pushes past Anthony. "Nate, son, please wait," Anthony says. His father sounds like a broken man. He doesn't have his usual disappointed tone. Nathan smiles and turns to face him with his jaw tightened up. He takes Nathan by the hand and they walk to the condo lobby and seat themselves in a couple of chairs. Anthony tells his son to listen closely. Nathan's cell phone is ringing, but he doesn't answer it; instead, he pushes some buttons to silence the call and save the number. Turning toward his father, Nathan smiles. Anthony watches as his heart breaks with mixed emotions of love and hate for his son. Nathan doesn't want to play any games with his father any longer, so he stands up. "Nate, Mother passed away peacefully three hours ago." His father sounds mortally depressed when he says it. In stark contrast to his father, Nathan feels as though he has been kicked in the stomach, like he is half dead. He feels as though he is hanging somewhere in outer space. Everything suddenly seems unreal. "How? I mean mother has been doing well, how could she leave me now?" He thinks as he sits down again. He could not stop the tears from coming, so he loosens his tie and stands up. His father is also in tears when Nathan turns to ask, "Why did you let mother die? You are a doctor... doctors are supposed to save lives. Why did not you save my mother?" Nathan sits down again having vented his frustration. He leans his head back against the wall with his eyes closed. Anthony does what any parent will do at the time: without words he holds his son as they both grieve for Heather. Nathan has a frightening thought that maybe his mother's death was something his marriage contributed. He could not calm himself. His father lets go of him and asks if he will be okay. Nathan's expression is blank when he goes to the elevator and pushes the up button.

Anthony tries to tell his son that he can't come to the condo because he has taken a restraining order against his soon to be ex-wife. Upstairs, Nathan is ready holding Tia and the baby by the time Anthony comes inside. Anthony watches them, puzzled. A little while later there is a knock on the door, and Anthony wonders why he has not been paged from downstairs. Nathan opens the door to two policewomen and tells them to come in. One of the police women says that they are there to see Mrs. Carter. Anthony steps in and tells them, "Just a minute..." Interrupting, Nathan says, "Dad, please. Let's get this cleared up."

"Mrs. Carter, we're sorry to come at a bad time, but we need to ask you about your fall last night, ma'am. Is there somewhere private where we can talk?"

Tia wipes her tears and says in a clear voice so everyone can hear, "I lost my balance as I was running down the stairs."

"Are you sure?" Nathan asks.

Tia is confused, "Yes! I'm sure. You were there!"

Anthony also asks, "Tia, is it true? Are you sure about that?"

Trying not to lose her patience, Tia says, "Yes, Daddy, just like I told Mother this morning. I was wearing high-heeled pumps. Did you not see the shoes I was wearing when you picked me up from the airport?" The old man smiles and says, "No. I don't always notice ladies' things."

The two policewomen left and Nathan asks her again. "What really happened?" Tia is getting upset with the repetition of the question.

"What do you mean what really happened? You were there with your tart! Is this some kind of a sick joke you and your tarts like to play? I'm done playing: they win, you can go back..." Tia realizes that Jayzel is standing there listening attentively.

Nathan picks up Jayzel and covers her ears. "Baby, please, can we go home and discuss this?"

Tia takes Jayzel away from him, but Nathan grabs her hand gently and says, "Baby, please don't go." Tia glares at him.

"Tia, I was on my way to a meeting with Shawn and Lyden when Nicole arrived at the house. The next thing I remember is you on the floor. I did not call Dad to pick you up. Honey, I have missed you and our daughter like crazy. Do you really think I would trade you and Jayzel for any woman? I did not sleep with her. I have not slept with her since I met you. Baby, please!"

Tia is more upset about the extremes Nathan will go to humiliate her. "Daddy, I need you to come with us. I have a bag packed for you already," Tia says.

Anthony looks coldly at his son. "Angel, thank you, but..." Tia does not let him finish. "Nathan," Tia interrupts, "Please, take Daddy's bag to the limo. We'll be downstairs shortly." Tia takes her father-in-law's hand. "I cannot say I know what you are going through with the loss of Mother. I am going to be selfish and say that I need you with me, Daddy. I will not go the cottage without you or leave you here alone."

Anthony knows that Tia needs him. "Daddy, I have forwarded all the calls to the cottage already. Steven and Jackie know that we are going to be at the cottage. They will be arriving tomorrow night. Daddy, please!"

"Of course, Angel," Anthony is a little confused. He is trying to sort out the sequence of calls and misdirections. He got a call from Nicole asking him to pick up Tia, but this morning Tia's lawyer also received a call from Nicole to meet Tia at her house. Anthony reminds Tia what her lawyer had said in the morning.

"Uh-huh," Tia says. "I would like to share something with you and Nathan at the cottage. Lyden is meeting us there with two other people, so come along, Daddy, please."

Anthony tries to protest, but Nathan says, "Dad, please come with us."

Nathan asks, "Tia, why is a private investigator meeting us at the cottage?"

"I'll fill you all in on things once we get there."

Nicole is happily chatting on her cell phone about a job well done as she reaches the Carter cottage. She has received a message to meet Nathan there. When Tia opens the door for her, she almost faints with surprise. Tia looks so elegant and beautiful, with her black slacks, black cashmere sweater, high-heeled black suede boots, hair pulled back in a neat ponytail and big gold earrings. Her make-up neatly hides any bruises from the fall. Nicole feels bad for her. She has always liked Tia.

"Hello, Nicole! Please, do come in," Tia says politely with a smile. Nicole nervously says, "You look terrific, Tia." Tia thanks her. Nicole is off-balance, uncomfortable since she is not expecting Tia to be there. Nathan has just put the baby down for her nap. Coming down the stairs, he sees Nicole, and shouts, "Get out now! Get out of my family home right now, Nicole! I'll not lose my family over you, Nikkie!"

Nicole is in tears as Nathan's words cut right deep into her heart. Nathan has always told her that, but this is not in private. There is hatred behind his tone and something else in his tone she does not recognize.

Tia says, "It's okay. I asked Nicole to stop by." Nathan has taken off his shirt and is wearing a white vest. His body looks powerful and muscular. He puts his arms around Tia, and gives her an enormous hug, lifting her off the ground as he normally does and sits her on the island. He takes a step back and looks at her then his father, who can not understand what is going between his son and daughter-in-law. "Baby, please! I am telling you the truth. I have not been sleeping with Nicole."

Tia stops him and says softly, "I don't care. I don't really want to hear what you do or don't do with Nicole." She goes to the kitchen and takes out four mugs from the cupboard. There is a knock on the door. Nathan sighs and goes to the door.

Opening the door to Christine Freeman knocks Nathan into a million pieces. He realizes that this is his Judgment Day. Nathan is more confused when Tia asks him to let Christine in the house. Christine smiles delightedly. "Hello, Nate!" she says as she walks in past him and settles next to Nicole. They are both puzzled about why they are here at the same time. They do not talk or make eye contact when Tia comes into the room bringing them both a mug of coffee. Nathan remembers her now. "Chris," he whispers under his breath. "How can Tia know?" he wonders. He tightens up his jaws as he closes the door behind him. He is still standing by the front door, trembling and wondering if anything else can go wrong in his life today. Tia comes and hugs him and says "it's okay. Everything is going to be okay."

Anthony Carter was affronted by what he saw, and it bothers him that Tia is so kind to his son. She has always made excuses for Nate, as she does for everyone else. Where others are critical, Tia makes an effort to excuse and forgive. She is generous to a fault. Anthony is in the kitchen when he asks, "What is going on?" He can't stand the suspense anymore. Nathan sits on the floor in tears. He speaks softly, "I am so sorry, Dad." Anthony asks, "What have you done now?" Nathan tells his father, "I am so sorry. I never wanted you or Tia ever to know about this." He stands up and says, whispering, "I lost Mother today... I feel like... I have lost the two of you, even though, you're here." He is looking at his father and at Tia. He walks back to the living room and says, "Five years ago, the three of us all lived in Toronto." He points to Nicole, Christine and himself. "We were just starting out. Rent and food was very expensive. We shared a one bed room apartment together as well as the bed. We were lovers. They both became pregnant.... I made... I told them both to get an abortion – at the same time." Anthony could not believe what his son is saying. It is beyond cruel.

"Chris left town. I never saw or spoke to her until today. Just before we left for Europe, I had Nicole followed. I learned about Jayzel's birth records. I saw Chris last night at our home and at the hospital. I realized that I was being set up. I thought I had pushed Tia down the stairs…, but I was not very certain of myself. I spent the whole night looking at and reading Lyden's report, but there was nothing there to help me. I did not sleep with Nicole yesterday. I was on my way out when Nicole came in with papers for me sign. The next thing I remember is…" He stops. His father slaps him across the face. Nathan almost falls as Tia begs and pleads with Anthony not to hit him anymore.

"Oh my God! How can you be so disrespectful and unkind? This says nothing about how Heather and I brought you up, Nate. We raised you better than this! How could you?"

Anthony left the house, consumed by his wife's death, his son's thoughtless behavior and Tia's willingness to forgive Nathan's transgressions. Tia runs after her father-in-law as Nathan sits on the living room floor with a bloody nose. Since Tia met Anthony and Heather Carter and got married, she seldom puts her needs first. She has made a few demands, but never admitted her own needs. Today, she needs Anthony's support to hold her family together. She does not know how to do it, she tells her father-in-law.

"Angel. I'm so very sorry. Nate gets away with everything! Who's there for you, Tia?" His question is blunt and to the point.

"I don't need much, Daddy," Tia says quietly, lowering her eyes and looking down at her hands. "I have everything I want. I can't let our family fall apart, Daddy." Tia glances back up at the house. She holds her hands out to him and they walk back to the house. Meanwhile, Nathan has cleaned himself up. "I do apologize for keeping you waiting, ladies," Tia says, as she sits down opposite from them, crossing her legs. "I am ashamed by my husband's behavior. I don't take kindly to individuals who go out of their way to hurt people the way Nathan has. You ladies have dragged me into your revenge scheme and may have caused my mother-in-law's death."

Nicole raises her head at Tia's words and asks her, "What do you mean about Mrs Carter's death?"

"Heather suffered a heart attack this morning, right about the time you two were acting out your revenge against Nathan and me." Anthony sits in a chair in Jayzel's room as he listens to Tia. Nathan is standing behind his wife and feels physically sick to his stomach. "You see, ladies... I'm not a doctor, but I'm sure any expert will tell you that my mother-in-law's death was caused by your inhumane behavior and your need for revenge. I have made a complaint against both of you. All the evidence that I have, along with the divorce papers you two served me this morning on Nathan's behalf will be forwarded to the Ontario Law Society and their ethics board. Nathan, would you be kind enough to show your ex-girlfriends out of our home, please?" Tia gets up and leaves the room and goes into the kitchen.

"This is my payback from the two of you?" Nathan stamps his foot. Nicole and Christine try to leave, but Nathan blocks the door. He pulls Nicole aside, "My mother died today. I will not lose my wife and children for whores like you two. Any further attempt against me and my family and I will press charges and have you both disbarred. Your attempt to break up my family has failed." He opens the door and tells Christine to get out. Nicole tries to talk, but he puts his right index finger on her lips, her whole body shakes with fear. "Relax, Nikkie," Nathan says as he leans his face against her ear and whispers, "Nikkie, I have always loved you." He walks her to her car and opens her car door for her, just like years ago in college the first time he kissed her. He watches her drive off. Nicole could not stop the tears from coming.

Tia is standing by the bottom of the stairs with Nathan's jacket. Nathan is on his knees begging before she opens her mouth. She knows, she has heard it all before. She taps his shoulders.

"I know how sorry you are, sweetie, but we are no longer married," Tia says in a soft voice. "I want you to leave, Nathan. I do love you so very much. Your actions took away mother from us today. I don't want to inflict any more pain on you today, but I cannot be here with you. I signed the divorce papers this morning, so we are done."

"No, no, no, baby," he says frantically. "Please don't say that, Tia, please, baby. You can't leave me today of all days. Baby, please, tell me what you want me to do. I will do it." He is in tears. He means every word and Tia can see it.

"I want you to leave, sweetie, now. We both need this time apart." She pulls away from his embrace and goes into the family room. Nathan runs upstairs almost out of breath as he calls out to his father.

The old man is in the baby's room when he hears his son. He knows what he is after, so Anthony meets Nathan in the middle of the stairs and sweeps him into his arms. He lets go of him, as they walk downstairs. Anthony says, "I cannot help you, son. You are a grown man with your own family, Nate." Anthony Carter has always overlooked his son's behavior with his wife, and his inability to be the son he and Heather raised. He remembers the first time Nathan came home with Tia. She was enchanting and mesmerizing and they all were captivated by her. Heather was dazzling and immensely appealing to Tia and her kindness: they all fell in love with her. She is an extraordinary young woman. He has often told Nate that. There are sobs of anguish.

Nathan sounds like a wounded animal. He reaches for the phone, and closes his eyes with the pain in his whole body. He calls a taxi, conceding gracefully. It occurs to him that his father holds him responsible for his mother's death, just like Tia does. He resents Anthony for not helping him. Heather would want Anthony to help Nate, to help with Tia. Nathan tries to act cool as he leaves the house, but he feels devastated. He has never felt so hopeless in his life, so lost. His father watches him in the taxi as it disappears down the road. It is ironic: when Nathan gets in the taxi, the song on the radio is by Leanne Rimes, "How do I live without you?" Nathan sits in the back of the taxi thinking the words of the songs describe his life with Tia. "How do I live without Tia?" he asks himself.

Anthony is shaken by recent developments in his family. When Tia reappears in the family room, he wants to hug her, apologize for everything. Tia asks that he sit down while she fixes something for him to eat. He picks up the courage to ask about her plans. Tia simply smiles. She feels she has burdened him enough since she arrived. She doesn't want to add more worry. Tia does not want to contemplate the events of the past twenty-four hours: she just wants to cry. She can not imagine how anyone could go to that extent to hurt her like this. She is stunned to hear what Nathan did to Nicole and Christine years ago. Heather has died today and yet Nathan has managed to turn the attention on himself once again. Tia has had it with Nathan.

"I don't know if I did say that I was the writer of a new show being televised in the fall on the CTV network. It's called *The Saga*. I'm also an executive producer on the show, Daddy."

Anthony senses she is dogging his questions. "Wow! That's nice. I'm so proud of you, Angel."

"Jackie is arriving in the morning. I have a meeting in the morning, so I was hoping you wouldn't mind picking her up for me and I will meet you back here. Jayzel's nanny should be here soon, too."

Anthony says Jackie can stay in the condo with him, but Tia says, "No, Mother would want all of us together, Daddy. I have discussed it with everyone already and we all agree that we should all stay here together until after." She pauses.

"It's okay to cry, Angel. I miss her already." Anthony says. Tia looks at him sympathetically and asks why things are falling apart.

Tia and Anthony did not eat very much as Jayzel kept asking for Nathan. Bath-time was rather difficult because the little girl was used to Nathan's silly songs and also his custom of singing to her to sleep. She misses him and truth be told, so does Tia.

Tia orders special flowers for Heather from Jayzel. She feels so tired by the time she goes to check on Jayzel that she falls asleep in the chair in the baby's room.

Nathan goes to their home in Orleans. He puts on the television and it is set at the Tree house Channel with a show that Jayzel likes on the screen. He tries to remember the name of the show, but he can't. He changes the channel to CNN; Larry King is on, interviewing Aerosmith. He goes to the kitchen and comes back to the living room just in time to see Aerosmith's video " I don't want to miss a thing." It feels like the knife is in his heart and the pain is unimaginable. Nathan Carter is on the floor crying and alone.

He has lost his beloved mother, and the only woman he loved more than life itself has finally had it with him. He sends diamond pearl earrings to Tia and Jayzel the next day, along with a hand-written apology to his father and his wife. His brother and sister both are in town, too. His mother's death comes as no surprise to any of them because she has been ill for most of the past three years. It is hard to say how many people will come to her funeral. His in-laws are arriving in two hours, so he has his assistant inform his wife and father that he will have Henry pick them up from the airport. He hopes that Tia will let him back into the cottage by now, but it has not happened. He is frantically worried; Nicole, too, is still in town for a pre-trail hearing, but they've not talked. He goes into her office to see her. She is on the phone with a client, so he goes and stands by the window. She has seen the obituary in the newspaper. It has said where the funeral will be. Nathan is sure she would like to attend. She always had a deep love for Mrs Carter. Nicole knows there is no point discussing anything that has happened in the past few days or her part played in the break-up of Nathan's marriage. She wants to explain, but Nathan will not let her. She has made no effort to talk to him. Right now, he looks like someone from another planet to her. He seems quiet and composed. "My mother's memorial service is in three days, Nikkie. I need you there with me, please."

"Outrageous!" Nicole says. "We have scarcely talked about… things," she pauses. "I am sorry, Nathan. I can't. I cannot come with you." Nathan pulls up a chair and sits down with an agitated look. "Nikkie, things have happened that I can't change. We need to move on. We've been best friends since college and we've been business partners a long time. We have also been more than friends. I cannot lose you, Nikkie." Nicole sobs quietly. "Tia and I are separated. I was not able to… the divorce that you and Chris helped her… As much as I want to blame people, I can't: it is my fault. I need you now more than ever. Please don't abandon me, too. Nikkie, you are all that I have. My marriage was the best and my wife was the best thing in my life since college, but I can't lose you, too."

Nicole knows there is no point in arguing with him. It is just going to drive them both insane. Nathan cries and she comes running to him, so nothing has changed; that's their relationship. It doesn't matter how much he hurts her, she always loves him. "I will call Ian and let him know," she says. Nathan walks over and kisses her on the cheek.

Tia's mother and father are unhappy to learn that Tia had kicked Nathan out of the house at a time like this. Tia's mother asks Henry to take her to see him. He is the only person at the office when Naana arrives. Nathan is not looking forward to this meeting at all.

"Hello, my darling, how are you holding up?" She asks her voice full of kindness and her eyes filled with tears and love. It made Nathan think of his mother and also of Tia. He has tried to put his mother and Tia out of his mind, but it is not easy. He stands and goes to the door to greet Mrs Sharp. She wears the same perfume as Tia. She puts her palm on his face and says, "Your mother would not want you working yourself to death, darling, living alone. Whatever it is, you and Tia will have to work it out. I have come to take you home, darling."

Nathan bit the side of his mouth as he fights back the tears. His mother-in-law is a kind woman. Any mother in her position would have berated him. Instead, she hugs him as he tries to tell her what he has done. "We have done things that we not proud of, it's okay. Bobby is talking to Tia. I cannot go home without you, darling," she says.

"Oh... Mother, she won't forgive me this time. I didn't do what she and father think that I did," Nathan cries.

It breaks Naana's heart seeing her son-in-law crying. She wipes his face just like she used to do with her children when they were young. She is still holding his hands as she helps him with his jacket and says, "Tia understands and knows that you are family, and that comes before anything. Jayzel has missed you, and she will forgive you, darling. Come on. It's not going to be easy, but she will, darling. You two need each other."

Nathan sighs and opens the door for his mother-in-law and they walk out his office together. He hopes to God that his mother-in-law is right about his wife forgiving him.

Chapter 43

Tia sits in the kitchen with her father listening to him tell her to grow up, that marriage is not like a football game in which she can give her husband a red card every time he does something she doesn't like. "I know all about Nathan's roommates back in Toronto five years ago. Brooke showed me the report. Young men do foolishness all the time. It is in the past, Tia, so let it be."

Tia feels like she is still living at home when all she wants is for the old fart to leave her the hell alone and mind his own business. How dare he talk to her that way! She wipes her face and nods, and nods. She has missed Nathan. The house has been rather quiet without him.

"Tia, you both have lost someone you loved very much. Don't let Nathan suffer like this, sweetheart, please. You need each other right now, more than ever," her father says.

Nathan feels like a stranger going back to the cottage. Naana takes him by the hand and says, "It will be okay." Bobby hugs him first when they arrive home. Jayzel is brushing Brooke's hair when she sees him, and runs across the room to him. He picks her up and throws her in the air. He has missed her more than words can say. It annoys Brooke as she straightens up her hair and says hello to Nathan. He sighs, then smiles, says "hello, Brooke" with a fleeting frown, and they both know why. His eyes meet his father's, though it takes whatever strength Anthony Carter can muster to smile and hug his son. Anthony tries to turn his thoughts away from the painful memories, though it is not easy. He asks how Nathan is holding up and Jayzel pipes up, "Fine, thank you!" Both men laugh.

Naana, pleased to see them laughing, says to Tia, "You did the right thing, darling." Tia has not slept in her own bedroom since her return from Europe. "She hardly ever sleeps now," Anthony informs Nathan, who agrees that she does look tired. Later, Nathan runs a bath for Tia. He leaves her in the bathroom to get milk for her. Brooke tempts him in the kitchen with a bottle of wine, but Nathan quickly pours the milk in a glass and dashes upstairs. He knows his wife well enough that he does not dare try anything romantic with Tia. Nevertheless, Nathan can't help wishing he could get in the warm tub with Tia and wash her back. He returns to their bedroom and sits down on a chair. It has been so long for Tia to be in the bath in the en suite, he thinks, so he investigates and discovers Tia is not there.

Expecting that she might be sleeping with Brooke, as they often do when they re-connect, Nathan tiptoes to the baby's room to check on her and finds Tia sleeping on the toddler's bed. Coming up behind him, Anthony whispers, "She has been sleeping there since we came to the cottage." Nathan picks up Tia and carries her down the hall into their bedroom, where she wakes. The past week has been, without question, the most agonizing week of their married life. He whispers, "I appreciate you letting me come home tonight. I realize how much I have compromised our marriage. Still, working side by side with Nicole as a business partner, I am making changes. Baby, please, you've got to forgive me. I've been lost without you and Jayzel."

"I did not want you here. It was a fucking disgusting thing you did with your tarts! Sleeping with two friends and getting them both pregnant at the same and then getting rid of the kids?" Tia said bluntly.

"You looked exhausted." Nathan said, looking apologetic. Tia sat up in the bed, "Nathan, did you hear what I said?"

Nathan had a feeling that he was standing on a volcano that was about to erupt. He sensed the tension and anger in his wife's voice. He did not know when her ferocity was going to be directed at him, but he needed to put that fire out as quickly as he could. His face turned icy, although he continued smiling. He decided to swallow his pride. He said innocently, "Babe, you've been through a lot the past week. Baby, listen to me. I have been a fool. I have no excuses for my actions in the past, but I cannot have you upset. I will do anything that you want, just please don't ask me to leave again." He paused and stood in the middle of their bedroom with an anguished expression. Tia could see how miserable he looked.

"Tia, I almost lost you when you fell.... The whole night I did not sleep, thinking what I could have done to prevent that. I believe in the closeness of family and all that entails. You are my wife. I am very much in love with you and the family we are building. I am on the same page with you and only you. Look, I'm not able to stop our divorce... Please Tia… I love you, and I miss you and Jayzel so very much." As she listened to him, Tia became more enraged. She said stubbornly, "Why do you repeatedly do stupid things, Nathan? It's been one foolishness after another. I am done... I am fed up, Nathan. I will not put up with you screwing around with your fucking disgusting whore you call a business partner anymore. You hear me? I am done with your lies and your goddamn whore. She is good enough to fuck around with, why don't you go and be with her? How stupid do you think I am? You are a lawyer and yet you sign your own divorce papers without reading them, and I'm supposed to believe that you have not been sleeping with your tart of a partner? You are fucking out of your mind! You leave me the fuck alone!"

The whole house woke up. Nathan stood still and quiet as Tia vented her anger, as she screamed and yelled. Tia's mother was heading to the master bedroom when she met Anthony who was equally unhappy with the screaming. Finally, Naana opened the bedroom door without knocking. Nathan and Tia were both startled when they saw her slam their bedroom door. "Tia Faith Sharp, that is enough! How dare you? You never ever speak to your husband in that manner. You have a little girl sleeping down the hall, a house full of guests and this is how you two kids behave?"

Nathan tries to apologize. His mother-in-law silences him. He quickly goes and sits on the bed with his wife like a naughty school boy about to get a time out. She turns to Nathan, "Whatever it is you have done, darling, you find a way to fix it before it tears us all apart. We all have lost someone we loved very much." Naana is in tears as she pauses to take a breath, "Heather adored you both. If she was here today, not only would her heart break to see you two kids at each other's throats, but she would also be very disappointed with you – as we all are." She left the young couple deeply troubled as she went back to her room.

Anthony, looking at his son with contempt, asked Nathan to come with him. His voice is as gentle as Nathan's eyes are blazing with anger. Nathan feels his father has been trying to poison his wife against him. The very idea seems in bad taste to Nathan. He knows that his father has odd reactions to stress and men who don't meet his standard. He has tried to avoid him completely the past week, but there is no way that he is leaving his wife and child alone. He is home to stay. His father looks understandably terrible, Nathan thinks. He wants very much to avoid the heated discussions about his marriage.

"I know I'm not a man enough for Tia and Jayzel, but I don't want it to hear it tonight, Dad. I will not be kept apart from my family. Please, Dad, not tonight," he says calmly.

Tia knows the Carter men too well. She does not want anger brewing between them. Certain that Nathan absolutely will not leave under any conditions, and equally certain that being thrown out of his home in front of everyone will be the outer limit of upset, Tia feels annoyed by the whole situation. Tia embraces Anthony, saying, "It is okay, Daddy. I am sorry. Now is not the time for this." No one could sleep after the couple's fight. An assortment of left-over Chinese food waits in the fridge in the kitchen downstairs. Brooke, Steven and Jackie trickle downstairs. Then the Sharps and Anthony join them. A few minutes later, Nathan trots downstairs in his pyjamas, pours some milk, warms it, and apologizes again to everyone about the noise and the disruption. When he returns to the master bedroom, Tia is sound asleep. He turns off the lights and goes back downstairs to help himself to some left-overs. The house seems suddenly peaceful and quiet, and he smiles to himself, happy to be home with his family. He sits at his desk for couple of hours, answering correspondence and working on his opening statement for an up-coming trial.

In the morning Nathan can see that his wife's eyes are full of sorrow. She is wearing her diamond stud earrings, her hair brushed over one shoulder, and the black dress she wore is unzipped. Nathan walks slowly towards her and zips up the dress. She looks so beautiful. She sits on the bed and tries to put on her high-heeled boots. She looks depressed. Nathan says quietly, "I have been incredibly stupid. It has been the most humiliating moment in our marriage: you felt betrayed and cheated by my actions. I swear to you, as I..." He paused. "Mother would have lost every bit of respect she had for me if she could see how sad you are now, Tia. I love you. Please, if not for our family, then for Mother." He put his hands out and she took them. He wiped her face, did his best to calm her. Tia and Nathan said very little to each other on their way to the church. Heather Carter knew a lot of people: her two older sisters and her father were there as well as many friends and colleagues she had known over the years. The funeral ceremony was very well attended. Nathan, Antony and Heather's father waited by the door to shake hands with friends. Nicole arrived late with her husband. The smile she and Nathan exchanged could have lit up the Province of Ontario. She and Ian shook hands with Tia, and Ian said, "I was in town for business. I saw the obituary in the paper yesterday. I called Nicole and we thought it would be a decent thing to come." Tia smiled frostily and thanked them for coming. "Poor fool," she thought of Ian.

Heather's father, her sisters, and Jackie all said a few words during the service. They all cast a pink rose on Heather casket beside the huge circle of white roses with the "Grandma" banner that Tia had ordered on behalf of Jayzel. They went to the cemetery immediately after the funeral to bury Heather. They watched in silence as the casket was lowered into the ground. It was so sad as Tia realized that Heather was really gone. It hit her like thunder, and she began to cry. For a moment, she was in Nathan's arms and her parents were happy to see them close again. The family had rented a conference room at the Hilton Hotel in order to accept the condolences of friends and family. It was an elegantly simple buffet. The waiters offered people coffee, drinks and wine.

Tia had not had any time to talk to Brooke since she arrived. The two friends wandered to the other side of the buffet. Brooke told her things are getting a lot better between herself and Jason. She suggests that maybe Tia should try and work things out with Nathan. Tia insists that she can not. She has thought about it, but she can't do it. She has her daughter to protect. Jayzel leaves the wake with her parents and Anthony heads to the airport to catch his flight to the Virgin Islands.

All Nathan thinks about is Tia: memories of how their life used to be kept flashing back to when Henry would pick them up and drop each of them off at work, first him and then Tia. The same thing in the evening: Nathan enjoyed rubbing cocoa butter on her feet and stomach every night before they make love. He remembers with pleasure the many evenings they ate out and the weekends when he liked to take her to Quebec City or to Toronto, where they spent their weekends either in Nathan's condo in Toronto and at a hockey game or a basketball game, or dancing sometimes at a night club. Tia always wore the sexiest dresses. Some weekends she would invite the associates to dinner in their house, and she couldn't keep her hands of him, flirting with him under the noses of their guests, and he was the same as they talked and laughed.

Nathan was happy being married to Tia. She often came to the court house and watched him at work; at their gym he was the envy of all the guys who came to work out there. Everyday with her was like having a different woman. Sex was fantastic, Tia was sexy, and everyday she did something romantic that blew his mind. How could he have thrown all that way? She was still living at his parents' condo, so he thought that was a good sign. She did not run back to her ex-boyfriend in England; Jayzel was in Europe with his in-laws; and his mother-in-law had called to say that Tia was coming to Holland, so maybe Nathan should also come and try one more time with Tia. She was almost six months pregnant.

Chapter 44

Guntar is at the airport to meet Nathan when he arrives. He informs Nathan that Tia is waiting in the car. Nathan thinks that is a good sign and he feels hopeful of a warm welcome from Tia, but as he sits in the back of the car, Tia closes her eyes and refuses to talk. Jason and Brooke are in the pool when they arrive at the house. It is a little awkward for Nathan, at first. Gertrude greets him from her wheel chair, a permanent fixture since her stroke a month ago. After dinner, Tia announces, "The last time we were in Amsterdam, I didn't get a chance to show Nathan the city. I think we should do that tonight!" They cruise the canals at night, just the two of them, and while they are enjoying themselves, Nathan tells Tia that he is happy to see her. Tia responds, "I can't forgive you, Nathan. I've tried, but I just can't."

The next day Tia, Nathan, Brooke, and Jason visit Gertrude's art gallery. Tia shows Nathan all the paintings and tells him some of the stories behind them. While they all view the paintings, Tia gets a call from Jaden. "Brooke, could you show Nathan around while I take this call? Thanks." Tia slips into Gertrude's office to talk to Jaden.

Brooke and Nathan have hardly said two words to each other since their wild weekend in the Ramada Hotel when they went to Casino de Hull. Jason observes the two of them laughing and out of nowhere he punches Nathan on the mouth. "Stay the hell away from my wife!" he exclaims. Finished with her call, Tia is just coming out of the office when she witnesses the whole little drama. Preferring not to let on that she knows about it, Tia slips back into the office.

"You had your fun with me and my wife. If you dare make a pass at her again I will break every bone in your body. I hope you enjoyed blackmailing my wife about the kiss the night before your wedding," Jason adds.

Feeling squeamish, Tia covers her mouth with her hands as she listens to the discussion in the main room. Tears sting her eyes as she listens to Jason's accusations. For her part, Brooke anxiously dreads that Tia has overheard everything. She shakes her head no to Nathan, but Nathan begins to laugh: "Jason, I love your passion: if any man put his lips on my wife I would…" he pauses for effect, then makes a slicing gesture before laughing again.

Jason grabs him and pins him against the wall. "You have about five seconds to let go of me," says Nathan threateningly. Jason lets go of Nathan, who turns to Brooke. "Brooke has been interfering with my family and I wanted her to see what it would feel like to lose something that means the world to her. Do you really think I would not fight for what's mine? The next time something like this happens, … Well! We will see who will laugh last!" Nathan strides away from them, laughing. Brooke, for once, is mercifully quiet. Tears slide down her cheeks as she approaches her husband, "Jason, I'm sorry." Unmoved, Jason stands silently next to her, lost in his own thoughts.

Tia pulls herself together and swings the office chair around to see Nathan standing there with a fat lip. She asks innocently, "Sweetie, what happened to you?"

"Jason Grey punched me and told me to stop making passes at his wife."

Tia begins to laugh out loud. "Well, a man has to protect his wife!" she observes through her laughter.

"Baby, I am in pain. I was not making passes at her. I'm here to win back my wife," he says sadly.

Tia couldn't believe it. It was clear to her that Nathan has not changed at all and will never change. She says, "Sweetie, I need to make a few phone calls. Why don't you go and make nice with Jason, hmm?"

Tia has learned to hide her emotions well from the people she loves. Learning that the people she loves are not what they seem is hard for her to overcome, but she is determined to enjoy her vacation before she goes back to Canada and begins her new life, once again alone. The four of them drive to Amsterdam tourist spots and they take another boat ride and have lunch on the boat with the other passengers. It is a little different compared to the last time Jason and Brooke took the boat ride in Amsterdam. Back then, it was just the two of them getting to know each other. Now Jason feels like he doesn't know his wife. It's been one lie after another: he does not believe her anymore; and he does not want to be around Nathan Carter, either. He is a cruel, cruel man. How could Tia still want to be around him? It makes him sick sitting across from them watching them laugh. It all looks staged to Jason. "Thanks for lunch, guys, but Brooke and I are going to get off here," Jason says politely. He does not want to go back to the house.

He feels so torn about being here in Holland, about his family connection to Tia and Nathan through Gertrude. He has been desperately terrified of himself, especially whenever he thinks of that morning when he almost went to jail for raping his wife. They've tried to make love since, but it's not the same and they have not made love since the last attempt. Brooke doesn't seem to care that they are married and living in the same home, and sharing the same bed, but nothing. On top of it all, Jason's career has suffered as a consequence of the incident, so much so that his wife doesn't even know that he is drowning in debt. Brooke puts her hands up and calls a taxi. She sits with her eyes closed trying to think of a way to turn things around with Jason. They constantly mistrust each other these days and she doesn't like it. Just before the taxi stops, she puts her hands on his thigh and says, "There is something I've been meaning to run by you, sweetheart, but there is never a right time." She is still sitting in the taxi when Jason gets out. She looks just as miserable as he does. He is horrified that she might want a divorce, a devastating blow on top of everything else. "I shouldn't have hit Nathan," he says as he helps her out of the taxi. "You should have done a lot more to him, darling," Brooke says ominously. For a minute Jason sees his old wife back and he smiles. He takes her by the hand as they return to their room together.

Standing by the window of their room, Brooke blurts out, "Jason, are you having an affair?" Jason, sitting on the bed taking his shoes off, almost has a heart attack. He drops the shoe and stares at Brooke in shock, mouth open in surprise. He wonders what else can go wrong today. She finally turns to face him, repeating the question: "You seem to have gone off me. We've not made love for a long time now," she observes softly.

Jason gets up off the bed and walks slowly toward Brooke: "I have not been having an affair. I thought you'd gone off *me*." Brooke hardly lets Jason finish his sentence before she wraps her arms around him and begins kissing Jason. With each kiss, they peel off a garment. They talk, just like they often do, after they make love. Brooke mentions, "I have been thinking about our future lately, darling. I enjoy working for my mother and being in a partnership with the girls at Urban Style. It occurs to me that we have been doing a lot more working and building our own empire and that we could be doing something to secure our children and our future."

Jason is aroused when Brooke says children. He didn't think that she wanted kids even though she adores Jayzel. He sits up in the bed and smiles. Brooke asks, "What is so funny?"

"So you want kids?" he asks with a naughty tone. Brooke jumps out of the bed, "One afternoon of wild sex is enough! I don't want to make babies right this minute!" She is already getting dressed when Jason begs her to come back to bed.

Tia knocking on the door makes Brooke and Jason laugh that it is not the maid coming to make up the room.

"I see, you two have had yourselves quite a tasteful afternoon," Tia teases. She closes the door behind her and sits on the bed. Jason is still naked with a woody under the sheets.

Tia says ruefully, "I have wanted to apologize for Nathan, and all that he has done."

Jason says, "It is forgotten."

"I can't forget like you two," she says softly.

Both Brooke and Jason are confused. Brooke lashes out, "then what the hell are you still doing with the son of a bitch? Did you not give him the divorce? Do you know how difficult it is to get a divorce?"

Tia laughs. Brooke is stunned. "Tia, you tell me what you are up to before I go wipe the grin off the face of that man you call a husband," Brooke insists.

"It's true. Nathan and I are divorced and we have been living apart since my return to Canada three months ago." Brooke looks at Jason, who is even more confused than his wife. Tia continues, "My mother-in-law's death has not been easy for me and I didn't want to add to my father-in-law's pain. We have been granted a divorce. Nathan knew about it, and he did his best to stop it, but it was too late."

"What do you mean Nathan did his best to stop it?" Jason asks.

"The day his mother passed, a lawyer that Brooke hired when Jayzel was born brought divorce papers from Nathan's office. According to the lawyer, Nathan had requested a divorce and had given his rights to the kids to me. Anyway, he was not aware of any of it as his partner, Nicole, got him to sign the papers by passing him a stack of papers needing his signature. So he just scrawled his John-Henry on each page without reading everything. It turns out Nicole and the lawyer that Brooke hired were Nathan's roommates years ago in Toronto. Nathan got them both pregnant at the same time and made them get an abortion the same day."

"No!" says Brooke. "Oh, no! It was Nicole who gave me Christine Freeman's number. I wasn't even thinking of the things she pointed out with regards to the law and she told me not to say anything to Nicole."

"It was their plan all long. Nathan told me he used to share an apartment with two girls who were lawyers and one of them had moved out. When I first met Christine, I noticed a photograph of the three of them in her office, which she tried to hide. In fact, it was the first thing that I saw before she let me in the office, so I went along with her game, and I hired someone to investigate her past for me."

Brooke, agitated, asks, "Why are you still with him, and why did you not tell me?"

"Brooke, I love you, but you have got to stop being bossy and overprotective of me." Jason starts laughing when he hears Tia's words.

Brooke frowns and Jason laughs harder. "You did not answer my question: why are you here with him?"

"I'm not *with* him. "You know how my parents are… my mother invited him to come. I just want to get my daughter and leave peacefully. I'm hoping to leave him something that will burn him until he dies. I have already bought a house in Stoney Creek, Ontario. It's a few hours from the Toronto CTV studio, where I will be working in three weeks. My producer's mother lives in Stoney Creek, not far from me and she can babysit Jayzel when I'm at the studio. Everything is all set. I plan to tell him about it two days before Jayzel and I leave."

"Listen, you are not going back to Canada. You are crazy if you think I'm gonna let you go," Brooke shouts.

"Now, Brooke," says Tia as she stands up. "You see, that's exactly what I mean about being over-protective. Be downstairs in an hour and we'll all go out to the Amsterdam Lacy night club. It's going to be a memorable experience, I promise!" Tia winks as she closes the door.

Jason and Nathan stand in the hall waiting for their wives when the maid approaches to say, "Miss Tia and Miss Brooke say you two should go ahead with Guntar and they will drive themselves to the club, later." Nathan was about to tell the maid to go tell his wife no, when Jason begins to whistle at the two girls standing at the top of the stairs wearing their sexiest dresses. Both Jason and Nathan have never seen the girls looking so good. As Brooke and Tia take their time walking down the stairs, the men do not take their eyes off them. Brooke tells Tia she wants to spend a quiet night by the pool with Jason.

"Oh – no, you don't!" Tia exclaims. "I am almost six months pregnant and divorced. This is the only time I have to go out and let my hair down. You are coming with me," she whispers.

"Damn! Baby, this is better than prom night," Nathan says.

Tia kisses Nathan on the cheek as she sits on his lap in the back of the limo and pours him a glass of champagne as well as one for Brooke and Jason. The night club is fully packed. Tia talks in Nederlands to the bouncer at the door, giving him two hundred Euros. The bouncer escorts them to a private area. Disco lights flash in the dark room, and the music is loud. Tia raises her hand and signals two sexy girls to come over.

"I told them that you are my sexy ex-lover, and that I'm pregnant, my feet hurt, and I want them to dance with you for me." The girls are all over Nathan already.

"I will rub your feet," Nathan says. He extends his hand and Tia takes it. "I don't want to go home. I want you to slow dance with me," she says.

Jason wants to take his wife home and rip her clothes off. He tells Brooke what he's thinking. "Later, darling. How about you dance with me?" She fans his face with her hands and kisses him gently on the lips. "I miss you so much, Jason. Making love today was just like the first night in the loft. Let's not let anything come between us again, Jason. I promise not to kiss any other man again if you will forgive me," she says.

"I love you too much not to forgive you, sweetheart," he says as he kisses her.

They were still kissing when Tia and Nathan returned to the table, so Tia said, "if you two have not had enough of each other this afternoon, I can get you a hotel room now, you know?" Brooke flushes with embarrassment and replies, "You are such a child, Tia!"

Both Jason and Nathan laugh. They enjoy a nice dinner. Tia has four girls come in after dinner and strip for them. Tia puts money in Jason's and Nathan's hands to put in the ladies' thongs. Brooke finds it a little uncomfortable and tells Tia she has had enough for the night, and that she wants to go home. When they return to the house, everyone is already asleep. Tia and Nathan say good night to Jason and Brooke. Tia heads to the pool area and lights a fire, then sits down on one of the lounge chairs. Nathan takes off her shoes and rubs her feet just like he had promised earlier. Tia takes his hands and kisses the back of them. Nathan has never seen this side of his wife. "Who are you? ..and what have done with my wife?" Nathan asks softly.

Tia begins to undress and says, "Come swim naked with me." He smiles, "I'd love to, but I can't. Are you going to forgive me and come home so we can get remarried before the baby is born?"

"Our son, Trey Anthony Carter, Nathan. Our son."

Nathan couldn't hold back the emotions he felt at that moment when he learned that Tia was carrying a boy. Part of him wished that his mother-in-law was right about Tia still being in love with him. There is no way this is going to be easy for him now if Tia refuses to come home and work things out. Nathan picks her up and says in a sexy voice, "You, Mrs Carter, I have been a fool, and you have punished me these last three months. What do you say?" Tia didn't respond. After a pause, Nathan says, "Okay, then. I will wait."

Tia and Nathan sleep through the better part of the day, leaving for England that evening to pick up Jayzel at the Sharp's. Jayzel has grown big in the few months they have been apart. Tia shows Nathan everywhere in London worth seeing. The day before they were to leave England, they were in Marks & Spencer's in Oxford Street. Tia tries on different sexy panties while asking Nathan which ones he likes. Of course, he loves all of them. Tia selects a few to purchase. When they return to her parents home, Tia's mother asks "Are you going to go home and put your marriage back together, or are you going to carry on with this foolishness?" Tia takes Jayzel and leaves the house. Naana tells Nathan not to worry, that it will be all right; Tia will calm down and come back; and then you two can sort things out. It has been three days, and Tia has not come home or called anyone. Naana visits Brooke's apartment, but Brooke says she and Jason were just about to come over and take Tia and Nathan out for lunch. It looks to them that Nathan had lost a lot of weight already. He tells them that he is going to go back to Canada the next day. He asks if they have any ideas where Tia would be at all, but recalling their conversation in Holland, Jason and Brooke lie and say "no". Nathan Carter is faced with the heartbreaking prospect of losing his family for good this time. However, he remains confident that it will all be straightened out once he talks to Tia.

Chapter 45

Kevin has not stopped thinking about Tia since the day she broke up with him. Nevertheless, he has kept himself busy during the last four years. He has always wanted to be a lawyer, so he went to New York City to take the bar exams, but did not pass them, so he returned to England before his visa expired. He is now divorced, holds a British passport, but has no Tia to fulfill his life. He wonders whether Tia's baby could be his. For Kevin, in the best of all possible worlds, the baby is his and he and Tia are together. He has not brought a gift for his sister Ola's little girl, so he goes to Regent Street and looks in Hamley's Toy Store for something appealing to a three-year-old. He wishes he knew Tia's address so he could send something to the little girl. A familiar voice that he knows but can not place rings out, very close to him, so he follows the sound. "I must be hearing things," he thinks. At the cashier's desk he is surprised to see Brooke, looking more beautiful than ever. She smiles and signals to him to come over. Tia, arms full of stuffed animals, is unprepared for this meeting and drops her purchases.

Brooke asks, "Hi Kevin! What are you doing in Hamley's?"

"I'm looking for a toy for my sister's child," Kevin replies.

Tia pays for her stuff and tells the sales girl to hurry up as she doesn't want get stuck in traffic.

Kevin asks, "How long will you be in town?"

Brooke answers, "They are leaving for the airport now. Why don't you come with us, Kevin? If you are not too busy?"

Tia, unhappy with Brooke's suggestions, says, "No, I'd like to spend a quiet time alone with you." Brooke gives her number to Kevin and suggests he call her later. He walks them to their car, but Tia does not say much to him. He stands aside and watches them drive off in a BMW convertible. It is a huge blow to Kevin: he has thought of nothing but Tia and her baby, but she does not say a single word to him.

In their new home in Stoney Creek, Tia sleeps with Jayzel in her room in the same bed. They both feel jet lagged and have been sleeping a lot more since they arrived back in Canada. Amy Hall is in Stoney Creek over the weekend visiting her mother, so she drives over to Tia's house, uninvited as usual. Tia is not expecting anyone, so she doesn't want to go to the door, but Jayzel is sleeping and the person at the door won't let up, so Tia reluctantly logs off her computer and answers the door.

"Honey, you still sleeping?" Amy asks. "Our promo for *The Saga* was aired two days ago. The buzz is already out. It is going to be huge, I tell you!" Amy exclaims. Tia smiles and closes the door.

"How are you holding up, kiddo?" Amy asks.

"Fantastic. How do you like the script I sent in for the next three episodes?"

Amy knows that Tia writes very close to home, but keeps it to herself because it is very juicy stuff. Now that everything is going to be aired nationwide, she is a little worried about potential legal matters.

"Well!" Tia says, "The suspense is killing me, Amy. Is it good, or do you need me to rewrite?"

"Honey, I love it! I love it! It occurred to me you write about things you have experienced and I take it your handsome ex-husband has not read any of the stuff you write about?"

"Your point?" Tia asks, handing her a mug of coffee. She drinks some of the coffee and changes the subject, "I love your house." Tia has become very impatient since her marriage to Nathan and hates when people won't say what's on their minds. "I do write very close to things that I know, feelings that I have shared and often things that my friends and families have been through. If is there a problem with the script and the network wants to pull us off the air, I need to know right now, Amy. I'm a single parent now. I cannot afford to be sued for my children because I cannot provide for them."

"Oh, no, Tia! Honey, they loved it!" Amy exclaims.

"If you are worried about Nathan, there is not a single character in *The Saga* who went to Stanford, played college football and became a successful lawyer on the show. So why should you care if he has read the stuff that I write or not?"

"Tia, I think you are very brave getting a divorce at six mouths pregnant and with a toddler, too. I am just concerned about you, honey. Your husband did not appear like a shit head to me. Any idiot can see you two are very much in love. Why the quickie divorce? Are you two filing for a bankruptcy?" she asks.

Tia laughs, and says, "Thank you, but Nathan is not up for discussion with you or anyone else. And we are not going bankrupt." Tia asks, "Do people really file for a divorce if they are going bankrupt?"

Amy raises an eyebrow and says, "I see I have to teach you the Canadian way. Do you have a television?" Tia points her to the living room.

"Since you're here… I don't suppose you want to join me for dinner? My daughter is sleeping." Amy suggests, "Why don't we order in some Chinese food?" Tia agrees and they sit down to watch television while they wait. Their promo came right after the six o'clock news. Amy screams like a teenager. As soon as their promo comes on the TV, Tia simply smiles. The phone rings: her father-in-law has seen the promo and loves it. He tells Tia, "I'm coming to Toronto next week. I'll stop by to see you." They do not talk about Nathan.

At the office, Tia's first in-coming call that day is from her mother, followed by a call from Nathan. They have not spoken since that fateful afternoon in England four days ago.

"I am coming to Toronto tonight. I want you to come home, baby. We will get remarried before the baby is born, just like we did with Jayzel. I've been out of my mind with worry. Baby, please."

Tia has been waiting for this call since her return to Canada, but she doesn't want to get into an argument with him. "I will see you tonight," she says, hanging up. She spends most of the afternoon in production meetings and she visits the set with Amy for the first time. It is a lot different from the news room. She meets some of the cast members. "You hold this glittering backdrop of celebrity and glamor in the palm of your hands, honey. They are nothing without you Tia, honey. You are *The Saga*," Amy says proudly. Tia has learned to like her the last few months. "The launch party is tonight. Do you need a date?" Amy asks.

"No, thanks Amy. I never date people that I work or do business with. My ex-husband is in town tonight. I will bring him before I cut down his big ego," Tia chuckles.

Amy puts her arms around Tia. "You, honey, are giving women everywhere hope. You British people sure do believe in girl power. Tia, I mean it: if you need anything at all, call me or my mom. You know? She loves Jayzel already and, of course, you have all the cable channels, she tells me!"

Tia has kept a lot of things inside her. Her writing is the only escape. There are times that she can not escape some of the things in her life. She loves her office and the privacy it provides. Nathan arrives at the CTV studio. The security calls Tia, and he is asked to sign in and is given a visitor's pass. He is asked to wait for Miss Sharp's assistant to escort him to her office.

He hates it when Tia is referred to as Miss Sharp. He is not anxious at all. He has everything planned, to go back to Tia's hotel, order dinner and tell her everything is going to be alright. They will be making wild passionate love before midnight. The security guard interrupts his thoughts as he alerts Nathan to the presence of Tia's assistant, a handsome young man. Nathan doesn't like him already. They take the elevator to the sixteenth floor. Tia is not in her office, so the assistant offers Nathan a drink. Nathan declines. Tia has photographs of herself, Brooke, and Kate on the window sill accompanied by a glass elephant figurine, and a collection of photographs of Jayzel. There is a photo of Tia, Jayzel, Naana and Heather on her desk. Nathan picks it up and looks at it. Nathan sits on the sectional couch and closes his eyes. He does not hear Tia enter the room. When he opens his eyes, Tia is sitting behind her desk, typing on the computer. He thinks she looks very pale. Getting up, he walks over to the desk and kisses her cheek. It is so soft; he does not want to take his lips off her cheek. "How are you?" she asks.

"Terrified – and lonely without you and Jayzel," he replies. Tia wants to throw herself into his arms and kiss him. God, how she has missed him! She didn't expect it to be this difficult. She is in tears when her assistant calls to ask whether she needs anything. Tia replies, "No. I will be heading out to the launch party soon with my husband. Good night, David. Please remember that I will not be here until Thursday afternoon." Nathan is relieved to hear Tia refer to him as her husband. They didn't stay very long at the party, just long enough to make an impression. They returned to Stoney Creek in the limo.

"Where are we?" asks Nathan.

"Home," replies Tia simply. He draws her gently to him and asks, "What do you mean, home?" Tia tells him to come in. She introduces Nathan to Mrs Hall and thanks her for staying with Jayzel, who is asleep in her own room.

"Tia, please tell me what's going on?" Nathan asks quietly, trembling with fear, heart racing. He puts both hands in his pockets to hide their shaking.

"Are you hungry? Do you want something to eat, Nathan," Tia asks as she takes the blender out of the cupboard. Nathan shouts, "I don't want a smoothie! I want to know what's going on! Now!"

"Sit down, Nathan," says Tia firmly as she points him to a chair. He refuses. She leaves him in the dining room to sit in the living room and take off her shoes. The baby is kicking hard, and Tia is rubbing her belly when Nathan joins her. He knows his wife can be fiercely independent, and he does not want to force the issue, but he can see that this has been what she wants. As Nathan scans the room, he notices the furniture has come from her old apartment in Ottawa. She must have kept it all in storage. The house, her luxurious job at the CTV studio, did not just happen a month ago. How could he have missed it? Tia has always been open with him. "Why would she do this?" he wonders. She looks almost half asleep. He glances up to see the lights on in the upstairs hall. Going upstairs, he can see Jayzel sound asleep in her room. It is painted in rich pink and lime tones. The baby crib is all dressed up in lime and filled with different types of stuffed animals. There are two dressers: one pink and the other one lime.

The next bedroom is plain: white walls with a queen-sized pine bed. The master bedroom has a cheater door to the bathroom. There are lots of candles everywhere. He opens the closet which is filled with women's clothes. The bed is unmade.

Returning downstairs, Tia has fallen asleep on the sofa. Nathan carries her up to the bedroom with the unmade bed and covers her. He now suspects Brooke knew where they were when he asked whether she knew Tia's intentions. Why did Tia go along with Christine's and Nicole's scheme? Why would a woman pregnant six and a half months seek a divorce and be isolated from everyone who loves her? Nathan has so many questions and he is not going to get answers from Tia right now. Looking at her fast asleep, she is a vision of perfection. He picks up the phone to call his private investigator, Lyden, and sees that his father has called a few times, which means he was aware of where his wife was all along. Nathan scrolls down Tia's call display. His father had been calling them everyday for two weeks now. He feels worse: what a miserable, rotten man his father is! How could he stand and watch him suffer like this? He is not actually surprised: Nathan has suspected this is what he wanted. Anthony still blames Nathan for Heather's death. It certainly seems like everyone is out to get him, and he feels broken up. He puts down the phone and sits in the chair feeling disappointed, and reeling from the truth that he has lost his wife. He can't imagine managing without her now. In the past three months he has lost his mother and his long-time business partnership with Nicole. To whom will he turn now? He's always had his mother's love no matter what he did, as well as Nicole's. It never occurred to him that he could lose the love of the key women in his life. There were tears rolling down his cheeks. Nathan made his mind up that he was not going to beg Tia to come back to Ottawa so they could get remarried. He decides to be exceptionally reasonable, not making a fuss about the way she has betrayed him. He fully understands the situation. He stays up all night watching Tia soundly sleeping. There is half a bottle of champagne that Amy had brought to Tia's house the day before. He pours some in the glass and drinks it. He sets the glass on the dining table. It is now five in the morning. He looks through the yellow pages and calls a taxi. By the time Tia wakes, he is gone, leaving no note at all.

Kevin Peters has got a job with a fellow Nigerian lawyer's office working as his legal assistant. He comes across Brooke Williams' card and gives her a call. They meet for lunch. Brooke does not waste time telling Kevin that Tia is now divorced and still very much carries a torch for him. His conscience tells him that Brooke's suggestion is ridiculous. He asks incredulously whether it is true that Tia still has feelings for him, especially after everything he did to her. Brooke has never been the one to accept boundaries, so she writes down Tia's address and advises Kevin to go to Canada and tell her that he still loves her and wants to be with her. Kevin puts considerable thought to what Brooke has said. He confides in his sister, Ola, who has always loved Tia and thought that she was perfect for Kevin. She tells Kevin not to think about Tia, who is about to have a second child with the ex-husband, but that he should follow his heart. Consequently, Kevin is in London Gatwick airport three weeks later boarding a plane to Hamilton International Airport to go see Tia. Of course, Brooke knows but does not warn Tia.

Anthony spends every second weekend in Stoney Creek with his former daughter-in-law. Tia is almost nine months pregnant and the baby is due any day. She and Nathan have not spoken or seen each other since the night her show first aired. Nathan has thrown himself into his work; he still lives in the same home he once shared with Tia and Jayzel; and everything has been left the same as the day they left. Since parting ways from Nathan, Nicole works as a Crown Attorney in Toronto and she is doing very well putting people behind bars. Nicole has gained a reputation as the Crown Attorney who never loses – until the day an actor-rapper by the name of Eric DeSante is charged with the rape and assault of his then seventeen-year-old girlfriend. Eric DeSante is also a cast member of *The Saga*, one of CTV's number one shows in Canada, which is also written by Tia Sharp, executive producer. Of course, Amy Hall immediately retains Nathan Carter to represent Eric. Nathan agrees under two conditions: that Tia must not be told that he is Eric's lawyer; and that he wants Tia at the court house for Eric's bail hearing. Amy informs Nathan that Tia has already written Eric out of the show the moment he was arrested, and that it would be impossible to get her to come to the court house to show Eric her support. However, she is able to offer Nathan a proposal which he likes better. The media whips into a frenzy when the judge grants Eric DeSante bail. Nathan and Nicole are on opposite sides of the court room. They do not talk to each other before or after the hearing. Nicole's office is filled with all kinds of flowers by the time she returns. She knows instantly who they are from without needing to read the card. Her heart has not stopped racing from the moment Nathan walked into the courtroom looking sexier than ever. Throughout the hearing, he behaves as if she doesn't exist.

There is a silence and a distance with which Nicole is unfamiliar. Because she has never accompanied Nathan to court, she does not know how domineering Nathan can be in the court room. She knows she has lost the battle even before it begins. Nathan does not make eye contact, though she catches a glimpse of him occasionally biting his lips like he does when he gets nervous. It saddens her to realize that she and Nathan are working against each other. She feels her dignity and strength slip away the moment she sees him enter the court room. Nicole has been unable to concentrate the whole day. Helplessly, she giggles like a teenager in love. The card reads: *You looked beautiful today, Nikkie. I've missed u. Let's have dinner soon. Love, Nate.* Nicole was in tears as she read the note.

Nathan is on the six o'clock news just like Amy has promised, and also like Amy promised, she has contrived to have Tia run into Nathan and the press. Showing more and looking sexier than ever, wearing her usual trademark over-sized sunglasses and carrying a black Chanel bag, Tia stops and smiles at him, before being swamped by the waiting press with flash photographers and a myriad of questions. Nathan runs to her aid and sweeps her into a limo just like he wanted. She is still sitting on his lap with her head down on his shoulders. Nathan tells the driver to head to Stoney Creek. He closes his eyes, deep in his own thoughts and rubs her back while the other hand runs through her long wavy hair. They can feel each other's hearts beat.

Mrs Hall opens the door as the limo parks in Tia's driveway. Nathan asks her to run a bath for Tia, which she does. Jayzel is already in bed, sleeping. Nathan gives Mrs Hall money to order Chinese food for them before she leaves. When the food arrives, Tia is still in the bath. Mrs Hall sets the table and arranges the food before leaving for the day.

Nathan warms a glass of milk and takes it to Tia, who is lingering in the tub. He washes her back while she drinks her milk. Then, he helps her out of the bath. She has not had a bubble bath for while. The last time she ventured into the tub, Tia got stuck in the bath, her big belly making it next to impossible to climb in and out of the tub. It is nice to have Nathan there to help her out of the tub. He slowly dries her with a soft towel and puts her in the bed. He rubs cocoa butter lotion on her like he used to do before Jayzel was born. He wants so badly to kiss her, to make love to her, her breasts look so lusciously full. She puts her fingers against his lips when he tries to kiss her, her mouth is warm and inviting when they slowly kiss. It's like the first time they kissed in his parents' cottage, long and sexy.

"Make love to me, Nathan," she moans. It is like nothing has changed. They make love and they both cry in silence afterward. Nathan asks, "Are you hungry?" Tia does not want food. She wants more and more of him, which he is happy to give her. Mrs Hall returns in the morning and takes Jayzel out to play.

Meanwhile, Kevin's flight is about to land as the flight attendant announces that everyone must put on their seat belts. The anticipation is killing him. He gets into a Blue Line taxi and tells the driver Tia's address.

Tia is awake, though it is after lunch already. She and Nathan have been making love all night and half of the morning, but they have not really talked. Mrs Hall brings Jayzel home from the park. When Tia finally comes down to the kitchen, Nathan is sleeping. When he finally came downstairs for lunch, Jayzel looked at him like a stranger. It broke his heart that she had forgotten him already. The door bell rang, so he went to the door.

"Can I help you?" Nathan asks the man at the door.

"Yes. I'm looking for my girlfriend, Tia Sharp. I was told this is her address."

Nathan does not get a chance to ask the man to repeat himself because Jayzel runs to the front door and into the man's arms. As Kevin picks up the little girl, his face is full of enthusiasm and excitement he pushes past Nathan. Nathan feels helpless standing there watching a stranger hugging and kissing his little princess. It is an unforgettable experience for both men, though for different reasons.

"Nathan! My water broke!" Tia cries out.

"Okay, honey. I'll get one for you." Nathan murmurs distractedly.

"Nathan! I'm in labor! My water is broken!" Tia exclaims. "Call Daddy, please."

Nathan hasn't heard half of what Tia has said. Mrs Hall and Kevin notice that Nathan looks like he is having an out of body experience, he looks so confused.

"Tia is in labor," Mrs Hall reminds him.

Kevin follows Tia's voice. He quickly puts Jayzel down and calls 911. Tia suddenly realizes that Kevin is in her house. She screams in pain for Nathan, who still standing at the front door in a state of shock. Kevin asks Mrs Hall to take the baby as he tries to calm Tia. Tia doesn't want him to touch her. She screams, "Leave me alone!"

Mrs Hall calls Amy, who calls Anthony. Luckily, he is in Toronto, so Amy tells him to wait for her, that she will pick him up. When the ambulance arrives, Nathan is still standing by the door. Tia tells Mrs Hall that Nathan normally freezes when he is in shock. Kevin goes in the ambulance with Tia.

Chapter 46

Nathan's phone rings. "Hi, Nate! It's Dad. Listen, Tia is in labor in the maternity ward at St Joseph's Hospital in Stoney Creek. Where are you?" Nathan hangs up on his father. The phone rings again, and he is about to tell his father where to go, when he sees Nicole's number.

"I need you, Nikkie," Nathan mumbles. His voice is broken. Nicole knows that something is wrong. She asks, "Where are you, Nathan?"

Nathan goes upstairs to dress. He thinks he understands now why Tia has moved to Stoney Creek. She has been having an affair all this time. The baby might not be his. That's why she is so willing to keep him out of the children's lives. It all makes sense now. Calculating, Nathan suspects he was the last person to learn about her pregnancy. The secret divorce… she must have known her boyfriend was arriving and wanted to hurt him more. How could she? Nicole arrives at Tia's house less than an hour later and advises him to go to the hospital, so that he can claim his child. He tells Nicole, "The baby is not mine."

"Nevertheless, you must go. It can change things," Nicole says persuasively.

Tia has been in so much pain during the last two hours that the labor feels like it will last forever. Kevin is by her side comforting her, even though she repeatedly asks for Nathan, but he is nowhere to be found. Anthony arrives with Amy, so he scrubs and goes into the delivery room. Graciously, Anthony thanks Kevin for being there for Tia. The contractions are five minutes apart by the time Nathan and Nicole arrive. They wait outside. When the baby arrives, Anthony comes out and tells them: a boy, six pounds seven ounces and Tia is asking to see Nathan. When Nathan enters the room, Tia is holding the baby and

Kevin is sitting on the bed. They look like a happy couple. He closes the door before they can see him and takes Nicole's hands and says, "Let's go." Nathan leaves without seeing his baby son.

Tia realized that perhaps she should not have insisted on the divorce. Last night, the magic was still there between them and she knew she was still in love with Nathan. She told her father-in-law, "I'm going to give it one more try. I have missed Nathan and I think I've let my anger get the best of me." Joyfully, Anthony says, "I will go and bring Nathan back." Tia sleeps after the baby is born. Kevin stays at the hospital and calls his sister and Brooke to tell them about Tia's baby. He returns to Tia's room where she is still sleeping. He pulls up a chair to sit and sleep himself. It has been an unforgettable experience. Anthony calls Nathan, but he does not answer, so Anthony calls Nicole. Nicole says that Nathan is at Tia's house at Stoney Creek. Anthony drives to Stoney Creek in less than ten minutes. Nathan is on a long distance call with Tia's mother, and the phone is on speaker. Anthony stands still in the dining room listening to what Naana Konadu-Sharp has to say to his disgraceful son.

"Nathan, my darling, I know all about your hot little affair with Brooke Williams." Nathan tries his best to lie his way out and protects his innocence, but his mother-in-law does not let him get away with it. "Darling, I was in Canada when your daughter was born and Tia fell sick in hospital. Brooke Williams is a beautiful young lady and you are a very handsome young man with needs. This is not a judgment or a way to shame you, or to belittle you. We are all human and grief sometimes makes us do things out of character. What is done is done. Nathan, you got married to a woman who was coming into the marriage from a past with a heavy load. You are a good man. You may have lost your way. Darling, you are a good father. Don't let pride and anger take away your family. Tia respects the importance of family and understands that no one is perfect. You must not follow your ego and pride. Darling, go to the hospital to be with your wife and child. Let this Mr. Peters know who you are. Nathan, it is time for you to fight and to take your family back home, if that's what you truly want. Stop blaming others for your own mistakes and for Tia's mistakes. I love you, son. Tell Tia and Tony that I will be in Canada in a week. It is important that you and Tia start to communicate. Tony has not had any time to grieve for your lovely mother's death because of you two kids. It's time you two grow up, darling."

"Thank you, Mother," Nathan murmured. Although, Anthony was disgusted with the revelation that Tia's mother had made about his son and Brooke, he managed to calm himself down and to ask for Jayzel.

"Nicole and Mrs Hall have taken her to the park," Nathan answers.

"Tia asked me to get you," Anthony says.

Since Heather Carter's death, Nathan and his father have become and remained bitter, angry towards each other. Their only common interest has been Tia and Jayzel. After issuing a tough ultimatum to his son, Anthony is determined that his son should do the right thing by his wife. The poor man is exhausted. He doesn't want Tia or his son to feel anymore anguish because it is destroying all of them.

"Do you want me to drive you to the hospital?" Anthony asks generously as he comes and stands next to Nathan, who is drinking champagne and doesn't make any attempt to respond to his father. Instead, he takes out his cell phone and dials a number. "Nikkie, I'm ready to leave now. I will be at the hospital. Pick me up from there," he says and hangs up. He puts the glass on the coffee table and walks out of the house.

Meanwhile, at the hospital, Tia wakes still so sore from the birth. She is looking out the window when the door opens suddenly and Nathan strides into the room. She beams with a smile. Expecting Kevin to be with Tia, Nathan had a big speech prepared to say to her. He looks pointedly across the bed at her. "I need a DNA sample of your child. I need to know whether or not I am the father." Kevin is in the bathroom and Anthony is outside the door in the hall. They both hear Nathan's request. "I will not raise your lover's child as my son!" He adds, "Tia, after all the bullshit you pulled in Europe, I will not do this again. Tia, you will have to find yourself some other poor slob to… to… " he pauses.

Tia is shocked by Nathan's words. Embarrassed, she narrows her eyes to fight back the tears and stares at Nathan. He is stubborn and unreasonable, but never this mean and hateful. Tia nods and looks out the window. She has been reveling in the excitement of having them all together as a family. For his part, Anthony is furious to hear his son diminish his wife in that manner. He comes into the room and puts his arms around Tia, saying to his son, "What is wrong with you, Nate?" He is outraged that Nate would accuse Tia of adultery, and the attempt to pass her lover's child as Nate's is utterly absurd. There is a phone by Tia's bed. She picks it up and calls the nurse.

"This is Tia Sharp. I would like a DNA test done right away on my son, Trey Anthony Carter," she requests.

It is not long before the nurse enters the room to swab Nathan's mouth. He asks the nurse when would the test be ready and she replies, "First thing in the morning. It is going to the lab now." Nathan storms out of the room, slamming the door. Anthony asks Tia, "Why would Nate ask for a DNA test?" Just then Kevin Peters emerges from the bathroom like a thief, who has just been caught with his hands in the cookie jar.

Tia is a little startled and asks, "Why are you here?" Anthony tries to leave as the whole day has been too much like a soap opera to him. Nothing makes sense anymore. Tia asks him to stay. Kevin asks if he could speak privately to her. Tia is enraged. She finds Kevin's presence intrusive and inappropriate. Annoyed again, she yells, "Kevin, I'm not going to ask you again! Why were you at my home earlier, in the labor ward with me, and now hiding in my hospital bathroom?"

"I wanted to pay you a visit," he mumbles. Anthony is a little uneasy with Kevin's response. "Who are you?" he asks kindly.

"Oh -um.. Tia and I used to... um date. Sir," Kevin stammers.

Suddenly, Anthony and Tia both understand why Nathan wants the DNA test. Kevin closes his eyes in anguish. Tia is not too pleased to see him. She asks how he got her address. He does not respond. Tia said, "Fine! I will call the police and let them handle this. I will not be stalked by you!" She lashes out at him.

"Tia, please! It was not my intention to intrude or to cause you any upset. Brooke..."

"Brooke!!!" Both Tia and her father-in-law exclaimed simultaneously.

"Yes, Brooke. She told me you were divorced and she gave me your address to come and see you. She said you are still very much in love with me," Kevin explains.

Tia spoke in French to her father-in law. The old man wasn't happy with the task Tia had given him, but he nodded and headed out of the room. Anthony quickly ran outside to see if he could find Nathan. Nicole was pulling out of the parking lot when she saw him and stopped the car. Nathan asked her to please drive, but she waited. Speaking French, Anthony asked if he could talk to Nathan. Whatever Anthony said to Nathan amused him, as Nathan was laughing out of control as he told Nicole "let's go." Tia told Kevin that she does not have feelings for him, not the kind of feelings he thinks. "You and I were together for over two years, Kevin." She was about to say we share a child together, but stopped. "Life is about making the right decisions for ourselves. You made one for yourself when you dumped me and got married to that girl so you could get a British passport. I have been very happy for you, but I am married with family now."

"Brooke told me that you were divorced," he argued.

Tia smiled. "I'm so sorry you came all this way for nothing. I am very much in love with my husband." She said it with a straight face, but Kevin neither believed nor cared. He thought Nathan Carter was an arrogant jerk, who treated his wife shamefully. Kevin shared his thoughts with Tia, and Tia laughed. Kevin was happy to see her laugh. "Your kids are so beautiful, Tia," he said. He was more relaxed and at ease when Anthony returned. Whatever Tia asked him to do he could not have done. She put on a brave face and smiled, but she was profoundly upset. "How could Nathan think that? We made love. We were like a family again," she thought. She looks physically and emotionally exhausted.

"Daddy, you look exhausted. Why don't you take Kevin home with you? There's lots of left-over junk in the fridge. You can bring Jayzel with you and we will all drive home together," Tia suggested.

Anthony, speaking again in French, advised Tia not to take Kevin home with him because he had caused far too much upset just by showing up. Anthony thought Kevin's presence would cause more upset for Tia and Nate. "Angel, please, reconsider and let me find a hotel for the young man," he pleaded.

"Nathan will be back in hour with flowers, crying and begging and I will do what I always do, Daddy. We are fine. It was out of jealousy what he said about Trey. I want you to go home and stop worrying." The old man smiled and asked Kevin to come with him, but Kevin declined, thanking Anthony for his kind offer. As the old man insisted, and Tia added her support for the idea, the two men left the hospital.

Anthony called Nicole before he left the hospital. Nicole informed him that Nathan was trying to get a continuance on his pre-tail hearing in the morning. She believed he's got it, and that he was on his way back to be with his wife at the hospital. Anthony thanked Nicole and hung up the phone. "You lie very easily to people, Nicole. Do you know why?" Nathan asked. Nicole tossed her cell phone into her purse. "It was not a lie. That's what we are going to do now, Nathan, just like I told your father. I did let Christine mess with our friendship. I will not do it again. I love you too much to see you this unhappy," she said. Nathan opened his arms for Nicole to come to him, and she did so without hesitation. He held her tightly. "I want to be here with you. Call Ian and tell him you are spending the night in town," he whispered.

Nicole pulled away gently. "Ian and I have been separated for a couple of months," she muttered.

Nathan asked, "When did this happen? Why didn't you tell me?" Nicole was quiet. "Nicole, we have been the best of friends since college. You and I have always shared each other's joy and pain. How could you not have told me?" Nicole was still quiet. "Nikkie, are you going to talk to me, or am I just going to guess? Answer me damn it! Nikkie," he yelled. Nicole still did not respond. She picked up her purse and walked out of Nathan's condo. He asked in a child-like way, "Have I lost you too, Nikkie?" It broke her heart. She stopped. There was a long silence. Nathan took her hands and said, "Please, Nikkie. I know I have often hurt you repeatedly in the past. Tell me what happened with your marriage. I want to help. I love you, Nikkie. I have not looked out for you as I promised that I would." He paused.

Nicole could see the man she fell in love with years ago standing in front of her. She remembered the night at the college, during a Thanksgiving weekend party, when Nathan almost got his face kicked because of her. She smiled. Nathan asked what was funny. He hates it when she does that. She was still laughing thinking about those times: like the time he would not let her come to his dorm room, so Nicole thought he was gay.

He kissed her; he didn't want to stop, but he was thinking about Tia. He pulled away and said he was sorry. Nicole said it was okay and that they should go to the court house and file for the continuance, so he could go and be with his wife. Nathan said only if she told him what was going on with her and Ian. They spent the rest of the afternoon talking about what they have missed over the last six months. It was late by the time they ordered take-out and made love in Nathan's condo.

Nicole said she was going home to Ian to fix her marriage. She advised Nathan to do the same. It was just like old times, except this time, Nathan felt bad for sleeping with Nicole, so he shared it with her: "I know your are in love with her," Nicole mumbled, "and I'm in love with Ian. I hope we are not too late to save our marriages." They both got dressed quickly and left the condo in opposite directions.

Chapter 47

Back in Stoney Creek, Kevin senses that Tia may still be holding on to her broken marriage. He worries less about her husband than her father-in law because of their close relationship. He calls Brooke and asks her advice. Brooke suggests that the strong bond between Tia and her father-in-law could make a difference if Tia decides to forgive Nathan and take him back. The father-in-law adores Tia.

"Yeah, that could be true, but I think Tia still loves me. She might be afraid to trust me after the way we parted. I'm going back to the hospital to spend the night with her and to make sure the husband doesn't return."

Kevin calls a taxi and goes to the hospital. He brings some flowers, but Tia is sound asleep when he arrives, so he lays the bouquet on her bedside table. He wishes he could kiss her. Pulling a chair close to the bed, Kevin begins to tell her all the things he has ever wanted to say to her. The door is ajar, and Nathan hears enough of Kevin Peters' love and regrets for Tia as he stands behind the door listening to every word. He does not hear Tia say anything in response. He does not hear her say that she loves her husband. Nathan strolls down the hall to the nursery window. He wonders which one of the babies is Trey. He is about to leave when he sees Kevin in the nursery holding Trey and kissing him. It looks like he is saying something to the nurse, but he can not hear the conversation or read the man's lips. Nathan is sure he has seen enough. He has had enough of Tia Sharp and Kevin Peters.

Tia mother's spends most of the morning with thoughts of Nathan and Tia on her mind. She calls Canada hoping that all is well with her daughter's marriage only to learn that Kevin Peters is still there, and in fact living as a guest in Tia's home. It enrages the very kind lady. She tells Anthony that she will not be coming to Canada, and perhaps they all should let Tia and Nathan sort out their own mess. Anthony agrees with her. She drives to the Gemini Real Estate office to see Brooke Williams. Brooke happens to be on the phone with none other than Kevin Peters. Naana Konadu-Sharp wasted no time telling Brooke that she knows all about Brooke's affair with Nathan. "You and Tia are like sisters and being as close as you two are, it is uncommon that you may often share the same man. Nathan and Tia have hit a rough spot in their marriage. Kindly leave them alone, Brooke. Your interference in my daughter's marriage is beginning to annoy me!" She got up and left before Brooke could spin any lies. Brooke was trembling when she called to warn Nathan.

"It's all over, beautiful," Nathan says. "I will not fight for something that is not mine. You wanted me out of your sister's life. I'm out. Kevin Peters is welcome to her." He hangs up. Nathan puts on his tie. A limousine is waiting for him to take him to the court house. The press swarm around him like honey when he steps out of the limousine wearing his trademark dark shades. He looks very sophisticated, well-groomed, and the press love him. He stops and removes his shades, answers one of the many questions they are throwing at him. "No, sir. I'm not here to ask for a continuance. We are ready to proceed." He smiles, replaces the shades, and moves inside the courtroom. Court room number eight is fully packed as Nathan enters. Nicole is not present as the Crown Attorney. She has stepped down because of a possible conflict of interest. Nathan has no objections and a trial date is set for two weeks from now. He meets the press with DeSante and his agent. The press want DeSante to address the rumor that he has been written out of *The Saga* because the studio believes he is guilty? Nathan doesn't like the question. He responds before DeSante can say anything. "My office has requested that the judge put a gag order on both Mr DeSante and his ex-girl friend. Until this case is tried, no one is guilty of anything! Please, let's be diligent about how we address this matter. Many women, young and old, are raped by people they love and trust each day in Canada." He pauses and adds, "I am a father with a beautiful baby girl. I have a sister not much older than Mr. DeSante's ex-girl friend. Let's think about them and how we try this case. We all want women to come forward and report any abuse no matter what! Being a celebrity makes no difference to the law in Canada.

"Let's not get confused with the Kobe Bryant case here, ladies and gentlemen." Kobe Bryant is an NBA superstar, who plays for the Los Angeles Lakers. Mr. Bryant was charged with the rape of an eighteen-year-old hotel employee in Colorado. Of course, Mr. Bryant claims it was not rape. The members of the associated press were stunned. They loved Nathan Carter more as he showed a respect for the victims – raped and abused women – and encouraged them not to hide away but to come forward. The press were very anxious to see how he was going to defend DeSante since he sounded very much like a prosecuting attorney.

Meanwhile, Tia was home with the baby. Nathan did not bother to return to the hospital. When the DNA report came, it proved that Nathan is the father of Trey. Anthony is even more embarrassed because his son sent a junior associate from his office to pick up the report. Tia wants Anthony to stay with her a little bit longer, but Anthony feels that Tia's mother is right about leaving the kids alone to sort out their own mess. He told Tia that he would return in three weeks. For his own part, Kevin could not be happier that Anthony was leaving. He has assumed the role of the father, feeding and changing the baby and reading to Jayzel. Jayzel calls him KC, a nickname he loves. Tia, though, is depressed. She has left several phone messages for Nathan, but he has not once returned her calls. She puts the TV on for Jayzel and there he is on the evening news. Tia wants to change the channel, but Jayzel says, "KC, come see my daddy on TV!"

Kevin hates Nathan even more as he watches and listens to Nathan field questions. He can see Jayzel's happiness when she sees her father on T.V. He has not realized how much the little girl has missed her dad. Kevin feels sad and jealous at the same time. Nathan is on TV almost every day until he wins his case. He is still on TV about his new case, a policewoman being accused of shooting a black teenage boy. Kevin is sick of seeing Nathan everywhere and living in his shadow. He has not had any time to talk to Tia at all. He's been in Canada for almost a month now, and wants to go home since he can see there is no future here for him. Brooke's number is out of service, so Kevin can not talk to her to find out where Tia's heart might be.

After a six-week break, Tia returns to studio for the first time after Trey's birth. She knows Nathan is in Toronto and decides that it is time to talk to him face to face, whether he likes it or not. The doorman is happy to see her as he opens the door for her to enter the building; she takes the elevator up and knocks on the door. She looks lavishly dressed for someone feeling depressed. She wears a silk dress with the back open, pearl stud earrings that Nathan gave her on her twenty-first birthday and a string of pearls on her left wrist. Her straight hair is pulled up, her back is to the door when he opened it. He knew it was her the moment he opened the door. It reminded him of the night he went to a night club with her, Brooke and Jason when they were in Holland. Sexy and much more. Nathan was nervously thumbing when she turned and finally said, "We need to talk." The door was wide open, but she could see that he was not alone and that he had company. He tightens up his jaw and says without looking at her, "I am very busy right now, Tia."

"I need to discuss something with you."

Nathan could feel his palms sweating. He knows Tia can be stubborn when she doesn't get her own way. He says to his guest, "I'll be right back, sweetie!" He closes the door and pushes the elevator button. He stands by the elevator door with his head down. He pushes the stop button half-way down and says quietly, "We are finished, Tia. You and I have nothing to discuss. I have complied with the divorce. Whatever problems you and your boyfriend are having has nothing to do with me!"

"You are being totally unreasonable, Nathan. For God's sake, how long do you want us to go on living like this?" Tia asks. "You are being a rotten father, the children and I have been punished enough. We all miss you and I'm still in love with you." She feels embarrassed by her admission.

"What do you want me to say, Tia? You wanted a divorce and the children to yourself! You have it all, Tia," he says finally. "I will not have my wife and the mother of my children behave like one of my..." He pauses and puts his hands on his head. "I am done with this argument. I have fought and fought for you since day one. I am done!" He pushes on the button for the elevator to go down. Tia feels she has made a fool of herself. Just when the tension between them has reached an almost intolerable level, the elevator doors open. Their discussion is an ugly one. She feels powerless and defenseless. She has no intention of putting her marriage back together by the time she gets home. The kids are both sleeping. At just six weeks old, Trey is a good baby, who usually sleeps through the night. If put to bed no later than eight o'clock, the little guy will sleep until five in the morning. He was not a breast-fed baby like his sister was. Kevin sent the babysitter home because he wants to talk to Tia. It seems that every time he makes an effort to plead his case there is something or someone there. Today he cooks dinner and puts Jayzel to bed early right after her bath. He finds some candles in the house, remembering how much Tia loves candles and jazz music. He takes a bath and goes to the guest room where he has been staying to put on his nicest shirt. He sits down nervously and waits for Tia, watching the candles melt away. There are so many thoughts in his mind. The last six weeks with Tia and the kids has been an amazing experience for him. He doesn't hear her come into the house. He thinks Tia is very brave and he is impressed by how she lives her life with the kids close to her heart. She has totally turned her depression around, though she looks sad tonight, he can tell. Tia clears her throat and says, "Kevin, Why are you still here in Canada? Taking on a role as an instant father?"

Kevin smiles and puts his hands out. She takes them and he dances with her. "I made dinner for you," he says. He pulls out a chair for Tia to sit down. "You were a good man, a romantic man, and it looks like a good father," she mumbles.

"I still love you, Tia, and now I've met the kids, I see myself in them. I know they have a Daddy," He pauses to pour some wine for her. She takes a mouthful of the spicy food and sips more wine. "I am happy to have you here, but you can't go back to our old relationship, Kevin. I'm in love with Nathan. I never thought that we would break up for the better," Tia says quietly.

"Tia, please, listen to me. I should have sat down and talked to you years ago about my immigration problems. I wanted to marry you.

My brothers and sisters all wanted me to marry you. I was not sure that you loved me enough for marriage and I was too much in love with you. I knew if I told you what I was facing, you would have married me without question. I couldn't do it, so I chose the easy way out." Tia wanted to tell him about Jayzel at that moment, but inexplicably she didn't. Instead, she sat back and listened to Kevin while he talked about his nightmare of a marriage and how he left and went to New York and by the time he returned to England a year later, his wife had filed for divorce and was telling everyone that he had run off with Tia. Tia thought that was funny: every time she went to Europe, Nathan thought she was having an affair with Kevin.

Tia can see how much Kevin cares about her and the kids, but she is not about to make any changes in her life, and she tells him that. He understands. Kevin has lots of photographs of the kids to take with him when he returns to England. Kevin often muses that Jayzel has so many of his own characteristics. He loves Tia and the children, and misses them terribly. He calls every day to talk to them and when Tia finally says she wants to try and give him another chance, he is more than ready to move to Canada. Tia suggests this to Brooke. Again, Kevin is faced with a dilemma: he has just started work with a Nigerian lawyer, who is going out of his way to train him while he attends law school. He discusses the problem with Tia and they agree that he should stay in England and come home at Christmas. Tia and the kids will come to England during the summer. He negotiates with his boss to get the whole month of December off, telling him that he has family in Canada. Kevin tells him that his son is barely a year old and that he misses his family so much. He shows his boss photographs of himself and the kids, so the boss agrees to one month away in Canada.

Tia drives to Toronto with the children to meet Kevin at the airport. Jayzel sees him come out of the doors first, and runs to him as he sweeps the little girl into his arms, hugging and kissing her. Tia is holding Trey, who has grown big, but who will not go to Kevin. Kevin feels sad that the little boy has forgotten him. Tia kisses him and Jayzel tells them to stop kissing and let's go see Santa. "She wants her picture taken with Santa," Tia tells Kevin.

"And give Santa my list," reminds Jayzel, putting her hands in her pocket to retrieve her list.

Kevin thinks she looks adorable in the matching pink coat and hat. Trey is not quite a year old and already he is walking, but still won't go to Kevin or let Kevin pick him up. Kevin is desperate to hold the little boy. The kids are asleep by eight and when Tia comes downstairs, Kevin is sitting on the sofa. She sits on his lap and begins to kiss him. She peels his sweater off and it's not long before they are on the floor making love. Kevin didn't expect that. "You have not changed one bit. I love that about you," Kevin says.

"I have missed your touch, Tia. I was devastated by your rejections. I almost didn't come. Ola told me that our passion would ignite once I got here." Tia notices he is still wearing the necklace she gave him years ago. He tells her, "That necklace and the big towel of the White House you got me when you went to Washington D.C., I still treasure them both. I never stopped loving you, Tia." Tia has an affectionate, fun-loving nature, while Kevin has had a strict up-bringing by his father. The average African woman that he has slept with in the past are nothing compared to Tia. He loves her more than ever, she knows. There is nothing dispassionate about Tia and their love-making. He tried hard to forget her, but he couldn't. His father has forbidden him to think about someone who has two children and who is divorced, but Kevin stood up to him and told his father that he loved Tia and the kids and that his father would be on the outside looking in if he could not reconcile himself to the relationship. Kevin's father has plans for Kevin to come to Nigeria after law school, so that he can help him get into politics. Kevin's father has suggested that he should look for a wife for himself from a good family from their own Igbo tribe, but Kevin has declined. He is very happy. Tia always lavishes on him all the love and affection a man could want and more. She has not changed a bit, he is certain. He stares at her thinking what a fool Nathan is to give up her and the kids. Kevin plans to do everything in his power to help her fall in love with him again. He will like it if she will agree to marry him, especially if it can happen before he returns to England. He knows that Tia's parents may not like him as much as they liked Tia's ex-husband, but he believes that once he is earning good money, they will like him better, and will want him with their daughter. He hopes once they see that he treats her and the kids with respect, they will not have any concerns. After all, Tia's mother is an African.

Chapter 48

Nathan has done nothing but work for the last nine months. He is now Canada's answer to Nancy Grace. While Nancy Grace is on CNN, Nathan is usually on CTV, the same network employing his ex-wife. Oddly, in all of this time, they have not run into each other once. They have not talked either since their nasty fight in his elevator nine months ago. Nathan tries not to think about any of them: his father, brother, and sister don't speak to him anymore, either. They are ashamed of him for abandoning his wife and children. He still lives in the house he once shared with Tia and Jayzel in Ottawa. Today, he is expected at the CTV studio in Toronto to comment on the trial of a prominent politician charged with fraud and inside trading. He got Nicole and Ian back together as he had promised by lying about their affair, and now they are his only friends since most of his colleagues hardly talk to him and none of them extend invitations to him since his divorce from Tia. He dates countless of beautiful women. For the last two months, he has been dating one of Canada's top super models from Toronto, and will be spending the Christmas holidays with her in Brazil. She has a photo shoot there, so Nathan has already rented a villa for them.

Having finished his interview, Nathan strolls to the studio where his girlfriend is a guest on a talk show. Santa hands out gifts to a bunch of kids, but Nathan doesn't pay much attention to them as he hardly likes children these days. Surprisingly, Jayzel runs to him and pulls him by the hand, saying, "You must come up and see Santa, Daddy." He doesn't know what to say, but manages to ask, "Where's Mummy, Jayzel?" She is too excited to answer. Meanwhile, Kevin is busy yelling at Tia's assistant, David, for losing Jayzel. Tia suggests "Santa was visiting one of the studios today. Maybe she's there." David calls security and is told that yes, Jayzel is with her father and they are talking to Santa. Kevin's anxiety escalates, so he yells, "You're fired!" at David, but Tia overrides Kevin and tells David, "You're not fired, but please hold all of my calls until I return." Kevin is unhappy that Tia has showed him up in front of her assistant, but Tia's response is practical: "You cannot go around and fire people who do not work for you! Unless you are the head of the CTV studios and I don't know it?" Tia puts Trey down for a second to tell Kevin to calm down. Tia adds, "This is a very secure building. It's not like England. Children don't get kidnapped from TV studios in Canada!" She hugs Kevin and tells him to relax. They turn around and Trey has disappeared, too. Kevin sees a man hugging Trey and Jayzel is talking to a beautiful lady. Kevin runs to them and shouts to the man, "Put my son down now, before I have you arrested for child kidnapping!"

Nathan can't imagine who this man must be. He is still rubbing Trey's back when Tia joins them. It is the first time Nathan has held his son and the emotion is like electricity for both of them. Trey is so relaxed. Kevin wonders why the little boy is not making a fuss. He doesn't like to go to anyone other than Tia and Jayzel. The man turns to face him and Kevin realizes he is talking to Tia's ex-husband. Kevin is well pissed off.

"You can't just take my kids whenever you feel like, you know?" Kevin screams. The whole studio hears him. Jayzel joins the group with Nathan's girlfriend. She is pulling the girl's hand to come and meet her mother. "Mummy, Mummy… This is Elizabeth, Daddy's friend. Isn't she beautiful, Mummy?" the little girl enthuses.

"Yes, baby. She sure is." Tia extends her hand to Elizabeth. Elizabeth wants to know where Tia bought her boots. Tia explains she picked them up the last time she was in Europe. Jayzel pulls Elizabeth away again for her to go meet Kevin. Elizabeth thinks why not go with Jayzel? Mrs Carter is way too sophisticated and much prettier than she had expected.

"Oh Daddy, you met KC," says Jayzel. Nathan smiles. "This is my Daddy's friend, Elizabeth. She is a super-model, KC. And she is so cool!"

Kevin choked on a smile. Nathan is on his knees as Jayzel kisses him on the mouth and nose and rubs both his cheeks. Nathan puts Trey on one knee and does the same as the little girl has done. "I knew Santa would bring you home, Daddy. I told the baby that Santa would bring you home for Christmas and he did!" Jayzel beams and hugs Nathan again and says that she misses him. Nathan's mouth is open in surprise. He has not realized how much the children must miss him. He expects that by now Jayzel would have forgotten him. He looks at Tia, who shakes her head "no"; Kevin and Elizabeth both see the gesture, but don't know what it means. Nathan closes his eyes in anguish. He picks up both children in his arms and sits on the floor with them: "Baby, Santa did not bring me home. I'm here to pick up Elizabeth. If you and Trey want me home... I will come and take you both to *Toys R Us* when I get back from South America with Elizabeth. I can't come for Christmas, baby. I'm so sorry." Jayzel is upset. "Daddy, you must! I will have milk and cookies, just the way you like 'em," she cries.

Kevin feels helpless as he looks at Nathan with the kids. "We have to go now, Jayzel," Kevin says with a level tone. "Say good-bye. Jayzel, we got to go now." The little girl hugs Nathan and says, "Good-bye, Daddy." She looks like she is about to cry. Trey is still in Nathan's arms when Elizabeth says, "Hey! Jayzel, how about your daddy and I cancel our trip so we can take you and your brother out on Boxing Day for shopping? Would you like that?" Elizabeth asks.

"No, Daddy must come home for Christmas," Jayzel insists. She holds Kevin's hand, "What is Boxing Day?" she asks. "Does Santa come on Boxing Day, too?" Kevin glances at Nathan with a look of barely hidden hostility, but Nathan ignores him.

"No, Jayzel. Santa doesn't come on Boxing Day," Tia says, though the idea is cute. She takes Trey from Nathan. "It was nice to meet you, Elizabeth," Tia says. Jayzel lets go of Kevin's hands just before they board the elevator and runs back to hug Nathan. He returns his daughter to Tia and places her in the elevator as he kisses her on the head and watches the doors close.

Nathan is heartbroken. He tells the driver to drop Elizabeth off at her apartment. Elizabeth is falling in love with him and she doesn't want his kids coming in between them. She tries to be understanding and says, "I've been thinking..." Nathan does not like the way the conversation is heading, so he immediately kisses her and says, "you know what? Why don't we go out to dinner as planned and you can tell me what you've been thinking at dinner." Elizabeth likes that, but she feels tired after the long day at the studio.

"That sounds good, but I'd rather go home with you and order out, if that's okay."

It's not okay with Nathan, but he tells the driver to take them to the condo. Elizabeth has known all along that Nathan was married with children. She didn't know his children were very young and his wife was like a super model of some kind. "Why was she in the CTV studio anyway?" Elizabeth wondered. Nathan is not a man who likes to explain himself to the woman with whom he is sleeping, but Elizabeth is different. She cares about him and likes to keep their relationship low key, not like the others who were press hungry, calling him every minute, telling him they love him before he even takes their clothes off. Things are easy and relaxed with Liz. He enjoys her company. "Sweetie, that was very nice what you said to my daughter, but I don't want to cancel our trip. Tia will probably go to the cottage with them to see my father. I don't plan to go because I don't get along with him, anyway," Nathan explains. This is the first time that Nathan has shared anything about his family with her and Elizabeth wisely does not want to push. Instinctively, she feels that a non-committal attitude is the right direction. Sex is great, but she senses he has put up a wall and doesn't want anyone breaking it down; she wishes she knew what happened in his marriage to make him so self-protective. She could tell that Nathan and his ex-wife are still very much in love. Since Nathan's divorce from Tia, he has learned many things about life. One of them has to do with human behavior and how to treat the opposite sex. It was a skill he didn't possess when he was married to Tia. He gently kisses Elizabeth on the forehead. "Don't try to figure out about me or my ex-wife. It's a love affair that will go on forever. It is also a very private one. I have come to adore you, Liz. Let's not spoil things by intruding in the past. I am in love with Tia, and I love my children more than words can say. I believe they will find their way back to me. God will not keep punishing us like this. I am sorry for telling you all this. It is not to hurt you, Liz. Never will I hurt you. In the past,

I have hurt so many people that I care about that I am determined never to be that man again. If you want to break up with me, I will understand."

Elizabeth Star is nineteen years old going on forty; she is exceptionally wise for her age. She grew up in the small town of Paris, Ontario. Both parents are still married. Liz knows how important it is to grow up in a loving family environment. Although she didn't know the circumstance between Nathan and his ex-wife, she, too, feels they will be reunited sooner than Nathan thinks. Nathan laughs out loud when she tells him that. She looks so sweet, and when she wants to be naughty, she reminds him so much of Tia sometimes.

"Liz, it is a nice way to dump me," Nathan says with a smile. She stands up and begins getting undressed, saying in sexy voice, "What makes you think I'm dumping you, Mr. Carter? I am going to rock your world before you leave me and go claim what's yours, Mr. Carter."

Back in Stoney Creek, Jayzel and Trey are sleeping and Tia is sitting on her bed with her laptop, writing as she often does. Kevin comes into the room and demands that they talk about what happened at the studio earlier. Tia shrugs, "Don't worry about it! It's over and done." Kevin is surprised at Tia's attitude. "I see a problem here, Tia, that we need to deal with once and for all to avoid any future misunderstandings with the kids," he screeches. Tia looks up at him and asks, "What are you talking about, Kevin?" He sits down on the bed beside her. "I want us to get married before I go back to England." He continues, "I want to adopt the kids as my own. I don't want... I don't want your ex-husband and his father hanging around my family." Tia writes and smiles and Kevin thinks she is on the same page as him. He is so relieved to see her still smiling. He begins to relax. They make love that evening and Kevin says, "I'm glad you agreed to my proposal earlier. Tia, once we are married, I want the kids to have my name. I will try to buy a home with my savings and we can all be together in England."

Tia opens her eyes and says, "I don't want to get married. When did I say I wanted to get married and move to England? What is this about changing the children's names?"

Kevin is shocked, almost speechless, "We discussed this earlier, we agreed that your ex-husband and his father should not be allowed to hang around the kids and to come and go as they please. Tia, you agreed to this!" he insists.

Outraged, Tia gets out of bed, puts on her bathrobe and leaves the bedroom. Furious, Kevin follows. "Did you change your mind already, Tia?" he demands to know. Tia thinks Kevin's so-called proposal is provoking. She wants to tell him a few home truths, but bites her tongue instead. "I didn't agree to any such thing, Kevin," she retorts. "I've got to go to bed. I have a meeting at the studio in the morning. Maybe afterward we can talk about Christmas and the kids." She kisses him on the cheek and goes back to bed still angry about his suggestion. "I'm in love with my husband. Why the hell would I want to get married to a man who traded me in for some stupid papers without a second thought?" she asks herself. She can't help thinking about Nathan and what he must be doing with that super model right now. It brings tears to her eyes. Kevin mistakenly things she is crying about their argument, so he lays next to her, gathers her into his arms and says, "Don't cry. I'm sorry. I guess I want things to move too fast. I got scared today when I saw him with the kids. Tia, I didn't mean to push things too fast. If you're not ready, it's okay. I will wait." Tia is in her own world. She misses Nathan, especially at this time of the year when she and Nathan fell in love at Christmas time. She and Nathan both loved the holidays. Tia has always believed that Nathan is "the one". She knew she loved him before she met him. She thought the divorce would encourage the mature side of him to grow up so they could build a strong home together. How could I be so wrong? What am I doing sleeping with a man I don't love? Deep in her heart, Tia knows Nathan also loves her. It is not going to be a good Christmas without him and her father-in-law, and she misses them both dearly. Anthony has been like a father to Tia since they met. She feels more at ease and at home with Anthony than with her own father. He respects her, doesn't treat her like a child, whereas her own father always says, "do as I say, Tia." He is always going to be in her life and in the children's lives no matter who I'm sleeping with, she wants to tell Kevin.

Liz is sound asleep. Nathan has not been able to get Tia and the children out of his mind. Jayzel has grown and Trey is not a baby anymore. He is walking and running, a handsome boy. How could I have done this to them? Everyone told me. She still loves me. I saw it in her eyes, she still does. "God, I need help," he cries hopelessly out loud. "I can help you," Elizabeth says. She is standing, completely naked, at the door of the bedroom. Elizabeth stands five foot ten inches tall with light brown hair and green eyes. The only difference between her and Tia is her height, and the color of her hair and eyes; otherwise, she looks just like Tia. Nathan, looking at her, thinks she has so many similar qualities as Tia. Looking at her makes Nathan misses his ex-wife even more. Nathan asks, "What are you talking about?"

Elizabeth returns to the bedroom wearing one of Nathan's shirts unbuttoned, just like Tia used to do. "I canceled my photo shoot in Brazil. We are going to do the shoot in the studio, instead, so you can spend Christmas with your children!"

"That is not a good career move, Liz. If you want to break into acting, you cannot cancel jobs at the last minute. I want you to call them back." Before Nathan could speak his mind, she had him in her mouth and he couldn't think. Afterward, she said, "I have surprises for you and your children. I will tell you all about it when I come pick you up on Christmas Eve." She runs off to the bathroom before he can respond.

Tia has finished her meeting and is heading home when Amy stops by with gifts for the kids. Amy has turned out to be a good friend. Their show is still number one in Canada. Tia made a proposal about the show being seen in Europe. The network executives were surprised at how much research she had done on all the countries in which she was hoping the show would air. Tia has already contacted most of the networks and the feedback is positive. Amy is so proud of her, although she feels Tia works too much and needs a break. Tia laughs, "Oh, I'm too old for romance!" Her father-in-law has given her some lame excuses about where he is going to spend Christmas. Tia does not take no for an answer and insists that he join her and the kids. She has rented a house on Turkey Point for them. Jackie and Steven are coming as they both have not yet seen Trey. Tia is also working on a private project. Elizabeth Star arrives to see her as she is wrapping things up with Amy. She tells Tia about her Christmas plans for Nathan and the kids and enlists Amy to help her convince Tia. Tia eventually acquiesces and says to Amy, "I do have more room left in the cottage that I rented in Turkey Point. I want you and your mom to join me and I'm not taking no for an answer!"

"I will come, but only because I want to make sure your brother-in-law does not to try to steal you away to Hollywood. I know all about your private project with him!" Tia laughs, and then asks Elizabeth if she can act at all. Amy raises an eyebrow and asks "why?" "Nothing, just wondering," Tia replies. Both Amy and Elizabeth are intrigued by Tia's reticence.

"I've been taking acting lessons. During my last shampoo commercial, the director's comments about me were so mean that I decided to take some lessons," Liz said. Elizabeth enjoys being a model, but acting has always been her passion and Nathan has been encouraging her to pursue it.

A snow storm is about to blow through the region. Tia leaves Toronto and goes to the farmer's market and buys everything she can get her hands on to feed an army of house guests. She calls her house, instructing the babysitter to get the children ready for the drive to Turkey Point.

Kevin has just finished making dinner when Tia arrives and says they should not delay: they ought to go before the snow begins in earnest. She has not mentioned Turkey Point until they are almost there. Kevin asks, "Why aren't we spending Christmas at home in Stoney Creek?" Tia explains there was not enough room for everyone, and that she wants everyone to be comfortable. Kevin doesn't quite understand what she means until her brother-in-law arrives Christmas Eve with his girlfriend, followed by Amy, her mother, Anthony and Jackie.

Kevin had always known that Tia is a family person, but this is too much, even for him. He feels like an outsider. He tries to talk to Tia about it, but there is never enough time. Anthony and Jackie take over the kitchen while Mrs. Hall reads to the children. Tia is busy with her brother-in-law while Amy drinks wine and watches TV. Kevin leaves the cottage and goes for a walk. The snow is beautiful: he wishes he could bring the kids out to play in it. Tia has certainly rented a beautiful cottage for all of them to enjoy the season together.

Kevin returns to the warmth of the cottage as he is not used to the cold weather. Anthony meets him by the door with a cup of hot chocolate. "You look cold, Kevin," he says. "Come sit by the fire with me, son." Kevin always thinks of him to be a kind man. He replies, "thank you, sir." Anthony returns, "Oh, call me Tony, please." He can tell Kevin feels out of place. "Tia tells me you are very good in the kitchen, too. Why don't you and I show all these lazy buggers what we can do?" Kevin smiles. First, he and Anthony put up the Christmas tree in the enormous living room, while Mrs Hall, Jackie and the kids decorate it. Kevin and Anthony connect while they cook: sirloin burgers, Pacific rim pork accompanied by ginger garlic stir-fry vegetables and pickled radish salad. Dinner is nice. Tia sits next to him and is very naughty with her hands under the table. Kevin loves that it was not as bad as he thought it would be.

Kevin finds the Carter's to be a very nice, close family. He can see why Tia loves them so much. He feels a bit jealous of the closeness they share. Jayzel and Trey are standing by the front door, all of Christmas Day, since the morning and Steven asks, "What are they looking at?"

"Santa was supposed to bring our daddy home for Christmas, Uncle Steven. I think he forgot about us," Jayzel explains, holding back tears. Steven turns to look at his father, who is busy in the kitchen with Kevin putting all the finishing touches on the Christmas dinner. They are heart broken when they realize why the children have been waiting by the door all day for their father to come. Steven sits by the front door on the floor and tries to cheer up the children, but it is no use. The children will not move from the door.

A long white limousine pulls up in front of the property. Steven asks Kevin whether he and Tia are expecting more guests for dinner. "Not that I know of," Kevin says as he dries his hands and steps to the front door. He cannot believe his eyes. His jaw drops open, and he is totally surprised. Initially, the kids did not see him, but Kevin and Steven both smile as they open the door.

"HO...HO...HO... I'm looking for Jayzel and Trey Carter!" Santa says, "Your Christmas wishes!"

Jayzel is star struck when she sees Santa standing there. The little girl's eyes are wide with excitement, Trey is busy drinking his bottle and looking out the door. He runs out the door. Jayzel, Steven, Kevin and Santa pass into the living room. "My Christmas wish was my Daddy, Santa. You forgot to bring my Daddy," Jayzel cries. "You gave me the wrong address, Jayzel," Santa says. "I went to Stoney Creek to find you and your brother, but you were not there. I've been looking all over Ontario to bring you and Trey your gift." Meanwhile, outdoors, Nathan's hands begin to tremble when he sees Trey running to him still holding his bottle. The little boy reminds him of his football days, the way he is running with the bottle. Nathan picks up the toddler and walks into the house with him. "Merry Christmas, baby," he says.

"Oh, Santa! Thank you... I knew you would not forget," Jayzel cries out. Nathan stands by the door holding Trey in his arms. Jayzel runs to him as he sweeps her into his arms and kisses her on the mouth and nose. Kevin's heart races as he turns around to see if Tia is there. "She obviously knows about this and purposely did not tell him," he suspects. He doesn't know what to do as he stands there hopeless and powerless watching Nathan with the kids and everyone circling around them except Tia. Kevin leaves the living room and retreats to the office, where he finds her on the phone. He is about to leave when she sees him and tells him to stay. She looks stressed and Kevin doesn't want to add to it. Instead, he stands behind her chair and massages her shoulders while she talks on the phone. A few minutes later, she puts down the phone. "I just closed a deal that will bring me and the children to England three months from now to work for the next eight months. Everything is coming together for us, Kevin. I was worried about the time apart. Now, we don't have to, we're all going to be together!" Tia exclaims as she kisses him. Kevin pulls away from her. "I've been worried, too," he murmurs. Tia draws him back towards her. "There is nothing to worry about! It is meant to be. This deal proves it. Now come here and give me my Christmas kiss before our army of house guests interrupt." Just as Tia predicts, Nathan walks in with the children. He extends his hand to Kevin and wishes him a Merry Christmas. He doesn't say a word to Tia, and he leaves with the children. Tia throws her pen down in anger and swings her chair around. Kevin senses that perhaps Tia didn't know he was going to be here.

"Tia, please… it's Christmas. Let's all put everything aside for the kids," Kevin says softly. Tia is upset with the way Nathan has been treating her. He knows how much it hurts her. Kevin assures her that it will not be as bad as it looks. Tia thinks that he has no idea how bad things could be. Still, Kevin insists that it will be okay. "I am surprised at you! Last week you wanted him banished. What's changed?" asks Tia.

"You, me, and the kids are family. That's all that matters. I was scared last week, Tia. I thought I was going to lose you all," he murmurs. "There is no reason why we all shouldn't get along. The kids love him. I know they love me. I am happy when you and the kids are happy."

Nathan thanks Elizabeth for all the effort she made for him to be able to spend Christmas with his family. "I want them back, Liz," he says.

"You will have them back. That Kevin guy doesn't deserve them," Liz remarks. "Your wife asked whether I could act," she says.

"Why do you always call Tia 'my wife'?" Nathan asks. Liz laughs. "Mrs Carter is very much in love, and crazy about you, just like you are about her. Even Miss Hall thinks so," she adds.

"Amy Hall is crazy," says Nathan dismissively. "When did Tia ask if you could act?"

"I was at the CTV studio on Friday taping a holiday special for the Children's Hospital Fundraiser Event and I saw her. I asked did she work there, and I was told that she is the writer and the producer of *The Saga*. Why didn't you tell me? I love that show!" Liz exclaims.

Nathan smiles proudly. "I went up to her office to ask her to help me surprise the children. My Dad had already agreed to play Santa for me. Miss Hall was there when she asked if I could act."

"She didn't say why?" inquires Nathan.

"No. My Dad thinks she may be writing something for me. He hopes it is not about me sleeping with you," she laughs.

"Tia is not that kind of mean person. I do agree with your Dad, though. She is a very creative lady." Nathan observes.

"I leave for England in two days to work," Liz says. "I am going to miss you dearly, Mr. Carter. Why don't you come here and give me something to remember you?" Nathan smiles enthusiastically.

Chapter 49

Since Kevin's return to England, it has been hard for him to be by himself. He is used to Tia and the children. He has become friendly with one of the young lawyers at the firm, Angela from Barbados, and very close in age to Kevin. A Christian woman, Kevin likes her very much and cannot fault her for anything. His boss advises him to be careful with his female workmates. Kevin doesn't really need his advice. When Angela asks about his family in Canada, Kevin explains that children are not his, and claims he is not really sure where he stands with his ex-girlfriend. "We hardly talk anymore. I'm getting fed up with the whole thing, already," he says with frustration tinting his voice. "She was supposed to arrive in London last week with the kids. I waited four hours like an idiot at the airport, but she didn't show." Angela asked whether Tia called. Kevin said, "No. I'm done with her." They begin seeing each outside of work. One day, Kevin's boss calls him into his office to talk to him about his relationship with the co-worker. Kevin unpleasantly tells the man where to go, and several weeks later he quits and files a law suit against the firm for unpaid wages, which he wins. When Kevin passed his bar exams, he writes to the British Law Society asking them to waive his two-year probational work experience requirement, arguing that the last five years he has worked to earn enough experience. The Law Society agrees with him. Now able to practice on his own, Kevin decides to move into immigration law. No stranger to immigration law through his own personal experience, he has also become very good in family law too, despite his training as a criminal lawyer. All three areas will serve him well in his practice.

Kevin remembers Brooke Williams worked in real estate, so he calls her. He is told that Brooke is out of the country indefinitely. Since the company has several commercial and residential properties on their listings, less than one hour after the call the agent emails some of their listings. Kevin views some of the properties. He has the money from his lawsuit settlement and wants to put it to good use. He sets up a small law office. He creates some flyers and puts them in all the African and Caribbean churches and colleges to advertise for clients who have immigration, housing, and welfare problems: all the things he and his family have experienced since they have been in England. Just a few days pass before Kevin has more clients than he can reasonably handle. He invites Angela to join him. Two weeks of working together and sleeping together is just too much for the both of them. Angela leaves to take up a job with a bigger law firm. Feeling he has made something of himself now, Kevin decides it is now time to go to Canada and to bring Tia and the children back to England with him. On the day he was going to end things with Angela and catch a plane to Canada, Angel informs him she is pregnant. Kevin doesn't have to think about it. He tells his brothers and sisters the happy news and when they all ask about Tia and the kids, Kevin replies, "We are finished! I'm getting married in a week. My child is going to grow up in the same house with me!"

Tia has been in a cancer treatment center in Toronto for almost four months now. Six months ago, on her way to England, she collapsed at Hamilton International Airport and was taken to the hospital. Amy Hall called Nathan. They were told that Tia was approximately twelve weeks pregnant and had miscarried. An irregularity had developed in her blood, and initially, it was thought that she might have leukemia. Nathan felt helplessly angry and utterly devastated. Amy called Kevin's law office in England, but she was told that Kevin didn't want to be bothered with Tia's problems and that she should not call again. This time, Nathan is not as afraid of the hospital as he has been in the past. He has taken some time to learn all he can about leukemia. He calls his mother-in-law and tells her that Tia needs a bone marrow transplant. The Sharp family are all distraught and terrified of the procedure. Tia's mother sounds like the whole world had ended. Naana's eyes fill with tears as she listens to Nathan describe what is needed. Everyone was tested, but her mother was Tia's perfect match, so she flew to Canada with Brooke. Nathan put the children into a day care, and he divided his time between the children and Tia. His father and sister both offered to help, but he refused. He went to the hospital day and night to do Tia's personal care himself. He also hired a personal support worker for her, and had a lady to do her hair and nails. The children were very happy with him. He told them that mummy was working overseas so they wouldn't worry. He takes them to court, if he needs to, and also to the gym. He even learns to cook and cleans the house after them. He was not comfortable living in the home that Tia had shared with her lover, so he kept a lookout for a new property. When he came across a vacant lot in the nearby village of Binbrook, he was pleased to learn that the lot was for sale. It happened one day while driving around with the children. He stopped the car to look at a hobby farm near the land. The children quickly ran to the fence to meet the horses. Nathan was standing in the middle of the land, lost in his thoughts, when a man yelled "Hello!" Nathan smiled. He apologized for trespassing. The man told him it was okay. He could tell Nathan had the whole world on his shoulders. He went to the children and gave Trey carrots to give to one of the horses.

Jayzel told the man that Trey is very shy. "My name is Jayzel and that over there," she pointed "is Daddy." The man shakes hands with Jayzel and says "Very nice to meet you, Jayzel. I am Chase." Jayzel was giggling, and remarked, "That is funny a name ...Is it because you chase the horses?"

"Well, how did you guess?" chuckles the farmer.

"You are a funny man. I like you." Jayzel told him.

Nathan came over and thanked the man for his kindness. "Oh Daddy, this is Chase. Do you know he likes to chase the horse? That's why he is called Chase, Daddy?" Jayzel exclaimed.

Nathan was embarrassed. Chase thought she was adorable.

"I see my land got your attention?" Chase asked.

Nathan smiled and said, "Yes sir."

Chase figured with cute little kids who love animals Nathan could not be a big-time city developer who would put a luxury condominium or a mini mall there. He told Nathan that he was born on the farm and lived there all his life. There is a conservation park five minutes from here. He pointed in its general direction. He asked Nathan, "If you don't mind me asking, what exactly are you looking for?"

"My wife has leukemia, and she loves the countryside and outdoor living. I have always wanted to build a home for us years ago, but things happened," Nathan replied. Chase's heart went out to him. Nathan asked if he knew of any building restrictions in the area.

"No, it all depends on what you want to build. I have a friend who works in city hall. I could find out for you if you like. We didn't want to sell to just anyone, but I think Jayzel here loves it already." Chase said.

Nathan gave him his card, and said to have his realtor call him right away. He needed it done quickly as time is not on his side. Chase sort of understood. Chase Page thought that Nathan looked familiar, but couldn't recall how he knows him. He watches them drive off thinking about what he could do for Nathan and the kids. He calls his buddy at the city offices right away to find about what the zoning restrictions. It wasn't until Chase was about to call Nathan back that he remembered that Nathan was the lawyer on TV. Nathan arranged everything since he was buying with cash. Chase introduced him to an architect friend of his. Chase Page was not just a hobby farmer: he knew people from all angles of industry and corporate life. He was a stockbroker, but the stress was killing him at the tender age of forty, so he retired. Nathan likes him, although he has never been friends with a homosexual man before, but he did not feel less than a man around Chase.

He shared with him and the builder the kind of home he wanted to build for his family. He didn't want any delays. They got the plans approved with Chase's help and it was no time before the foundation was finished. Nathan and the kids went every afternoon to the site. The children would play with animals while Nathan got his hands dirty. All the contractors liked Nathan's laid-back, down-to-earth personality. He was nothing like the lawyer they often watched on TV.

It was also a way of coping with Tia's illness. He learned and bonded with all the people who were bringing his family home to life. He spent any spare time he had at the site until the house was built. Nicole has been worried: she and Ian both have offered to help by taking the children on weekends, but Nathan always declines the offer. His father has done what any father can to reach out to him. Nathan stubbornly would not talk to him.

For six months, every two weeks, Tia has chemo treatments. Tia's body couldn't handle the chemo-therapy. She would vomit like Lake Ontario after each treatment. Nathan was by her side every single time. The bone marrow transplant was successful. Tia has lost a large amount of weight and all her hair has fallen out. The after-effects were a lot harder than the chemo itself. Her body will get so hot and then so cold at any given time. She could not go to sleep for more than three hours without waking in the sweat of nightmare. Again, Nathan was there to hold her. Tia's mother and Brooke moved all their furniture from their Ottawa home to the Binbrook home for Tia's home-coming. Nathan has been at her side the past seven months, but they have not talked very much. She would often cry in pain that she wished to die. Nathan would then pick her up and hold her in his arms and tell her that she is strong and that she is too mean to die. Tia would tell him how much she hates him and he will smile and kiss her in reply. He has grown to love her even more now. He knows that once she is out of the hospital, he will again be outside looking in, but he feels okay with it. He pleads with his mother-in-law not to bring his personal belongings to the Binbrook house as it is Tia's and the children's home. Naana Konadu-Sharp tells him it is high time for all of them to put the past behind and to move on. Tia has her last rehab session and as she waits in her room with Brooke, she confides in Brooke that she feels like she has died and been given a new life. She has no idea where it is heading.

She has always known how to fight and to go on when all the odds are against her. Now, she is so afraid of each passing moment. Her mother and Anthony have just entered the room and they both heard her. It was the worst they have seen her. Anthony clears his throat and says, "Now, you listen to me, Tia Sharp Carter, you are not going to go soft on me, Angel. I have held my heart in my hands all these months. We all have. You are the glue that bound us all together. I have missed you, Angel, and I don't want to hear any talk of you can't do this and that. The only woman who made Nathan Carter cry can't do this?" They all laugh.

Because Tia had difficulty balancing herself, she was released from rehab in a wheelchair. She notices that her father-in-law has gone past the highway 20 exit where she lived in Stoney Creek. Anthony was driving more into the countryside past Binbrook Beach. He turns into a farm and drives past newly planted trees to what looks to be a secluded estate. The automatic gates open and Anthony drives in. Tia turns her head back to see the gates closing. It is a spectacular estate on over seven acres of property on a secluded country lot. Tia wonders why they are there. A small Pomeranian dog greets the car when it stops. Coming outside, Brooke picks up the little dog, calling it "Hope", as if the dog knows her.

Her mother and Anthony help Tia out of the car and into her wheelchair. Brooke plops the little dog on Tia's lap and she, too, is surprised by the dog's cuteness. She forgets to ask why they are there, and whose adorable dog is this? The little dog could not stop licking Tia and she is amused by the dog. They all move inside the house. It has a very high ceiling like a loft with warm earth-toned colors. Very spacious hallways, beautiful hardwood floors, boxes piled here and there convey the notion that the owners have just moved in. An ornate marble fireplace provides the backdrop for Tia's furniture from Ottawa in the family room. She puts the dog down and asks her mother to stop pushing the wheelchair.

"What is going on and why am I here?"

Jayzel comes running into the house and puts her hands on her mouth, saying "shush!" Trey follows, "Is quiet time. Daddy is working. Shush, quiet time, quiet time." The little boy repeats his message, but the children do not know their mother is in the wheelchair. Tia has lost a lot of weight and wears a scarf on her head. She suddenly begins to sob as she sees her children for the first time in almost a year. Jayzel said, "Please, don't cry. My daddy doesn't like people who cry all the time." Trey thinks Tia has a cool bike, one to sit in. Jayzel says authoritatively, "That is not a bike, silly baby. It's a wheelchair. It's what old people use to move around when they can't walk."

Trey asks his mother, "Are you old?" Tia smiles and says, "No, baby." The children realize that she really is their mother and they both run toward her and take her in their arms, almost tilting the wheelchair. Tia is still crying when Trey says, "Oh no! My Daddy will be sad if you cry, Mummy." Tia's mother and Anthony, too, are in tears as they watch Tia and the children. Kate, Jaden and their son, James, are also present for the home-coming. They discover Brooke in the kitchen eating. Tia asks, "Why are we here?" Jayzel says, "It's our new home. We helped. Daddy and Chase made it for us. Do you like it, Mummy?" The dog jumps up on Tia's lap and Trey says, "Hope, you leave my Mummy alone!"

Everyone laughs. Tia is so overwhelmed she forgets to ask Nathan's where-abouts. She sits in the wheelchair and watches the children and Brooke eat lunch and laugh. They both have grown big. Her mother had disappeared somewhere in the enormous house. Tia wants to go home to her house in Stoney Creek, so she asks if Nathan is around. Her mother says from behind her, "He is on his way down. He has just finished wrapping things up with his assistant." She wants to help Tia transfer into the sofa but Tia says she prefers the wheelchair. "I am so sorry, everyone," Nathan says as he joins the gathering.

"Oh, no Daddy, you been a bad boy?" Trey asks to the general amusement of everyone present.

"Why are the children living here?" Tia asks with accusation creeping into her voice. Nathan can see she is not happy. He goes behind her chair and leans on her shoulders, "Let's go outside for a walk around your new home. Outside, we can talk. I'll answer any question you have. It's been an emotional and traumatic time for everyone, Tia. Please, I promise I'll be on my way soon."

Tia calmly agrees. Nathan pushes her out of the house into the backyard of the house where there is a pool with a hot tub. Different types of annual and perennial flowers newly planted emulate Heather's garden at the cottage. It almost brought tears to Tia's eyes. In the far corner to the east side of the backyard, she could see a tree house. "Did you build that?" Tia asks, pointing at the tree house.

"Yes!" Nathan says with a grin. "That's a club house for the children. There is a big dog house for Hope, too. You want to see?"

"Are you serious?" Tia asks incredulously, smiling.

"I'm totally serious." His face says he is. It looks more like a big doll house than a dog house. There is a wooden bench and table, too. Nathan sits down. "I figure you can be here writing while the children play. There is a lot of room left in the house and outside for you to do whatever you wish. I wanted to bring a little bit of everything that you love into the home for you and the children."

Tia was not prepared for this kind of home-coming, and she began to cry.

Nathan asked, "Why are you crying?"

"I have missed the most beautiful experience in my children's lives. I am never going to get that back," she wailed.

Nathan knew and understood how she was feeling. They both were quiet with their own thoughts for awhile and soon Tia stopped sobbing to say, "This is a beautiful home, Nathan, but I would rather go back to my house in Stoney Creek." Nathan was angry but he tried not to show it. "Whatever you want is fine with me, Tia," he replied.

"What do you want, Nathan?" Tia asked, frustrated.

Nathan smiled. "Come on, let's get you inside." He got up to push the wheelchair, but Tia told him that it was okay and he should sit.

"I want to know what you want, Nathan!" she insisted.

"I have you alive, Tia," he paused. "The children are very happy, everyone is very happy with the miracle that we've all been given. I can not ask for more."

"Stop it, Nathan!" Tia raised her voice. "Why do you do this every time? Am I that difficult for you to talk to me?" she asked. "Nathan, I really don't remember much, but you have been there with me throughout this ordeal." Tia was sobbing again.

Nathan tried to fight back his own tears and everything he's been keeping inside him, but he couldn't any longer. Looking into Tia's eyes and hearing her asking him questions that he has asked himself, he was unprepared to articulate the answers. The tears were rolling down his face as he stood up and pushed the wheelchair. Tia asked again for him not to push her, but he was already in the house in a room which looks like an office or a library. One cannot tell with all the unpacked boxes of books, but there was a white sofa close to the fireplace. He pushed her near it and transferred her into the sofa. He could tell she was upset with him. He sat very close to her.

"Tia, I have been angry for so long, I'm not even sure when it all began. I somehow managed to live with my anger and hide it from you when we were married." He was speaking to her in a clear, soft voice, and she wanted to wipe the tears off his face and hug him and tell him that it was okay. He went and stood by the window. He had his back turned to her and he did not hear her walking towards him. She sat on the window seat and took his hands. "Tell me what you've been angry about and how you've managed to hide it so well, Nathan." She was serious.

"I will sit down and talk to you, Tia, soon, but not today. Today, you are home with your family. I want you to enjoy it. I built... my children and I built this home for you to show you how much we love you. Tia, I took a little piece of all the homes that you have lived in and loved." He pointed out to the window where there was another spot of all kinds of flowers. I remembered Grandmother Gertrude's home. There's also a small one just like your mother's... she helped me put all the plants together for you. I love your mother, Tia, very much.

The last few months she has been more than a former mother-in-law to me. She knows I'm not a perfect man. She knows all about things that," he paused, "things that I have done in the past, things you are not aware of and still she loves me just like my mother did. I have everything that I want. I could not ask for more." He took her in his arms and held her for a long time and when he let go of her, he said, "I am happy to have you home and to be in good health. I'm going to say good-bye to the children now. The 403 highway to Toronto will be closing tonight for some maintenance, so I must leave now before the road is closed."

"You love me so much, but every chance that we get to talk, you run, Nathan," Tia spat.

He smiles. "I'm not running, Tia. I meant it... I will sit and talk to you and answer all your questions. I just thought you might want to be alone and I as much as... I want to have you all to myself, I do understand," he says with a sigh.

"I can't deal with this alone, Nathan. I need you," she says with desperation.

Nathan felt sad because he felt the fear in her voice and it broke his heart. He swept her into his arms and sat on the sofa with her on his lap as he often liked to do. "I know we cannot do what we've done in the past. I cannot run away, Tia, from my family, like I have in the past. There is a matter that needs my attention in Toronto. You know what? Let's go get some lunch and we can discuss whatever you and the children want afterward," he said.

"No. I want you to tell me one thing first," Tia said emotionally. "How did you cope with everything?" He put his forehead against hers and closed his eyes, "God helped me." Tia thought that was funny. She laughed so loudly that her father-in-law, who was worried that the couple may be up to their usual fighting again, almost hard a heart attack. When he began running towards Tia's voice, he was relieved to see them both laughing, and it looks like things are getting back to the normal life they once shared. Tia's mother and Brooke followed. They were equally happy to see them in each other's arms, laughing. Brooke has never been the settled type: "Now that you two have made everyone miserable with your stupid divorce. I love her so much. I hate him. I love him. When do I get to plan another wedding for you two? This time it will have my own contract that says you two are crazy!" She screeched. Anthony has always liked Brooke and her no-nonsense attitude to say things others won't. He says, "I agree with her." Both Tia and Nathan began again, this time laughing even louder.

For Tia's mother, she was so happy that everything was settled. She, too, has come to respect her son-in-law. She has always loved him as Tia's husband, but more so as a son now. It warms her heart to see him laugh as he has not had much to laugh about in the past year and a half. She has pleaded with Anthony to forgive his foolish ways and to remember that he was a good boy. Anthony told Naana that if Heather were here she would probably say the same thing. Nathan's hands begin to tremble. Tia notices and says, "Please don't go soft on me. I love you very much. Please don't doubt how much." She gently squeezes his hands and he smiles.

"Today, I thought about our first meeting at Holland airport years ago. I could not get it out of my head. What a journey it has been for us!" he exclaims. "I love you, Tia Sharp. I have more to share with you."

Chapter 50

The same day that Tia was released from rehab to go home, Kevin and Angela Peters welcomed their daughter. For Kevin, it was a bittersweet moment, as it brought back the memories of the afternoon that Tia gave birth to Trey. Angela and his family thought he was crying because of the intensity of his emotions, but in actuality, he wishes with all his heart that Tia had given birth to their child. He calls the little girl Princess, and he falls in love with her as instantly as he did with Tia's children the moment he holds his baby. Angela couldn't have asked for a better relationship between father and daughter. She knows Kevin has only married her because of the pregnancy, a fact he often denies, but five months later, she became pregnant again and this time they are expecting a baby boy, and Kevin feels over the moon with happiness. He has not thought of Tia and the kids for months. In fact, it is almost like they never even existed. He cuts down his workload so he can spend more time at home with his pregnant wife and the baby. He enjoys being a father to Princess. It is hard to leave her to go to work.

Five days ago Kevin Peters was leaving a court house in London when he runs into none other than Jaden Blake.

"Hello, Jaden," says Kevin cordially.

"Hey, yourself! Tell me something, man... What's it feel like to abandon someone you claim to love when that person is facing death? What's it feel like to abandon your own child? Hmm?" says Jaden enigmatically. Jaden didn't pause for a response, and went his way. Kevin, on the other hand, did not understand Jaden's questions and felt insulted, but he didn't pursue it.

Today, Kevin's former employer called him to congratulate him on the news about his son. Kevin wonders how he knew of the baby sex. They had just had the ultra sound done today, and only himself and Angela know the details. He has not told his brothers and sisters that he and his wife are expecting a son in four months. He has not spoken to his former employer since he sued him for unpaid wages and won, almost two years ago. Mystified, Kevin sends him an email to ask how he knows about the sex of his unborn child? Within fifteen minutes he gets a reply telling him that Tia Sharp did not die of cancer and that Jayzel was his and Tia's biological child. Kevin almost had a heart attack he was so surprised at this disclosure. He pulls himself back into his chair and keeps reading the rest of the email.

He learns that Angela knew about Tia's illness and that Jayzel is his biological daughter. Kevin keeps a box of photos in the closet of his office containing pictures of Tia and the kids. He retrieves the box with a rapidly beating heart. He opens the box and the first picture he takes out is Jayzel's. Kevin has a photograph of Princess and Angela on his desk and when he puts the two photos side by side he can barely tell the two girls apart. Kevin screams like a wounded animal. He goes to the British Law Society's website and finds Jaden Blake in its directory. Kevin calls him and begs him not to hang up. He tells Jaden that he had no idea that Tia had cancer and likewise that Jayzel was his biological child. "I've just learned all of it from my former employer," Kevin says.

Jaden said that he was sorry, that he couldn't talk just then because he was on his way out to the airport to join his family and he hangs up the phone. Instinctively, Jaden believed Kevin, so he called Kate and told her Kevin's pathetic tale.

Anthony Carter and his son have not seen eye to eye since Heather's death. Nathan has felt that his father and ex-wife hold him responsible for his mother's death. Although, his father has never come out and said it, Tia has, plenty of times. It is something that has haunted him the most, of all the disappointing things he has done in his life. Nathan feels he will not get the chance to make it right. He thought about the day his mother died when Tia blurted it out in their Ottawa home: "Your selfishness, your stupidity, and your ex-lovers' needs to seek revenge on us may have caused Mother to have that heart attack." That was what Tia said before she asked him to leave their home. Nathan drank some of his tea.

"Daddy, it's still quiet time?" Trey asks. Nathan puts down his coffee mug and picks up the little boy. He asks, "Why do you think it is quite time?"

"Because you look so quiet in the kitchen by yourself," his son says.

Nathan smiles and tells Trey, "No, it is not quiet time. I am thinking."

Trey asks, "Why are you thinking, Daddy?"

Nathan kisses him on his forehead and says, "Daddy has done things he's not proud of and he likes to think about it sometimes." Anthony has just walked in and heard most of the conversation between his son and grandson, bringing tears to Anthony's eyes. Growing up, Nathan Carter was the most thoughtful young man. Looking at little Trey reminded him so much of Nathan as a youngster. Even at college when he and Heather would go and visit, people approached them to tell them how kind and humble Nathan is. Anthony often wished he knew what changed his son so radically. The past year and the half he has become that young man again. He did the impossible when Tia got sick and Anthony is so proud of him. Although, they hardly talk these days, Tia's mother has advised him that it is time for the Carter/Sharp family to heal and stop the feuding.

"There you are, my two quarterbacks!" Anthony exclaims. Nathan has not seen his father this happy in a long time. He smiles and puts Trey on the ground and watches him run into the old man. "Nate, I was just talking to Mr. Page." Nathan wondered what his father could be talking to Chase about? He interrupted and asked his father if there is something wrong. "No, no. Son, the weather is very good today. It's Angel's first day at home. Chase wanted to know if you would mind if he comes and barbecues for you and your family. I hope you don't mind, son. I told him it would be a fantastic idea, and maybe afterward we can play football. You and I can teach young Trey, here how to be the next Carter quarterback. What do say, son? Is that okay with you?" his father asks again. Nathan didn't have to think twice. He reached for the phone and told Chase that he is going to ask his wife if it's okay. Anthony was proud of him, and he told him so right there. He hugged him and said "You're a good boy, son. Heather would've been so proud of you if she were here." There were tears rolling down both their faces when Trey reminded them that crying is not allowed in the house, and they both began laughing. Tia was in the library with Kate, Brooke, and Tia's mother, unpacking the boxes when Nathan came in and spoke in French to Tia. His mother-in-law smiled when she heard what he has asked his wife. Tia tells him to let her check with the others first. Nathan says this is her home and they are her guests. Tia asks if it is okay with him as she doesn't know Chase and he smiles: "Why don't you run it by your sisters? Chase is on the phone, so I can – " but Tia takes the phone and says, "Hello, Mr. Page. I am Nathan's wife. Yes, sir, we would love it if you come and barbecue here, as long as we get to help." Chase replied, "Of course! You must call me Chase." Tia is not feeling like a house guest after talking to Chase. "You just called yourself Nathan's wife... Does this mean you two are going to get remarried before we go home?" Brooke demands.

Kate is embarrassed, but can not help laughing. Nathan bites the side of his lips and smiles. He transfers Tia to her wheelchair and pushes her into the kitchen. Tia is not able to reach the counter tops. Nathan asks what she wants, and she replies that she wants to fix something. Chase is coming to barbecue for them. Nathan suggests, "Why don't you make the salad, baby? Dad, you can make the Chinese cabbage and bean sprouts that Kate and Brooke like so much. I can make the spaghetti and Parmesan spinach for the children." Tia begins to laugh and says, "Sweetie! I will ...um... make the pasta. I don't want you to burn the house down on my first day home."

"Angel, Nate can cook," Anthony assures Tia, though she is still laughing at the idea of Nate in the kitchen. " Of course, Nate can cook, Daddy!"

"Mmm ... huh... you wait and see, baby. I am going to make stir-fry just for you so you can eat your words," Nathan winks at his father as they trade a high five.

Tia is very quiet, so Nathan asks what is wrong.

"I miss her," she mumbles. Nathan glances at his father. Anthony thinks she is talking about the child she and Kevin were going to have, that she miscarried more than a year ago. So did Nathan. "I wish Mother were here. She always enjoyed all of us under one roof." The Carter men were both relieved. "I am sorry for everything that Nathan and I have put you through, Daddy," Tia said to her father-in-law. Nathan felt the same way, but unlike his ex-wife, he finds it difficult to admit when he is wrong.

Anthony pulls a chair closer to Tia and he asks Nathan to come and join them too, please. Anthony Carter is a wise, kind man. "Perhaps, I should have had this talk with you two kids a long time ago. I love you both very much. There's been times that... I wished that you two were kids, so I could take my belt to you," he smiles. "You are both equally stubborn, but you love each other. I only have one thing to say, and that is communication with one another in your relationship is essential. There is no more sorry. We are family, though not a perfect one. I'm so proud that we are all acting like a family now. Angel, is right. Heather would have..." he paused. Nathan stood up and tapped his father on the shoulder and admitted that he too misses his mother more than ever now.

Brooke comes in with Jayzel, all dolled up. "What is it with you Carter and Sharp families? You are too emotional! Are we going to have this barbecue or what?" She spat. "Jayzel and I are hungry!"

Anthony told Brooke ten minutes, and she left with Jayzel.

Chase has barbecued a feast. He is Nathan's first friend that Tia has met. Nathan didn't have many friends. He knows a lot of people and has a lot of associates, but not many friendships. He and Nicole had a friendship, Tia thought. It was a nice dinner. Afterward, Trey and Kate's son James were playing football. Nathan asked Jayzel if she would like to play. "No, Daddy. It's not lady-like to be dirty," the little girl remarked. Both Tia and Nathan turned to Brooke, and simultaneously ask, "What have you been teaching my daughter?"

"Jayzel has always been my little darling whether you two like it or not," Brooke told them. "Come, darling, let's go paint our nails."

"I am going on record now to say that I hate your sister," Nathan mutters.

Tia can see nothing has changed during her absence. She is happy to see Jaden and Kate so happy, but she can sense there is a distance between Kate and Brooke. Tia asks if everything is okay with them. Kate lies, "Oh, I've had it with her bossy ways. It's like you left home and now she thinks she can boss me about like she used to do with you. I told her where to stick it! She don't like my attitude. Don't you let her spoil Jayzel," Kate warns Tia. Tia laughs. Everything is unreal to Tia. She has not thought of Kevin or asked about him all this time. She suspects it is one of those things that should be left alone, though she did grieve when she found out she lost her child with him. "Maybe it is all for the best," she is telling her mother. She is able to talk to her mother about things now. Her mother is not an old fart, as she often thought when she was growing up.

"I feel like I've been born again. I can't explain, mother. When I was leaving England to come and work for Nortel, years ago, I knew I was going to meet Nathan. I told the girls when we were in Holland, and they thought I was crazy." Her mother smiles. "I know you think I don't respect Nathan. I like to yell at him a lot. But I have always loved him, before I even met him. Does that make any sense to you, Mummy?" Tia asked.

"Yes," Naana says. "Tia, true love also requires hard work, too."

"You and Daddy make it work. Nathan and I... We..." she pauses. Naana tells her there is no such thing as a perfect man. "There are good men. Your father is a good man and Nathan is a good man, but they are not perfect men, just good ones." Tia raises an eyebrow and blusters, "Daddy is nothing like Nathan, Mummy. You have no idea what Nathan has put me and the kids through."

"Tia, listen to me. Marriage and family comes with huge responsibilities. Often our husbands only thinks with their libidos, not with their heads like women do. Everything that Nathan has done, your father has done a lot more, darling. I'm still there, but he could be even having another affair, while I'm here." Naana shakes her head. This is not what Tia wants to know, that her father is a good man. He will never cheat on her mother the way Nathan does. She is shocked to hear what her mother has revealed about her marriage. How could she keep it to herself if her father is such a man? Naana knows what is going on in Tia's mind. "Tia, not everything in a marriage is out in the open for others to see the way your marriage is. When children are involved, you think of them first. You learn to forgive," she explained. Tia thought her life is a nightmare. She had no idea that her parents' marriage is full of lies, too. She picks up the courage to ask if her mother is in love with her father, or has she stayed with him all these years because of her and her sisters.

"Darling, I will not stay with any man because of you girls. I'm in love with Bobby, just like the first day at college, when we first met," she says with a smile.

Tia asks her mother how she copes with her father's cheating ways. "You don't. How does one cope with betrayal? The more flowers and gifts he brings me, the more he promises not to do it again. I forgive until it happens again," Mrs Sharp tells her daughter.

"What do you mean 'until it happens again'? Finding Nathan in a hotel room was more than enough for me. How could you put up with Daddy's shenanigans?" Tia asks.

Naana chuckles. "You got divorced because you found Nathan in a hotel room?" her mother asks with disbelief.

Tia is quiet. "I was sick of his whole friendship with his ex-lover and business partner, Nicole Bright. I just couldn't take anymore of her meddling, Mother. I couldn't. I figured divorce would let him see what we have is the real thing."

"Tia... you discuss matters like these with Nathan. You don't just leave him. He thought you were sleeping with Kevin, and you did not set him straight. Tia, you two cannot go on living like this. He has been out of his mind with worry about you. He won't let any of us help you or the kids. Nicole and Ian pleaded with him to have the kids on weekends, so did Amy Hall and her mother. Elizabeth Starr offered too, but he won't hear of it.

"Tia, your father has being having affairs, one after another, since you were born. Nathan is good a man. I do hope you two get back together and fix things because darling this is not a good reason to get a divorce. Were you happy with Kevin?" Her mother asks pointedly. Tia laughs, "Believe it or not, Kevin made me see how much I was in love with my idiot of a husband. My divorce was a mistake. Daddy went and told him the day Trey was born, but Nathan was too jealous to listen. I tried to talk to him afterward, for him to come home but he wouldn't, and now I don't know. I don't want him back because I'm sick or for the kids. Mother, I want my husband home for me and only for me," Tia declares. Her mother sighs. She advises Tia to discuss with Nathan her expectations of him. Tia feels good talking to her mother, though she wishes her father would change his cheating ways. Her mother deserves a lot better than that old fart! The sky looks especially bright, remarkably wholesome, and she can not remember the last time she sat outside. It seems to her that she has been in hospital for half of her life. Trey has so much energy playing football. Tia wishes she could borrowed some or it as she was tired already. Nathan notices Tia's fatigue, so he thanks Chase for coming.

"I must go and take my wife inside and put her down. She looks very tired," Nathan says softly. He is almost out of breath now playing football with the boys. Chase tells Antony, "You have a good boy there. You must be very proud of him." Anthony replies, "Yes. Yes, I am." Nathan stands behind Tia's wheelchair and bends over to put his chin on her shoulder. He says softly, "You look exhausted. May I take you inside now?"

His voice made Tia shiver. "Please do," she says, feeling breathless as his hand slides under her waist, when he lifts her up and places her in the sofa in the family room. He asks if there is anything Tia wants. Tia has been wanting to talk to Nathan alone since she left the rehab center to come home. There has never been the right moment, with friends and family around all the time. Nathan can see she is preoccupied with her own thoughts as she didn't respond to his question. He wants so desperately for her to tell him what she is thinking about, even if it is about Kevin Peters and the child she lost – he wants to know. Not knowing is the worst, he thinks as he covers her with a blanket.

"Thank you," Tia sighs with a smile.

"Do you mind…. if I…um.. stay a little while longer with you and the children?"

"I'd love it if you could stay. I thought you have a murder trial to work on?"

"It's over already."

"What was the verdict?"

Nathan enjoy discussing his cases with her. It is one of the things he missed most about Tia since their divorce. He smiles. "We won, mainly because the prosecutor is inexperienced. I took advantage of it. It was frustration, immaturity and some anger, but not with malice in the legal sense. They didn't have enough evidence to support a conviction for second degree murder."

"Are they going to retry for manslaughter?"

"I'm not sure at this point. They bent over backward to encourage my defense's strategy. In short, my client got a free pass to get out of jail. I get to be home with my family. I'm just happy it is over. I didn't think my client was going to be inexorable," he said dully.

"You sound a lot more like a prosecutor, not a defense attorney."

"No, I just hate it when prosecutors don't follow the law to get a conviction. This is a case that they should have won easily." He turns to look at Tia and asks if she is okay. Tia reaches for his hands. Her hands felt cold, so Nathan asks if she is cold. "My body gets cold and warm most of the time, like it doesn't know which it would like to be."

"I'm going to call Father to take a look at you."

"It's okay. Daddy knows all about it. It's the after-chemo effect and it will soon pass, I'm told." It breaks his heart to see her this way. Tia has persevered through leukemia, so anything is possible Nathan thinks. He gets on the sofa behind Tia and holds her, caressing her back. Nathan ends up falling asleep instead of Tia, but Tia enjoys their alone time together. She is certain that she wants Nathan home for good. She wishes that he will want the same things she does. She knows sooner or later they will have to discuss everything that has happened over the last few years. She prefers it to be later, mainly because she fears the subject of Kevin Peters may have cost her the man of her dreams. Nathan is not one to forgive and forget easily. Her heart rate beats faster and Nathan felt her heart pounding. He wondered why the sudden change. "Tia... sweetie, are you alright?" His voice is soft and he shivers as he lifts her on top of him. There were tears rolling down her face. He is afraid to ask, so he wipes away her tears with his thumb and assures her that whatever it is, it will be okay. He is here for her and the children for anything they need.

"I don't want to force you to talk to me, Tia, but I hope you will, whatever it is worrying you."

"I'm fine. I'm overwhelmed with everything that has happened. I'm happy to be here with you." She pauses. "I don't want you... home out of pity."

Nathan chuckles, "You're very stubborn, Tia Carter. I'm home – in case you don't know – I never stopped loving my wife. This is a desperate man's attempt to try and win back his wife, his whole family. Pity has nothing to do with it!"

"You're doing a terrible job!" Tia joked.

"Oh- yeah? Well, I have hardly begun my campaign. Just wait until I go on national television to plead and apologize in public for the whole Province to hear, to ask for you to take me back. Viewers will be begging you to take me back just to get me off the air!"

"You're crazy, Nathan Carter!" It was just like before they got married. He always knew how to take her pain away and make her laugh. That is one of the things that made Tia fall in love him. Tia told him that.

"I thought that you fell in love with me because of my sophisticated, irresistible charm."

Tia chuckles and kisses him on the cheek and holds on to him.

Chapter 51

Tia's mother went to Holland to spend sometime with her mother. Gertrude has been in poor health too for a few months, but is doing a lot better now. Jayzel and Trey went to the nearby African Lion Safari with their grandfather and Mrs Hall. Nathan is in Toronto because of a trial.

The Saga is returning to television a week before Thanksgiving. Tia has everyone worried as no one knows what she has written, or whether she has written anything at all. She calls Nathan and asks for Elizabeth Starr's number. Nathan tells her that he is in Hamilton with Amy Hall and that he will be home in less than ten minutes. He parks the car, and get out and begins to kick the shit out of the car. Amy is on her cell phone when she looks out the window and sees Nathan kicking the car. She opens her door to get of the car and says, " It's okay, I didn't think you'd know how to change a car tire. It's a good thing that I know how," she teases.

Nathan looks up and says, "What planet do you people in television come from anyway?"

Amy realizes that he is upset about something to do with his phone call.

"Mr. Carter, your wife holds my job in her hands. I know how much she loves you, so I'm going to be as kind to you as I can be. You are a fucking nut case!" Amy gets back in the car, starts it, and tells Nathan to get in, that she is driving.

"Yeah, well, I am a nut case!" Nathan replies and they both begin to laugh.

Tia has already asked her assistant David to call Elizabeth Starr to arrange a meeting for tomorrow morning with her and Amy at the her office. Amy tells Nathan as the gates open how much she loves the new house. She asks if Chase is married or seeing anyone. Nathan quickly forgets about his worries and begins to laugh at Amy.

"What? What's the big joke?" Amy asks. Nathan can only reply with laughter.

"Aw, shit, Nathan! You're being an insensitive jerk!" Nathan laughs harder in response.

Inside the house, Tia pulls Nathan toward her and kisses him. He is still laughing and Tia makes a childish face and says, "My baby, insensitive? Never, Miss Hall!" She is still kissing him. Amy has had it with their never-ending romantic ways, so she leaves to get herself a drink.

"I did not come here to watch you two make out like two horny teenagers."

"Oh, Amy, by the way... Do you remember Elizabeth Star?" Tia asks.

Nathan lets go of Tia's hands, but she pulls him back and wraps both arms around his waist. Amy turns with a quizzical look.

"The model you wanted to know if she could act. Wasn't she sleeping with Handsome here?" Amy points to Nathan.

Nathan tightens his jaw, "Thank you very much, Miss Hall!"

Tia decides to end the tension. "Yes. Well, um, I have a part for her. I think the viewers will love her... That is, if she can act."

Amy exclaims, "I knew it! I knew it when you asked. She's a babe, alright! But can she act?"

"I want to hire my father-in-law as medical consultant on the show. There are going to be a lot of medical issues this season. I have to re-write the season. It was sent to the studio and the cast members earlier this morning. I want to touch on some things..." she pauses, sits down. "Amy, you have always said *The Saga* is a glowing, heartwarming story. I'm beginning to see it now. I have seen the numbers

The Silent Sisterhood

in Europe, and they love the show there, too. The part I want Elizabeth to play is a young nurse."

"Now, that is one sexy nurse! You are going to have all the young men going to the hospital now, Tia," Amy remarks.

Tia and Nathan both laugh. Tia reaches for Nathan's hands. He doesn't know what his wife is going to say, but he is certain he is not going to like it. He knows her too well. She begins by rubbing his back. Then, Tia sits on Nathan's lap.

"I think she can pull it off. She will be playing a young, single mother... um... who has cancer." Tia says softly. Amy is quiet, and Nathan is not too pleased, either.

"I want you to listen to me. She is a super model. Most of our audience knows her. They have seen her commercials, glittering celebrity, and glamor. Elizabeth's character – I'm hoping – will shape and change the show. Our viewing audience will see her as a strong, single mother faced with the heartbreaking prospect of death."

Amy's face lights up and she says, "Your wife is a fucking genius! New viewers will be drawn in to the story!"

Tia continues outlining her proposed plot: "The devastating illness develops as the story evolves. In the midst of it all, a scandal erupts, threatening a budding romance between her character and her doctor. As I see it, they have a chance to build a happiness they both could never have dreamed of."

Amy loves it. "Were you working on this plot line before you got sick?"

"I did... I was, but the character had AIDS. Cancer is more something I can write about," Tia explained.

Amy asked, "Who do you have in mind to play the child?"

"Well, I was thinking of Jayzel... Jayzel and Elizabeth have a good chemistry. Jayzel is no stranger to the camera, but I have to discuss it with Nathan and Jayzel first."

Nathan's knee-jerk response is, "No! Tia, please..., no! The next thing you will want to put me in the story as the husband, or the father, who abandons them. Tia, this is too close to home. I will not have you relive everything we've already been through on television."

"I love it!" says Amy, clapping her hands gleefully and thinking of the ratings.

Nathan stands up and says, "I will get an injunction against your studio if anything about my family is – " he pauses to look at Tia. "You are a talented writer, Tia, but there are other ways to do this. Baby, please. I cannot be on opposite side of the court room battling with my own wife. I just barely got you and the children home, so let's not do this. Tia, we both made a promise."

Tia says, ignoring Nathan, "The ex-boyfriend is a doctor." Tia laughs and tells Amy to go get herself a glass of wine while she and Nathan sort things out. "By the time you come back, we'll be making out like two horny teenagers!" Amy can not believe it. At every moment, she expects the show is going to go off air for sure: "Tia Sharp, you are a – "

Nathan screams at her to stop encouraging his wife, before she can finish saying what she wants to say. Although, Nathan has not talked to Tia about the effect her illness has had on him and the children, Tia knows and the more he plays it cool that he is okay, the more she can see that they need to find a way to deal with it as a family, though perhaps not through her writing. She shares her thoughts with Nathan. She also makes it clear that she will not re-write the story.

"It's my life's work. Nathan, it's like being told to stop being in love with you, which is impossible. I don't want our relationship to be like the past when we wouldn't discuss things, and let things get out of control."

Nathan listens to her. He can see the growth of love she has for him now, but the thought of her reliving the event of her illness on her show terrifies him. He doesn't want Jayzel on the show either.

"Jayzel is going to be a doctor, like father. I don't want her following you and Steven in your show biz world. Tia, I will not know how to protect my little girl from the show biz world," he asserts.

"Sweetie, she can still be a doctor. I want my family close by me. I need you to convince Daddy to move here with us, Nathan. I cannot have him living in the condo in Ottawa all alone. Make him see that Mother will want us all to be under one roof as a family. I need him, sweetie, here with us, please." She pleaded with him. She is in tears, and Nathan does not like to see her in tears.

Nathan doesn't want his father living with them because he has not lived up to Anthony's expectations. This is his opportunity to show his wife that he is the man of her dreams. His father is just going to get in the way. Nathan knows Tia can be stubborn when it comes to his father. She will be devastated if he tells her that he doesn't want his father to come and live with them. Tia can see Nathan is struggling to hide something from her.

"What are you thinking about, Sweetie?" she asks lovingly.

Nathan is quiet and doesn't respond right away.

"Daddy loves you, Sweetie. He is so proud of you. Please, don't let your jealousy get in the way of what's right for our family. He is hard on you because your are his first son. I see you do the same with Trey, and Jayzel runs you around her cute little fingers," she says.

Nathan smiles as he takes her hand and kisses it. Amy is standing in between the door watching the couple and wondering why they got divorced. Tia has never said why.

"Do you two ever keep your hands off each other at all?" Amy asks.

"Chase has a partner, so you leave me and my wife alone and mind own business about what we do." Nathan snaps at her as he leaves.

Amy observes that Tia's husband can be a jerk sometimes. Then, Tia and Amy spend the afternoon discussing the set and the script. By the time they are finished, Anthony and the children are already home, so Amy and her mother join them for dinner. After dinner, Nathan gives his children a bath and reads to them. He doesn't read the fairy tales most parents read to their children that age. He is reading *The Human Body* to them. At the end of their reading time, Nathan says, "We are finished with the heart." He asks if Trey can tell him what the heart does. Jayzel sits up in her bed and puts her hands up and says, "Oh, Daddy, ask me. I know!" Nathan asks Trey again.

"The heart is a pump! Daddy, you know that!" Trey says.

Tia glances at her father-in-law and smiles. Nathan kisses the little boy on the cheek and gives him five dollars. He turns to Jayzel and asks if she can tell him what the skin is.

"The skin, Daddy, protects the body from getting hurt, Daddy," the little girl says.

"That's right, baby," he says as he gives her ten dollars and kisses her.

The children run and put their money away. Tia notices they have so much money and asks them how they got it.

"We earn it. When we give Daddy knowledge, he give us money, but we can't spend the money, Mummy," Jayzel told her mother. Tia asks why not. "Money goes to the bank, silly," Trey giggles.

"Did you know, you get more money, when you keep your money in the bank, Mummy?" Jayzel asks.

Tia is very impressed with how Nathan has trained the children in her absence. She has missed a lot in the short time they've been apart. She can see why he says Jayzel is going to be a doctor. Tia is in the master bedroom when she hears the knock on the door. Nathan opens the door to ask if Tia needs anything before she goes to sleep. They have been sleeping in separate rooms. Tia walks to him and says, "I hate sleeping alone. I sleep better when you hold me," she murmurs. He picks her up and puts her back into bed and climbs in next to her. He kisses her on the cheek and tells her to get some sleep. Tia confesses that's not what she meant. Nathan replies that he knows what she wants and she is not going to get it.

"I only make love to my wife, and you're not my wife. My sweet mother would be turning in her grave right now, knowing that we are in the same bed and divorced. I want us to get remarried, Tia, with an iron-clad clause that says you are never going to divorce me – no matter what stupid thing I may do. I want to make love to you everywhere in this house."

"I'm not going to sit around and let you go around sleeping around on me, Nathan. I won't."

Nathan sits up in the bed. He sighs, " I know, baby. I have no intentions of – " he paused. "I will never do anything to us, or our family. I don't mean you and the children, all our family in Europe. I'm not the same man that you married, who would cheat on you with anyone. I hope you believe that. I'm the man you saw in your dreams before your left Europe, years ago, Tia. I'm in love with you still. I hope you are with me, too."

"I want to get remarried to you for the same reasons, too. I just don't think I can handle your whores."

"I promise to only whore myself to you and only you. If you marry me." He looks so sweet. He smiles and kisses her. As he pulls away, Tia tries to feel him up and kisses him endlessly.

He told her, "You are not going to have your way with me this time, Miss Sharp. I can go without longer than you think. I will only make love to my wife and only my wife," he says firmly. "Stop arousing me before you get raped!"

She laughs and says, "Wow! We will see who can't keep their hands off someone. I can go longer if need be. I'll do whatever it takes to seduce you."

"You can try all you want, baby. I'm not going give in to your advances. You have no shame, Tia!"

"Shame is what you're doing refusing to make love to me until we are married. Mother would want you to put a smile on my face. Come here and give me a kiss," she teases. He brushes her hair away from her face, and she tries one more time to arouse him. He gets out of the bed, "I'm going to bring you some milk to help you go to sleep. I've become used to a life of celibacy, so do your worst, Miss Sharp!"

Back in England, Kevin drives to Tia's parents' home to find no one at home. A neighbor tells him that they are away until the new year, spending the holidays in Holland. Kevin leaves his card for them. He goes to his office, but he does not know whom to call. Later, he finds himself on his driveway, sitting in his car, feeling enraged. There is a new American show that his wife likes to watch on ITV. As he enters the house, Kevin sees she is laying down in the sofa in their living room watching the show.

"Oh my God," she says. "You must see this. The little girl on the TV and her brother – their mother had cancer and their father left the mother and got married to some tramp." She tearfully retells the story, even though Kevin is not paying attention to her.

"Hush, they are finished with the advert," she says. She turns her attention back to the television where a distinctive voice that Kevin knows comes out of the box. He asks his wife if there is anyone in the house with them and she tells him to hush. He hears the voice again, this time from the television and there she is: Jayzel on *The Saga*. That's the show Tia writes and produces in Canada. The show she was trying to bring to England years ago, when they were together. It looks to Kevin that he knows the actress who plays Jayzel's mother, but Kevin could not remember where he has seen her before. There is a scene in a house that looks just like Tia's kitchen in Stoney Creek. The mother is making breakfast, Jayzel enters asking how she feels today. She has grown, Kevin thinks and there is a cute little boy who plays Jayzel's brother in the show. They sit down to eat and when the little boy picks up the spoon with his left hand, Kevin realizes that it is Trey. He recalls Trey is a leftie just like Tia. His heart rate begins to rise. He watches the show with interest and it looks like everything that Tia and the children went through has been put on her show. It is art imitating life. His anger boils over and over. He can not control it. He picks up a glass and throws it right into the television. The TV glass breaks and some of it cuts Angela as she is too close to the TV. Kevin is out of the house already before she can ask him what is the matter with him?

Kevin Peters arrives at his sister Ola's house. Ola is a nurse and she, too, loves *The Saga*, although she has no idea that's the show Tia writes and produces. She knows Tia works in television, but Ola does not know what Tia does. Ola gives Kevin a bottle of beer and he puts down the beer as he watches her reverse her taped show and Kevin tells her he needs to talk to her now and that it is urgent. He tells his sister about the incriminating email and phone call from his former boss implicating his wife in keeping him away from Tia and the kid. Ola has always loved Tia; in fact, she still keeps in touch with her. It was just last week they were on the phone for hours.

She asks, "Why did Tia never say anything about the baby? What was her intention?"

Kevin reminds her about his first marriage to obtain his papers to be able to stay in the country. "I think she left because she was pregnant and thought I would not want the baby. I knew she was mine when I first held her, when Jayzel was a baby. I told Aaron about it. I was with him when we went to see them at Tia's parents place. I was too ashamed to asked if the baby was mine. The day that I first arrived in Canada she went into labor and her son was born. The husband thought the little boy was mine. That's why he asked for the DNA test and left them. She did not dump me. She collapsed on her way to me, and her family was told that I wanted them to leave me alone, that I don't want anything to do with her!" Kevin is openly crying, " Ola she was three months pregnant with our second child, mine and hers."

He turns the TV back on. "*The Saga*, that is the show that Tia writes and produces. It is the show that she was trying to bring to England, so we could be together as a family." He froze a scene on the TV screen with Jayzel and Trey. "That's my kids on TV playing our life, reliving everything for people to see what a bastard I am, Ola." The horror on Ola's face was indescribable.

"My life in England had been the sick revenge of a man who used me as a fucking dog and refused to pay for my service. You know, in his witness statement in court when I sued him, he told the judge that I had a wife and two kids in Canada and I laughed at him. I remember Angela asking if it was true. She never once said that she knew I had a child and that message after message was sent to me. Today, I learned that we were going to have a son. Angela and Adam decided to let me know that I had abandoned the woman I love." He was crying as his sister's sweet face projected her dismay.

For Nathan and Tia, life couldn't better for them as a whole. They have settled in very comfortably in their new home with Anthony. Living with his father is not as bad as Nathan thought it would be. They are a lot closer now as father and son. Nathan only regrets his beloved mother is not around to see them happy. He puts down the morning papers he is reading as he feels Tia's foot under the table in his crotch. "God help me," he says to himself.

He gets up to leave the breakfast table and she corners him, putting both arms around him whispering to him that she is wearing nothing under her silk bath robe. She slowly kisses him and reminds him that there are two more weeks before they get remarried. "It looks to me that you are ready to throw in the towel, baby," she teases.

He brings his lips to her's and kisses her lightly and winks that no chance in hell is he going to lose this challenge. She pulls him in for one more kiss before she strips her bathrobe off and walks slowly upstairs. "God, I can't wait to be married to make love to my wife," he says.

Tia yells to him to have a good day at work and she loves him. He chuckles and shakes his head.

Epilogue

Tia Sharp remarkably survives the overwhelming odds of cancer. Tia was right: when something belongs to you, it will always find its way back to you. Nathan's and Tia Carter's love triumphs over tragedy and betrayal. They will find strength in their love and their family to continue their unforgettable journey once again as husband and wife and go on to have four wonderful children.

Anthony couldn't be more proud of his son, as Nathan becomes a doting father and husband. Mrs Sharp always knew that the man who intruded on her in New York City, years ago, would be the son-in-law she always wished for her daughter.

The friendship that Tia, Brooke and Kate share will also extend to their husbands as they, too, join and protect their wives and children when the saga continues in infused with life's experiences. The Sharp's and the Carter's will build a future filled with love, romance and hope with their unique and fascinating friendship with their friends.

Amy Hall and Tia Carter will also build a ground-breaking television production company in Canada.

Lisa Sharp, Tia's younger sister, will come out of the shadows of her powerful mother and sister to build her own dynasty as well as to motivate her younger sister Claire to realize her dreams of becoming a great artist.

The Sharp/Carter amazing saga continues... in *for ever never dies*.

T.S